THE TRAFALGAR GAMBIT

THE TRAFALGAR GAMBIT

CHRISTOPHER G NUTTALL

Text copyright © 2014 Christopher G Nuttall
All rights reserved.
No part of this book may be reproduced, or stored in a retrieval system, or transmitted in any form or by any means, electronic, mechanical, photocopying, recording, or otherwise, without express written permission of the publisher.

ISBN: 1502885794
ISBN 13: 9781502885791

http://www.chrishanger.net
http://chrishanger.wordpress.com/
http://www.facebook.com/ChristopherGNuttall

Cover by Justin Adams
http://www.variastudios.com/

All Comments Welcome!

PROLOGUE

(Heinlein Colony; Two Years Before Vera Cruz.)

"Well," Ira said. "Aren't you glad you came all this way?"

Jill Pearlman hesitated, then glanced out over the water. The sun had set hours ago, but the moonlight illuminated a warm lagoon, with water lapping gently against the sandy shore. It was completely isolated from the colony five miles to the south, largely unseen by human eyes. Ira had boasted he was the first person to set eyes on the lagoon.

"Yes," she said, shaking her head. "But did we have to come all this way?"

Ira grinned at her, his teeth gleaming white against his dark skin. "Yup," he said. He turned, then moved towards the beach. "Come on!"

Jill watched him run, shedding clothes as he moved, then blinked in surprise as she realised he'd stripped himself completely bare. His ass winked at her as he paused on the very edge of the shore, then splashed into the water. She hesitated, unsure if she wanted to skinny-dip, then ran after him, almost tripping over his trousers and the gun he'd left on the beach.

"It's warm," he called. "Come on in!"

"Coming," Jill said.

She removed her shirt and trousers, then hesitated before adding her bra and panties to the pile of clothing. Ira was fun, and she knew her parents approved of him, but she wasn't sure she wanted to allow their relationship to get so intense so quickly. And yet…she pushed her doubts to one side and splashed into the water. It was warmer than she'd expected, now that the sun had gone down. But it was definitely lovely.

"I told you so," Ira said, as she swam out to meet him. His eyes flickered to her breasts, then looked back at her face and remained fixed there. "It's lovely out here."

Jill let out a sigh as she flipped over and stared up at the rising moon. She'd pitched all sorts of fits when her parents had announced that the Heinlein Society was setting up its own colony world – and that they would be among the first colonists. They'd wanted to leave overpopulated and overregulated Earth, but all Jill had been able to think about was leaving her friends behind. And Earth's facilities. She'd fought, for nothing.

And I'm glad I lost, she admitted, in the privacy of her own mind. *This isn't Earth.*

The colony was only three years old, but the settlers had already created a number of farming settlements, including the homestead Jill and her family worked. Life was slower than it was on Earth, without entertainment movies or VR downloads, yet there was something about it that made her feel content, something she'd never truly felt on humanity's homeworld. And her relationship with Ira felt better, more wholesome, than anything she'd had on Earth. She didn't feel any pressure to move faster or to have loveless sex with him…

She turned and smiled at Ira, then dived under the water and swam away from him, daring the young man to follow. Heinlein had few higher forms of life; the settlers had introduced various breeds of fish as well as cows, sheep and pigs, monitoring their progress as they swarmed and multiplied in the endless oceans. Jill had been told that, one day, they would be able to fish as much as they liked, but for the moment they were restricted in what they could take from the waters. Not that she really cared, she had to admit. She preferred lamb or beef to fish.

Ira caught up with her as she stopped and rested her feet on the sandy seabed. Jill turned to reach for him…and froze as the moonlight revealed *something* in the water. For a moment, she was convinced she was seeing things. Heinlein had no sharks or dolphins, nothing that might be dangerous to human swimmers. And yet…the water ripped where the shape had been, just under the surface. Something was definitely there.

"What?" Ira asked. He was more sensitive than any of the boys she'd known on Earth, more able to read her moods. "Jill…"

"Look," Jill stammered. The shape seemed to be growing larger. "What is *that*?"

Ira turned, just in time to see the shape burst through the surface and out into the open air. It looked humanoid, but it clearly wasn't human. Jill screamed in shock as it faced them, one long leathery hand reaching out towards the humans. Water dripped from its skin as it stared at then, as shocked to see the humans as the humans were to see them. Jill shivered, feeling suddenly cold, then started to back off towards the shore. Heinlein had no higher life forms, she knew. And yet she was staring at evidence of…what?

"Get back to shore," Ira said, through clenched teeth. "Hurry!"

They'd been stupid, Jill realised, as she splashed through the water. It suddenly seemed very difficult to move. They were so far from the colony homesteads that they couldn't hope to attract attention, no matter how loudly they shouted. Behind her, she heard Ira calling out to the creature, trying to speak to it. Jill reached the shore and turned, just in time to see the creature advancing towards Ira. Panic overcame her and she ran for his clothes, then scooped up the gun in one hand. Her parents had drilled her again and again until she was an excellent shot, cautioning her that she might need to be able to defend herself one day. But they'd never envisaged *this*…

Ira started to back off…and the creature followed him, its leathery hands waving frantically, as if it were trying to say something. But Jill couldn't hear a sound, apart from a very faint rasp that echoed unpleasantly on the air. She couldn't understand what she was seeing. Was the creature actually *intelligent*? Or was it a previously undiscovered form of life? The planet was big, after all. There might be *anything* outside the colony's walls.

"Get back to the farm," Ira ordered. "Tell them about…"

He stumbled and fell backwards into the water. The creature kept advancing towards him, its hands reaching out as if it intended to pick him up and carry him into the deep waters. Jill shouted, but the creature showed no reaction. Desperately, she lifted the gun, snapped off the safety and fired, just once. The creature stumbled as her bullet struck its head…

…And collapsed back into the water.

CHAPTER
ONE

The devastation stretched as far as the eye could see.

Admiral Sir Theodore Smith stared down as the shuttle made its way towards London, struggling to keep his face and emotions under control. Like all of the officers and crew in the Royal Navy, he had sworn an oath to put himself and his body between his country and war's desolation. But the scene below the shuttle was proof that he and his fellows had failed to keep Britain safe. The country had been devastated.

He sucked in his breath as he looked down at what had once been towns and cities, fertile countryside and harbours. The aliens hadn't targeted British soil directly, but it had hardly mattered. They'd landed a massive warhead in the Atlantic Ocean, which had triggered tidal waves that had washed over Britain and Ireland, Spain and Portugal. No one had anticipated an attack on such a scale, not even after Vera Cruz. Uncounted millions were dead, millions more were unaccounted for. The country hadn't suffered devastation on such a scale in all of living memory, if ever. Not even World War II had come close to slaughtering so many British citizens.

A feeling of horror, mixed with despondency, grew in his breast as he tracked the passage of the tidal waves eastward. Penzance and Cardiff, Bristol and Bournemouth, had been drowned beneath the massive tidal waves. The Brecon Beacon National Park, where the British Army had put its recruits through hell for hundreds of years, had been washed away into nothingness. Only the presence of Ireland, he knew, had kept more of the western coastline from being drowned under the waves. And yet the devastation had still not come to an end. So much water had been vaporised and thrust into the upper atmosphere that it had yet to stop raining over parts of the country. Floods were an ever-present threat.

He'd seen pictures, of course, broadcast over the datanet by reporters eager to claim the first scoops from the devastated zone. There were images of horror, of dead bodies piled up as the tidal waves receded or looters making their way into the devastated areas to loot, yet those images hadn't seemed quite real. Devastation on such a scale was far beyond his imagination, even though he'd been a serving naval officer for what felt like an eternity. And yet, now, he knew he wasn't even looking at the worst of it. Far too many countries had lost millions of lives in the wake of the alien attack on Earth. And entire complexes in space had been destroyed with all hands.

Down below, he knew, there were thousands of refugee camps for survivors, policed by the military. There had been nothing like it in Britain since the Troubles – and even the Troubles, at their worst, had been on a much smaller scale. The social fabric that made up the British nation had been badly damaged, perhaps shattered. He'd accessed news sites as the shuttle made its way towards Earth, only to discover a non-stop liturgy of horror. Food riots, protests against refugees...outright defiance of the government's authority. No matter how he tried to be optimistic, part of him couldn't help wondering if he was looking at the final days of mankind.

The devastation faded slightly as the shuttle picked up speed, heading towards London, but it wasn't *normal*. Floods covered large tracts of land, a small army convoy made its way through devastated fields and a large refugee camp covered what had once been a farm. If the Troubles hadn't taught the government the wisdom of making sure Britain could feed itself, Ted knew, it would have been a great deal worse. But it was already bad enough...

He sighed as London came into view, then winced in horror as he saw the flooding. London had always been vulnerable to floods, but the safety precautions seemed to have failed in the wake of the alien attack. Or perhaps it was the rain, part of his mind noted. London was on the wrong side of the country to have a tidal wave marching up the river, smashing everything in its path. One of the datanet interviews had been with a scientist who had claimed the aliens had deliberately set out to melt the icecaps. Ted couldn't help wondering why the aliens would have bothered.

But they live below the waves, he thought, as the shuttle slowed to a hover over London, then dropped down towards Heathrow Spaceport. *They might see advantage in drowning the human race, then taking our world.*

Raindrops splashed off the shuttle's portholes as it touched down, sending shivers running down Ted's spine. He'd travelled in space, even flying cloudscoop missiles through Jupiter's atmosphere as a young man, but he'd never been comfortable flying through the rain. He knew it was safe, yet part of him had always been scared. It was funny how he'd never had any problems in space...

He rose, then looked towards his travelling companion. "Lieutenant?"

Lieutenants Janelle Lopez looked up at him, her eyes dead and cold. Ted felt a flicker of pity, despite the certain knowledge there were people outside the shuttle who were far worse off. Janelle had blighted her career through pressing for assignment to *Ark Royal*, the Royal Navy's outdated space carrier, when assignment to *Ark Royal* was normally reserved for officers and crew the Royal Navy couldn't be bothered to discharge. She might not even have been promoted if *Ark Royal* hadn't proved to be the only ship capable of standing up to the aliens in open battle. And yet she'd proved herself under fire...

But it isn't her service that brings her to London now, Ted thought, as he helped her to her feet. The fire had gone out of her when she'd discovered her lover was dead – and who he'd really been. *And I wouldn't have brought her here at all, if it had been up to me.*

"Come on," he said, gently. "It's time to face the music."

The hatch opened, revealing puddles of water gathering around the shuttle. Ted hesitated, then let out a sigh of relief as a pair of armed soldiers appeared, one of them carrying a spare umbrella. Ted took it, then used it to cover both himself and Janelle. The soldiers looked thoroughly wet and miserable as they beckoned Ted to follow them towards the terminal buildings. He couldn't help noticing that the spaceport was largely disused, despite the urgent need to bring supplies into the city. Two of the terminals seemed to have been converted into makeshift refugee camps.

"There's a VIP transport for you, sir," one of the soldiers said, once they'd checked IDs against a central database. He pointed to a large black car, waiting just outside the terminal, with an armed escort on either side. "You'll be taken directly to Downing Street."

Ted swallowed as he saw the soldiers. "Is it really that bad out there?"

"It's worse," the soldier said. His voice was dead, as if he had been pushed to the limits of his endurance and there was nothing left, but duty. "If the flood levels keep rising, we're going to have to move millions more people out of London to higher ground. Damned if we know how we're going to do that, sir. We had a riot in Soho yesterday that saw several thousand people dead. We had to stack the stiffs in a pile and use lasers to burn the bodies to ash."

Ted nodded, unsurprised. There was no way that millions of dead bodies could be stored for later identification, not now. Hundreds of thousands, perhaps millions, of people would never be accounted for, their fates utterly unknown. The prospect of never knowing what had happened to his family gnawed at him, yet he knew there was no choice. Thousands of decomposing bodies would spread disease at horrifying speed.

He climbed into the rear of the car, then settled down and watched as the driver started the engine and followed the soldiers out into the streets. London was awash with water, even on streets he would have thought immune to flooding. It had been years since he'd driven in London, but he was fairly sure the driver was taking the long way round. But then, if some streets were impassable he would have no choice.

"My God," Janelle said. It was the first thing she'd said since boarding the shuttle. "*Look* at it!"

Ted followed her gaze. It had once been a park, he was sure, a place for young children to play while their parents watched. Now, it was a muddy refugee camp, with prefabricated buildings providing limited shelter against the rain. The refugees themselves were largely older citizens, young women or children. The young men, Ted knew, would have been drafted to help with the floods. Many of the refugees had torn clothing, nothing more than whatever they'd been wearing when the attack began.

"We've been having some problems feeding them all," the driver said, as he drove past the camp and down towards Downing Street. "I believe there are plans to move them all to Scotland, but no one really knows if it will ever happen."

Ted shuddered, remembering some of the disaster management plans he'd seen during his stint at the Admiralty, after his promotion. None of them had made encouraging reading – and, judging from the scene before him, they'd simply been swept away by the pressure of events. Some of the plans had even talked about triage, about allowing the elderly to die while lavishing what resources were left on the young men and women who would be required to rebuild the world. He couldn't help wondering if the system was no longer capable of even separating out the younger men and women and sending them out of danger.

But there is nowhere safe these days, he thought, morbidly. *The aliens could return at any moment to finish the job.*

The thought was a knife in his heart. Operation Nelson had been a success, tactically speaking. *Ark Royal* and her multinational task force had hammered the aliens, smashing dozens of alien starships and occupying – for a few long days – an alien world. It had been a tactical masterpiece. But they had returned home to discover that Earth had been attacked, millions of humans were dead and that the war might be on the verge of being lost. A second attack on Earth might prove disastrous.

He frowned as the car turned into Downing Street, catching sight of the protestors at the far end of the road. Some of them waved banners demanding more food or supplies for the refugees, others preached genocide and demanded attacks on alien worlds. Ted understood what they were feeling; he had to admit, in the privacy of his own thoughts, that he shared the desire for revenge. But he also knew that mutual destruction would be pointless.

But how can we come to terms, he asked himself, *when they don't even talk to us?*

The car came to a halt outside Ten Downing Street. Armed policemen, their faces grim and pale, checked their IDs again before allowing them to exit the car and run up the steps into the very heart of British Government. Inside, it felt curiously musty and abandoned, as if the vast army of civil servants who made the government work had been withdrawn. It was quite possible they had, Ted knew. The contingency plans had insisted on establishing a command and control centre some distance from the disaster zone, even if the Prime Minister and the Monarch remained in London, symbolically sharing the plight of their people. But it wasn't quite the same.

"Admiral Smith," a voice said. Ted looked up to see a man in an elegant black suit. "I'm Giles Footswitch. The Prime Minister is waiting for you."

Ted placed the name as they passed their coats to the equerry, then followed Giles Footswitch through a solid metal door and down a long flight of stairs into the secured bunker that served as the Prime Minister's command and control centre. Cold air struck him as they reached the bottom of the stairs and passed another pair of armed guards. Inside, the conference room was nearly empty. The Prime Minister sat at one end of the table, staring down at the latest set of reports. His face was so pale that Ted couldn't help wondering just how long he'd been hiding out in the bunker.

"Prime Minister," he said, carefully.

"Admiral Smith," the Prime Minister said. He rose, then stepped slowly towards Ted. "I must apologise for the welcome or lack thereof."

"I understand," Ted said. The normal ceremonies when an Admiral visited Downing Street had to be put to one side, under the circumstances. "I..."

"Take a seat," the Prime Minister interrupted. He turned, then returned to his seat. "The others will be here soon, I think."

Ted obeyed, motioning for Janelle to take the seat next to him. The Prime Minister's eyes rested on her for a long moment, then he looked away with a very visible shrug. Ted understood. Normally, the lover of Prince Henry would be a subject of considerable political importance, but now it hardly mattered. Millions were dead, millions more were missing...there was no time to worry about the Prince's former girlfriend. And the Prince himself was dead.

"I wanted to thank you for your service," the Prime Minister said, quietly. "It may have been overshadowed, but I still want to thank you."

"Thank you, Prime Minister," Ted said. "We did our duty."

"Others will disagree," the Prime Minister said. His voice betrayed no trace of emotion, beyond a deadness that was more worrying than outright hatred. "You should be ready for it. Love can turn so quickly to hate."

Ted nodded. He'd been a complete unknown before the war. After the first battles, he'd become a household name all over Earth. His fame had been great enough for there to be no other prospective commanding officer for Operation Nelson, despite having a reputation as a drunkard. Indeed, he'd *beaten* alcohol's grip on his mind. But now…there was no hiding the fact he'd been hundreds of light years from Earth when the planet was attacked. It was quite possible that the men and women who had loved him before the start of Operation Nelson now hated him for not being there.

He looked at the Prime Minister and sighed, inwardly. The man was utterly exhausted, sitting in a bunker, cut off from half of his staff and struggling to cope with a crisis that could bring Britain to her knees. That had *already*, in many ways, crippled the entire country. Ted was tempted to suggest that the Prime Minister took a nap, perhaps with a sedative pill, but he knew the Prime Minister wouldn't want to do anything of the sort. He was just far too aware of his role as elected leader of the country.

"The bunker network was badly damaged by the flooding," the Prime Minister said. It was such a total departure from the previous line of conversation that it made no sense. "We worried that the entire network would be flooded before realising that it was largely safe."

"Yes, Prime Minister," Ted said.

"I stay here because of the danger," the Prime Minister added. He sounded almost as if he were pleading for understanding, or forgiveness. "No one has ever presided over such a disaster, not ever."

Ted shared a long look with Janelle. The Prime Minister sounded as if he were losing the ability to think clearly under the pressure. It would be hard to blame him, Ted knew, but right now the country needed clear-sighted thinkers, not tired politicians. But there was no way he could say that out loud, not to the Prime Minister.

"Prime Minister, the latest figures are in," Giles Footswitch said. "I…"

"Leave them," the Prime Minister ordered, quietly. There was no room for dispute in his tone. "We can go over them later."

Ted felt the silence grow until it felt truly awkward, but held his peace. The Prime Minister clearly agonised over each and every death, asking himself if there was something he could have done to prevent the slaughter. Even now, more men and women – British citizens – were dying, some though starvation, some through being caught looting. By contrast, Giles Footswitch didn't seem to understand that each of the figures had a name and story behind it, or maybe he'd just chosen not to think about it. At some point, the numbers became so high that they were just...*statistics*. It was impossible to truly comprehend the sheer weight of the losses the country had suffered overnight. To try to understand was to court madness.

He looked up as the door opened, revealing the First Space Lord and a man wearing a General's uniform. Ted didn't recognise him. Both of the newcomers looked tired; the First Space Lord, in particular, wore an expression of numb shock. Ted couldn't help fearing for his life, once the immediate crisis had come to an end. It was the Royal Navy that was responsible for protecting Britain from attack and it had failed.

"Gentlemen," the Prime Minister said. "Please, be seated."

He sounded more in control of himself now, Ted noted, as a handful of other men and women entered the bunker. The Leader of the Opposition – Deputy Prime Minister, for as long as the War Cabinet remained in session – sat facing the Prime Minister, the others took whatever chairs were available. Janelle shifted uncomfortably beside him, clearly unhappy at being at the same table as so many high-ranking politicians and military officers. But there was no time to move her out of the room.

"General Steward," the Prime Minister said. "You may begin."

CHAPTER
TWO

"I've been in worse places," Wing Commander Kurt Schneider said, just loudly enough to be heard. "Haven't I?"

"It sure isn't the Academy," Rose pointed out. His lover looked visibly ill-at-ease, something she'd never shown before. "This is a foretaste of hell."

Rain crashed over the ATV as it crunched its way towards the refugee camp. The camp itself looked alarmingly like a POW camp, perhaps one of the detention centres that had been set up during the height of the troubles and used to house everyone the government of the time hadn't liked. It was surrounded by barbed wire and guarded by armed soldiers, none of whom looked very pleased to be standing in the mud, rain dripping off their uniforms. And, behind the wire, there were a dozen prefabricated colonial buildings, providing emergency shelter for thousands of refugees.

The ATV screeched to a halt, allowing Kurt to see the inside of the camp clearly. Hundreds of refugees milled around, almost all of them women, their faces bleak and hopeless. The only men in the camp, he saw, were very old men or very young boys. A news report they'd picked up on the way in had stated that men from twelve to fifty had been conscripted into the armies of labourers trying to help keep back the floodwaters. He said a silent prayer for his son as he stood up and made his way towards the hatch. Percy might have been doing well in the CCF, but he hadn't been remotely prepared for the greatest disaster to hit Britain in centuries.

But then, none of them had been prepared for the alien attack.

Outside, rain lashed down from high overhead, turning the ground into a sea of mud. Tiny rivers of water ran downhill, adding their weight to the floods growing in the valley, drowning human homes and farmland under an endless tide. He shuddered, recalling the farms that had once supplied his country with food. No one had been short of food since the Troubles, since the British Government had worked hard to ensure the island could feed itself, once again. But now there were food shortages everywhere. The emergency food supply had never been designed for a crisis of this magnitude.

Rose scrambled out behind him, struggling to unfurl her umbrella as the rain intensified, drenching her uniform jacket. Kurt allowed her to cover him as they walked towards the gate, where four soldiers stood with loaded weapons. The reports had also warned that two refugee camps had been overwhelmed by looters, who'd killed and kidnapped girls as well as stealing food supplies and vanishing into the countryside. Kurt swallowed inwardly as the soldiers raised their weapons, clearly ready to shoot. The entire country was under martial law.

"Identify yourself," one of the soldiers snapped.

"Wing Commander Kurt Schneider," Kurt said. He held up his palm, allowing them to scan the implant inserted into his right hand. It contained both his naval ID and his travel authorisation, something that bothered him more than he cared to admit. He'd never needed authorisation to travel anywhere within Britain before the war. "I have an appointment."

The soldier relaxed, slightly. Kurt had never been a groundpounder, but he'd worked closely enough with both the army and the Royal Marines to recognise a soldier from the Territorial Army, probably someone – like Kurt himself – who had done his time and not expected to return to the uniform. But everyone with military experience had been called back to the colours after Vera Cruz, after humanity had realised it had a new and deadly enemy on its hands.

"There are rules," the soldier said. He waved a hand towards a tiny building just inside the gate. It was no larger than a heavy-lift shuttle. "You may go no further into the camp than there, sir. Your family will be brought to you."

Kurt stared at him, puzzled and alarmed. "Why?"

"We've had too many people trying to sneak in and abuse the refugees," the soldier said, as he motioned for his mates to open the gates. "There were some quite nasty incidents until we sorted out the problem cases from the ones who could actually follow orders. Things will get worse before they get better."

He snorted, rudely. "And we had some MP come around a day or so ago to make a speech to the refugees," he added. "Fucked if I know what he had in mind, sir. But the refugees almost lynched him after the third condescending promise to address their concerns as soon as possible."

Kurt swallowed. The thought of his daughter in a place like this was almost more than he could bear. Penny was sweet and young and innocent and...*trapped*. Their home was gone, washed under by the tidal waves or floods. Kurt himself would be expected to return to *Ark Royal* within the day, where he would resume his duties. It all seemed so pointless if he couldn't look after his children. And his wife was gone.

The thought gave him a pang as he stepped through the gates and looked around, taking in the handful of refugees who sat in the mud with listless expressions. It was painful to admit that Molly and he had been growing apart for years, even before he'd been recalled to duty, but it was something he had to face. Their last face-to-face meeting had been far from pleasant: Molly had once held social ambitions and she'd thought the award for Kurt's role in capturing an alien starship would help her to achieve them. But the money had been running out long before the aliens had attacked Earth...

And he had no idea what had happened to his wife. There were countless millions missing, utterly unaccounted for; Molly could be dead in a ditch, her body buried under piles of mud, or she could be in one of the refugee camps, so completely out of it that she hadn't even been able to give her name. And why hadn't she been with the children when the shit had hit the fan? Where had she been when the first missile struck the water and sent tidal waves washing out in all directions.

"Kurt," Rose said softly, "do you want me to wait outside?"

Kurt hesitated. He had no idea how he would introduce Rose to his daughter, let along what the two women would make of one another. To

Penny, Rose would be the Other Woman, the person who had broken up her parents relationship. It wouldn't be true – not entirely true, he had to admit – but he doubted they would get along. And yet, he needed her support more than he cared to admit.

"I think you'd better come in," he said, as they reached the solid metal door. "But let me do the talking."

He hadn't been sure what to expect in the visiting chamber, but inside it was nothing more than a damp room with muddy trails on the floor. There were no chairs or tables, merely a sodden rug that someone had put on the floor and then used to try to wipe up the mud. Kurt looked around, hoping to see something that would make it look less like a prison cell, but saw nothing. In the end, he leaned against the metal wall – it felt like a starship's bulkhead – and tried to relax. But it didn't take. He'd faced the aliens in combat without flinching, he'd chewed out the Heir to the Throne himself, yet part of him just wanted to run now. He didn't want to see what living in a refugee camp had done to his daughter.

The door opened again, revealing two girls. Kurt started, then remembered that the babysitter – practically a live-in maid – had been trapped in the refugee camp too. Molly should have taken care of her children, the nasty part of his mind noted, before it was washed away by a sudden surge of love and pity. Penny looked...old, as if she'd grown up way before her time. Beside her, Gayle Parkinson didn't look much better.

Kurt was across the room and wrapping his arms around his daughter before his mind had quite realised what he was doing. Penny smelt... *unpleasant*, as if she hadn't been able to wash for several days. The trousers and shirt she was wearing were two sizes too large for her, while her long blonde hair lay in unwashed strands. Her face was tired and worn, just like Gayle's. And she clung to him as if he was her only hope.

"Dad," she said, finally. Tears were streaming down her face. "I...I thought you would never come."

"I'm sorry," Kurt whispered, cursing himself. He should have refused the call to return to duty, or simply deserted after it had become clear that Molly was neglecting the children. It might have been possible to transfer to one of the squadrons defending Earth, if he couldn't leave the military altogether. "I'm so sorry."

He should have been with his children, he told himself. He should have been with them as they struggled to escape the tidal waves and find safety elsewhere. He should have escorted them deeper inland, perhaps to their grandparents home in the Scottish Highlands, well away from the floods. Or perhaps they should have moved to one of the asteroid settlements that were heading out of the system at STL speeds.

Penny shuddered against him, then started to cry, a sound that tore at his heartstrings. She hadn't cried like that since the day she'd managed to get lost in the countryside, when she'd been a little girl. Beside her, Gayle flopped down and sat on the muddy floor, her torn shirt showing far too much of her breasts. Rose knelt down next to her, then started to chat to her gently. Kurt ignored them as best as he could. Penny was trying to speak.

"The ground shook," she said. "The water came so quickly we didn't have time to run. All we could do was get upstairs and pray. The house is ruined."

"It doesn't matter," Kurt said. He smirked, suddenly. The emergency legislation rushed through Parliament would make sure they wouldn't have to continue paying the mortgage now the house was effectively destroyed. "All that matters is that you're safe."

"We ran as soon as the waters fell away," Penny said. "We didn't know where to go, so we tried to head uphill. The rain came soon afterwards, catching us in the open. There were men all around us and…"

She shuddered again. Kurt stared, wondering just what had happened – and wondering if he dared ask. The news from Britain alone was a non-stop liturgy of horror. Law and order had broken down completely in vast swathes of the country, despite martial law and the deployment of armed soldiers. Refugees had been beaten, raped, shot or simply driven away by locals who considered them nothing more than plagues of locusts. Had his daughter been threatened…or raped? He didn't want to know.

He shuddered, too. Normally, there would be therapists to help children overcome the horrors of their past. He'd never thought too highly of them even before he'd joined the military, where there was often no time to reflect on previous battles. But now, he would have happily taken Penny to see a psychologist, except there weren't any. The millions of refugees would have to come to terms with their experiences on their own.

"We ended up here, eventually," she concluded. "The army took Percy at once, told him that he had to help build dykes. I haven't seen him since. Gayle…stayed here with me, but we were told she might have to go to another camp when they move us away from here."

"I'll do something about that," Kurt promised, although he wasn't sure what he *could* do. The emergency services were utterly overwhelmed dealing with the crisis. "What happened to your mother?"

"I don't know," Penny said. "She wasn't in the house when we had to flee."

Kurt cursed Molly under his breath. Where the hell had she been? Why hadn't she been with her children? There should have been enough warning for her to get back home before the missiles started to strike the planet itself. But then, the road, rail and air transport networks would have been shut down as soon as the aliens entered the system. It was possible that she'd tried to make it home and failed.

And she'd left her children in the hands of a babysitter not much older than themselves.

"I wish I'd been there," he said, truthfully. But what could he have done? Beaten his wife to force her to do as he wanted? "What do you do here?"

"Nothing," Penny said. She waved a hand listlessly in the air. "There's nothing to do here, apart from sit in the mud. No games, no toys…I saw a mother slap her daughter when she kept complaining about not having her VR headset. Others kept offering to go build dykes themselves, just to get out of the camp, but the soldiers refused. They said we have to stay here."

Kurt understood. The population of Britain had been sharply reduced by the aliens. Young women who could bear children had to be protected at all costs, while men – inherently less vital – could be sent out to labour on the front lines. But it was still unpleasant to think of his daughter being kept in the camp, earmarked to serve as a brood mare if the population didn't recover naturally. He couldn't help wondering if female naval personnel would also be required to serve as mothers, even if they wanted to put their careers first…

You're exaggerating, he told himself. *It isn't that bad.*

But it could be, he knew. The population of Britain before the attack had been seventy million, thanks to a steady rate of emigration to Britannia and the other British possessions outside the Solar System. Now...the most optimistic estimate suggested that ten million civilians had died in the attack, with millions more likely to die in the coming months as sanitation broke down and disease spread widely. Or food supplies ran out, or were murdered by their neighbours, or shot under martial law...his imagination provided too many possibilities, none of them good. It was his duty to protect his children and he'd failed, miserably.

There was a sharp knock on the door. "Visiting hours are over," a harsh voice snapped. "Get your arse in gear and get out of here."

"I wish I could take you with me," Kurt said. A mad scheme crossed his mind – take his daughter back to the spaceport, then ship her to *Ark Royal* – but he knew it would never work. And it would probably get himself put in front of a court martial board and shot. "I'll be back as soon as I can, I promise."

"I understand," Penny said. She was trying to be brave, but he could see just how scared she was underneath. "And please give Percy my love."

"I will," Kurt said. He'd sent Percy a message, but there was no way to know if he'd read it, not now. "But if you see him first, give him *my* love."

He winced at the thought. The planetary datanet had been sharply reduced ever since the attack, something he had thought to be impossible. Once upon a time, there had been nowhere on the planet where someone couldn't log into the datanet and do everything from send v-mails to download VR simulations for their headsets. Now...Penny's world had been sharply reduced, until all she knew was inside the wire. She couldn't send a message to her brother, let alone her friends...if any of them were still alive. He didn't want to know.

Penny held him for a long moment, then started to cry again. Kurt kissed her forehead, then gently disengaged her from his body and half-carried her towards the door. Outside, the rain was falling harder. The predictions he'd seen, he recalled as he put Penny down, had suggested that it would be weeks before all the vaporised water in the upper atmosphere finally washed its way to the ground. He watched the two girls as they hurried back towards one of the shelters, then turned and walked back through the gates to the ATV. The soldiers saluted as they climbed into the vehicle and left.

"She offered herself to some thugs," Rose said. There was a sombre tone in her voice, very unlike her normal demeanour. "They would have raped them both otherwise."

It took Kurt a moment to realise she was speaking of Gayle. "I didn't know," he said, wondering why Penny hadn't told him. But she wouldn't have wanted to talk about it, would she? "I…"

He shook his head. "I'm going to request reassignment," he said, shortly. "I don't want to go back into interstellar space, not now."

Rose frowned. "You may not have a choice," she said. She sounded understanding, but also concerned. "Kurt…"

"I don't care," Kurt said. He'd practically deserted his family when the call-up came. Now, there was no one left to look after his children. "My family…I can't leave my daughter here, not now. I'm damned if I'm going back into space when I can take her somewhere else."

He turned and looked out the window as the ATV drove down a road that had once been considered a safe place to learn to drive. Now, it was awash with water, just like the refugee camp. He shook his head, then nodded in grim resolution. Penny was not going to stay there, no matter what he had to do. She was his daughter…

…And he'd failed her enough already.

CHAPTER
THREE

"The situation is grim," General Stewart said. His voice was almost emotionless, but there was a strong hint of Lancashire in how he spoke. "We are facing the greatest crisis in British history."

Ted listened carefully as the General outlined the situation. The western part of the country had been badly hit by tidal waves, apart from the parts shielded by Ireland, and millions of people had been displaced. It was worse in Ireland, the General noted, but that was no consolation. Food supplies were stretched to the limit, law and order were breaking down and entire regions had slipped out of governmental control. Several cities had been effectively smashed flat.

"Gloucester and Winchester have been effectively annihilated," the General droned. He nodded to the map, showing the path the waves had taken as they slammed into Britain. "A number of rivers have broken their banks and may even change course permanently, ensuring we can no longer even rely on our maps. Farmland has been ruined, farmers have been displaced and the rain is making it hard to coordinate relief efforts."

"We cannot expect any help, either," the Prime Minister said. "The Americans have lost most of their ports along the eastern seaboard, making it harder for them to send emergency food supplies to us. France and Germany escaped the worst of the blows, but have their own problems with the rain."

Ted nodded, unsurprised. Any government that prioritised assisting another country's population over its own would be in deep trouble with the electorate, if it lasted long enough to face a general election. It was quite likely that Britain would be unable to hold an election for several years, at best. The entire country had been thoroughly shaken up and there was no census, no idea how many voters had survived or where they were living. It was a nightmare.

"The situation isn't much better in space," the First Space Lord said. "The aliens hit the cloudscoops orbiting Jupiter as well as a number of asteroid-mining and shipbuilding facilities. We're facing a shortage of HE3 at the very moment we need it desperately to power our fusion reactors. Given enough time, we could rebuild and draw on cloudscoops in the settled star systems, but I don't think the aliens will give us time."

"I can't disagree," Ted said. The aliens had pounded Earth's orbital installations badly, crippling the human race's ability to produce new starships and weapons of war. There were other shipyards outside Sol, he knew, but the aliens might go after them next. "But they didn't follow through their offensive to actually *take* Earth."

He looked down at his hands, thinking hard. In hindsight, Operation Nelson had been easy – too easy. It was clear, now, that a sizable portion of the alien fleet had been tasked with attacking Earth, perhaps even seizing the planet if the defenders had been overwhelmed. He ran through the possible course vectors in his head, trying to decide if Nelson had forced the aliens to attack ahead of time or if it had distracted them from taking Earth. But there was no way to know.

"The bottom line," the Prime Minister said, "is that the war is on the verge of being lost."

Ted sensed Janelle tensing beside him. He knew how she felt. Defeatism wasn't something the Royal Navy tolerated, not since the dark days before the Troubles. But cold logic suggested the human race was in deep trouble. The aliens had crippled humanity's ability to make war, while their own industrial base was undamaged. Combined with their frighteningly advanced technology, they had a very definite advantage that would only grow more pronounced as the war raged on.

Japan, he thought, recalling history lessons. Japan had launched a war – two wars – against the United States, but in neither case had the Japanese been able to prevent the American industrial base from making good America's losses and then burying the Japanese under a tidal wave of mass production the Japanese had simply been unable to match. Midway wasn't the battle that had doomed Japan for the very simple reason Japan had been doomed by the decision to go to war. And yet…the Japanese had believed they had no choice.

And the aliens have more settled worlds than us, he thought, morbidly. *Does that give them a larger industrial base?*

"The tactical analysts were very interested in your reports from Target One," the First Space Lord said. "In particular, they were interested in the suggestion the aliens have more than one political faction."

Ted straightened in his chair. "Yes, sir," he said. "The data does seem to support that conclusion."

"They even attempted to open communications with us," the First Space Lord added. "Do you believe they are potential allies?"

"Unknown, sir," Ted said. "We simply don't have enough data to speculate. They may be a national grouping in their own right or they may be an oppressed minority, hoping we will save them from their enemies. They may be able to assist us or they may be unable to do more than provide us with limited intelligence."

"Intelligence is something we need," the First Space Lord mused. "We have been unable to get anything out of the prisoners, Ted, and our work on their computer systems have produced more questions than answers."

Ted nodded. They'd pulled a starchart out of the alien computers that had led *Ark Royal* and her task force to Target One, but they hadn't learned anything about alien political factions…assuming, of course, it wasn't an elaborate trick. Most of the data they'd accessed was meaningless gibberish, he'd been told, something utterly useless without the key to read it.

The Prime Minister cleared his throat. "It has been decided, however, that opening communications with Alien Faction Two may well be our best chance for survival," he said, shortly. "Admiral Smith; you and a small task force will be charged with travelling to alien space and attempting to open communications with the aliens."

"Yes, Prime Minister," Ted said.

He had no illusions. There was no easy way to tell the difference between Faction One and Faction Two, save by watching and waiting to see if the alien ships opened fire. They'd be poking their way through alien space once again, utterly unaware of where they were going or what was waiting for them, hoping and praying to get lucky. It didn't strike him as a suitable military strategy at all.

But it was also the only one they had.

He took a breath. "Will we be travelling alone?"

"Politically, the world is divided," the Prime Minister said. "It is unlikely anyone will commit any major starships to the new task force. No one has broken ranks openly, at least not yet, but there have been dark rumblings that some nations are considering trying to broker private deals with the aliens. They might prefer to be Churchill rather than Petain, but…"

He shrugged, expressively. Ted had no difficulty understanding his meaning. It was better to resist than to be a collaborator, but if resistance was truly futile why not be a collaborator and hope for a chance to regain independence in the future? He wondered, absently, which nation would be the first to jump ship and sell out to the aliens. Japan? The Japanese had been hit by worse tidal waves than the UK. Russia? They'd been tapped out by the war. Or France?

But the French fought well in both Operation Nelson and the Battle of Earth, he thought, crossly. *They're not going to betray us now.*

"I believe they may assign diplomats to the mission," the Prime Minister said. "But I don't expect them to make a full commitment."

"They'll put home defence first," the First Space Lord rumbled. "It will be hard enough avoiding panic when people realise we sent *Ark Royal* away again."

"Yes, sir," Ted said.

"There is a second aspect to your mission," the Prime Minister said. He nodded towards one of the men Ted didn't recognise. "Doctor Russell?"

Ted studied the man thoughtfully. He didn't *look* like a doctor – and, if he *was* a doctor, why wasn't he out on the streets, helping the wounded? Doctor Russell wore a black suit, somehow managing to look elegant even in the bunker, and had shaved his hair close to his scalp. His eyes were hard and cold.

"I trust that everyone here is cleared for this information," Doctor Russell said. His voice was as cold as his eyes. "I shouldn't have to remind you that certain matters are classified well above most security clearances…"

"Everyone here is cleared," the Prime Minister snapped. "And besides, it may not be long before the truth comes out."

"Yes, Prime Minister," Russell said. He nodded to Ted. "As you know, one of the great successes of the *Ark Royal's* first long-range mission was to recover a number of samples of alien life from their colony world, both living and dead. The living aliens were transported to a secure facility on Luna where they were examined, while we attempted to communicate with them. In the meantime, the dead aliens were transported to another facility on the edge of the Solar System."

Ted felt a chill creeping down his spine. Whatever Doctor Russell was about to say, he suspected, he wasn't going to like it.

"Our principle purpose was to crack the alien genetic code and untangle the mysteries of their biology," Doctor Russell continued. "Our *secondary* purpose was to develop a biological weapon that could be used against them, if necessary."

Janelle gasped. She wasn't the only one. It was clear, Ted realised, that several of the people at the table, the men and women trying to steer Britain through the greatest crisis in British history, hadn't heard anything about the project until now. The Leader of the Opposition looked particularly shocked. Even the First Space Lord looked disgusted.

"This was not an easy task," Doctor Russell continued. If their reaction surprised or annoyed him he showed no sign of it. "The alien biology is completely different from anything native to Earth. We might have prayed for a *War of the Worlds* scenario, where our diseases bring them down, but it is flatly impossible. Our diseases will not infect them under any circumstances. However, we did find something new."

The Leader of the Opposition looked revolted. "Are you saying you developed something that will kill them all?"

"We believe so," Doctor Russell said, flatly. "I'll spare you the details. Suffice it to say that we uncovered alien germs and viruses within the alien bodies and cultivated them ourselves, then modified their genetic codes to make them more dangerous. The aliens should have no natural resistance to the newly-created disease."

Ted shuddered. Humanity had managed – barely – to prevent the genetically-engineered disease genie from getting out of its bottle. God knew there had been several terrorist plans to build tailored diseases to wipe out everyone they didn't like, with the diseases targeting physical features like black skin. But there was so much intermingling these days that such a disease would almost certainly spread out of control.

On one hand, he had to admit, a virus targeted on the aliens would be unlikely to infect humans. But, on the other hand, the aliens would definitely retaliate in kind.

"This is madness," the Leader of the Opposition snapped. "You're talking genocide."

"I'm talking *survival*," Doctor Russell said. "The aliens started this damn war. They haven't told us what they want; hell, we can't even *surrender* to the bastards. If it's a choice between them or us, who do you want to survive?"

General Stewart looked grim. "Can you guarantee the aliens will be affected by your disease?"

"I believe it will work," Doctor Russell said. "But…"

The General held up a hand. "I am not qualified to discuss the morality of using biological weapons tailored to exterminate an entire race," he said. "Perhaps the Archbishop of Canterbury would be better placed to give us a ruling. However, there are a number of practical problems. For a start, we give our military personnel tailored boosters to make it harder for them to get ill. How do we know the aliens don't do the same?"

He went onwards before Doctor Russell could interrupt. "And then we would have to infect one of their settled worlds," he added. "How do we do that, practically?"

Doctor Russell glared. "I was planning to infect one of the POWs and return him to an alien world…"

"Hell, no," Ted said. "You're talking about abusing a prisoner in our custody…"

"I'm talking about *survival*," Doctor Russell snapped. "What do our moralities matter when we're staring at the end of the line?"

Ted met his eyes. "The situation isn't disastrous," he said. "Not *yet*."

"It will be," Doctor Russell predicted.

The Prime Minister cleared his throat, loudly. "The deployment of biological weapons – and strikes against the alien civilian populations – will be held as an absolute last resort," he said, firmly. "However, we will need to continue to research such weapons, just in case."

He turned to face Ted. "Admiral, you will be assigned a new task force and a diplomatic mission," he said. "I expect you to depart within the week."

"*Ark Royal* requires at least a month of heavy repair work," Ted said, evenly. The aliens had proved disconcertingly adaptable. Having discovered their weapons didn't damage the Old Lady's hull they'd copied a human weapon that did and deployed it with great effect. "And her crew will need time to rest, recuperate and come to terms with everything that's happened since their return to Earth."

"Time is not exactly on our side," the First Space Lord said. "I suggest you expedite matters as much as possible."

Ted sighed. *Ark Royal* was heavily armoured, her saving grace when the aliens had attacked her with plasma weapons that had ripped modern carriers to shreds. They could blow weapons and sensor blisters off her hull, but not harm her innards. And yet, the heavy armour that had protected the carrier was also a weakness when it came to repairing the ship after the battle. The armour had to be cut off and then replaced piece by piece.

"We'll do our best, sir," he said.

"You can have first call on yard services and engineering crewmen," the First Space Lord promised. "And whatever else you need."

A few hundred more carriers just like her, Ted thought. It was clear the aliens had chosen their weapons carefully, intending to slice through human naval fleets like a knife through butter. And it would have worked, too, if *Ark Royal* hadn't remained in service. The aliens had evidently missed her when they'd done their survey of human space. But it would be years before another heavy carrier joined the fleet.

"Doctor Russell and his team will accompany you," the Prime Minister said. "If negotiations fail, or simply don't get off the ground, you may need them."

Ted felt sick. The whole concept of biological weapons was obscene. It was the sort of nightmare the Royal Navy was meant to stop, not seriously consider deploying. And yet, even putting morality aside, was there any guarantee the weapons would spread to the entire alien population? Ted rather doubted it. Humanity had dozens of settled worlds; the aliens, if their records were to be believed, had more. They'd slaughter one planet's population, but the remainder of the alien race would survive…and know, beyond a shadow of a doubt, that humanity had tried to exterminate them.

"Yes, Prime Minister," he said. If nothing else, he could make sure that Russell and his team didn't do anything stupid – or anything likely to make the war worse than it already was. "I won't let you down."

The Prime Minister nodded. "You have another appointment, Admiral," he said. He rose to his feet, signalling the end of the meeting. "The King wishes to speak with you – both of you."

Ted winced, feeling Janelle's sudden apprehension. Some bastard in the crew – and Ted intended to keelhaul the blighter when he figured out who – had leaked the news of her relationship with Prince Henry to the media. And some *other* bastard in the media had spread it far and wide, perhaps calculating the British public needed a diversion after the alien attack had devastated large parts of the country. It was thoroughly absurd, all the more so with millions dead and millions more lost without trace, but the media had still tried to lay siege to *Ark Royal* anyway. The only explanation that made at least some sense was that the reporters were trying to pretend that everything was normal.

Idiots, he thought, as the room rapidly emptied. *Nothing will ever be normal again.*

"Yes, Prime Minister," he said. It wasn't as if they could decline an invitation from the King, no matter how much his young aide would have preferred to avoid it. "It will be our pleasure."

The Prime Minister smiled tiredly, perhaps recognising the lie. "Good luck, Admiral," he said. His voice was utterly tired, tired and depressed. He'd been in charge during the greatest disaster to hit Britain, ever. No matter how many decisions he made, the ultimate resolution wouldn't come from his office. "We need to end this, as quickly as possible. Whatever we have to do…"

Ted nodded, understanding the Prime Minister's dilemma. Peace with the aliens would come at a price, of that he was sure. And the aliens – or

Faction One, at least – had never shown any interest in *talking*. Biological warheads might be the only way to force the aliens to the peace table…or at least ensure that humanity remained alive to mourn the genocide that had been wrought in its name. He knew that to be true…

But he didn't like it. And he hoped he never would.

CHAPTER

FOUR

One of the curses of being born into the Royal Family, Prince Henry had decided long ago, was that one was expected to visit other countries and pretend to like them. It wasn't so bad when visiting a modern country like America or France, but a less-developed or traditionalist country could be an uncomfortable place to visit. He still had nightmares about the water houses in Malaysia, where there had been no air conditioning, or the tents in Southern Arabia where his staff had been strictly segregated by sex. And complaining hadn't been allowed, no matter how uncomfortable or unpleasant it became. It had been one of the many things he'd hated about his life.

But he had to admit it was also good practice for being an alien prisoner.

He lay naked on the uncomfortable bed, staring up at the transparent canopy. Outside, thousands of brightly-coloured fish swam through the water, showing no fear of the aliens or – for that matter – the human in the cell. And it was a cell, he knew, even if there were no locked doors or handcuffs. The only exit involved swimming through murky water and somehow getting up to the surface before he drowned. Henry knew he was a good swimmer, but he would never be as good as the aliens. They drew oxygen directly from the water through their gills.

The cell wasn't exactly uncomfortable, although the aliens didn't seem to understand what humans needed to survive and prosper. They hadn't provided him with any clothes, either out of a misplaced paranoia over what he would do with them or through a simple lack of awareness that humans *needed* clothes. The aliens never wore clothes, as far as he could tell, at least outside combat situations. Given their biology, it was quite likely they had never developed any form of nudity taboo. Henry had rapidly grown used to being naked in front of his visitors. It helped that they were very definitely not human.

He sat up as water splashed around the entrance, then swung his legs over the side of the bed as an alien clambered up into the compartment. As always, the alien seemed largely uncomfortable in the cell, even though the atmosphere was warm and moist enough to pass for Malaysia. He couldn't help comparing its movements to a strange mixture of wet dog and wetter seal, before it turned to peer at him with bulging, utterly inhuman eyes. Henry had the feeling that bright light would disorientate the alien – its eyes were designed to see underwater – but there was no way to be sure. He didn't have anything, apart from his wits.

"Greetings," the alien said.

Henry rose to his feet and affected a bow. "Greetings," he replied. "Have we seen each other before?"

"Yes," the alien said.

There were humans, Henry knew, who would have been offended by the suggestion that every member of a particular ethnic group looked alike. And it *was* stupid; it was quite easy to tell the difference between two different humans. The only exception to that rule, at least in Henry's experience, was an asteroid where every single person was a clone of the asteroid's founder or his wife. But the aliens didn't seem to care. They all looked alike to him and, no matter what he did, he had never been able to even tell the difference between male and female aliens.

They might have the same problems with us, he told himself.

The alien seemed to flow into a sitting position. "Sit," it ordered. "Please sit."

Henry nodded, wondering just where the aliens had learned their English. His best guess was that they had recovered a tutoring console, perhaps from Vera Cruz or one of the other smaller colonies out along the rim of known space. They seemed to have a good grasp on the basic structure of the language, but they had real problems with understanding the differences between requests, commands and warnings. And that, he suspected, was just scratching the surface. It was possible that humans and aliens would never come to understand one another.

He sat cross-legged and faced the alien, wondering just what the alien saw when it looked at a human. A faceless monster, an animal... or another intelligent being? Humans saw monsters when they looked at aliens, Henry knew, although he wasn't sure how much of that sensation had been dictated by experience. He was looking at a representative of a race that had devastated several worlds, occupied more and taken countless humans as prisoners.

"You will explain your government, please," the alien said. "How do they come into power?"

Henry hesitated. It was hard enough explaining democracy, let alone the strange combination of meritocracy and aristocracy that made up the British Government. He rather doubted he could make it comprehensible to the aliens. But he had to try.

"When we want to select new leaders," he said, "we ask people to support them. The person with the most votes wins the election and becomes the leader for the next few years."

There was a long pause. He wondered, suddenly, how the aliens handled *their* government.

"Explain your government," he ordered. It had taken him some time to realise that the aliens responded better to bluntness than politeness. He wasn't sure if they didn't need the social lubricant politeness provided for humanity or if words like 'please' or 'thank you' confused them. They'd certainly never punished him for asking questions or being rude. "How does it work?"

"All talk," the alien said. "All decide. All do."

Henry frowned, puzzled. Was the alien being deliberately evasive or was it unable to express its true meaning in English? Or was he simply not understanding what he was being told?

He took a breath. Weeks – he thought it was weeks, although it was hard to be sure – of captivity had left him uncertain of anything. It was growing harder to recall that there had ever been a world outside the cell, where he'd struggled to be a starfighter pilot and achieved his dream, only to be captured by the aliens. And the aliens didn't have the slightest idea who they'd caught. He'd been careful not to say anything that might suggest his true identity to them.

"I understand," he said. If the alien was feeling talkative, he could at least try to learn something from it. "Why did you decide on war?"

The alien moved, oddly. Henry wished, not for the first time, that he knew how to read their body language. A human might have been laughing at him or preparing to throw a punch, but the aliens were completely inscrutable. He braced himself and pressed onwards.

"Your people attacked us," he said. "Why?"

"Attacked. Us," the alien said. As always, the computer-generated voice was completely atonal. "You. Attacked. Us. Faction for war won."

Henry felt his eyes narrow. There was certainly *evidence* the aliens had more than one faction; he'd been at Target One when the aliens had fired on one of their own ships. But what had the War Faction won? And why did they think humanity had attacked them first?

"We didn't even know you existed until you attacked us," he said. "Why didn't you talk to us?"

"Faction for war won," the alien repeated.

It – or he – spoke as though it explained everything. And perhaps it did, Henry realised. It was far from uncommon for humans to be rushed into war against another group of humans without sober reflection. If the aliens had some reason to think that humanity had started the war, it might explain their reluctance to actually *talk* to human representatives. They'd see the human race as aggressive, as needing to be pruned back before opening discussions. But how had the aliens come to that conclusion in the first place?

"We don't have to fight," Henry pointed out. "We could have the land; you could have the sea. There'd be nothing to fight over."

"Faction for peace...*uncertain*," the alien stated. "Aliens. Started. War."

Aliens, Henry thought. *They must mean us.*

"But what happened?" He asked. "And why?"

The alien said nothing. It rose to its feet, inched back towards the entrance and dropped into the hole. There was a splash as it hit the water and then vanished, somewhere within the murky depths. Henry stared after it, wondering just what had happened, then stood and walked back to the bed. There was little else to do, but sleep and dream of Janelle. He couldn't help wondering just what had happened to her...

And Ark Royal, he thought, numbly. *Did she make it back to Earth or did the aliens kill her?*

His thoughts were interrupted by splashing from the entrance. One alien – a new one, if he were any judge – clambered into the room, then knelt down and held out a leathery hand. It was so odd that Henry stared in disbelief. He'd never seen the aliens needing assistance to climb out of the water and into the room. But, as the next person came out of the water and removed the mask covering her face, he understood. The newcomer was human. And female.

He looked at her, then flushed and looked away as he realised she was naked. She was probably a handful of years younger than him, he decided, probably just pushing eighteen rather than twenty-two. Her long brown hair clung to her body as she wiped her skin, trying to get the water off her flesh. Henry understood the feeling all too well. The faint smell from the ocean water suggested it was far from clean.

"There's a shower over there," he said, pointing to the corner of the room. "It's clean water."

"They never supply towels," the girl said. She sounded rather amused. "I should complain to the management."

Henry snorted, then looked back at the alien. It looked back at him, then stepped into the water and vanished from sight. Henry shook his head in disbelief, then tried not to look at the girl as she washed the ocean water from her body and hair. His body was insisting on reminding him just how long it had been since he'd slept with anyone.

And are you going to betray Janelle so quickly? His thoughts mocked him. *Or are you going to try to excuse your behaviour?*

Shut up, he thought. He *knew* his father and grandfather had both had their affairs – being in the Royal Family made it impossible to keep anything quiet for long – but he was damned if he were going the same way. Honour wasn't just the name of a famous American movie heroine, after all. *I'm not going to cheat on her.*

30

"My name is Jill, Jill Pearlman," the girl said. Her accent was definitely American, Henry decided, although it was thicker than the last American accent he'd heard. Was she from one of the colonies? The Americans had been enthusiastic colonisers after the discovery that Terra Nova wasn't the only Earth-like world out there. "Who are you?"

Henry hesitated. Everyone knew him as Charles Augustus. It might not have been the brightest name to pick for himself, but it had worked. And yet, here and now, he didn't really want to hide behind a mask. It wasn't as if *Henry* was an uncommon name.

"Henry," he said, simply. He studied her, trying hard to keep his eyes on her face. It was possible she was an American starfighter pilot, but he rather doubted it. She just looked too young. "Where did you come from?"

"Heinlein," the girl said, bitterly. "I started the war."

Henry stared at her. There had been a flurry of interest in the Heinlein Colony on the datanets after the discovery of artefacts from the colony on Alien-1, but he'd been struggling to get through the Academy and he hadn't been paying much attention. From what he recalled, the colonists had wanted to set up a homeworld far from the United States and its colonies, claiming they were tainted with a political disease. They'd boarded a ship, jumped through the tramlines and vanished. No one had seen anything of them until Alien-1.

"I see," he said. "What happened?"

Jill looked down at the floor, then sat next to him on the bed. "We were swimming," she said, slowly. "Ira and I...we went to have some fun away from the adults. Ira spent all of his free time exploring, so he knew where we could go. There was this lagoon."

She broke off, bitterly. "We went skinny-dipping," she admitted. "It was Ira's idea."

"I'm sure it was," Henry said. "And then?"

"We saw this creature rise out of the water," Jill said. "It was one of them" – she waved a hand to indicate the aliens – "but we didn't know it at the time. We thought it might be a dangerous creature. I ran to get the gun and shot it. It fell back into the water and vanished."

She rubbed her eyes with her bare hands. "They didn't believe us in the colony," she said. "There hadn't been any traces of higher life forms on

CHRISTOPHER G NUTTALL

Heinlein, none at all. They didn't believe us until the aliens arrived and attacked in force."

Henry cursed under his breath. The aliens settled the seabed first and *then* moved onto the surface, if all the projections and observations were correct. Humans, meanwhile, settled the land and rarely paid any attention to what was lurking under the waves. It was quite possible, he decided, for two separate colony missions to occupy the same world, without ever realising the other one was there. If they'd both checked for other life forms and found nothing, would they even bother to check again?

"And it started there," he mused. "They must have been as astonished as you."

"I don't know," Jill said. "I hid when they attacked; my father fought desperately to protect the colony. But they overwhelmed the defences and took the survivors prisoner. They just...took me away from the other captives one day and sent me here. I haven't seen any other humans since then."

Henry considered it. "What do they want from you?"

"They just ask questions and try to master English," Jill said. She made a face. "I was not a very good teacher."

"I don't think English is an easy language for them to learn," Henry said. How many of humanity's words were bound up in unspoken assumptions that simply didn't apply to the aliens? "But you did very well."

He looked down at his hands, thinking hard. The war was an accident. The whole war, which had killed hundreds of thousands of people and presumably aliens, was an accident, the result of a disastrous First Contact. And yet...how could he get back to Earth to report to his superiors? And even if he did...

They could have talked with us at any moment, he thought, bitterly. *God knows Earth would have happily disowned the colonists if it would have prevented a war. Instead, they started to plan for a war that would have crushed us within months, if the Old Lady hadn't remained intact. They took a minor incident and turned it into a pretext for all-out war.*

"The war hasn't been going well," he said, slowly. "How long have you been here?"

"I don't know," Jill said. "I used to count my...well, *you know* – but the aliens accidentally destroyed my markers and I lost count. Several months, at least."

Years, Henry thought. *They would have needed time to prepare their weapons and tactics to launch the invasion.*

He looked up at the greenish light filtering down from the ceiling. It was the same as it was yesterday and the day before yesterday. The food was the same, the water was always bland and completely tasteless, there was next to nothing to do…it was easy to lose track of just how long he'd stayed in the cell. His hair might not have grown out long enough to suggest he'd been imprisoned for months, but it was still longer than it had been.

Jill caught his arm. "There's a war on?"

"They attacked Vera Cruz nearly a year ago," Henry said. he wasn't sure of the precise timing. "Then they stabbed inwards and advanced on Earth, taking New Russia and several smaller colonies at the same time. We stopped them, then launched a deep-strike raid on the alien colonies. I was on that raid…"

He shrugged. "I don't know what happened next," he said, "but I do know some aliens tried to communicate with the fleet."

Jill stared. "They did?"

Henry nodded, sourly. Humanity's First Contact protocols had obviously failed, although if the aliens were in a warlike mood they might not have paid attention. But building up a common language was obviously going to take time, time they didn't have.

"it failed," he said. "Other aliens stopped them."

He looked up at her. "Did they try asking you questions about Earth? Anything *tactical*?"

"Of course not," Jill said. "I don't *know* anything about Earth."

"But it suggests they want to learn from you, rather than just suck you dry," Henry said. The aliens had kept Jill for at least a year, perhaps longer. They could have killed her by now if they'd not thought they had a use for her. "And we have to try to convince them to talk to the rest of humanity. Get some proper diplomats and language experts here, talking to them. We might be able to come to an agreement."

Jill frowned. "And what if they don't *want* to come to an agreement?"

"I don't know," Henry said. He thought, briefly, about how the aliens had treated occupied worlds. New Russia had been occupied, but the aliens had largely left the human population alone. But it could have just been a tactical decision to avoid starting the genocide until after the humans were thoroughly defeated. "I just don't know."

CHAPTER
FIVE

Ted had known, intellectually, that London had more than its fair share of underground tunnels and bunkers. Ever since the invention of flight, it had been necessary to hide large parts of the government underground, just to ensure some continuity after the country came under attack. Nothing, not even the Troubles or the development of orbital bombardment weaponry had deterred the government from protecting itself.

But he couldn't help wondering just how safe and secure the network was, after the tidal waves and floods. Parts of the power grid seemed to have failed completely, leaving some of the tunnel sections dark and gloomy, while he could hear the sound of water dripping in the distance. No one had anticipated London being flooded, not since the tidal barriers had been put into service. And no one had anticipated alien bombardment. It was all too easy to imagine a crack in the rock and concrete above their heads widening enough to allow a flood of water into the underground network. They'd be washed away by the water before they realised what was happening or wind up trapped in a subsection of the complex, waiting helplessly for the air to run out.

He shook his head, angrily dismissing the thought, as they passed through a series of secure airlocks and emerged in the basement of Buckingham Palace. It was a secure complex too, he knew, although it had been centuries since the affairs of the nation were directed from any of the Royal Residencies. And now most of the Royal Family had been moved into the countryside, with only the King and Crown Princess remaining in London to share the sufferings of their population. They thought it made good press.

Ted snorted, cynically. The Royal Family would never starve; Buckingham Palace was safe, secure and *warm*. There would be emergency transport out of London if the aliens returned or rioters threatened the palace itself. Somehow, he doubted that many of their subjects would be impressed.

He looked around, interested, as the equerry led them up a flight of steps and down a long corridor, the walls lined with portraits of monarchs from a bygone age. There were countless display cases everywhere, showing off the presents given to the monarchs by foreign visitors; several of them, he couldn't help noticing, had been stripped bare, their contents shipped to bunkers well away from the coast. The contents of the palace were a vital part of Britain's heritage, he knew, something that had to be preserved. But it was hard to take such concerns seriously when he knew millions of people were starving.

Janelle caught his arm as they approached a large pair of wooden doors. "Admiral," she said, very softly, "I don't know what to say."

Ted nodded in agreement. There *was* a formal protocol for meeting the monarch, but most of it had already been put aside for the private meeting. The last time he'd met the King, it had been when he'd been awarded a whole series of medals for *Ark Royal's* victories against the alien foe. Everyone who had been anyone in British society had been there. Now, they were having a private meeting…he shook his head, gently. Under the circumstances, it seemed absurd to think of protocol.

"Be polite," he advised. Offhand, he knew of no naval officers who had regular private meetings with the monarch, even though they technically worked for him. "And try not to stare *too* much."

The doors swung open and the equerry stepped through. "Admiral Sir Theodore Smith," he announced grandly, leaving out the list of letters Ted was entitled to have after his name, "and Lieutenant Janelle Lopez."

Ted smiled and stepped through the door. Inside, it resembled a comfortable sitting room rather than the heart of a monarch's kingdom. There were several chairs and a sofa, drawn up around a blazing fire, and a drinks dispenser in one corner. It was, he realised with a flicker of insight, a place for the royals to be *people*, rather than figurehead rulers for their nation. And the man ahead of him, wearing a simple tunic and shirt, was King Charles IV of Great Britain, Emperor of Britannia and Prince of Nova Scotia.

He had looked more impressive the first time Ted had met him, Ted mentally conceded, but he'd also looked stressed, knowing that he was permanently on camera. Even Ted, who had tried to spend the last two decades on *Ark Royal* shutting out the rest of the universe, had known just how intrusive the media were around the Royal Family. The King and his family had never been able to relax, never been able to do anything for fear it would reflect badly on them – and there was nothing that could not be made to look bad, given time and carefully handling by an unscrupulous reporter and team of editors. But there were no cameras here, not at the heart of Buckingham Palace. The King could be himself.

It would have been impossible to tell he *was* the King, Ted decided, if he hadn't known ahead of time. He looked middle-aged, the very picture of a mature adult, but lacking the dignity offered by his formal robes and the crown he'd worn during the award ceremony. His hair was grey, slowly shading to white. He'd never bothered to have his face rejuvenated, Ted noted. Was it because he wasn't vain enough to have cosmetic surgery or was it because his protocol officers insisted it was beneath the King's dignity to have himself redesigned to look younger? There was no way to know.

"Admiral," the King said. His voice was very calm, very controlled. "Please don't stand on formality, not here."

He motioned Ted to a seat, then bowed to Janelle as she hastily curtseyed. "Please, relax," he insisted. "Elizabeth and I have been waiting for you."

He motioned for Janelle to sit on the sofa, next to his daughter, then sat back in his chair.

"I appreciate you coming to see us," he continued. "We weren't sure if you'd be able to make it."

We weren't given a choice, Ted thought. But he understood. The political issues surrounding Prince Henry were a minefield, even if the disasters that had struck the country had pushed the Prince's life and untimely death onto the backburner. It wasn't the King who would make the decisions, despite being the boy's father. The Prime Minister was the one who would have to decide how best to present Prince Henry's death to the world. Or maybe it had been some bureaucrat in the Civil Service who had made the final call.

He looked at the two girls and felt a stab of pity. They made an odd study in contrasts; Janelle was dark-skinned, with dark hair cropped close to her scalp in accordance with naval regulations, while Elizabeth was blonde, her hair hanging all the way down to the small of her back. The Princess was several years older than her brother, he recalled, but it had been an open question which one of them would actually succeed their father. He couldn't help wondering, from the way the Princess held herself, if she'd been in two minds about taking the throne. But Henry had very definitely *not* wanted to become King.

"I would like to hear about my son's final moments," the King said. "And about his life on your ship."

Ted hesitated then recollected what he could and launched into the tale. Henry had been a starfighter pilot, with all the strengths and weaknesses of men and women who had known their next mission could be their last. He'd lacked the discipline of the Royal Marines or the engineering crews, but he'd been a skilled pilot and *Ark Royal* had been happy to have him as part of the crew. And it wasn't a lie, he knew. Prince Henry would have gone far if he hadn't been killed by the aliens.

"He was a good pilot," he concluded. It was unusual for pilots to serve more than three years in the cockpit, but Henry could have gone on to become a CAG – Commander Air Group – or aspired to frigate command, if he'd wanted to stay in the navy. "And he is deeply missed."

"And you were fucking him," Elizabeth said. Her voice was icy cold. "Did you know who he was?"

"*Elizabeth*," her father snapped.

His daughter stared at him with bright blue eyes. "It has to be asked," she said. "You *know* how many…"

"*Elizabeth*," her father repeated.

"I didn't know who he was," Janelle said, quietly. "As far as I knew, he was just…Charles Augustus, a starfighter pilot."

The King shook his head. "Charles Augustus," he muttered. "In hindsight, the media will make it out to be blindingly obvious."

"But you were screwing him," Elizabeth insisted. "Did he never tell you the truth?"

"No," Janelle said. Her fists bunched for a long moment, then she forced herself to relax. "I never knew."

Ted eyed the girls with some concern. Janelle had been upset – more than upset – after Henry had died, even before he'd told her who her lover had been. He'd actually broken his own rule and given her compassionate leave, even though all it had meant in practice was that she got to stay in her cabin rather than carry out her duties. In hindsight, perhaps he should have kept her busy, with tasks that would keep her mind off her woes.

There's a reason married couples aren't allowed to serve together, he thought, morbidly. *If one of them dies, the other becomes useless – even dangerous.*

Princess Elizabeth, on the other hand, sounded bitchy – and yet he knew she had good reason to worry. Her brother would have had no shortage of suitors, Ted suspected, and most of them would have been more interested in claiming a royal title than in Henry himself. Elizabeth herself would have the same problem, perhaps made worse by the uncertainty over which of the royal children would inherit the throne. She would never know if anyone who showed interest in her cared more for her – or for the title. Ted felt a flicker of sympathy for the girl, despite her rudeness. It was very hard to blame her.

"The Prince never revealed his true identity to anyone," he said, as reassuringly as he could. Princess Elizabeth was young enough to be *his* daughter, but he knew next to nothing about being a father. "No one knew until they caught up with the news broadcasts from Earth,"

The King cleared his throat. "Be that as it may," he said, "it still raises uncomfortable questions."

He looked at Janelle. "Did either of you discuss the future?"

Janelle shook her head, staring down at the floor. "No," she said, quietly. "We knew we could die at any moment."

Ted winced, inwardly. Shipboard romances were hardly uncommon – and far from forbidden, as long as regulations were honoured – but they rarely lasted long. The sheer intensity of a sexual affair between two young people under constant threat of death didn't always survive when they returned to Earth or resigned from the military. Ironically, he knew, if they'd met before the war, their romance might have survived. *Ark Royal* had been held in a stable orbit near Earth. The crew had never expected to do more than maintain the ship. They'd certainly never expected to go to war.

The Princess snorted. "You just made love to him without considering the future?"

"I'm not trapped in a goldfish bowl," Janelle snapped, showing a flash of fire. "I didn't even know it might be a concern."

Ted winced. *That* had been a low blow. The Princess couldn't have an affair with *anyone*, male or female, without the media turning it into a circus. Her lover's life would be dissected ruthlessly, anything he had said or done in the past would be used against her...and the relationship would probably shatter under the pressure. The Princess could never afford to relax, let alone have a relationship that she knew might never go anywhere. It would wind up becoming a nightmare, even if her partner had been everything she wanted in a man.

"But it has *become* a concern," the Princess snapped back. She glowered at Janelle. "Are you pregnant?"

Janelle spluttered. "What?"

"All naval personnel have contraceptive implants," Ted said, quickly. "No one can get pregnant on a naval starship."

"But there are already speculations that you are carrying Henry's child," the Princess insisted. "Your life will never be the same."

"Then they will have to swallow their words when they see I am very clearly *not* pregnant," Janelle pointed out.

"Then they will start claiming that you have had an illicit abortion," Princess Elizabeth said, darkly. "They have already claimed that I have had five different abortions in the past."

Janelle recoiled, shocked. "Seriously?"

"Yes," Princess Elizabeth said. "And apparently I've had twelve different lovers."

She snorted, rudely. "I must have been asleep," she added, "because I can't remember *any* of them."

The King cleared his throat, loudly. "I would have liked to welcome you to the family formally," he said, addressing Janelle. "I believe you would have added something we desperately need. But it would probably be best for you if the whole...*affair* was forgotten as quickly as possible."

But it *wouldn't* be forgotten, Ted knew. Janelle had become a Public Interest celebrity the moment someone had revealed her relationship with Prince Henry to the media. Short of changing her name, or at least shipping back out as quickly as possible, there was no way the media would ever let her rest. At least Ted had managed to bar reporters from *Ark Royal*, despite objections from the Public Relations Department. No one wanted them to tell the universe just how badly the Old Lady had been damaged by the aliens.

"I agree," Janelle said.

Princess Elizabeth leaned forward. "Did you *love* my brother?"

"I...I don't know," Janelle confessed. "We were happy together, but..."

Oddly, Ted noted, the Princess seemed happy with the answer. Or perhaps it wasn't odd at all. There were no shortage of social climbers who would happily claim to love the target of their affections, even when it was blatantly clear they had no interest in anything beyond the title and the prestige that came with it. But the media would tear their lives apart anyway, looking for something they could use to shock and beguile the British public. Janelle might have had a very lucky escape.

But that shouldn't be a problem now, he thought. *The country has far more serious matters to worry about.*

"I have reviewed the files," the King said. He looked directly at Ted. "I do not believe that you – or any of your crew – can reasonably be held responsible for my son's death. He wanted to live the life of a starfighter pilot, without using his rank to his advantage, knowing the risks that he would face. His death..."

He broke off, clearly upset. Ted remembered the files and understood. The King had opposed his son going into the military – and then into the line of fire. It would have been relatively simple to assign Prince Henry to one of the squadrons defending Earth...although *that* might have been a mistake. Those squadrons had taken more than 80% casualties when the aliens had attacked. Henry had followed the path he'd chosen, the path that had allowed him to earn rewards – and punishments – without his rank being taken into consideration and, in the end, it had killed him. But he'd died bravely and well.

And they will use it to bolster the position of the Royal Family, he thought, cynically. Buckingham Palace employed a small army of PR experts, hoping to shape the narrative before hostile editors – or merely ones looking for a scoop – started to try to shape it for themselves. *Henry's death will make it seem as though they are sharing the same risks and burdens as everyone else.*

"There will be no Board of Inquiry," the King continued. "I believe, in any case, that you will be leaving Earth again, far too quickly."

"Yes, Your Majesty," Ted said.

He sighed, knowing the King wasn't speaking his own words. It was quite possible the King felt otherwise, that he wanted his son's death investigated carefully before passing any kind of judgement. But the decision would have been taken by the War Cabinet and the King would have had to follow orders, particularly now. The country couldn't afford an open squabble between the King and Parliament.

"I wish you the very best of luck in talking with the aliens," the King continued. "It may be our only hope of a lasting peace."

He looked at Janelle. "I am truly sorry for pulling you into our lives," he said. "I have no doubt that, if my son had survived, he would have taken steps to ensure you were protected or simply never identified. Henry, whatever his faults, was a decent person."

"That is beyond doubt," Elizabeth said, frostily.

"You are free to call us at any time, should you wish to chat," the King continued. "And please know that we do not blame you for anything."

"Thank you," Janelle said.

"But it won't be an easy few months for you," the King warned. "It has always been so for those who come too close to the Royal Family."

He rose to his feet. "You would be well-advised to remain on the carrier for the next few months, if possible," he added. "There are few other places the media won't go – and they're searching for a distraction. If they think your life will make a good distraction…"

"They already have," Janelle said, bitterly.

"She will be safe on *Ark Royal*," Ted said. He stood, then saluted the King. "Thank you for your time, Your Majesty."

The King snorted. "Good luck, Admiral," he said. "Make peace with the aliens, if you can; if not, make them pay for everything they've done to us."

CHAPTER
SIX

"We have two new squadrons of pilots joining us this afternoon," Rose said, as the shuttle landed neatly in the shuttlebay. "They'll need to be brought up to speed on carrier procedures as quickly as possible."

Kurt barely heard her. Every time he closed his eyes, he saw the refugee camp and the refugees, trapped behind the wire like prisoners. The reports they'd picked up as they made their way back to the spaceport had been far from reassuring. At least one camp had collapsed under the rain, drowning hundreds of refugees, while the supervisors of another camp had been arrested for abusing their charges. The sooner he got his children – and Gayle – out of the camps, the better.

Rose elbowed him. "You're not listening to me!"

"I was," Kurt protested.

"I just told you I was planning to hold an orgy in the briefing room with all the new pilots and you *agreed*," Rose said. "Or should I let you explain it to the Captain afterwards?"

Kurt sighed, rubbing his eyes. "I'm sorry," he said. He'd zoned out completely. "I'll try to pay attention in future."

Rose eyed him for a long moment. "There are two new squadrons of pilots joining us this afternoon," she said. "Did you hear *that* part?"

"Yes," Kurt said. "I…"

"Then you know we also have to work them into the ship's training cycles," Rose said. "All of which have to be worked in around the repair work. And then they have to be checked out on the simulators…"

Kurt rose to his feet as the hatch opened. "Deal with it," he ordered. "I hereby appoint you acting CAG, to hold the position until relieved or confirmed by the Captain."

Rose stared at him. "Kurt..."

"I need to speak to the Captain," Kurt said. He walked through the hatch and stepped down onto the solid deck. "You can handle the new pilots, can't you?"

"Kurt," Rose said, "I can handle it, but it's your job."

Kurt understood. Rose loved flying. She was in line for a post as CAG, but it would have taken her off the flight roster permanently, at least unless the carrier needed an extra pilot more than it needed a flight supervisor. Few pilots considered seeking promotion until their reflexes started to dull, while they came up with inventive excuses to *avoid* promotion as long as possible. It never failed to confuse anyone working their way towards starship command.

"I need to speak to the Captain," he said. He wanted to take her in his arms, but he knew he didn't dare, not when the shuttlebay was full of spacers and yard dogs from the nearby shipyard. There were just too many witnesses. "You can handle it, can't you?"

"I can," Rose said. "But you're not going to do anything stupid, are you?"

"I'm a CAG," Kurt pointed out. "Stupidity is abolished when one is promoted out of a cockpit."

Rose rolled her eyes, then strode past him and through the hatch that led down towards Pilot Country. Kurt smiled at her retreating back – starfighter pilots tended to act like overgrown children until they were on the verge of burning out – and then turned and made his way towards the hatch leading up to Officer Country. The starship's metal corridors were jam-packed with spacers and pallets holding dozens of spare parts, several brought out of long-term storage for the Old Lady. Others, he knew, had to be specifically reengineered for the ancient carrier.

He nodded to a pair of Marines as he strode past, who nodded back. Most of the Marines assigned to the Royal Navy had been redeployed down to the ground, reinforcing the military units struggling to cope with the sheer scale of the crisis, but *Ark Royal's* Marines had remained onboard as part of the ship's damage control teams. Part of the reason the Old Lady had such a large crew was to keep up with repairs, if necessary. The modern carriers had indulged in more automation than some officers suspected was healthy.

It took longer than he'd expected to reach Officer Country. The laser warheads the aliens had used – they'd stolen the idea from humanity, something that bothered him more than he cared to admit – had done considerable damage to the interior of the starship and several sections had been closed down entirely while the repair crews worked their magic. Kurt wondered, absently, what they'd do about the armour plating, before dismissing it as something outside his remit. The Captain and the XO had to worry about repairing their ship. Kurt only had to worry about his pilots.

He felt a flicker of guilt as he passed through the hatch and into Officer Country, making his way up to the Captain's cabin. Rose was perhaps the most experienced officer, save himself, left on the ship. Once Kurt left, it was quite likely she would be pushed into taking on the CAG job, no matter her personal preferences. He knew she'd hate it – and hate him for leaving her. But his family came first...he gritted his teeth, silently promising to explain everything to Rose after he'd spoken to the Captain. He owed her an explanation.

The hatch opened when he pressed his hand against the sensor, revealing the Captain and the Chief Engineer standing in front of a holographic display. Kurt shook his head as he stepped into the cabin and realised that the display showed just how badly *Ark Royal* had been damaged. Most of the internal damage could be repaired fairly quickly, he was sure, but it was the armour that posed a real problem. It was just unlike anything the Royal Navy had produced for over fifty years.

"We're going to have to slim down armour from these sections," Chief Engineer Anderson said. He sounded pleased, despite the situation. His expertise with one particular starship, and none whatsoever with the more modern starships, had ensured his career had stalled until *Ark Royal* had been called into battle. "We can use the armour plating to patch the holes in the hull here, here and here."

He jabbed at the display as he spoke. "I'm hoping for some additional armour plates from Mars, but they're stalling on delivery," he added. "And we might have to reshape them ourselves when we get them anyway."

Captain James Montrose Fitzwilliam nodded, thoughtfully. "Draw down the armour," he ordered. "The Admiralty wants us gone in a fortnight at best."

"They'll be lucky," Anderson predicted, dourly. "I'd honestly prefer to replace at least half of the ship's systems with completely new gear."

"And we don't have the time," Captain Fitzwilliam said. "Do your best, please."

He looked up at Kurt. "One moment, Commander," he said. "We're just finishing here."

Kurt nodded. Captain James Montrose Fitzwilliam had, according to scuttlebutt, tried to use his connections to edge Captain – now Admiral – Smith out of command when the war had begun. The Admiralty, in an unusual display of perceptiveness, had left Smith in command, but assigned Fitzwilliam to him as his XO. Somehow, the two men had learned to work together and Fitzwilliam had replaced Smith as Captain of the Old Lady when Smith had been promoted to Admiral and put in overall command of Operation Nelson. The doubts some of the crew had once had – Fitzwilliam was young, handsome, rich and aristocratic – had faded when they'd seen him in action. He *was* a competent commanding officer.

"We're getting emergency supplies rushed to us from Britannia, but we really need some of the older Chinese shit," Anderson continued. "Half of our modern systems don't talk to the older stuff we use as the backbone for our systems; hell, we really should modernise the whole ship, but we just don't have time."

"I'll speak to the Admiralty," the Captain said. "They can trade with the Chinese."

Anderson smiled, then switched off the display. "I'll keep you informed, Captain," he said. "But I honestly doubt we will be ready to meet our scheduled departure date without slimming the repairs down to the bare minimum."

Kurt swallowed. *Ark Royal's* one great strength was her solid-state armour, the walls of metal that had protected her when more modern carriers had simply been ripped apart within seconds by alien weapons. If that armour was weakened...but the aliens, he knew, had already found a way to break through the armour. They'd be building more such warheads even now, he was sure, and arming their ships in readiness for the final thrust towards Earth.

"Thank you," the Captain said. He watched the Engineer stride out of the cabin, then turned to Kurt. "What can I do for you?"

And it had better be important, hung in his voice.

"Captain," Kurt said. For a moment, his nerve almost failed him – and then he remembered the refugee camp and gritted his teeth. "I would like to submit my resignation."

The Captain studied him for a long moment. "Denied," he said, finally. "You can take it to the Admiralty if you like, but I don't believe that any resignations are being accepted at the moment."

Kurt felt cold despair – and rage – boiling up inside of him. "Captain," he said, "I would ask you to reconsider."

"And I would tell you the same thing," the Captain said, evenly. He pointed Kurt to the sofa, then turned and walked to the drinks dispenser. "Do you take milk in your tea?"

Kurt blinked. "Captain?"

"I want to know if you take milk in your tea," the Captain said. He poured a mug of tea for himself, then turned to look at Kurt. "Do you?"

"Yes, thank you," Kurt said. The Captain serving him tea? It was unprecedented in his career. Had he entered the twilight zone? "Sir..."

The Captain passed him a mug. Kurt studied it, trying to keep his eyes away from the Captain's calm gaze. It was branded with *Ark Royal's* pennant and, below, the ship's motto. *Zeal does not Rest.* At one point, it would have seemed an absurd motto for the ship, but now it fitted perfectly. *Ark Royal* had carried almost the entire weight of humanity's war effort within her solid-state hull.

"I do not believe you would seek to resign without cause," the Captain said, as he sat down facing Kurt. "Why do you want to leave the service?"

"My children are in a refugee camp," Kurt said, slowly. He wasn't sure why he wanted to tell the Captain anything, but if he was refused permission to resign his only choice would be desertion. In times of war, it carried the death penalty. "They're...not in a good state."

"Few people are, these days," the Captain said. "Do you think you can take care of them on the ground?"

"With all due respect, sir," Kurt said, "you don't have children."

"I do understand the impulse," the Captain said. "And I understand your desire to protect your children at all costs."

"My wife is dead and my children are in a fucking prison camp," Kurt snapped, before he could stop himself. The tidal wave of bitterness threatened to overcome him. "I can't leave them there!"

The Captain leaned forward. "Do you think you're the only naval officer with family in refugee camps?"

"They should be doing something about them," Kurt said. "I...I can't *think* for worrying about my family. They're all I have left."

"It has only been two weeks since the battle," the Captain said. "I believe they're planning to separate confirmed family and friends of military personnel, but right now the system is utterly overloaded. People are dying because we can't get medical supplies from one place to another..."

"Which is why I have to take care of them," Kurt insisted. "Who *else* is going to do it?"

The Captain met his eyes. "If you are discharged from the Royal Navy, you will promptly be conscripted into one of the semi-volunteer units fighting to keep as much of the country intact as possible," he said. "You *may* wind up operating a refugee camp. Or you may be ordered to help dig ditches or fill sandbags or something else that will take you away from your family once again. I hear that even prisoners have been forced into helping with relief efforts."

And if I desert, I might wind up helping anyway, Kurt thought, recognising the unspoken warning.

"And you cannot really be spared," the Captain added. "You are one of the most experienced CAGs in the navy, certainly the most experienced officer on *Ark Royal*. I cannot replace you before we depart for..."

Kurt stared. "We're leaving? Again?"

"Yes," the Captain said, flatly. "Do you make a habit of interrupting your commanding officers?"

"No, sir," Kurt said. He'd known Captains who would have blown a fuse at the mere thought of being interrupted by one of their subordinates. "I…"

"Quite understandable," the Captain said, blandly. He took another sip of his tea, then looked up at Kurt. "I can arrange for your children – and anyone else you wish to name – to be moved to a better location, if you like. They will be cared for. But I cannot accept your resignation right now. The country needs you."

"The country needs to take care of my children," Kurt muttered, sourly. "I was promised…"

"I don't think anyone anticipated such a staggering attack," the Captain said. "Everyone assumed we would have to deal with a few thousand wives and children who had lost their husbands and fathers. We could have handled that, if necessary."

Kurt couldn't disagree. One of the few advantages to being part of the Naval Reserve was having a guaranteed pension for his wife and family, if he died while serving in the navy. It was a far from perfect arrangement, but it would have helped Molly avoid an immediate financial crisis while she looked around for work for herself. But the system had been crushed below the tidal waves that had ravaged the coasts of Britain and Ireland. It was unlikely his pension would ever be paid now, if he died on active service.

"I will have your family moved, if you send me the details," the Captain said. "I'm due to visit Earth in a couple of days anyway, so I'll have it done then. In exchange, I want you to get back to your duties and carry them out in a professional manner."

"Yes, sir," Kurt said. He felt a little reassured. "Are we actually planning to depart in a fortnight?"

"The Admiralty's orders admit of no flexibility," the Captain said, flatly. "I expect we will be carrying repair technicians and shipyard drones with us when we finally weigh anchor and make our way towards the tramline. It will be a far from easy voyage."

Kurt nodded and finished his tea, then put the mug to one side. The Captain's steward would pick it up for washing, if he hadn't already been assigned to repair work. Maybe *that* was why the Captain had produced the tea himself, unless the Captain had wanted time to think and gather himself. Kurt's request to resign had to have surprised him.

"Get your flight crews ready as quickly as possible," the Captain ordered. He tapped a switch, activating the holographic starchart. Far too many stars gleamed red, signifying alien occupation. "You never know when the aliens might put in an appearance."

"Yes, sir," Kurt said. The aliens hadn't bothered to try to hold the Terra Nova system, but they still had a strong presence at New Russia. They might be planning another attack at any moment. He rose to his feet, then strode over to the hatch. "And thank you."

He stepped through the hatch and made his way slowly back to Pilot Country. Several new pilots had been assigned to *Ark Royal* since their return from alien-controlled space, although they'd simply been slotted into pre-existing squadrons rather than used to build up entirely new formations. Adding two new squadrons...he'd been too distracted to pay much attention to the paperwork, but he had the very definite impression that most of them were new pilots, just recently graduated from the Academy.

Wonderful, he thought, as he reached his office. *Just like Prince Henry*.

"Kurt," Rose said, as the hatch closed behind him. "What did the Captain say?"

"Get back to work, you slacker," Kurt said. He smiled, despite feeling no sense of humour at all. "Or words to that effect."

Rose's eyes narrowed. She was far from stupid and knew when someone was trying to distract her. "And what did you say to him?"

"I told him I wanted to resign," Kurt said. He felt another stab of guilt at the brief flicker of pain that crossed her face. "He told me I couldn't – but that he'd help with the children."

"I'm sorry," Rose said. Her voice was curiously flat. "But at least the children will be safe."

She looked...*torn*. Their affair, which had been born out of the certain knowledge neither of them would see Earth again, hadn't faded away when they'd returned to their homeworld. She'd come to have feelings for him, Kurt knew, and he'd come to have feelings for her too. And yet, it was something they could never admit, not openly. Their affair was still in direct breach of regulations.

"I hope so," Kurt muttered. The Captain was well-connected. But even the aristocracy had taken a beating when the tidal waves had washed over Britain. It was quite possible the Captain wouldn't be able to do anything to help his children. "But we have work to do."

Rose stood, walked behind him and pushed him down onto the deck. "First, you need to relax," she said, firmly. Her hands started to massage his back, kneading out the aches and pains that had been tormenting him since he'd learned what had happened to his family. "And then you can get back to work."

CHAPTER

SEVEN

"I say, my boy," Uncle Graham said. "You look like a drowned rat. And smell like one too."

Captain James Montrose Fitzwilliam sighed as he stepped into the library. There was at least one over-bred idiot in every aristocratic family, the result of too much inbreeding or a complete lack of discipline when they were children. Uncle Graham had been an idiot when James had been born and he hadn't really improved since. But then, he'd never been forced to actually work for a living.

"It happens to be raining out there," James said, with as much patience as he could muster. It wasn't much. Winchester Hall had escaped the tidal waves, but the never-ending rain had ruined the gardens and turned the grass into a muddy ocean. The refugee camp established on the fields outside the walls only made matters worse. "And I didn't have an umbrella."

"I know, laddie," Uncle Graham said. "We haven't been able to play cricket for *weeks*."

James sighed, again. There were times when he understood just why the republicans wanted to get rid of the aristocracy. If people like himself genuinely earned their places – and he recalled how he'd tried to gain command of *Ark Royal* and shuddered – there were quite a few aristocrats who did nothing to make themselves worthy of the rights they claimed from the British State. Uncle Graham should have been sterilised as soon as it became clear that he wasn't going to improve. Fortunately, no one had expressed interest in marrying him.

He strode past his uncle and into the next room. Uncle Winchester was seated at his desk, going through a large stack of paperwork. Beside him, his secretary took notes, her face illuminated oddly by the firelight. The flames burning in the fireplace, James decided, were almost hypnotic. It was enough to make him want to forget the disaster that had struck the country outside the walls.

"James," Uncle Winchester said. He nodded to his secretary, who stood and walked out the door, closing it firmly behind her. "You're late."

"The roads were completely flooded," James said, shortly. He'd been in combat. He wasn't going to be intimidated by Uncle Winchester. "I had to divert quite some way before I got to the estate."

"You should have taken a shuttle," Uncle Winchester said. He looked James up and down, then nodded shortly. "Take a seat, please."

James sat. "The shuttles were required for distributing emergency supplies," he said, curtly. "I was damned if I was going to take one away from its duties just to get here on time."

Uncle Winchester didn't bother to argue. "I got your request," he said. "Are you sure this is what you want to do?"

"Yes, Uncle," James said, firmly.

He sighed. The CAG wasn't the only officer or crewman with family in refugee camps. A quick check had revealed over three hundred registered dependents in various camps, along with several thousand deaths. He'd asked Uncle Winchester to take the Kurt Schneider's family into his home, but also to ensure the remaining family members were protected. It was his duty as a commanding officer to take care of his men.

"It has been done," Uncle Winchester said. "The young girls have been given rooms in the Hall; the young man has insisted on remaining with the volunteers. And everyone else has been placed on the priority list for transport elsewhere."

James nodded. Thankfully, large parts of the country remained untouched by the tidal waves, allowing the government to start setting up proper holding facilities for the refugees. It would be a long time before they had anywhere *decent* to live – abandoned and second homes were already being tapped under the Disaster Relief Act – but they would be safe, at least.

"Thank you," he said.

"This leads to another question," Uncle Winchester said. "Do you want them to be added to the Emergency Evacuation List?"

"*What* Emergency Evacuation List?" James asked. "If this building comes under attack…?"

"No," Uncle Winchester said. "The list of people we plan to take away from Earth if the war is not concluded soon."

James stared at him. "Uncle…?"

"*Formidable* was just commissioned at the Britannic Yards," Uncle Winchester said, slowly. "She was originally intended to be named *Prince of Wales*, but the Admiralty wanted a replacement for the carrier they lost at New Russia. Unfortunately, she isn't any better armoured than her namesake. Putting her in the line of battle, here and now, will simply give the aliens more targets to engage. We have other plans for her."

"Other plans," James repeated, feeling a sinking sensation in his chest. "Do I want to know?"

"We also rushed two large colonist-carriers through their trials," Uncle Winchester continued smoothly. "They were intended for the Boer Republic, but we seized them for ourselves. They're both designed to set up a separate colony without the need for supplies from Earth…I believe the Boers intended to pull a Heinlein and just vanish from the rest of human space."

James put two and two together. "And that's what you intend to do too, isn't it?"

"Correct," Uncle Winchester said. "*Formidable* will escort both ships, crammed with our best and brightest, through the tramlines and as far away from the aliens as possible. All three ships are designed for several years of independent operations, so they should be able to get quite some distance before they start looking for a new world to settle. Once they do, of course, they will start building up a force that can retake human space."

"Or simply avoid the aliens indefinitely," James observed.

"In the long run, that is unlikely to be possible," Uncle Winchester said. "We have no idea how fast the aliens intend to continue their expansion, but eventually they will discover the colony. There *are* plans to build a colony without any form of high technology, yet even *that* would eventually be detectable. Ideally, the colony will develop new weapons and technologies that can be used to take the war back to the aliens."

James swallowed. The aliens had shown themselves to be innovative, first in creating weapons intended to scythe through humanity's most modern starships and then, when confronted with *Ark Royal*, building weapons that had blasted their way through the Old Lady's armour. Somehow, he doubted humanity's enigmatic opponents would sit on their hands and stagnate while the refugees rebuilt a technological base and advanced well ahead of them. They'd certainly have far more resources than a single planet settled by a few hundred thousand humans.

"Chancy," he said, finally. "And what happens if they *do* stumble across the colony?"

"The colonists die," Uncle Winchester said. He sighed, loudly. "Given five or ten years, James, we'd kick their assess. The boffins are going nuts over all the discoveries from the alien battlecruiser you captured. *Genuine* original science is being performed. Some of them are even talking about ways to duplicate the tramline effect or use gravity-based drives to power missiles and starships. But we won't have time to put more than a handful of new weapons into production before we get crushed by the aliens."

He sighed, again. "Right now, humanity's entire fleet is down to twelve carriers, not counting *Ark Royal* or the modified freighters. We're making some progress on protective armour that will stand up to alien weapons, but it will still take months to get it into production and use it to coat the remaining ships. We have more frigates and destroyers, yet they're not enough to make a difference. The bottom line, James, is that we are on the verge of losing this war."

James leaned forward. "We don't know how badly the aliens have been hurt," he said, slowly. *Ark Royal's* various missions had taken out at least twenty alien carriers, although post-battle analysis had suggested some of them might be repairable. "For all we know, we might have seen the worst they can throw at us."

"But we *don't* know," Uncle Winchester said. "Have we taken out their entire fleet – or have we only scratched the surface?"

"I don't know," James said.

He recalled the projections the analysts had devised when they'd discovered and attacked Target One. They'd pointed out that Target One couldn't have produced carriers for itself, suggesting there were other shipyards located somewhere deeper in alien space. But where *were* the shipyards? If they could be destroyed, the war might come to an end.

"We do have the vague hope of contacting another alien faction," Uncle Winchester said. "But if it fails, we have to plan for the worst."

"Yes, Uncle," James said.

"This plan must remain a secret," Uncle Winchester warned. "There will be panic if *any* word gets out."

"That's why the media has been discussing Prince Henry, despite the floods," James said, in sudden understanding. "You're using it as a distraction."

"Essentially," Uncle Winchester said. "The floods themselves are one hell of a distraction, of course, but the media is helping by trying to" – he smirked – "distract people."

James snorted. He'd reviewed the datanet channels while the car had made its slow way to the house and most of them had been broadcasting entertainment programs from a bygone age. Soap operas had always disgusted him, but maybe he just wasn't the viewer demographic they were made for. But if they showed mundane lives…their viewers, surely, would *have* mundane lives.

Or maybe he was just missing the point.

"Most people just want to relax and forget their woes, or wallow in woes belonging to other people," Uncle Winchester added. "Or some of them want to feel reassured that life will return to normal."

"But it won't," James said. Even if the war ended tomorrow, even if humanity came to a peace agreement with the aliens, it would be decades before life returned to *anything* like normal. Humanity would have to rebuild from the war, then come to terms with the fact that they were no longer alone in the universe – and that some of their new friends wanted to pick a fight rather than talk. "Surely they know better than that."

"Most people are idiots," Uncle Winchester said. He paused. "James, there *was* a reason I asked you here, today."

James lifted his eyebrows. He'd suspected as much. Strings had been pulled to arrange for him to visit Winchester Hall, strings that had been in motion long before he'd approached his Uncle to ask for a favour. Those strings wouldn't have been pulled if they hadn't wanted something from him that went above and beyond the call of duty.

He settled back, cursing inwardly. There were days when he understood *precisely* why Prince Henry had sought to join the Royal Navy under an assumed name.

"*Formidable* – and the entire colony mission - will need a commander," Uncle Winchester said. "I'd like you to take command."

"I should have expected that," James said, slowly. "You do realise my carrier expertise is limited to *Ark Royal*? *Formidable* is a very different kettle of fish."

"You won't be expected to take the ship into battle," Uncle Winchester assured him. "All we want you to do is find a new world and set up a colony there."

"Except you have no more idea than I do of what might be lurking at the far end of the tramlines," James pointed out. "We might discover a second alien race, far more hostile than the first. Or we might discover the aliens themselves, trying to block our escape. You need a commander who knows more about modern carriers."

"We need one who understands the urgency of the situation," Uncle Winchester grated. "I would hesitate to nominate someone else..."

"But you should," James said. "I had to learn the limits of my capabilities the hard way."

"So you did," Uncle Winchester said. "And there were other reasons to put you on *Ark Royal*. But those reasons are gone now, if you are to be believed, and it is time for you to move onwards."

James took a breath. "Uncle," he said. "I won't desert *Ark Royal* or Admiral Smith, not now."

His Uncle studied him coldly. "It is your duty to go where you are sent," he said, after a tense moment. "I will not accept you trying to escape your duty for sentimental reasons."

"I'm the commander of *Ark Royal*," James said. "She's due to depart in twelve days – and isn't *that* going to be a right headache? There is no time to prepare another officer, even Commander Williams, to take my place."

He stood and walked to the windows. Outside, rain pelted the glass sheets and ran down towards the flowerbeds below, but he could still see the refugee camp outside the walls. A few hundred people resided there – even he hadn't been able to pull an exact number from the datanet – after losing their homes and everything they owned to the tidal waves. Three weeks ago, they had been civilians, the people he was pledged to defend. Now, they were nothing but helpless refugees. How many of them, he wondered, had donated money to charities intent on helping people from Africa or the Middle East? Had they ever thought they would end up like the victims of endless civil wars and religious conflicts?

"And I owe it to the people down there not to run," he added. "There are no guarantees of survival, Uncle, but I am damned if I will run."

"The issue here is not bravery or cowardice," Uncle Winchester said. He tapped the table to underline his words. "The issue here is the survival of the human race itself."

"Or the British part of it," James pointed out. No one would repeat the mistakes of Terra Nova in a hurry. He smiled at the thought, then sobered. "Do other countries have their own plans?"

"We assume so," Uncle Winchester said. "The Americans had a colonist fleet that was due to depart just before Vera Cruz. It was placed on hold and nothing has been seen or said about it since. There are some indications that France and Brazil are planning their own departures, but we don't know for sure. They may just be considering moving additional settlers to their colonies in the wake of the Battle of Earth."

James nodded. Moving to Britannia – on the other side of Earth from the aliens – would seem very attractive right now. They'd been lucky, he knew; the aliens had deliberately avoided firing on the orbital towers, even though they were easy targets. If the towers had fallen, the death toll would have been far higher. It suggested the aliens were far more than just mindless killers. Perhaps there was a way to coexist with them after all.

But if Earth fell, Britannia wouldn't last much longer.

He took a breath. "Uncle," he said, as he turned to face the older man, "I respectfully refuse to take command of *Formidable*."

Uncle Winchester slowly rose to his feet. "Are you refusing the promotion?"

"My duty is with *Ark Royal*," James said. He fought hard to control his growing anger. "I have no intention of fleeing Earth…"

"You have a duty to ensure the human race survives," Uncle Winchester snapped. "You will be in command of a carrier, with a full complement of fighter pilots and starfighters, protecting two colonist-carriers and a genetic databank. The human race will live on where you choose to settle. It's your damn duty to take command of the fleet."

"There are others who are better equipped to take command," James said. Understanding clicked in his mind. "And most of them have ties to the aristocracy. Offer to take their families along and they will probably be *happy* to take command of the fleet. You will get to maintain your social structure indefinitely, provided you don't forget the lessons of the Troubles. And the very best of British luck."

He turned and started to make his way towards the door. "I won't mention this to anyone, Uncle, but I won't be involved. I can't."

"Very well," Uncle Winchester said. "Go back to *Ark Royal*. Resume command. Prepare for your deployment…which may very well be your last. And do everything in your power to establish a peaceful outcome to the war."

"Yes, sir," James said.

"You'll need these files," Uncle Winchester added. He picked a datachip off the desk and tossed it to James. "I was going to ask you to pass them to Admiral Smith, but seeing you're still in command…"

"Thank you," James said. "Do you know who will be appointed the Ambassador?"

"That's still being haggled over by the Foreign Office," Uncle Winchester said. He snorted in a remarkably child-like manner. "Some of the mandarins want an experience diplomat, preferably someone who cut his teeth making deals with the Americans or the other spacefaring powers. Others want someone more used to handling African or Middle Eastern powers…"

"That would be disastrous," James said, quietly. "They're too used to negotiating from a position of strength."

He sighed. After the economic storms of the mid-21st Century, large parts of Africa and the Middle East had become backwaters. The old nation-states were long gone, replaced by states built on religious, racial or ethnic lines. None of them were any match for a spacefaring power; if they caused trouble, the standard response was to send in Special Forces or call down strikes from orbit. No one, these days, wasted time trying to rebuild entire nations. If their people wanted better nations or rulers, the thinking ran, they could do it for themselves.

It was heartless, some said. But all previous nation-building attempts had failed.

"Deals are being struck," Uncle Winchester said. "I believe there will be an answer soon enough, James. Until then…"

He shrugged expressively. "Get your ship ready for combat, Captain," he added. "I have a feeling that these negotiations will be far from easy."

CHAPTER
EIGHT

As always, it was hard to tell how long it had been from the moment the aliens had left him alone with Jill to when they returned to his compartment. Henry knew he'd fallen asleep twice – being a starfighter pilot *had* taught him to sleep just about anywhere – but he honestly wasn't sure how long he'd slept. But it had given him time to think and bounce ideas off Jill, once he'd told her what the researchers had established about the aliens. She'd picked up a great deal herself, merely from watching them closely.

"I don't think they want us to mate," she said. "I've never seen them show anything resembling sexual interest in anyone."

"The researchers say they mate like fish," Henry agreed. "The women eject eggs into the water; the men eject sperm and the two match up away from their parents, like tadpoles."

Jill considered it as she lay back on the bed. "I wonder what that does to their society," she mused. "Ira and I spent all the time we had together kissing and stuff. They won't do anything of the sort."

Henry couldn't disagree. His sex life had always been more circumscribed than anyone born outside the Royal Family, but that hadn't stopped him spending most of his waking hours plotting how to have sex. But so much of humanity's culture, morality and society was built around sex, one way or the other. How would an alien race that didn't have the same built-in urges as the human race grow and develop?

"They won't have any concept of bastardry," he said, finally. "The children might be brought up by dedicated teachers, rather than their natural parents. Hell, they may not even have husbands and wives, as we understand the term."

He scowled, remembering his history. One of the most promising royal marriages had shattered after one of the participants revealed that he'd sired a bastard child. Another prince had been tormented by suggestions his father wasn't his father, although Henry had sometimes wished *his* father hadn't been his father. He could have left the Royal Family with a clear conscience and gone elsewhere.

Jill sighed, her breasts rising and falling as she breathed. "How strange," she said. "And yet…why should we expect them to be like humans?"

Henry looked away from her. It was unlikely the aliens had realised just how many problems they were causing him by putting a naked and beautiful girl into his cell. There was little difference between alien males and females, as far as anyone could tell; they certainly didn't mate like humans. But part of his body kept reminding him just how long it had been since he'd lain with Janelle. And he had a sneaking suspicion she felt the same way.

He shook his head, firmly, then strode over to the entrance and peered down into the murky water. It smelt funny, as always, but he'd grown used to it by now. There was nothing underneath the cell, as far as he could tell, apart from a source of light. The eerie green glow pervaded the water, marking the cell's location. And yet, he had no idea why it was there. It wasn't as if the aliens needed light to see underwater.

"We shouldn't," he said. There were hundreds of human cultures and societies, even though all humans shared the same biology. It was unlikely the aliens would have a culture humans would understand completely. *They* were probably equally perplexed over some of the materials they'd pulled from their conquests. "They're nothing like humans."

Something *moved*, deep below the waters. Henry stepped back, just in time to avoid an alien coming up and out of the water like a performing seal. It should have been an absurd scene, a literal fish out of water, and yet the alien moved with an eerie grace that belied its odd appearance above the water. They would make poor soldiers, Henry considered, particularly away from the sea. But they wouldn't have to fight on the land to win the war.

The alien shivered, spraying water droplets everywhere, then turned to face him. Great yellow eyes met his, almost glowing in the dim light. Henry resisted the urge to take a step backwards as the alien squelched its way around the entrance and up towards the bed. Jill sat upright, her eyes flaring with alarm, just before the alien stopped and lowered itself to the floor. Henry hesitated, then walked back to the bed and sat next to Jill. She looked calm, calmer than he would have expected. But then, she'd been an alien captive for years.

"We must talk," the alien said. As always, it used an electronic speaker. "We must understand you."

It sounded more comprehensible, Henry noted. He'd always assumed the aliens had been studying human technology, including the teaching machines that could be found on almost any asteroid colony or small colonial homestead. Given time, they could have used the teachers to learn English and a great deal else about humanity, even though the machines contained nothing of tactical value. But the machines had also been designed for humans. It seemed equally possible that the aliens might have been unable to use them properly.

"We must talk too," Henry said. He took a long breath. "This war started by accident."

The alien seemed to recoil, slightly. It took Henry a moment to realise that it was connected – somehow – to its fellow aliens. Telepathy? There had been no sign the aliens were able to read minds. Or perhaps he was just over-thinking the issue and the alien was using communications implants. It made sense, Henry knew. The aliens might know the humans were trapped, unable to leave without drowning, but they'd want to supervise anyone who went into the cell. Henry might try to take the alien hostage.

"The War Faction states otherwise," the alien informed him. "State your case."

Jill crossed her arms under her breasts. Henry wanted to tell her to remain still. It was unlikely the aliens could read human body language, although they had definitely had a chance to download medical or psych textbooks from the colonies they'd overrun, but there was no point in taking chances. One of the most common human tactics in sensitive negotiations was to have one of the ambassadors an expert in reading people. A good one could tell a practiced liar from a honest man.

"We settled the same world as your people," Jill said, carefully. "It never crossed our minds that someone else might be living under the waters."

That was true, Henry knew. The Survey Protocols the various inter-stellar powers had formulated had never been intended to look for a race that lived underwater. No one had seriously believed that intelligent life *could* develop underwater, let alone develop technology and everything else that a spacefaring race would need. Survey ships looked for radio signals, glowing lights at night time and all the other signs that matched humanity's own pattern. They'd never thought to look under the waves.

And that raises another question, Henry told himself, sourly. *What if there are other colonies shared with the aliens – and we don't know about them?*

It seemed unlikely, he knew. Very few human colonies had one ship dropping off the colonists and no further contact with the rest of humanity. Most colonies were founded by nation-states, after all. But the aliens… who knew how they thought? Once they had ensured enough food in the oceans, they could settle a world and develop a colony without further contact from the homeworld. Maybe they believed in allowing a colony world to build up its population before they started to turn it into an industrial powerhouse.

"We believe that all races start in the waters," the alien said. It *definitely* seemed to have mastered English. "Did yours not?"

"No," Henry said. Technically speaking, humanity's very distant ancestors had crawled out of the waters, but he had a feeling it would only confuse the aliens if he brought that up. "We started on the land."

"But you killed one of our people," the alien said. It was impossible to tell if it was speaking of Jill personally or humanity in general. "That is not the sign of a peaceful race."

Henry shuddered. The alien had died…and its compatriots had mounted an immediate counterattack against what they'd assumed to be a hostile raiding party. A tragic mistake had rapidly turned into a night-mare, with tempers running high on both sides. And yet…

"You didn't attack us at once," he said. It was impossible to be sure, but he suspected that Jill had been a prisoner for over a year. But no one was quite sure when Heinlein had been destroyed. "Why not?"

There was a long pause, as if the alien was mentally debating what it should say. "War Faction stated that war was inevitable," the alien said, slowly. "Peace Faction outvoted."

Henry's eyes narrowed. There had been no shortage of human political factions that had turned a minor incident into a major crisis just to secure their own power, but he had the odd feeling he was missing something. The aliens couldn't be *that* close to humanity, could they?

Jill uncrossed her arms. "Which faction are you?"

"Peace Faction," the alien said. "Further attacks did not come. Suggested shortage of hostile intent. War Faction unimpressed. Found your worlds. Attacked them."

Henry considered it, slowly. "The War Faction believed we were hostile," he said. "And so they planned a war against us?"

"Yes," the alien said.

"And the Peace Faction did…what?" Henry asked. "Why didn't you try to talk to us?"

"Consensus for war," the alien said. "No talks until threat removed. Threat proved harder to defeat than War Faction believed. Attempted to convince War Faction to talk. War Faction refused. Attempted to talk to you directly. War Faction intervened."

Henry remembered the alien cruiser, killed by another alien ship, and shivered.

"War Faction is locked on war," the alien stated. "We must talk."

Henry looked down at his hands. He might have been intended to serve as nothing more than a figurehead, but he *did* have a working knowledge of politics and diplomacy. It was impossible to be sure, once again, yet he thought he understood. The War Faction had believed humanity to be a threat and convinced the rest of its race to support preparations for a short victorious war. And the other alien factions, assuming there were more than two, had gone along with it. They might not have viewed humanity as a lethal threat, but they might have wanted to negotiate from a position of strength or even support the war in exchange for other compromises. Henry had seen enough backroom dealing in Buckingham Palace to know that votes could be bought, often for the most surprising prices.

And then the war had gone badly and some of the aliens had started having second thoughts.

Jill frowned. "How was the decision made?" She asked. "Who voted?"

Henry looked at the alien, interested.

"All voted," the alien said. "But voting blocs split."

Henry puzzled over the statement, then pushed it to one side until he had more data. The alien clearly thought he understood the underlying assumptions, that he possessed knowledge of a culture he lacked. Perhaps he, too, would have the same problems explaining human culture and society to the aliens. They'd put a naked man in the same cell as a naked woman without ever understanding why that might be a problem.

We need more data, he thought, recalling all the briefings they'd been given. The researchers had come up with hundreds of theories, but none of them had actually been proven. He was looking right at a source of data and he couldn't even think what to ask. *How do these bastards think*?

"My people want peace," he said. The human race had nothing to gain from a war with an alien race, particularly if they could agree on a border instead. Hell, they could share the border worlds without bumping into one another. "You need to talk to us."

"We have tried," the alien stated. "It failed."

"It failed because your War Faction stopped it," Henry said. "You could try again."

The alien eyed him unblinkingly. "And your people would *listen* to us?"

"Yes," Henry said. "They will listen."

"Take us with you," Jill said. "We can tell them you want peace."

"The War Faction does not want peace," the alien said. "That is why it is called the War Faction."

Henry blinked. Had that been a *joke*? Or was the alien making a simple statement of fact? It might mean something more to the aliens, to their way of thinking, than it did to the humans listening to it.

He took a breath. "Space is immense," he said. "There is room for both of our races to grow and thrive. You would gain more by working with us and trading with us than you would gain from fighting with us. Take us with you, let us talk to our people, and we can convince them to talk properly."

The alien shivered, very slightly. "It will be considered," it said. "They will debate it."

Jill smiled. "How does your government work?"

"All talk," the alien said. "All decide."

"You said that before," Henry said. He rose to his feet and started to pace the cell. "But how does it work?"

"All talk," the alien repeated. "All decide."

Henry scowled, then peered into the murky water, catching sight of a handful of strange-looking fish as they swam past. The sight reminded him of fishing in the Scottish Highlands, one of the few memories he had that weren't tainted by the media or gold-diggers. Fish had swum in schools, if he recalled correctly, making their way through the water until they were caught by humans…

He stopped dead. Did the *aliens* swim in schools?

Communism had never worked – for humans. There was plenty of evidence that proved communism was nothing more than a repulsive historical nightmare – for humans. The communists eventually needed to create tools of coercion to make people behave, which in turn eventually created a dictator or a dictatorship of the party, of those judged ideologically sound enough to hold power. Or it simply fell apart, if done on anything above a very small scale. There had been a handful of asteroids ruled by communist regimes. None of them had lasted very long.

But would it work for the aliens?

The briefings had speculated on just how living under the water might have shaped the alien character. They'd have access to an infinite supply of food, ensuring there was no need for distribution networks or mediums of exchange like money, and they could simply swim off and find another school if they found the current one distasteful. Could they actually make a government for the people, of the people, work? Humans had real problems with unfettered democracy. The aliens might have managed to make it work.

And then...

Ethnic streaming, he thought. After Terra Nova, the human race had quietly resolved to separate planets by ethnic and national groups. Too many ethnic groups in close proximity led to war, ethnic cleansing and eventually genocide, particularly if they were historical enemies and had leaders keeping the old hatreds alive. *What would that do to the aliens?*

"The War Faction," he said, slowly. "It controls entire planets, doesn't it?"

"Yes," the alien said.

Henry swallowed as everything fell into place. The aliens had social groups, but they were united by shared politics and ambitions, not survival. Minor disputes could be tolerated, he suspected, but larger disputes would end with the disgruntled minorities heading off to join other schools of thought. Given enough time, the schools would become echo chambers, with members repeating the same beliefs and perceptions over and over again. The War Faction presumably believed that humans were a colossal threat. They weren't paying any attention to any evidence that might suggest otherwise...

Because it would be forbidden, he thought.

The aliens had spread out through the tramlines, just like humanity. They'd used their own form of ethnic streaming to settle other worlds, just like humanity. And, in doing so, they'd made it harder for the schools of thought to even *hear* about other ideas, let alone adapt and adjust their own in light of new evidence. The War Faction had presumably been warlike long before they'd discovered the human race, just like the humans who had believed in building up the various interstellar navies. And then they'd stumbled across proof they were right all along.

"We have to talk to our people," he said. "Can you arrange a meeting?"

"We would have to pass through space controlled by the War Faction," the alien said. It had clearly been in silent contact with its supervisors. "It will not be *safe*."

Henry smiled. "We don't mind danger..."

"Speak for yourself," Jill muttered.

"...And we will take the risk, in hopes of forging a peace," Henry said. "But can you convince the War Faction to see reason?"

"They will talk," the alien stated. "Other factions will also talk. A decision will be reached."

Henry glanced at Jill and winced. If he was right, the War Faction would be reluctant to listen to reason. They'd think they had good reason to continue the war.

"We will depart soon," the alien said. "You will be transferred to a ship."

"Thank you," Henry said. "Can we discuss other matters too?"

The alien looked at him. "We can," it said, finally. "But we will have to leave soon."

Henry nodded, then sat down facing the alien. If he was right...he thought he knew what questions to ask now. And if he was wrong...

He shook his head. At least the aliens were mounting a peace mission now. And maybe the other factions could convince the War Faction to stop the war.

Sure, he thought. *And maybe pigs will fly.*

CHAPTER
NINE

"Admiral on Deck!"

"As you were," Ted ordered, as he strode into the briefing room. The entire senior crew of *Ark Royal* had gathered to meet him, as per his orders. "We don't have much time, so take your seats and we'll catch up on the formalities later."

He took his seat at one end of the table, then tapped a switch, activating the holographic display. A starchart appeared in front of them, human-held stars in green, alien-held stars glowing blood-red. The tramlines were also marked; standard tramlines in gold, alien tramlines in silver. He took a long moment to study the display, then turned his attention to his subordinates.

"Operation Trafalgar, Ladies and Gentlemen," he said, without preamble. "The overall objective is to make contact with Faction Two and attempt to enlist their aid against Faction One. In the event of the first objective failing or Faction Two being unable or unwilling to assist us, our secondary objective will be to attack the centre of alien space here."

He tapped a switch. Their target, a star further into unexplored space than any human starship had ever ventured, glowed brightly on the display.

"The analysts, using the same algorithms that located Target One, believe that this star has an excellent chance of being the alien homeworld," he continued. "In any case, the alien homeworld is almost certainly in the general area. Our orders, in the event of us failing to make peace, is to carry the war right into the heart of alien territory. This will not be easy."

That, he knew, was an understatement – and he could tell from the hastily-guarded faces that his subordinates knew it too. Any heavily-developed world would have fixed defences, but it would also presumably have a number of heavily-armed starships defending it. No one knew just how many ships the aliens possessed, yet it was unlikely they would leave their homeworld undefended. The analysts had hinted the aliens might have drawn their forces down to attack Earth.

Wishful thinking, Ted thought, sourly. It sounded good, all right; it sounded too good to the true. He would have liked to believe the alien homeworld was practically undefended – fixed defences wouldn't prove *that* much of a problem – but he knew better than to plan on such an optimistic assumption. The fact that several analysts were trying to do just that worried him more than he cared to admit.

"I won't lie to you," he said. "The situation is dire. We are staring total defeat in the face – not just us, but the entire human race. Our deep-strike into alien territory may mean the difference between survival and total defeat. *Ark Royal* is the only carrier who could hope to pull the mission off against determined alien opposition."

He took a breath. "We should all pray that we can make contact with Faction Two and convince them to help us," he added. "But if not...you've all seen the records from Earth. The aliens have devastated humanity's homeworld. We...are charged with doing the same thing to them if we fail to make peace."

Once, he knew, the concept would have horrified him. He'd resisted the urge to bombard alien settlements during their earlier missions. Now...now, he couldn't help feeling curiously unconcerned about alien casualties. It bothered him, too, that he wasn't more bothered by the prospect of committing genocide.

And there were the bioweapons, of course. But those would be held in reserve for the final days.

"We will be departing in eight days," he said. "By then, I want the flotilla ready for anything from peace to war."

He sighed. The last two days had been an endless series of briefings with the Admiralty, the Foreign Office and various diplomats from the spacefaring nations, all trying to argue over what peace terms the human race should consider acceptable. Ted had pointed out that humanity wasn't in a good state to demand peace terms; they'd be lucky, he'd argued, to agree to a return to the pre-war status quo. The diplomats had not been amused, but the Prime Minister had backed him. He'd promised that the Ambassador would have been carefully warned to make the best deal he could, not hold out for an ideal deal the aliens would certainly reject.

"Ambassador Horace Melbourne will be joining us as the designated Ambassador-In-Chief for the mission," he continued. "He will be accompanied by two other diplomats from other spacefaring powers. I trust you will all make him and his staff welcome."

No one groaned out loud, but he sensed their irritation and dismay. *Ark Royal*'s sleeping quarters would have to be altered to make room for the Ambassador and his staff, all of whom would probably demand quarters in Officer Country. The crew would be trading bunkrooms and cabins for the next few days, with the humble midshipmen and junior officers getting the worst of it. Ted knew precisely how *he* would feel if someone kicked him out of his cabin and felt a flicker of sympathy. But it couldn't be helped.

"I'll reassign cabins later today," the XO said, briskly. She'd been in line for her own command after the end of Operation Nelson, but there was no time to train up a new XO for *Ark Royal*. "We should be able to handle it professionally."

"He'll want your cabin," Fitzwilliam said, dryly. "Admiral, I should lodge an official protest."

"They wanted to take the *White Elephant*," Ted said. "I think they'd be better off on *Ark Royal*."

He had to smile at Fitzwilliam's expression. The *White Elephant* – she was actually called the *White Star* – had been an attempt to build a five-star passenger liner for interstellar tourists. But the market hadn't been ready for her and she'd been placed in storage, then reactivated as a possible troopship for the war. Rumour had it that she was staggeringly luxurious, which would have suited the ambassadors perfectly, yet she was hardly a warship capable of standing in the line of battle. It was far more likely that the aliens would just blow her away without even noticing.

"They have to be out of their minds," Fitzwilliam muttered.

"In the event of us having to go to war, we will tell them to remain in their cabins," Ted said, bluntly. "I'd prefer not to have to send a ship back to Earth with them if it can be avoided."

He took a breath. "And, with that in mind, are we ready for war?"

Fitzwilliam looked at Anderson, who shrugged.

"Most of the internal damage has been repaired, now we were able to call on spare parts from China and several other nations," Anderson said. "There's enough redundancy built into the systems to allow us to operate without the remaining subcomponents. However, the main sticking point remains the armour. We will simply not be able to get new solid-state armour in time for departure."

He sighed. "With your permission, Captain, I'll strip it from several inner hull locations and use it to patch the holes," he added. "But our hull will still be weak in those points."

Ted considered it. "Will it be a major problem against alien weapons?"

"Laser warheads burn through our full armour anyway," Anderson said. "The real problem is the plasma cannons some of their warships carry. They may be able to make a dent in the weakened armour…and, of course, they can sweep the hull clear of sensors and weapons."

"By now, they'll know about our weaknesses," Fitzwilliam commented, bitterly. "Admiral, I think we have no choice, but to run the risk of using reduced armour."

"See to it," Ted ordered. It was risky, he knew, but the alternative was worse. "And weapons?"

"We've updated the mass drivers and railguns," Anderson said. "I'm actually working on ways to use railguns as small mass drivers, but I think they'd be better reserved for close-in point defence. The last thing we want are aliens firing more laser warheads at us."

"No disagreements there," Ted said. "What other problems are there?"

There was a pause.

"Crew morale is in the pits," Commander Williams said. She looked irked at having to discuss it in public, but she didn't have a choice. "Not to put too fine a point on it, morale was sky-high until we returned to Earth, whereupon it crashed badly. At least thirty percent of the crew had family or friends caught up in the tidal waves and either killed or rendered homeless. Or missing. Morale has improved since the Captain made arrangements for his crew, but it's still pretty low."

She frowned. "And there are a great many angry crewmen out there," she warned. "If we do happen to host a bunch of alien diplomats…"

"There might be incidents," Ted finished. He had no idea if the aliens would consent to sending diplomats onboard *Ark Royal*. Even if they did, he wasn't sure if he would trust them not to bring any unpleasant surprises with them…there, he had to admit, *White Elephant* would have come in handy. "If we do wind up playing host to alien diplomats, have the Marines guard them at all times. The last thing we need is a major diplomatic incident."

He looked down at the CAG, "Kurt?"

"We are seriously below complement for starfighter pilots," Schneider said, flatly. His voice was grim, yet curiously dispassionate. "Right now, we have three and a half squadrons, two of which are made up of pilots who have never flown outside simulations and training exercises. We were better prepared for war when we sailed off to attack New Russia. And I have been unable to convince the remaining home defence squadrons to cut loose any pilots. In short, we don't even have starfighters for the escort carriers."

Ted winced. After the first attack on Earth, it had been hard enough to convince the Admiralty that *Ark Royal* needed a handful of frigates and escort carriers as part of the flotilla. If the escort carriers hadn't been so useless in the line of battle, he suspected he would never have received approval. But then, without starfighters, they were damn near useless anyway.

Commander Williams frowned. "What's the bottleneck?"

"Pilots," Schneider said. He looked down at the table, almost guiltily. "Admiral, right now, we have starfighters without pilots."

"I know," Ted said. The Royal Navy had produced Spitfires and Hurricanes in vast numbers, perhaps intending to sell some of their production line to other interstellar powers. But it was pilots that was the true bottleneck. A starfighter was useless without a pilot. "Do you have a solution?"

"Only one," Schneider said. "I'd like to draw from the lead class at the Academy."

"They're *kids*," Fitzwilliam protested. "They won't even have completed the goddamned *accelerated* training course, let alone the full training period."

"Yes, sir," Schneider agreed. "But we don't have anywhere else to look."

He met Ted's eyes. "There's a big difference between flying a shuttle-craft and a starfighter," he warned. "If the pilots are too used to one craft, they won't be prepared for the other. I don't think we dare use shuttle pilots until they've been retrained and we simply don't have the time. And every other experienced pilot is tapped already."

Ted nodded, slowly. The Admiralty was unlikely to agree to assign three new front-line squadrons to *Ark Royal*, let alone the escort carriers. Using student pilots was one hell of a risk – they might wind up shooting each other instead of the aliens – but he saw no other option either. There was no way they could recruit pilots from other nations. They'd have the same problem as shuttle pilots, with the added disadvantage of believing they were prepared for war.

"Go to the Academy and ask for volunteers among the top-scoring pilots," Ted ordered, finally. "Make sure they understand this is a voluntary mission…"

He broke off. Starfighter pilots were *always* supremely convinced of their own skill, even when they'd managed to land so badly they'd broken the landing struts. It was unlikely that the best student pilots would *refuse* the mission, no matter how often they were told that refusing would not reflect badly on their careers. There were times, he thought, when starfighter pilots were allowed too much latitude. But now, with death increasingly likely for each pilot, they could be tolerated.

But if they prank my crew, he thought, remembering one incident on *Formidable* before her destruction, *I'll bring back the lash.*

"Aye, sir," Schneider said. "I don't think we will have any trouble finding volunteers."

"I don't think so too," Ted said, dryly. He looked around the compartment. "Are there any other issues we need to resolve?"

"The crew could do with a day or two of leave," Commander Williams said. "Right now, far too many of them are approaching burn-out."

"Sin City is gone," Schneider pointed out. "I thought we were going to have riots when *that* hit the datanets."

Ted nodded. The aliens, for reasons known only to themselves, had targeted Sin City with a long-range missile. There was no military reason for the attack; Sin City might have been a wretched hive of scum and villainy, but it had no military significance. And half of the servicemen who might have been visiting had been on active duty instead. All the aliens had done was kill a few thousand prostitutes, visiting civilians and force an emergency evacuation of the rest of the complex. It didn't seem like an effective use of a missile.

Unless they wanted to target our morale, he thought. Every enlisted crewman – and not a few officers – in every interstellar navy was intimately familiar with Sin City. One had been able get anything there for a price, from straight sex to VR simulations that covered the deepest darkest fantasies of the most depraved human mind. *Do they know us well enough for that?*

He shrugged. It didn't seem relevant.

"Assign them passes to Luna if they have places to go," he said, finally. Sin City wasn't the only den of ill repute, merely the best-known one. "But we can't tie up shuttles to Earth, not now. They'll be needed for recovery work."

"Aye, Admiral," Commander Williams said.

Ted nodded. "Are there any *more* issues?"

There were none.

"We will greet the ambassadors in several days, I assume," Ted said. "As I said, we have to put up with their presence, so…try to be polite, even if they *are* taking your cabin."

He stood. "Dismissed," he said. "Captain Fitzwilliam – a word?"

Fitzwilliam nodded, then waited until the compartment was empty, save for Ted, Fitzwilliam and Janelle. Ted gave her a look and she nodded, then headed through the hatch, which closed behind her. He felt a moment of concern – the bright and lively girl who had requested assignment to *Ark Royal* was gone, replaced by a stranger – but knew she had to work through her problems on her own. Perhaps it would have been kinder to urge her to change her name and emigrate to Britannia.

"Admiral," Fitzwilliam said. "Do you believe this mission can succeed?"

"I hope so," Ted said. "But we won't know until we try."

"We could have completely misinterpreted the data," Fitzwilliam added. "Or the aliens could be trying an elaborate trick."

"It's possible," Ted said. It was the Flag Captain's job to play devil's advocate. "But do we have many other options?"

He looked up at the display, charting the route to the alien homeworld – if it *was* the alien homeworld. The researchers had written hundreds of papers, each one arguing for or against the conclusion. But the only way to know for sure was to go and see. Ted was confident his command could slip through the alien rear, remaining undetected until they launched the attack, yet he knew there were too many things that could go wrong. Murphy would make an appearance at the worst possible moment.

"You'll get a confidential briefing soon," he warned. "If we make peace, well and good; if not, there are options."

"Yes, sir," Fitzwilliam said.

Ted was reminded, suddenly, of just how young his Flag Captain actually was. He'd used his family connections to try to take command of *Ark Royal*, yet – when thwarted – he'd shown the sense to actually *learn* from Ted, rather than doing his best to undermine Ted's command. And, when he'd been handed the opportunity to relieve Ted and take command for himself, he'd rejected it.

If he was my son, Ted thought, *I couldn't be prouder.*

"Many of those options are not good," he added. "They could make the war worse."

He had a sudden vision of humanity's worlds burning, one by one, as the aliens wreaked a terrible revenge. And of alien worlds burning too. The limits humans had imposed on international and interstellar conflicts meant nothing to them – and why should they? They weren't human.

Fitzwilliam snorted. "It can get worse?"

"It can," Ted said, firmly. He paused. "What arrangements did you make for the crew's families?"

Fitzwilliam flushed. "I had them moved to the estate," he said. "They'll be as safe as possible, even if *we* won't be."

"Good thinking," Ted said. He normally disliked any form of string-pulling – although he was honest enough to admit that might be because he'd never been able to do it for himself – but he had to admit that Fitzwilliam had done well. "Will they have time to send letters to their families?"

"I believe so," Fitzwilliam said. "But Admiral…the camps were shockingly disorganised."

"Yes," Ted agreed. Someone should have supplied footballs or board games or even tried to take additional volunteers out to work. "The emergency protocols were completely overwhelmed. No one expected a disaster on such a scale. Even a terrorist nuke would have been easier to handle."

"It would have been worse if they'd gone after the towers," Fitzwilliam said. "Do you think that's a good sign?"

Ted sighed. "I hope so."

CHAPTER
TEN

The Academy felt…*different* to Kurt as he walked through the long corridors, cut into the lunar rock, and made his way to the conference room. Once, it had been a place of fun as well as a place of serious training. The pilots he'd trained beside had worked hard and played harder. Weekends had been spent at Sin City, if they won passes in shooting competitions , where alcohol, gambling and girls had been available in large numbers. It had been hard, but it had also been fun.

Now, fear ran through the air and the students looked harried. Their training courses had already been cut down to the bare minimum, concentrating on flying skills to the exclusion of all else. Kurt knew – he'd been involved with designing the Accelerated Training Courses – just how dangerous it was to allow the students loose after a handful of months of training, yet it seemed worse now. The students looked as though they expected monsters to chase them down the corridor if they stepped on a crack in the floor.

He sighed, inwardly, as he stepped into the compartment. Perhaps it was the sense that it could have been the Academy, rather than Sin City, that had been destroyed. The Royal Navy had other training facilities, but none so extensive and capable. Or perhaps it was the grim awareness that starfighter pilots and carrier crews had borne the brunt of the war so far and couldn't expect to live long. Kurt and Rose were two of the longest-surviving pilots and they'd only been at war for a year.

"Attention," the Proctor snapped. The trainees in the room rose to their feet and saluted, poorly. Clearly, training had slipped even further than it had before he'd departed for Operation Nelson. "Commander?"

Kurt took the stand and studied the trainees carefully. They looked so *young*; the boys looked barely old enough to shave, while the girls barely seemed to be growing into their adult forms. It was his cynicism, he told himself bitterly, but it looked to him as though they were younger than Pèrcy and Penny. Perhaps it wouldn't be long before Penny was offered a chance to go to the Academy, now the war had reached Earth. Percy's name was already down for the next intake.

And they were scared. It was clear from the way they held themselves, from the way their eyes twitched and hands clenched when they thought he wasn't looking. He could hardly blame them for being scared, he knew; he still feared, if only for his family rather than himself. But there was no time to allow fear to master them. They were needed.

"Take your seats and relax," he ordered, deliberately informal. The trainees obeyed, sinking into their seats with every appearance of relief. "Officially, I am not here."

He watched as some of the students exchanged glances, then looked back at him. The last time he'd spoken to a batch of recruits, they'd included Prince Henry…not that he'd known it at the time. Was there someone else, equally secretive, in the bunch before him or was he simply being silly. The media had made such a song and dance about Prince Henry's brave attempt to be a normal person that it was unlikely anyone else could hide for long.

"And I will be blunt," he continued. He caught the eye of a girl young enough to be his daughter and looked away, keeping his reactions under tight control. "I don't know what you will have seen or heard on the data-nets, or the official news bulletins. The truth is that the war situation has developed not necessarily to our advantage."

A couple of them recognised the quote, he saw. The others probably thought he was indulging in deliberate understatement. Once, the students would have read histories of war and learned about their chosen field. Now, they had no time for anything, but starfighter training and endless simulations. They no longer had time to study history.

"My ship needs starfighter pilots urgently," he added. "You are the top-scoring pilots in your grades. If you are interested in joining my ship and entering active service as quickly as possible, you will have the chance to do so now. You will skip the final tests and examinations and go straight to the front lines."

He took a breath. "This is deadly serious," he warned. "I won't tolerate any form of misbehaviour onboard the ship. You'll be training endlessly with more experienced pilots, both in simulators and out of it, until you are flung into actual combat. And there is a very strong chance you could die within the first few seconds of fighting. You simply don't have the experience to know what you're doing.

"Normally, we would never consider this, any more than a father would consider giving his son the keys to the car without making sure he passed the driving test," he concluded. "If you choose to stay here and complete the training course, you may do so. It will not be counted against you – and it may well be the wise choice. But if you feel that you can handle it, that you're willing to risk everything to serve your nation now, report to the shuttlebay at 1900hrs. You'll be picked up there."

He nodded to the Proctor, who stepped forward. "Dismissed!"

The trainees rose to their feet and headed out of the door, some moving as fast as they could without running, others dragging their feet as if they wanted to stay and speak privately to Kurt. But that wasn't an option. He strode out of the room and headed to the transit tubes, where he knew he could catch a train to Luna City. Commander Williams had ordered him to take a few hours off, even if he had to wander the city rather than visit a brothel or a gambling hall. He'd spent several minutes devising ways for Rose to accompany him before reluctantly conceding she couldn't be spared from her duties.

It had been a long time since he'd visited Luna City, the first of the major settlements built on Luna and a politically independent entity. The Moon itself was a patchwork of cities, corporate installations and mining stations, some as independent as Luna City, others belonging to a nation back on Earth. It had often puzzled Kurt why the Royal Navy hadn't put its training centre closer to Clarke Colony, but there was probably some reason for it that only made sense to bureaucrats. Perhaps they'd wanted the trainees to experience Luna City rather than Clarke or Armstrong.

Or perhaps they weren't thinking at all, he thought, as he stepped out of the train and though the airlock into the first dome. Someone had scrawled *This Place Has No Atmosphere* on top of the airlock, he noted with some amusement. It was a droll reminder of just what would happen if the giant dome broke. *Bureaucrats rarely bother to consider what they're doing before it is too late.*

Inside, Luna City looked like any small town in Britain or America, save for the giant dome overhead that kept the atmosphere within the settlement. Unlike many of the other installations, most of the city was on the surface, despite the risks. After what had happened to Sin City, he couldn't help seeing, half of the population seemed intent on moving elsewhere. A number of shops were closed, the digital library was only open for half hours and the bars were the only places that seemed to be operating 24/7. Shaking his head, he stepped into one of them, only to discover it was almost deserted. The only occupants were a number of children in a booth in the far corner, snickering to themselves.

I feel old, Kurt thought, in a moment of self-pity. How long had it been since he'd felt so untouched by the outside universe? *And they're young enough to be my grandkids.*

He looked up, sharply, as a man sat down facing him. "Commander Schneider," he said, simply. "Welcome to Luna City."

Kurt blinked in surprise. The newcomer had a face so bland it was instantly forgettable, with short brown hair and a wide innocent smile. He wore a simple black tunic, just like almost all of the other adult residents of Luna City, complete with a dangling oxygen mask and emergency air supply. Kurt didn't recognise him at all.

"Thank you," he said. He didn't have it in him to be polite, not now. "Who *are* you?"

"My name doesn't matter," the man said. He waved to the waiter, who walked over to the table. "What can I get you?"

Kurt frowned. He was tempted to order one of the most expensive alcoholic drinks on Luna, but alarm bells were ringing at the back of his mind. Combat instincts were warning him to prepare to fight or flee for his life.

"English Breakfast Tea," he ordered, instead. "Why are you buying me drinks?"

"Have patience," the man said. He looked at the waiter. "I'll have a hot chocolate with vanilla essence and whipped cream on top."

The waiter nodded and retreated.

"We've followed your career with some interest, Commander," the man said. "You're quite the hero."

"You're a reporter," Kurt guessed. "I don't have anything to tell you."

The man smiled, as if Kurt had said something genuinely funny. "I'm afraid not, Commander," he said. "But you might be happier with the reporter."

He leaned back in his chair until the waiter returned, carrying a large mug of hot chocolate and a steaming teapot. Kurt watched the waiter go, then reached for the teapot.

"I'd give it time to settle," the man advised. "This isn't Navy-Issue Tea, you know."

"I'll call you Fred," Kurt decided. "You *look* a Fred."

The man snorted, then removed something from his uniform belt and placed it on the table. Kurt's eyes narrowed. A static generator was largely unknown outside the military or intelligence services, at least in Britain. He had no idea if Luna City had any import/export restrictions that covered counter-surveillance technology, but it wasn't something he would expect the average person to possess.

"You may be interested to know," 'Fred' said, "that we can no longer be overhead or recorded. We exist in a bubble of static."

Kurt stared at him. "Who the fuck are you?"

Fred shrugged, then reached into his belt again and produced a small terminal. "You may find this recording of some interest," he said. "Watch."

Kurt took the terminal and pressed play. A moment later, a pornographic scene appeared in front of him, showing a woman straddling a man and riding him for all she was worth. For a moment, he was puzzled...and then he recognised the woman. It was Rose. And the man underneath her was *him*.

He half-rose to his feet. "How the hell did you get this?"

"That would be telling," Fred said. He smiled as Kurt loomed over him. "I would advise you to sit down and pour yourself some tea. Or order something stronger if you wish."

"Go to hell," Kurt snapped.

"Sit down," Fred repeated. He watched as Kurt slowly sank back into his chair. "I trust you recognise the participants in our little version of *Starfighter Pilots Gone Wild*?"

"Fuck you," Kurt snarled.

"It seems more like you've been fucking her," Fred pointed out, mildly. He took a sip of his hot chocolate. "Let's be blunt, shall we? You've been having an affair with one of your subordinates – one of your *direct* subordinates. That will earn you, at the very least, a dishonourable discharge from the Royal Navy. Pretty awful, wouldn't you say?"

"Get to the point," Kurt said.

"Pour yourself some tea," Fred urged.

He smirked, unpleasantly. "That piece of footage is the icing on the cake," he said. "We have enough evidence of your affair to utterly ruin you. You'd be dishonourably discharged at the very least; Rosy-Posy would also be discharged. And what would that do, I wonder, to your family? Right now, thanks to your wife, you have fuck-all in the way of savings. Your only source of income is your salary from the Royal Navy."

Kurt glared at him, helplessly. He was right.

"A dishonourable discharge means you wouldn't be able to claim a pension," Fred pointed out, clearly enjoying himself. "You might even do prison time, which would probably mean a spell in the most dangerous part of the country right now, picking up debris from the tidal waves. And then…what would happen to your handsome son and pretty daughter?"

"I…I don't know," Kurt confessed. He wanted to believe the Captain would continue to protect them, but would that be possible if their father was dishonourably discharged from the Royal Navy? If not…he recalled some of the horror stories and shuddered. He was damned if he was allowing Penny to slip into prostitution, even to feed herself. And Percy… would he be able to follow his dream if his father was booted out of the Navy? "I…"

Fred leaned forward. "Do you understand the position you're in?"

"Yes," Kurt grated.

He forced himself to pour a cup of tea, add milk and then take a sip. It tasted fetid. Fred watched him with some amusement, then leaned forward and recovered the terminal. Kurt cursed himself for not pocketing it, even though he rather doubted it was the only copy in their hands…whoever *they* were. Reporters wouldn't use blackmail as a source, would they?

"Excellent," Fred said. He made a show of rubbing his hands together with glee. "You have a choice. You can follow our orders or your little porno show becomes the subject of the nightly news. I imagine that millions of people will download the videos in the first few minutes. Your partner has been quite honoured since *Ark Royal's* first return to Earth and…well, do you know how much *Playboy* offered her for a nude photo-shoot?"

"You'd be sued," Kurt pointed out, weakly.

"Ah, but you would have to find us first," Fred countered. "And who are *we*?"

Kurt said nothing.

"You will be departing on *Ark Royal* within the week, we believe," Fred said. "One of us will be accompanying the fleet. You will be given orders and expected to carry them out, whatever the risk. Once you have returned to Earth, all copies of the recordings will be turned over to you and you will be free."

Kurt gritted his teeth. He wanted to punch Fred, to knock that smug smile off his face, but he knew it would be pointless. Fred could destroy him and his family, just by uploading the footage to the datanet. By the time it was removed, if it ever was, his life would have been ripped apart. He'd be lucky if he was merely kicked out of the Navy…

And there was Rose too. She'd admitted she wanted to stay in the Navy for life, even though she only had a few years of starfighter piloting left. She could become a CAG in her own right or switch to command track and aim for carrier command. An experienced starfighter pilot would make a good carrier commander. But it wouldn't happen if the recordings were released. She'd lose her career, at the very least. At worst, she'd join him in a detention cell and then a clean-up crew.

He took a breath. "How do I know you'll keep your word?"

"You don't," Fred said. "But what I will say is this; you can refuse now and have your career ruined, or you can do one simple job for us and then you will be free, You will have literally nothing else to offer us."

"I don't trust you," Kurt admitted.

"Of course you shouldn't," Fred said. He reached into his belt, then produced a card, which he passed to Kurt. "You will receive a message from this account, every so often. When you get it, go straight to the observation blister and wait. You'll get your orders there."

He picked up the static generator and dropped it back in his belt, then finished the mug of hot chocolate in one swallow. "It's been a pleasure meeting you, Commander," he concluded. "And I hope your career continues to rise."

Kurt watched, helplessly, as Fred rose to his feet and walked off, leaving a handful of coins on the table. They were Luna Currency, Kurt saw; usable everywhere and damn-near untraceable. Fred couldn't have made the point more blatantly if he'd tried. There was no way Kurt could find him and his associates for himself – and, without any way to get at them, he had to do as they said or accept losing everything.

He cursed himself as he finished his tea. If he hadn't been so convinced they were going to die, he told himself, he would have refused Rose's advances. He hadn't been on the outs with Molly at the time…had he? But he'd survived the battle and he'd kept the affair going, despite the ever-increasing risk of being found out. And now disaster had finally fallen.

If he made a full confession, the blackmailers would be caught. Fred had told him that at least one of them would be on the starship. They could set a trap and catch him. But it wouldn't be enough to save his career, even if Rose was spared. And he wouldn't be able to support and protect his family if he was discharged from the Navy.

He didn't have a choice, he knew. He had to do as they ordered.

His terminal bleeped. It was a message from the Commandant, informing him that fifty-two trainee pilots had accepted the offer of an early start to their duties, despite the risk. All of a sudden, it seemed utterly unimportant.

You fucking idiot, he told himself, savagely. *What the fuck were you thinking?*

CHAPTER

ELEVEN

"Admiral," Janelle said, "Ambassador Melbourne and his staff just signalled us. They'll be landing within thirty minutes."

"Finally," Ted muttered. He'd hoped to have the ship ready to go before the planned deadline. Instead, the Ambassador and his staff had cut matters very fine indeed. "I'll be down in the shuttlebay to greet them."

He had no doubt, as he pulled on his dress uniform, that the Ambassadors would expect a full greeting party. But they were going to be disappointed. Ted couldn't justify pulling a honour guard of Royal Marines out of Marine Country, let alone divert his senior officers from their duties to greet the Ambassadors. Instead, it would be just him. If nothing else, it would give him a chance to see how the Ambassadors reacted to what they would probably consider disrespect.

"Don't forget your cap and sidearm," Janelle warned, as Ted inspected himself in the mirror and reluctantly concluded he looked presentable. "And you should wear your medals, sir."

"No, thank you," Ted said. He'd been given several medals by Britain and dozens more from all around the world. There was no way he could wear *all* of them on his chest, certainly not in a public gathering. Protocol officers were still having fits over precisely how many medals he should wear at any one time. "There's no point in trying to impress them."

He sighed. Janelle had been moved into his cabin, her own having been assigned to one of the Ambassadors and his aides. The first person who joked about it, he had promised himself, would be spending the rest of the cruise cleaning toilets with a toothbrush. But it did have the advantage of allowing him to keep an eye on Janelle. She was still doing her duties, but it was clear her mind was elsewhere. Perhaps leaving the solar system entirely would be better for her.

"They're almost here," Janelle said. "The shuttlebay is preparing to receive them."

Ted nodded, then walked through the hatch and down towards the shuttlebay. Janelle followed, dogging his heels like an overeager puppy. Several crewmen saluted him as he passed; others, carrying large boxes of spare parts and other components, merely nodded. Ted smiled, remembering the days when he had been a junior officer. They'd competed to carry the larger boxes, knowing it spared them from having to salute every superior they met along the way. It was astonishing how many junior officers thought they were the first ones to invent that dodge.

And it keeps them busy too, he thought, wryly.

He stepped through the airlock into the shuttlebay, just in time to watch as the shuttle nosed its way through the hatch and settled to the deck, the giant shuttlebay doors closing behind it so the compartment could be pressurised. The shuttle looked older and more battered than he would have expected from a diplomatic shuttle, but all forms of aerospace transport were in short supply right now. Chances were the original craft had been detailed to recovery work and hadn't been returned to their owners yet.

"The shuttlebay is pressurised," Janelle said. "Admiral?"

Ted sighed. Having reporters onboard his ship had been bad enough, but he knew from scuttlebutt that ambassadors could be worse. They combined the very worst of politicians and reporters, wanting to have things all their own way while being too ignorant to understand just what they were giving away. Or maybe he was just being paranoid. He knew the British Government wouldn't have selected an idiot or a team of idiots to handle delicate negotiations with the aliens. The files had certainly suggested otherwise.

He led the way into the shuttlebay and stood to attention as the shuttle's hatch cracked open, revealing a pair of grim-faced aides. They blinked at Ted, clearly having expected something more formal, then stepped down and onto the deck. Behind them, the Ambassadors and their staffs followed, their faces schooled to reveal nothing of their thoughts. Ted saluted them, then relaxed. It was important that none of the Ambassadors thought they could walk all over him.

"Admiral Smith," Ambassador Melbourne said.

"Ambassador," Ted replied. "Welcome onboard *Ark Royal.*"

Ambassador Horace Melbourne didn't seem put out at the lack of a formal greeting party. He was a short man, older and fatter than Ted would have expected wearing a simple shipsuit with a Union Jack mounted prominently on his right shoulder. Behind him, the American, Chinese and French diplomats wore similar clothes, although with their own flags. It had been decided, apparently, that there was no point in wearing any form of formal dress. The aliens would be unlikely to understand the importance of a suit and tie.

"It's a pleasure to be here," Melbourne assured him. "We're quite enthused about the chance to handle the diplomatic negotiations."

He smiled, then turned to indicate his companions. "Let me introduce Ambassador Lawrence Tennant, of the United States of America, Ambassador Luo Wenkang of China and Ambassador Pierre Gasconne of France. Between us, we represent the major powers of Earth."

"That's good to hear," Ted said. The aliens *might* have nation-states of their own, but there was no doubt that *humanity* definitely had different nations and nationalities. An agreement that suited Britain might not be accepted by the other spacefaring powers. But with four ambassadors involved, it was likely they could come up with a compromise the entire human race could accept. "With your permission, we will show you to your quarters and get you settled in for the voyage."

He felt his eyes narrow as others came out of the shuttle. One of them, a young girl who couldn't have been much older than Janelle, didn't ring any alarm bells, but the presence of Doctor Russell definitely *did*. The bioweapons project was an international research effort, Ted knew; it was the only way to avoid accusations that Britain was covertly breaking the ban on genetically-engineered biological weapons. And he had the feeling that having the Doctor assigned to his ship meant that *someone* anticipated having to use the bioweapon against alien-settled worlds.

"This is Doctor Polly MacDonald," Ambassador Melbourne said, introducing the girl. "She is currently one of the senior researchers at Selene."

Where they keep the alien captives, Ted thought. He made a mental note to read the girl's file as quickly as possible. Had she figured out a way to understand the aliens or was she as blind as the rest of them? He'd need to talk to her – or have Janelle talk to her – as soon as possible, *without* the Ambassadors listening in.

"Welcome onboard," he said. "I look forward to hearing about your work."

Polly MacDonald smiled. She was pretty, with curly red hair and a freckled face, but it was clear she was also very smart. Ted had a cynical view of most Earth-side universities – they tended to specialise in turning intelligent young people into fools and ideologues – yet he knew that Selene wouldn't have tolerated an idiot becoming a senior researcher. Selene was focused around results, rather than academic ideals. It had produced some of the best inventors of the last fifty years.

"Thank you, Admiral," she said. Her voice had a Scottish lilt, although it was almost buried under a more cosmopolitan accent. "It's always a pleasure to talk about it to someone interested."

Ted nodded, then frowned inwardly as more aides and assistants flowed out of the shuttle. Each of the Ambassadors, it seemed, had at least five or six people assigned to them by their government, several with redundant job portfolios. That, at least for the Chinese Ambassador, probably meant that some of the aides were actually meant to keep an eye on their nominal superiors. The Frenchman might have the same problem.

"If you'll come with us," Ted said, "we will escort you to your cabins, then you can join me and my senior officers for dinner later."

"Ah," Ambassador Melbourne said. "The very best of naval cuisine."

"Of course," Ted agreed, dryly. He barely managed to keep himself from smirking openly. If they were expecting a nine-course banquet with all the trimmings they were going to be very disappointed. There was no way he was going to host such a gathering when there were millions of people starving down on Earth. "Please. Come this way."

———

Kurt stood on the balcony and silently watched as the Ambassadors and their staffs made their way towards the airlock. The Ambassadors seemed to take it in their stride, but some of their staff were clearly ill-at-ease onboard the giant carrier. Kurt had never felt it himself, yet he did understand the feeling. The carrier could be disconcerting to a new starfighter pilot, let alone civilians who might not even have flown in space before. Faint quivers ran through the deck as the engineers tested the drives, while there was a constant *thrumming* in the background. Kurt had to concentrate to hear it now – he was so used to it – but it would be a while before the newcomers were able to tune it out automatically.

And one of them was…what? A spy? A reporter?

He'd barely slept since returning to the carrier as he worked the problem time and time again, trying to think of a way out. But everything seemed to be sewn up neatly. If he admitted the truth to his superiors, he would have to admit he had no idea who his contact was supposed to be – and he'd still be in deep shit for breaking regulations so blatantly. They might have escaped more than a sharp reprimand, he knew, if they'd broken off the relationship after escaping the alien trap. But instead they'd kept it going…

Kurt gritted his teeth. Honour demanded one thing, duty demanded another…and his crippling fear for the safety of his family demanded a third. He didn't dare risk losing his post, not now. Percy and Penny – and Gayle, he supposed – needed him. And it wasn't just *his* family, he knew. Rose would lose her career too. What would happen to her if she was kicked out of the Navy in disgrace?

The thought kept tormenting him as he watched the remaining aides making their way through the airlock. Which one of them was the spy? And what did he or she want?

I won't do anything that threatens the ship, he told himself, firmly. But he already knew he'd crossed that line when he didn't laugh in Fred's face. His weakness alone was a threat. *But what else can I do?*

He stepped backwards as the last of the aides vanished from sight, then turned and walked through the hatch. A handful of crewmen waved cheerfully at him as they passed, but he ignored them, his thoughts elsewhere. He was so wrapped up in his own thoughts that he barely noticed when he reached Pilot Country. Someone – probably one of the more experienced pilots – had scrawled *Welcome To The Nursery* on the hatch. Kurt hadn't had the heart to hunt down the culprit and force him to spend several hours removing the mark. He tended to agree with the mysterious vandal.

The simulators were occupied, he noted, as he glanced into the exercise room. Rose, to give her full credit, had taken over much of the work of preparing the maggots for flight duties, which meant putting them through so many simulated exercises that they spend their nights dreaming of flying through space in a starfighter. Kurt glanced at the statistics, noted there had been a slight improvement over the last few days, then sighed. It was too likely they'd overwork some of the newcomers and be forced to let them rest.

"Things aren't what they used to be," a voice said.

Kurt jumped, then spun around. Jake MacFarlane stood there, looking surprised at Kurt's reaction. The pilot hadn't been on *Ark Royal* for the first desperate battles against the aliens, but he'd joined the ship in time for Operation Nelson and the attack on Target One. He'd been a young puppy back then, someone who had trained alongside Prince Henry. Now, he was effectively a veteran pilot.

"They never were," Kurt pointed out. *He'd* had the full training course. MacFarlane had had the Accelerated Training Course. The maggots in the simulators hadn't even had *that*. But then, MacFarlane had clearly learned something. Or he would have died. "How are you enjoying your promotion?"

MacFarlane sighed. He'd been assigned to serve as a Squadron Commander, but it was very much a poisoned chalice. Almost all of his pilots were rank newcomers.

"I feel I should be sending them to their beds without supper," MacFarlane said. "They're *kids*."

Kurt nodded. He'd had the same reaction.

And he knew that far too many of those kids were going to die.

———

"I was surprised, Admiral, at your reluctance to serve alcohol," Ambassador Gasconne said. "It does tend to make diplomatic dinners go smoothly."

"Unless someone gets drunk and forgets diplomacy," Ambassador Tennant pointed out. "I was there when the Ambassador from Argentina got drunk and practically challenged the Ambassador from Brazil to a duel. Smoothing that over took a great deal of work."

Ted shrugged. It had been nearly a year since he'd touched a drop of alcohol, but there were times when he felt the urge to take a drink howling at the back of his mind. Alcohol had comforted him when his ship had been nothing more than a floating museum piece, yet when he'd actually had to go on active service he'd forced himself to stop drinking. It hadn't been easy.

And if Fitzwilliam hadn't been there, he thought, *I would have fallen back into a bottle and stayed there.*

He looked around the table, smiling inwardly. The Ambassadors hadn't seemed too put out by the food, but some of their aides were clearly doubtful. Ted had read their files, though; the Ambassadors were veterans of secret diplomacy, men who made deals well away from the media or the general public. They'd understand that it wasn't all fine wines, fancy dinners and public relations. But they wouldn't normally take their staff with them on such missions.

"The Navy is officially dry," he said, simply. It wasn't entirely true, yet he'd banned alcohol from the flotilla and made it stick. Someone probably had an illicit still somewhere – it was practically tradition - but as long as they were careful, Ted wouldn't be forced to take notice of it. "We have to set a good example."

"It could be worse," Ambassador Melbourne said. He nodded towards the dishes on the table. "I had to attend a meeting in Arabia once, years ago. They tried to feed me something made of greasy fat with a tiny piece of meat and piles of steaming rice. I later discovered it was goat."

Ted had to smile. The ship's cooks had done their best, but there was a shortage of fresh food from Earth these days. Most of the meal had come from processed biomass grown in the ship's hydroponic farms or recycled from the waste disposal systems. There were civilians who refused to eat anything recycled, all too aware of what it had been recycled *from*.

"We don't have goat on the menu," he said. "But we had to produce the meat in a vat."

"Understandable," Tennant said. "We can't afford to eat now when people are desperately looking for food down below."

Ted nodded. America had been badly hit by the tidal waves, but America simply had much more room to grow food and house refugees. Even so, it would be years before the country recovered, if it ever did. The latest reports suggested that applications for emigration, just like Britain, had skyrocketed over the last few days. Earth no longer felt safe and tranquil.

"But I should ask," Fitzwilliam said. "What do you plan to offer the aliens?"

"It depends," Melbourne said. The Ambassador shared glances with his compatriots. "Ideally, we want a return to the pre-war status quo, with a border demarcation and embassies that will prevent another war. Unfortunately, as we have no idea *why* they started the war, we may have to adapt to circumstances. At worst, we will have to cede the occupied worlds to them permanently in exchange for peace."

"The Russians will love that," Fitzwilliam pointed out. "Don't you have a Russian representative on your staff?"

"Yes, Peter Golovanov," Melbourne said. "But the Russians declined to send a formal Ambassador. Peter is…just an observer."

Ted frowned. International diplomacy wasn't something he had much experience with, apart from commanding a multinational fleet during Operation Nelson, but it seemed odd for the Russians to refuse to take part in any negotiations. Or had they assumed that the diplomats would be forced to cede the occupied worlds, including New Russia, and refused to take part on the theory that agreements wouldn't be binding if Russia didn't sign them? It wasn't a question he could ask at such a gathering.

I'll talk to the Ambassador privately, later, he thought.

Fitzwilliam changed the subject, hastily. "Doctor," he said, "do you think we can actually communicate with the aliens?"

"We have devised ways to convert our voices into something they can hear," Doctor Polly McDonald said. "But we have problems actually *communicating* with them. Some of the prisoners are more cooperative than others, yet we haven't been able to get them to talk properly. I think their society is so different from ours that some of our concepts don't make sense to them."

She smiled, charmingly. "I have been able to discuss mathematical concepts with them," she added. "They can do their sums, so we're not dealing with a race of drones, but we just can't get some of our ideas across to them. We may never be able to understand them completely."

"Wonderful," Melbourne said. "And to think I thought negotiating with religious fanatics was bad."

CHAPTER

TWELVE

"I suppose it could be worse," Fitzwilliam said.

Ted nodded in agreement as he sipped his tea. The flotilla was due to depart in two hours, but the final preparations had yet to be made. Between the diplomats, their aides and the researchers, Ted had had very little time to pay attention to the repair work. Fortunately, the Old Lady had a good commander and a brilliant engineer.

"Yeah," Ted agreed. "But we're still going to be in trouble if the aliens target the weakened parts of our hull."

He shrugged. "Apart from that," he said, "how do we stand?"

"We've kidnapped a few dozen yard dogs," Fitzwilliam said. "I think one of them is planning to file charges when we return to the solar system."

"I don't blame him," Ted said. Technically, the Royal Navy had the legal authority to pressgang whoever it needed to keep the ships running, but it had never been asserted before the war. The yard dogs would share the same fate as the naval officers, without any of the legal guarantees of protections and pensions for their families. "But as long as he does his duty here, we won't worry about it."

"The XO had a few words with them all," Fitzwilliam said. "And I've made arrangements for their families too."

He shrugged. "Most of them have families on the asteroids," he added. "The remainder are being offered safer places to live."

"Good thinking," Ted said. "And the crew?"

"The old sweats are doing fine," Fitzwilliam said. "But I do worry about the starfighter pilots, sir. They're nowhere near as trained as the last batch – and *they* took terrifying losses."

"I know," Ted said. He shook his head, bitterly. "But what else can we do?"

"I also think the CAG is on the verge of burning out," Fitzwilliam added. "I had a briefing with him two hours ago and…he seemed monumentally distracted. He's seen far too many pilots die under his command."

Ted couldn't disagree. Fifty years of relative peace had ensured that the Royal Navy's greatest losses came from accidents, not enemy action. A single death would have been cause for a full-scale enquiry into everyone involved, with careers suspended until the truth had been wrung out of them and new procedures had been put into place to prevent a repeat. But now…two carriers had been lost in the opening months of the war and it had only grown worse from then onwards. The Royal Navy alone had lost over thirty thousand personnel in just under a year.

He sighed. There had never been any shortage of volunteers for naval service, quite the opposite. Even a junior crewman could jump ahead of a civilian spacer if he did his ten years and then went into the private sector. But the Royal Navy had always been picky about who it selected to train as starfighter pilots, until now. The floodgates were opening, yet pilot training facilities had not been prepared for the sudden influx. It would be years before the situation changed.

"Keep an eye on him," he ordered, finally. "And the rest of the crew?"

"Stressed, but determined," Fitzwilliam said. "Moving their families helped, sir."

"Good thinking on your part," Ted reminded him. "And so we're ready to leave."

He keyed a switch, activating the starchart. Their planned route was far too close to the previous route they'd used to get into alien-held space, but there was no choice. The analysts had argued – and, for once, Ted agreed with them – that there was nowhere else they might have a reasonable hope of encountering Faction Two. Given the ambush the aliens had tried to spring, they'd concluded that Faction Two lay down one of the unexplored tramlines. Ted had privately noted that it was equally possible that Faction Two didn't have the firepower to keep Faction One out of its space…if, of course, they weren't misreading the data completely.

"We think there's a life-bearing world here," he said, pointing to one of the stars two jumps from Target One. "It's as good a place as any to start."

Fitzwilliam frowned. "It's still chancy as hell," he said, doubtfully. "But it has to be done."

Ted understood his feelings. The alien navigational data might be completely unsecured, for all the humans knew, yet it was hard to pull any sense out of it. Certain points – the tramlines in particular – were easy to verify, others were much harder to comprehend. Did the aliens really mean life-bearing world by that particular icon or was it a warning to stay the hell away from that particular star system? The only way to find out was to go look.

"Yes," he agreed. "It has to be done."

He tapped a switch, altering the display to show the flotilla. Six warships – two escort carriers, four frigates – kept station with *Ark Royal*, while a colossal Fleet Auxiliary hung behind them, crammed with everything from missile warheads to boxed starfighters. The transport would remain under cloak at all times, Ted knew. They couldn't risk losing her to alien fire, not when it would cost them far too much.

"They're ready to go too," he said. "We can leave on schedule."

"And just keep the repairs going while we're underway," Fitzwilliam said. He rose. "With your permission, Admiral, I will prepare my ship for departure."

"Please do," Ted said. The words caused him a pang. He would never be commander of the Old Lady – or any other starship – again, no matter how long his career lasted. An Admiral had no business occupying a command deck. "I'll be in the CIC in twenty minutes."

He watched Fitzwilliam leave, then sighed. What would he *do* after the war? He wouldn't be allowed to stay on *Ark Royal*, that was for sure; the carrier would still be a vital part of the Royal Navy. It was possible he could parley his military record into a high rank at the Admiralty, maybe even First Space Lord, although the thought of kissing political buttocks was repulsive to him. Or he could resign and write his memoirs.

It wouldn't happen, he knew. Nothing would ever be the same again.

Shaking his head sadly, he finished his tea, rose to his feet and walked through the hatch.

————

There had been a time, James Fitzwilliam conceded, when he'd thought of *Ark Royal's* bridge as crude, a memento of a bygone age. The Old Lady simply lacked the elegance of modern carriers, let alone the sheer consideration that had gone into designing her to look smart as well as efficient. But he'd come to love it over the months since he'd assumed, to feel that there could be no other command deck for him. It had a reassuring solidity that more modern carriers lacked.

But that could be because modern carriers can't stand up to the aliens, he thought. They looked good, alright, but the aliens could blow them into flaming debris within seconds. *We won't be building carriers like that again.*

He sighed inwardly as he took his seat and surveyed the main display. There were plans to build a whole new generation of armoured carriers and battleships, but it would still be years before the first ship left the shipyard and went to the front lines. Until then, *Ark Royal* was unique, utterly irreplaceable. And, if the Admiralty hadn't been willing to gamble, she would probably have remained tied to Earth, defending humanity's homeworld against the scum of the universe.

And would it have made a difference, he asked himself, *if we had stayed in orbit around Earth?*

He'd reviewed the records of the Battle of Earth. The main thrust of the alien attack had fallen on the planet's fixed defences, but they'd managed to find time to devastate the unified carrier fleet in passing. *Ark Royal* might have made a difference – or she might just have been blown apart by alien laser warheads too. There was no way to know what would have happened if she'd been there. But he knew he would always ask himself if they'd made a mistake in haring off to attack Target One.

Angrily, he pushed the thought aside. Endlessly dwelling on the past was pointless. What was done was done. It could not be changed. All that mattered was adapting to the world as it was and then moving forward. There was no point in thinking otherwise.

"Commander Lightbridge," he said. "Are we ready to depart?"

"Yes, Captain," Lightbridge said. As always, he seemed remarkably cheerful. "Drives are online; all systems read nominal. We can depart on your command."

Anderson needs a reward, James thought. *And so do the people who designed the ship before she was built. All that damage and she's still operational.*

He looked down at the status display, then up at Lieutenant Annie Davidson. "Signal the Admiralty," he ordered the communications officer. "Inform them that we are departing on schedule."

"Aye, sir, Davidson said.

"And then signal the remainder of the flotilla," James added. "Give them a countdown to our departure."

He settled back in his chair, feeling the starship quivering around him. Anderson had tested and retested everything, but he'd expressed private concerns over some of the components they'd had to hastily repair or replace. The Old Lady was built for constant modification – her designers had assumed naval technology would continue to advance indefinitely – yet some of her older systems were completely incompatible with newer systems. Anderson had said it time and time again, hammering the point home. There had been no attempt to modify and modernise *Ark Royal* while she'd been floating in the Naval Reserve and they were paying for it now.

The ship quivered again, a feeling that echoed through his bones and then faded away into nothingness. He couldn't help feeling a quiver himself, recalling just how blithely he'd turned down Uncle Winchester's offer of a way out of the nightmare. He'd meant every word he'd said to the older man – he was damned if he was deserting Admiral Smith now – and yet part of him wondered if he'd made a mistake. But there was no going back now.

Maybe they'll send the fleet out anyway, he thought, sourly. *Whatever else happens, things are going to change for humanity.*

He took a breath. "Bring the drives up to full power," he ordered as the countdown reached zero. "And then take us towards the tramline."

"Aye, Captain," Lightbridge said. A low hum echoed through the ship, growing in power as the drives started to propel the Old Lady forward. "We are underway."

"Prepare to launch the drones as soon as we cross the tramline," James ordered the tactical officer. "Do it just like we practiced."

"Aye, Captain," Commander Keith Farley said. "The drones are ready for immediate launch."

James nodded, feeling sweat trickling down his back. The aliens hadn't tried to occupy Terra Nova, but they might well have pickets in the system, watching humanity's starships as they moved towards the front lines. Ideally, the drones would pose as *Ark Royal* and her flotilla long enough for the fleet to slip away under cloak and then make its way towards the very edge of the Terra Nova system. Once there, away from any alien pickets, they would start advancing towards Target One.

Again, he thought, wryly. *But will they have bothered to repair the defences and station war fleets in the system to meet us?*

It was the old question, he knew. Just how many ships did the aliens *have?* There was no way to know, yet he suspected that if the ships *Ark Royal* had encountered during Operation Nelson had been assigned to the attack on Earth, Earth would have fallen. It suggested that the aliens either had publics that refused to allow home defence to be minimised or internal security problems of their own. Perhaps there were several alien groups and the one fighting humanity had to watch its back at the same time.

Are they watching the back doors into their space, he asked himself, *or are they gathering their forces for one last try at Earth?*

James had never considered himself a strategist. Uncle Winchester was the long-term thinker in the family. But he thought he understood the alien tactics. They'd devised a weapons mix they'd thought would be sufficient to overwhelm humanity – and they would have been right, if *Ark Royal* had been scrapped. Their advance through humanity's star systems had been smooth, clearly intended to mop up resistance as they went along, rather than a blitzkrieg towards Earth. And then they'd been slapped back by *Ark Royal* and had been forced to reconsider their options.

And the bastards are alarmingly innovative, he thought, remembering the nightmarish moment when laser warheads had burned into his ship's hull. *Just like us.*

"Captain," Lightbridge said, breaking into his thoughts. "We are approaching the tramline."

James nodded, feeling his gut twist uncomfortably. He would have preferred to sneak through the tramline to Terra Nova, but it had been unlikely that the aliens wouldn't be watching the Old Lady and her fleet… if, of course, they had pickets in the Sol System. It was what *James* would have done, if he'd had the ships to spare – and as long as they remained stealthy, there was little fear of detection.

"*War Hog* is to jump," he ordered. The frigate already had her orders. "And the remainder of the fleet is to go to tactical alert."

Alarms howled through the giant carrier as, on the display, the icon representing the frigate crawled towards the tramline and vanished. It was unlikely, James knew, that the aliens were preparing an ambush. They probably didn't have an entire fleet under cloak in the next system. But he knew better than to take anything for granted, not now. He silently counted down the seconds in his head until the icon snapped back into existence, seemingly untouched.

"Captain," Davidson said, "local space is clear."

James nodded, relieved. "Take us through," he ordered. "And then launch the drones."

He hated the moments when he couldn't do anything, when all the orders were issued and all he could do was wait for them to be carried out, but there was nothing he could do about them. The carrier shivered as she passed through the tramline, then the lights automatically dimmed slightly as the cloaking device activated. As long as the aliens didn't have a picket alarmingly close to the tramline, they shouldn't have noticed the carrier cloaking. Her signature had been replaced by a drone.

"Drones are deployed, sir," Farley reported. "Everything looks nominal."

Unless the aliens attack the drones, James thought. *They'd learn very quickly that nothing was remotely nominal about them.*

"Send the drones off on their cruise," he ordered. "And keep monitoring them for glitches."

He rose to his feet and walked over to Farley's console as the drones moved further and further away from the ship. Terra Nova hadn't even *tried* to hail the fleet, even though the planet was within a few light minutes of the tramline. According to the last report, Terra Nova had gone underground, with all radio transmitters confiscated by the various governments. James rather doubted the governments had managed to secure all the transmitters, but it hardly mattered. The aliens knew perfectly well where Terra Nova was, if they wanted it. And the planet was effectively defenceless.

"The drones appear to be working perfectly," Farley said, after ten minutes had passed. The display updated as the drones curved away from their mothership. "They're starting their loop around the system now. They'll return to the tramline in three days and go silent. It'll look like they jumped out of the system."

"Good," James said. He returned to his command chair and sat. "Helm, take us towards the transfer point, under cloak. Be sure to keep a distance from *any* contact, no matter how weak."

"Aye, sir," Lightbridge said.

James settled back into his chair. It would take hours to reach the planned transfer point, then days to cross the alien-held system to the next tramline. Normally, starships sought out the least-time courses, but they were the easiest ones to predict and picket. The aliens would have their work cut out for them if they tried to picket all possible courses. They'd need thousands of ships or sensor platforms to make it workable.

Which won't stop them leaving listening posts in a few sensible locations, James thought. *That's what we do, after all.*

He keyed a switch. "All hands, this is the Captain," he said. "We will remain under cloak, as planned, for the foreseeable future. I expect all of you to remember the silent running protocols."

Closing the channel, he thought rapidly. The crew would be tense, he knew, but there was nothing he could do about that. There was something about being under cloak that made it harder for people to concentrate and left them whispering to one another, even though everyone knew sound didn't travel through space. The XO would do her best to arrange activities for the crewmen, once they ran out of repair work to do; he hoped it would keep everyone distracted.

And stop our guests from complaining, he thought. The Ambassadors had taken their quarters in stride, but their aides had complained loudly. Perhaps they just hated the thought of having to share a cabin with their superiors. James, who had to share a cabin with his XO, found it hard to be sympathetic. And he was quite prepared to murder Uncle Winchester if he suggested that something untoward had developed between him and Commander Williams.

"Keep us on course," he ordered, pulling up a tactical exercise. At least they had even more data on just what the aliens could do. But who knew what they'd kept hidden from humanity until it was too late? There was too much speculation and not enough hard facts. "Inform me the moment anything changes."

Shaking his head, he activated the exercise and went to work.

CHAPTER
THIRTEEN

"That was a major balls-up," Kurt said, glowering at the assembled newcomers. Half of them looked as though they were going to start crying. "If the aliens had attacked us like that, you would all be dead. And so would the crew of this ship."

He sighed, inwardly. Why was it a surprise, he asked himself sarcastically, that the trainee pilots had bigger egos than piloting skills? There was an old joke, after all, that if a pilot didn't know who was the best pilot in the sky it sure as hell wasn't him. But it couldn't be tolerated, not now.

This was a bloody stupid decision, he thought, morbidly. But he still couldn't see any workable alternative, save drafting pilots from the remaining home defence squadrons. *And most of these pilots are going to end up dead when we first face the aliens.*

"Get some rest," he ordered, "then we will have a proper debriefing session and go through each and every one of your mistakes. In particular, you might want to think about the simple fact that there is no 'I' in 'team.' You are *part* of a team and if you can't *act* as part of a team, you'll be put on the benches and flogged. Dismissed!"

He watched them sidle out the room and sighed, bitterly.

"I don't think you're allowed to flog pilots," Rose said, as soon as the compartment was empty. "There are regulations against making yourself or someone else unfit for military service."

"It's amazing what regulations permit, if you look at them in the right way," Kurt said, shortly. Rose was the last person he wanted to speak to at the moment. "It's semi-legal to put someone in an airlock and threaten to decompress it to teach them a lesson."

Rose snorted, then strode over to the hatch and locked it. "We need to talk," she said, turning to face him. She rested her hands on her hips as she glared. "What is wrong with you?"

Kurt started. "Wrong with me?"

"You've been moping around like a depressed donkey for the last week," Rose snapped. "I think I've been doing a shitload of your work in getting those incompetents ready for battle and cleaning up their messes. You've barely been present at training sessions that don't involve you personally and..."

She took a breath. "And you declined my advances over several days," she added, her voice softening. "Kurt...what is wrong with you?"

Kurt stared down at his hands. He wanted to tell her...and yet he didn't dare. But that, his conscience prodded, was a cowardly attitude. Her career was at stake too. Hell, for all he knew, the people who were blackmailing him had also made advances to her, although that would have been harder. He'd been the only one to leave the ship and go to Luna City. In hindsight...

His blood ran cold. In hindsight, how had the blackmailers *known* he was going to go to Luna City?

Rose took his hands and guided him towards a chair, then pushed him into it. His mind blurred, part of him remembering him kneeling before her and taking him in her mouth, part of him recognising her concern as friendly, rather than sexual. He wanted to cry, to lose control completely and start screaming at the bulkheads, but somehow he held himself under control. She didn't deserve to watch him come apart at the seams.

"Kurt," Rose said, quietly. "What happened on Luna?"

Kurt swallowed, then decided to be honest. "I was ambushed," he said. "And blackmailed."

Rose's eyes suddenly went very hard. "Blackmailed with what?"

"Us," Kurt said. "Our relationship. They said they'd tell the entire universe if I didn't do as they said."

Rose stood upright, letting go of his hands. "Shit," she said, as she started to pace the compartment. "What else did they say?"

Kurt ran through the whole story from start to finish, then put his head in his hands. It was over. He'd ruined her life as well as his own. God knew it would have been smarter to desert and take her with him. Or perhaps...

"They say they have proof," Rose said, slowly. "What proof do they have?"

"Footage of us...making love," Kurt said. "They must have been spying on us for quite some time."

"Or maybe they got lucky," Rose said. "Where was the footage taken?"

Kurt hesitated, trying to place it. He should have studied it more carefully when Fred had waved it under his nose, instead of trying to recoil in horror and denial. If he'd taken the terminal and its compromising recording for himself...he thought hard, trying to recall the details. It had looked like a hotel room...

"The hotel we went to in Sin City," he said, finally. "I think..."

Rose snorted. "Such footage can be faked," she said, snidely. "How many times did you go to Sin City as a young man and fuck the latest entertainment star in a VR environment? I believe that fucking Princess Elizabeth is quite common among some of the younger generation of pilots. They just plug in the right simulation and fuck away."

"The footage would be perfect," Kurt reminded her. "They'd have everything just right, from your breast size to my hairy chest."

"My breasts are a matter of public record," Rose sneered. "I had to be measured for the flight suit, remember? Given sufficient access, it would be easy to come up with footage that would be practically perfect in every way."

She walked back over to him and patted his shoulder. "It might seem bad," she said, "but it isn't a total disaster."

"It is," Kurt said. "The allegations will trigger another investigation, just like the one into Prince Henry's death. They will uncover time we spent together, more than could reasonably be justified. And then they will put us on the stand and ask us if we were in a relationship..."

"We're also heroes," Rose said. She snorted. "Ok; they find out proof we've been fucking during our off-duty hours. They try to charge us with breaking regulations. The public crucify them. They'd be much smarter to ask us both to resign with honour and bury the entire scandal under the rug."

"I wish I shared your optimism," Kurt said. "The evidence could also make it suggest the regulations were bent for us. That would *also* be a political headache."

He sighed. The British Aristocracy had learned, the hard way, just how dangerous favouritism – or even the appearance of favouritism – could be. Kurt and Rose might not be aristocrats, but they *were* heroes – and the appearance of letting them off lightly because of their heroism could cause the government a whole series of problems. It was a toss-up if the government would let them resign gracefully, throw them out on their ears or send them to a work crew in the worst-hit parts of the country.

"Let's go through this," Rose said. "Someone is trying to blackmail you. What do they want?"

She went on before he could say a word. "They don't want money," she continued, "or they would have demanded it before you left Earth."

"I don't have much," Kurt said. "And money is practically worthless right now."

"So whatever they want," Rose said, "is more likely to be a major headache. Did they give you any specific orders?"

"Merely that I would receive a message," Kurt said. "And that when I received the message, I was to go to the observation blister and…see who met me there."

"That means they have someone on the ship," Rose said, slowly. "Did they realise we were fucking during Operation Nelson – or earlier?"

"Or the newcomer is part of the ambassadorial party," Kurt said. It hadn't occurred to him that someone on *Ark Royal* had betrayed them. It should have, he knew. *Someone* had ratted out Prince Henry and Janelle Lopez, after all. "And whoever it is has a great deal of access in places that are meant to be secure."

Rose sat down next to him. "So we have…three options," she said, after a moment. "They're reporters, they're someone involved with the government or they're interstellar spies."

She frowned. "Reporters aren't big on delayed gratification," she added. "And besides, blackmail could open them up to all manner of interesting criminal charges. You and they might end up sharing the same cell. That leaves a government conspiracy or international spies. I'd lean towards the latter."

"But if they were in the government," Kurt objected, "they could make sure we were both jailed..."

"They also wouldn't need to resort to blackmail to force you to do what they wanted," Rose countered. "If they're the government, why bother with blackmail when they could just issue orders? You're not the Admiral. I don't think they'd need something out of a Z-List Evil Government Conspiracy Theory Movie to get you to do whatever they wanted."

She paused. "And that suggests international involvement. But for what?"

"They knew I was going to Luna City," Kurt said. "How would they know that without having access to the naval datanet?"

"There's no shortage of international officers at the Academy," Rose reminded him. "And where *else* could you go for a short leave?"

Kurt frowned. She was right. There had been no shuttles to Earth, Sin City was closed and anywhere else would have consumed half of his leave time just getting there and back. Luna City was the only logical destination. And, given access to the city's public access datanet, the blackmailers could probably have tracked him right up to the moment he entered the cafe and sat down. Fred might even have been hard on his heels.

"And there was a possibility you'd be summoned elsewhere too," Rose added. "Weren't you on the list of people to attend a conference on countering alien starfighter tactics."

"I was uninvited," Kurt said. "Too much work to do here."

Rose wrapped her arm around his shoulder. "You have to go to the Admiral," she said. "*We* have to go to the Admiral."

Kurt stared at her. "But..."

"This is an international spy mission being carried out under his nose," Rose said, flatly. "If you keep quiet about it, you'll probably wind up carrying the blame for the whole affair – assuming, of course, that we survive. And if that happens, you and I will be lucky not to be put up against a bulkhead and shot. But if we help the Admiral catch the spies, we will be able to request a honourable discharge as a reward."

"Your career will be destroyed," Kurt said. He cursed himself under his breath. "Rose…"

"Shut up," Rose said. "I'm a big girl. I made the decision to fuck you because I believed we would die soon and I didn't want to die without feeling some human contact. If we'd stopped it then, it would probably have been fine. You could have gone back to your wife and I could have found someone nearer my own age. Instead…we developed feelings for each other."

She poked him with her finger, making him wince. "You're not a rapist," she said, "and I am not a helpless victim. We got ourselves into this mess and we're damn well going to do whatever it takes to get out of it with our skins and reputations intact. And if that means baring everything for the Admiral…well, we can do it. We don't have a choice."

Kurt shook his head, slowly. She was right, he knew, and if it had been just him at risk, he would have done so without a second thought. But his children were also at risk.

"And what will happen to them," Rose asked when he said that out loud, "if they discover their father is branded a traitor? Because that's what will happen if you surrender to blackmail and do as they tell you."

She stood up, then pulled him to his feet. "Kurt, I know how you feel," she said. "But you can't let fear blind you, even if it's for your children."

Kurt sighed and leaned into her embrace. "How can you be so cold about this?"

"One of us has to be," Rose said. She sighed. "You're the one who taught me to consider a situation and evaluate it thoroughly if there's no need to act immediately. And this situation needs to be considered carefully. They think they have you by the balls – and they're right. That's what's stopping you from thinking properly."

She gently pushed him away from her, then straightened. "Get yourself cleaned up in the head," she ordered. "And then we will go see the Admiral."

Kurt nodded, cursing himself once again. Perhaps they could have escaped notice completely if they'd broken off the affair after their first return to Earth. He was fairly sure there were at least three other couples who'd had an affair, then been separated by being assigned to different ships. But *he* had been stupid. No matter the problem with Molly, no matter the growing awareness that he and his wife were slipping and sliding towards divorce, he could have prevented himself from having an affair with a subordinate. There was always Sin City and its endless chains of brothels.

He stepped into the washroom and studied himself in the mirror. His face looked pale and wan, reminding him that he'd slept poorly for the last few days. He turned on the tap, poured water into the bowl, then washed his face thoroughly. It didn't make him feel any better. His life was about to change, which was bad enough, but he'd also damaged his children's lives…

"Come on," Rose ordered. She looked presentable, surprisingly so. "There isn't time for you to do your makeup."

"Oh, be quiet," Kurt grumbled. "Rose…"

Rose stopped and looked at him. "Yes?"

"I'm sorry," Kurt said. "I…"

"I think we have already established it wasn't entirely your fault," Rose snapped. "It was me who made the first move, not you. Yes, you fucked up; I fucked up too. And now all we can do is make a full confession and take the consequences."

———

"I can't say I'm too happy with the stress tests," Anderson said. "The modified Puller Drive is developing power fluctuations at odd moments."

Ted studied the display, wishing he knew more about how the system actually worked. The math, he'd been told, was too complex for the average spacer. Even engineers only mastered the bare bones, although they knew the hardware inside out. Or maybe the boffins were just keeping it to themselves to ensure they weren't subverted by someone from outside the system.

"I see," he said. "What will this mean for us?"

"At best, we may have to replace the whole system when we get back home," Anderson said. "At worst, we may lose the modified drive in the heart of alien territory."

Ted swore. Humanity's Puller Drive had been heavily limited, compared to the alien drive system. The ships had been modified after an alien system had been captured intact, but *Ark Royal* had never been designed to have her drive modified. If they lost the alien drive system, they would have to pick their way home – if possible – along a course that would be easily predicable. The aliens would have no trouble intercepting them before they could make it back to human space.

"That could be bad," he said. If they had time, he would have ordered an immediate return to Earth. But that would have delayed the mission for weeks, perhaps months, and crippled the ship as they tore the drive housing apart to replace the drive. "Can you keep it in check?"

"I think so, but if we take another pounding the drive might come apart completely," Anderson said. "It won't be good, sir."

"No," Ted agreed. "It won't."

He looked at the starchart, thinking hard. The tramlines they needed to use to reach Target One were alien; they couldn't be accessed without an alien-designed drive. But if they didn't use them, they'd have no hope of reaching Target One without travelling through too many unexplored and potentially occupied star systems. They had to rely on a drive system that was on the verge of breaking down.

"Keep me informed," he ordered, finally. "What about the other matters?"

"The sealed compartments have been assigned to the research teams," Anderson assured him. "But we don't have any idea what the aliens would consider acceptable quarters."

"We know they like it hot and moist," Ted said. The alien captives had been given temperature controls and shown how to use them. They'd been happiest, it seemed, in temperatures that made Australia seem cool. "Make sure you separate their system completely from our own."

"Aye, Captain," Anderson said. He reached out and rubbed the bulkhead. "The Old Lady will do her duty."

Ted had to smile. He'd been assigned to *Ark Royal* because the Royal Navy hadn't wanted the embarrassment of sacking a knighted hero. Anderson, on the other hand, had been assigned to *Ark Royal* simply because there was nowhere else for him. His skill with the outdated systems – to say nothing of jury-rigged spare parts from every interstellar power – wouldn't fit on any of the modern carriers.

"I know she will," he said. So far, there had been no sign of the aliens, but he was sure that would change. In their place, he'd picket the systems between Terra Nova and Target One, if only with a couple of starships. "I have faith in her."

The hatch bleeped, then opened. Ted lifted his eyebrows when he saw both the CAG and one of his squadron commanders, looking like naughty children. He half-expected to see a Marine escorting them into the office. But they were alone.

"Admiral," Schneider said. "We need to talk with you."

Ted had a sudden sense of doom. "Very well," he said. He nodded to Anderson, who picked up his terminal and left the compartment. "Talk."

CHAPTER
FOURTEEN

"Let me see if I've got this straight," Ted said, once the halting explanation had come to an end. "You've been having an illicit relationship since Alien-1, you've continued with the relationship ever since returning to Earth…and you are now being blackmailed. Correct?"

"Yes, sir," Schneider said.

"You absolute idiot," Ted said.

He shook his head in disbelief. Everyone knew that the regulations on sexual relations onboard ship were skirted more than anyone cared to admit, but there were limits. A relation between two people of different ranks would always suffer from a power imbalance, raising the prospect of coercion and naked force being used to push someone into bed. How could a relationship develop properly when one party could punish the other at will? And that, he knew, didn't even take into consideration the damage it would do to morale.

Everyone would be looking at Schneider's past decisions now, hunting for any signs of favouritism he might have shown towards his lover. She'd survived when so many others had died, Ted knew. Had she been deliberately kept out of the line of battle? And how many others had died when she should have died? He might have done nothing to help or hinder her career and it would still be disastrous to both of them. They should both be thrown into the brig, pending an investigation and court martial, followed by dishonourable discharge.

"It's at times like this," Ted continued, "that I wish we'd kept the lash, rather than rum and sodomy. What the hell were you two thinking?"

Rose Labara met his eyes evenly. "We were thinking we were about to die," she said, simply. "We did not believe there would be any future for either of us."

Ted understood. He'd almost crawled into a bottle when it seemed the aliens had them trapped in a dead end. Schneider and Rose had found what solace they could in each other's arms – and if it had stopped there, it would probably have gone completely unnoticed. But instead, they'd kept up the affair and finally run into real trouble. Someone was using their affair as a weapon against *Ark Royal* and her crew.

"There may not be," he said, bluntly. He silently awarded them both points for coming forward, even at the cost of their careers. "I doubt either of you can look forward to a comfortable life in future."

"Yes, sir," Schneider said. Oddly, he sounded a little relieved. "We will face whatever judgement you choose to mete out."

"I'm glad to hear it," Ted said, dryly. "I'm going to call the Captain and Major Parnell. The latter, in particular, has some counter-intelligence experience. You are going to sit down with him and go through *everything* that happened, right from the start, in the hopes of locating whoever is trying to blackmail you. Once this affair is finished…"

He paused, meeting their eyes. "Once this *matter* is finished, I will make my decision concerning your future," he warned. "I suggest you don't try to hold anything back."

"Yes, sir," they said, together.

"I can't afford to take either of you off active duty and toss you into the brig, no matter how much you deserve it," Ted added. "However, I will expect you to remember just how much trouble you're in and refrain from doing *anything* that might arouse suspicion. You will not meet in private for any reason. Do you understand me?"

The two lovers exchanged glances, then nodded reluctantly. Ted was old enough to be Schneider's father – barely – but he wasn't so old he'd forgotten what it was like to be in love. They *had* to have developed feelings for one another or they wouldn't have stayed together after their first return to Earth. Being told they could not see one another would *hurt*.

But they could have done a great deal of damage if they'd been caught earlier, he thought, crossly. He had never been one to care about what his crew did on their time off – he knew standards had slipped a great deal while *Ark Royal* had floated uselessly in the Naval Reserve – but this was different. This could have seriously damaged his ship's reputation.

He considered his options, briefly. It was the Captain who would have the final responsibility for deciding their fate – or it would have been, if the two pilots hadn't been mixed up in blackmail and espionage. Fitzwilliam could have punished them how he saw fit and the Admiralty would not have objected, not when they were reluctant to cast doubt on a Captain's role as master of his ship. But with intelligence staffers mixed up in the whole affair...Ted knew they might be offered amnesty in exchange for cooperation. Or they might be put in front of a court martial board afterwards anyway, no matter what they did.

"Dismissed," he said, quietly. "I expect you to inform me the moment they get in touch with you. And don't fuck up."

He watched them leave, then tapped his console and called both Fitzwilliam and Major Parnell to his office. The Marine had a nasty scar running down the side of his face that hadn't been there before, Ted noted, but he didn't ask any questions. Everyone, even the Marines, had been suffering badly from emotional whiplash since the return to Earth. They'd probably resorted to boxing matches to keep their skills up.

"We have a problem," he said, bluntly. He recorded all conversations in his office, thankfully. "You need to listen to this."

Captain Fitzwilliam said nothing until the recording came to an end, then swore. "Someone is trying to blackmail one of *my* crewmen?"

"Yes," Ted said, shortly. It was a particularly nasty case, he had to admit. Schneider wasn't the only one at risk. His family – and his lover – would also be imperilled if the recordings were released. "And they may have more complex motives than money."

"It is a pity we don't have the original recording," Parnell observed. "It would be informative to have some idea of just where they were filmed."

"That raises another set of questions," Ted agreed. "What are we dealing with here?"

Parnell considered it slowly. "I think they're right and its someone international," he said. "A spy – probably more than one – is on the ship."

"Wonderful," Ted said. "We have three foreign ambassadors, thirty-two foreign support staff of various ranks and a handful of others."

"But the spy might be a British crewman," Parnell said. "Although in that case approaching Schneider and applying blackmail might be unnecessary."

He shook his shaved head. "They will need something they believe Schneider can get for them," he added. "Otherwise there would be no point in playing the blackmail card too soon."

"Those stupid idiots," Fitzwilliam said. "What the hell were they thinking?"

"That they didn't have long to live," Parnell said, quietly.

He looked down at the deck, thinking hard. "With your permission, Captain, I would like to bring a couple of other Marines into the loop and start working on ways to catch the spy," he said. "He'll have to make contact with Schneider at some point or the whole affair will be worse than useless. When he does, we'll have an opportunity to catch him and cart him off for interrogation."

"Which will open a whole new can of worms if the spy is on an ambassador's staff," Fitzwilliam pointed out. "They have diplomatic immunity."

"Diplomatic immunity is not a licence to spy," Parnell countered. "We might not be able to try the spy and throw him out the airlock, but we could put him in the brig until we returned to Earth."

Ted nodded. "We need to know why they're doing this," he said, softly. "What do they have in mind?"

"Sabotage the ship?" Parnell suggested. "Or perhaps make it impossible to come to terms with the aliens?"

"They'd have to be out of their minds," Fitzwilliam said. "The war is on the verge of being lost!"

"Some people rarely believe that disaster, even a lost war with an alien race, can touch them," Parnell said. "That's why the Barbary States sometimes send raiders over to Europe, even though they can expect massive retaliation from orbit. Their leaders are so secure in their own power they think nothing and no one can touch them."

"…Idiots," Fitzwilliam said. He smiled, suddenly. "Although I know a number of aristocrats who act like that, I suppose."

He met Ted's eyes. "What do we do with them?"

"I'd suggest offering a honourable discharge in exchange for cooperation," Parnell said. He held up a hand before Fitzwilliam could say a word. "I know you will want to throw the book at them, Captain, but we don't want to discourage others from coming forward."

"I see," Fitzwilliam said. "But if we're not going to tell anyone about this…*affair*, Major, how will they know we were merciful?"

"Some details may be released later, once everyone is safety dispersed," Parnell said. "And I would caution you against believing that something will remain secret indefinitely. This affair certainly did *not*."

"True," Ted said. He looked at Fitzwilliam. "A honourable discharge?"

Fitzwilliam nodded, once.

———

As a child – back when dinosaurs roamed the Earth, according to Percy – Kurt had stolen some money from his mother. He'd had a good reason at the time, he'd thought, but guilt had overwhelmed him almost at once. Eventually, he'd returned the money and made a full confession. His mother had been furious and confined him to the house for the next month, but he'd felt better after admitting his guilt. He'd done something wrong and knew it, no matter how he tried to convince himself otherwise.

He felt much the same, now, as they made their way to the gallery. It was far from *private*, he knew, but it was rare for pilots to eat outside Pilot Country. He knew his life had been irreparably damaged, that he might have dragged down Rose and his children too, yet he felt better for having confessed. The die had been cast and now he could think clearly again. He led the way into the compartment, took a large cup of coffee from the dispenser and sat down at a table on the far side of the room. Rose sat, facing him, a second later.

"That was very brave," she said.

Kurt snorted. *Bravery* was one of the defining traits of starfighter pilots, along with a reckless disregard for danger or official flying regulations. Most of them were written by desk jockeys and pasty-faced bureaucrats, none of whom had any real experience flying starfighters. Flying a starfighter into the teeth of alien fire took *real* nerve. But he'd never really done anything that risked his family before.

"I suppose," he said, finally. He wanted to hug her, to tell her that it would be all right, but he knew he could do neither. "And I'm sorry."

Rose pointed a finger at him, like the barrel of a gun. "Stop apologising for everything," she said, tartly. "I made my own decisions."

Kurt took a sip of his coffee, grimaced at the taste and then took another sip. "Yes, but I'm the one being blackmailed," he said. "That makes it my fault."

"I think you're the most vulnerable," Rose pointed out. "You have a family – and the higher rank. I could just have told them to piss off."

She was right, Kurt knew. If she'd been willing to throw him under a bus, she could have claimed he'd pushed her into sex, promising promotion as a reward. It was quite likely it would have worked too. Senior officers were *expected* to handle themselves better than their juniors.

He jumped as a hand fell on his shoulder. When he looked up, he found himself staring into the eyes of Major Parnell. The Marine looked… emotionless, no pity or anger in his eyes.

"You're nicked, my lad," the Marine said. "We need to talk."

"Yes, sir," Kurt said. He looked at Rose. "Go put them through another training simulation."

He allowed the Marine to lead him through the ship's corridors and into Marine Country, where he was unceremoniously pushed into a small room. There was nothing inside, but a metal desk, a pair of chairs and a water cooler. The table was completely bare.

"Sit," Parnell ordered. He strode around the desk and sat facing Kurt. "I said *sit*."

Kurt sat. The chair was thoroughly uncomfortable.

"You're in a right spot of bother," Parnell said, bluntly. "The good news is that the Admiral and the Captain have agreed that you and your…lover will be offered a honourable discharge at the end of the deployment. Once discharged, any footage your friends might have of the pair of you will become about as worthless as a standard piece of voyeuristic crap."

"Oh," Kurt said. Having footage of a civilian caught in sexual acts on the datanet would be embarrassing for the victim, but hardly newsworthy. It was more than he'd dared hope for, which probably meant it came with a price. "And what is the catch?"

Parnell smiled. It didn't touch his eyes. "The bad news is that you'll be expected to do *everything* in your power to help us identify the people trying to blackmail you," he said. "And I mean *everything*."

He tapped the table. "I wish you'd brought this to us before we left Earth," he added. "We could have followed up leads right there and then. Instead…we will only be able to focus on this ship and crew. Tracking down the people behind your friends will be tricky."

"Yes, sir," Kurt said.

"I know you probably weren't thinking too clearly," Parnell added. He jabbed a finger at Kurt to make his point. "You'd just been shocked badly. However, this is the time to think clearly. We are going to go over *everything*."

He settled back in his chair. "You're not under arrest," he warned. "However, I am obliged to warn you of several things. This conversation *will* be recorded and it *will* be entered into the official investigative log. Should you be caught in a lie, it will be held against you when the Admiralty and MI5 consider your position. My very strong advice would be to tell the truth, the whole truth and nothing, but the truth."

He paused. "I suggest you pour yourself a glass of water," he added. "This could take quite some time."

Kurt nodded and obeyed. When he returned to his chair, Parnell had a datapad open in front of him and was skimming the pages, clearly looking for questions to ask. Or was he just pretending to be distracted? It was impossible to tell.

"First question, then," Parnell said. "Precisely what happened on the day you were told that someone else had footage of your sex life?"

Kurt braced himself, then went through the entire story. Parnell was a good interrogator, he rapidly discovered; every time he was unsure about a detail, he asked questions until it was clarified to the best of Kurt's ability. Kurt hadn't realised how much he'd seen or heard until Parnell teased it out of him, although much of what he hadn't realised he'd forgotten was largely useless. Fred's identity was still a complete mystery.

"It sounds like a professional," Parnell said. "Did you hear an accent?"

"No, sir," Kurt said.

"Definitely a professional," Parnell said. "You probably wouldn't have noticed an accent if he worked his tones to sound like you. Chances are his face was the result of some cosmetic surgery too. He'd change again as soon as he left Luna City, making it impossible to track him down."

Kurt swore. "Is it hopeless then?"

"I wouldn't say that," Parnell said. "Where was the footage taken?"

"I think it was in Sin City," Kurt said.

Parnell lifted his eyebrows. "And what were you doing in Sin City?"

Kurt glared at him. "What do people *normally* do in Sin City?"

"They don't normally bring their partners," Parnell pointed out.

"We wanted to share a hotel room without having to be discreet," Kurt said. It had been a fine weekend, marred only by the fact they'd had to split up to return to the Academy. And by the fact the hotel manager kept offering to send a girl – or a boy – up to their room. "You know their reputation for secrecy."

Parnell snorted. "That is a joke, right?"

"…Yes," Kurt said.

"Tell me," Parnell ordered. "How do you *know* the footage was shot in Sin City?"

Kurt took a breath. "It was the hotel room," he said, firmly. "It wasn't my office or quarters at Luna Academy."

"There are – there were – no shortage of intelligence officers prowling through Sin City," Parnell muttered. He glared down at the desk, then looked up. "How long did you spend there?"

"A weekend," Kurt said. "We booked in Friday evening and left Sunday, mid-afternoon."

"And where else did you go?" Parnell asked. "Or did you just stay there?"

"Yes," Kurt said. They'd been reluctant to go anywhere else, knowing they might be seen by someone else from the Academy. "We ordered room service and stayed together."

"She must really like you," Parnell said. "Of course, losing Sin City means following up that angle of investigation won't be easy."

Kurt cursed. The aliens, deliberately or otherwise, had destroyed Sin City. Anyone who might have been involved in planting cameras in hotel rooms was probably dead.

"Maybe they did it deliberately," he mused. "What if the blackmailers are working for the aliens?"

Parnell shrugged. "It seems unlikely," he said. "They wouldn't need to blow up Sin City to cover their tracks. All it would take is a knife in the back."

He stood. "We'll be doing this again tomorrow," he added. "I suggest you make sure you free up some time on your schedule. We will be going over this time and time again until they actually get in touch."

Kurt nodded, reluctantly. "Yes, sir," he said.

CHAPTER

FIFTEEN

"Wake," an atonal voice said.

Henry jerked awake, his eyes snapping open. Four aliens stood in the prison cell, their massive eyes watching him warily. Three of them, he noted with some surprise, wore clothes that resembled wetsuits, while the fourth was as naked as always. Jill started – she'd cuddled up to him as they slept – and sat upright, no longer bothering to try to cover her breasts. It was all Henry could do to keep his body from betraying his awareness of her nakedness...

But then, being stared at by alien perverts would cool anyone's lust, he thought, as he stood. The aliens had never entered the compartment while the humans were sleeping before, as far as he knew. *I couldn't perform under their gaze.*

"Put. On," one of the aliens said. It pointed to a large bag on the floor. "Now."

Henry picked up the bag and opened it. Inside, there were a pair of masks attached to a set of canisters. It reminded him of the scuba gear he'd used as a child, before he realised that that was precisely what they were. If the aliens wanted him to swim outside the prison cell, they'd have to give him a source of breathable air as well as a mask. But...he looked up, through the transparent ceiling. Just how deep below the water were they? It was far too easy to imagine them being struck by the bends as soon as they reached the surface...and he had no idea how to explain the prospective danger to the aliens. All they could do was endure.

"Pass me one of them," Jill said. She took it from him and pulled it over her face with casual ease. She'd used the masks before, Henry recalled, although the aliens had never let her keep them. "You put it on like this."

Henry followed her lead, wondering just where the aliens had found the gear. Had they taken it from Heinlein, one of the other colonies or had they simply produced it for themselves. He pushed the questions aside seconds later as he felt the mask seal itself around his face, then heard a hiss as he started to draw air from the canisters. The air smelt slightly moist, but it was breathable. Or so he hoped. It would be the height of irony if the alien attempt to keep him alive ended up killing him.

One of the aliens splashed down into the water and vanished in the murky water. The others beckoned for Henry to move forward and enter the water himself. Henry hesitated, but – knowing there was no choice – he made his way forward and jumped down. The water was warmer than he'd expected, like dropping into a warm bath, but it felt faintly slimy against his skin. Perhaps it was just his imagination, he told himself firmly, as Jill jumped down beside him. He certainly *wanted* to believe it was his imagination.

Jill glanced at him, her face unreadable behind the mask, then lowered her head until she was under the water completely. Henry followed, cursing mentally as his vision blurred and then cleared as the mask started to compensate. It was hard to see much in the gloom, apart from lights in the distance, but he could at least keep sight of Jill. Something about the water bothered him, although he couldn't place it. Moments later, the aliens swam past and motioned for the humans to follow. Henry braced himself – it had been years since he'd swum outside a swimming pool – and forced himself to swim after them. It rapidly became clear that the aliens were far better swimmers than humanity. They clearly needed to hold back just to keep the humans with them.

The alien city slowly came into view as they swam overhead. It reminded him of images of sunken towns and cities on Earth, except it was clearly a thriving metropolis. Aliens were everywhere, swimming in groups of three or more, surrounded by fish that hovered near them as though they were daring the aliens to try to catch and eat them. From time to time, an alien did just that, snapping a fish out of the water as easily as a shark would catch a minnow. Other aliens would roll over in the water and stare at the humans, their enormous eyes tracking their alien guests with ease. Several actually swam alongside the humans until they lost interest and turned away.

We're being paraded, Henry realised. He'd been in enough parades to know they weren't always about the person in the lead car. *But why?*

He pushed the thought aside and started to study the alien buildings, trying to see how they worked. Some of them were made from stone, carefully assembled below the waves; others were made of something that looked like emerald, although he suspected it wasn't *real* emerald. It could easily have been a trick of the light. He thought he saw hundreds of tiny crab-like creatures scuttling along the seabed, moving in and out of the houses as if they owned the place. The sheer diversity of life below the seabed was remarkable.

A hand caught hold of his and pulled him forward. He looked up into the eyes of an alien, who seemed more annoyed at the delay than anything else. There were no threats, at least as far as Henry could tell, but he got the message anyway and forced himself forward. Jill and her escort had almost vanished in the gloomy distance.

It felt like hours, his arms and legs aching in a way they hadn't since Basic Training, before they finally reached their destination, a tiny craft sitting on the seabed. It looked like a weird shuttle, one of the lunar buses that could only operate in low gravity, or perhaps a minisub. Henry felt himself yawn, despite the mask, as the aliens pushed him towards the hatch and forced him into the ship. Jill was already there, her mask discarded and lying at her feet. Her hair was so damp that it clung to her shoulders and breasts. But Henry was too tired to stare.

There were no aliens in the compartment, Henry realised, as the hatch slid closed beneath them. It was a prison, just as much as the prison cell they'd been forced to leave. A dull whining echoed through the craft as it came to life – for a moment, Henry was convinced his first impressions had been right and it *was* a shuttlecraft – and then started to move. It shivered from side to side as it passed through the water, his ears popping within seconds. They were clearly rising up towards the surface...

"The bends," he said, cursing his own ignorance. He wasn't even sure what the bends *were*, let alone how to cope with them without a pressure chamber. "If you feel pain..."

Jill looked bleakly at him. "What can we do about it?"

Henry swallowed. "Suffer," he said.

His ears popped again as the craft shook violently, then started to rock steadily. He couldn't help being reminded of a motorboat on the ocean... had the alien craft already reached the surface? If so, maybe they'd only been a few dozen metres below the waves, not deep enough to make the bends a serious danger. But would the aliens have known to show their captives so much consideration? God knew a couple of aliens humanity had taken captive had died soon afterwards, their captives utterly unable to treat them properly.

The craft rocked one final time, then bumped against something and came to a halt. A hatch in the side of the compartment cracked open – Henry swore inwardly; he hadn't even noticed it was there – allowing bright sunlight to stream into the craft. Henry cringed back, covering his eyes. It had been so long since he'd seen anything, but the dim greenish light of his prison cell. A shadow moved in front of the hatch and he froze. Outside, the aliens were gathering.

"Come on," he said, trying to put a brave face on things. He'd never wanted to be a groundpounder. "Let's go meet our adoring public."

Jill took his hand and they stepped through the hatch together. The bright sunlight revealed a tropical lagoon, not unlike the seas of Target One, but surrounded by strange white alien buildings. Water sprayed everywhere, as if it were the midst of a swimming pool, leaving the air hot and moist, just the way the aliens liked it. They needed it, Henry realised, as he looked at the jungle in the distance. The sunlight suggested the world was hot enough to please the aliens, but maybe not moist. High overhead, the sky was so brilliantly blue that he felt an ache in his heart. Would he ever see Earth again?

The entire city was *covered* in aliens, each one lying on the rooftops like dozing seals, staring at the humans as they were gently escorted through the alien city. Water lay everywhere, running down the floors and back into the seas...as a child, part of his mind noted, he would probably have regarded the alien city as a giant adventure playground. Not that he'd ever been allowed to play in any such playgrounds, of course. The Heir to the Throne – if they ever sorted out the issue of which of his father's children should succeed the Throne – could not be allowed to risk himself on roller coasters or theme park VR rides. They'd been reluctant to allow him to attend the Academy as a grown man!

He was tempted to wave at the spectators as they reached the edge of the city and walked towards a shuttlecraft, sitting on a launching pad. It was little different to a human design, he noted, although it looked to be a heavy-lifter. The escort paused outside the hatch, as if the aliens were consulting with their fellows, then opened the hatch. Inside, there was yet another tiny compartment suitable for human prisoners.

"They must prefer to live in the water," Jill said, as they were pushed inside. The hatch closed firmly behind them. "Do you think their starships are full of water?"

Henry considered the possibility. It was true that post-battle assessment teams had found a considerable amount of water vapour in the ruins of alien starships, but cold logic suggested the aliens *couldn't* use water throughout their ships. They'd run the risk of shorting out entire compartments if their innards were exposed, even minutely. He tried to imagine the response of the Royal Navy's engineers to deliberately flooding the fleet's starships and decided they'd probably want to strangle the idiot who suggested it with their bare hands.

But the aliens might not have a choice, any more than the Royal Navy had a choice about supplying its crewmen with oxygen.

"It's a possibility," Henry said. The shuttle seemed to quiver, then launched itself into the air. "But it would be dangerous."

He shook his head. He'd been told, more than once, that dolphins were smarter than they seemed, but dolphins had never attempted to grow hands and leave their marine environment for dry land. It didn't seem possible for them to even make a start on developing their own technology. Their environmental niche was a prison as much as anything else, with the added disadvantage they'd never know what they were missing. Unless the Uplift Project actually received the go-ahead...

But then we wouldn't be able to deploy cybernetic dolphins, he told himself. *There would be objections from vested interests.*

The gravity faded away to nothingness, leaving them drifting up into the air. Henry blinked in surprise – the aliens definitely had the technology to produce artificial gravity – and then resolved to ignore it. Jill looked green, though, just like some of the early starfighter trainees who had never developed their space legs. Eventually, they'd been sent back to Earth and told to apply somewhere that didn't involve regular space travel. The aliens might have been trying to use it to disconcert them.

"They probably don't have any problems with zero-gravity," he said, trying to distract Jill from her feelings. "If they're born under the water, they probably take to it like…"

"A fish to water?" Jill asked, weakly. She swallowed, hard. "I was asleep for the trip to Heinlein, Henry. I never went into zero-gee properly."

"It's not quite what it's made out to be," Henry said. There had been one zero-G parlour in Sin City where visitors were encouraged to enjoy making love in reduced or no gravity, but it wasn't as popular as he'd thought. "It can be fun, but…"

"You'd get sick at a delicate moment," Jill guessed. She floated up to the ceiling, then pushed herself back to the ground. "It would probably be rather unromantic."

"It was," Henry said. The whole experience had been a lesson in orbital mechanics, rather than something sexual. "But there are plenty of ways to have fun in zero-gravity."

The shuttle shuddered, then quivered gently. Henry felt the bulkhead carefully, remembering how *Ark Royal* had quivered against his fingertips when the main drive had been active. Unless he was very wrong, they'd just docked with a much larger starship. But it was clear the starship didn't have a gravity field of its own. They'd have fallen down towards the floor if the bigger ship had one.

If there is a bigger ship, he thought. Running two gravity fields together was asking for trouble, unless there was enough power to manipulate both fields to prevent problems. The Royal Navy tended to forbid it unless there was no alternative. *I could be wrong…*

The hatch clicked open. A wave of moist air, smelling of something fishy, rolled into the shuttle. Outside, he saw a pair of aliens, floating in the air as if they belonged there. Henry sighed, then pulled himself through the hatch, carefully only to use tiny motions. Jill, less practiced in zero-gravity, accidentally pushed herself right out of the shuttle and headed for the far bulkhead. Henry winced, remembering the first few days of his own zero-gravity training, as she hit the bulkhead and bounced off. One of the aliens caught her and half-carried her towards the hatch, using tiny handles built into the bulkheads to propel itself forward. Henry followed, realising that he'd been right. The aliens definitely preferred low-gravity environments.

He frowned as the first hatch led to a second hatch, which opened up into a larger compartment. A bed was pressed against the wall, while two computers – civilian teaching machines, he realised – had been left against the spare bulkhead. They'd probably still be working, despite the moisture in the air. Teaching machines were designed to survive small and resentful children. Henry had heard that one of them had been dropped from a helicopter and survived the fall.

"You will rest," the alien said. "We will leave now."

Henry turned, fighting to control his movements. "Where are we going?"

"Your people," the alien said. It pointed one leathery hand towards the bed. "We will talk. You will prepare to speak to them."

Henry nodded. After Target One, the human race would be suspicious of any alien ship attempting to make open contact. But they'd find it a great deal harder to ignore a human voice, broadcasting openly. And then…Henry smiled at the thought of the aliens meeting a proper set of human researchers, complete with computers and the ability to consider how best to speak at leisure. The communications barrier would be broken soon enough.

"We'll sleep," he promised.

"I'm not sure how," Jill muttered. She still looked green. "How do we stay on the bed?"

"…Bugger," Henry said. The aliens had dragged a bed into the chamber, but it was largely useless without a gravity field. He looked around for something they could use to tie themselves down, only to discover there was nothing. "I'm not sure."

Jill laughed, weakly. "Do we just sleep floating in the air?"

"It looks that way," Henry said. There was a second problem. As far as he could tell, there were no streams of air moving through the compartment. Carbon dioxide, exhaled from their mouths, would gather around them, eventually making it impossible to breath. Or so he thought. It had been a very long time since he'd studied survival in zero-gravity environments. "I think one of us will have to sleep while the other fans them."

"See if there are any atmospheric controls first," Jill said, once he'd explained. "They gave me some controls back when I…"

She broke off, shuddering. Henry wanted to put his arms around her and give her what reassurance he could. *He* could go back to Earth and be reunited with his family, his friends and his lover. But Jill would never see her friends and family again. The aliens, either through a mistake or cold-blooded malice, had slaughtered almost all of the Heinlein settlers.

"You have a nap," he said. He hated himself for saying something so useless, but what else could he do? "I'll look for controls and then fan you."

"Thanks," Jill said, weakly. She paused. "Do you think we're being watched here?"

"Probably," Henry said. "We're aliens, remember. They'll want to keep an eye on us."

But that was normal for him. He'd been watched almost his entire life, with his family and the media ready to pounce on any form of misbehaviour…even if it was something that would pass without comment for anyone born outside the Royal Family. Regular beatings would have been kinder, he'd often thought. At least he could have told someone about an abusive parent and been understood. But what did one do when the entire system was abusive?

Janelle and I can just run, he decided, finally. *We can go somewhere else and change our names. No one would know who we'd once been.*

CHAPTER
SIXTEEN

"*War Hog* has transited back, Captain," Farley reported. "Local space seems clear. Long-range sensors reveal no sign of alien activity."

James nodded, studying the report. There was little of value in the first alien-ruled system they'd invaded during Operation Nelson, save for a handful of asteroids and a tramline that led deeper into alien space. It would have been completely useless, he knew, if they hadn't had the alien-designed drive. He didn't find it a reassuring thought.

"Take us through the tramline," he ordered. "Full tactical alert."

He looked at the status display and shuddered. His starfighter crews were in their craft, ready to launch at a moment's notice. Gunnery crews and damage repair teams were on the alert, braced for anything from an alien attack to total drive failure. Everything looked perfect...and yet he knew it was nothing of the sort. The only crews at full capacity were the damage control teams. They'd had a lot of practice.

They vanished from the Terra Nova system as they crossed the tramline and reappeared in an alien system no one, not even the aliens, had bothered to name. He watched the display as passive sensors listened, watching for signs of alien activity, but picked up nothing. The system was as dark and cold as the grave. But that didn't prove the aliens weren't there, he reminded himself, sharply. They could easily have their drives and weapons deactivated, leaving them pretending to be holes in space.

"Local space seems clear," Farley said, again. "No alien contacts, sir. Not even a stray signal."

"Take us on our assigned course," James ordered. At least there was no need to play games with drones right now, thankfully. The aliens had either lost them completely or had a solid lock on their position a multitude of drones wouldn't be able to shake. "And continue to monitor for signs of alien activity."

The silence was baffling – and worrying. He'd known the aliens had never had much of anything in the system prior to the war, but he would have expected a picket ship at the very least. Unless there *was* one and they'd simply missed it...there was just too much space for a single enemy ship to hide in, given time. All he could do was make his way to the next tramline and pray they remained undiscovered. Target One was still ten days away on their course.

And if we take the least-time course we risk being detected for sure, he thought. They might have wrecked most of the Target One system, but the aliens would probably still picket it, knowing that its tramlines led deeper into alien space. *No, we have to remain stealthy and pray the cloaking device works as advertised.*

His console bleeped. "Captain, the drive fluctuations actually reduced this time," Anderson reported. "Everything was largely nominal."

"Thank God," James said. The frigates and escort carriers would be able to escape, he was sure, but not the giant carrier. Stranding her in a useless star system would suit the aliens very well. "Continue to monitor the situation."

"Aye, Captain," Anderson said.

And hope we don't have any more soap opera business, James thought, as he closed the connection. There were times when he didn't know how Captain Smith – *Admiral* Smith – had survived remaining on *Ark Royal* while she'd been stuck in the naval reserve. Some of his crew had been dedicated, others had been disciplinary problems who'd needed to be discharged as soon as possible. Most of the problems had faded away when the aliens attacked Vera Cruz, but a handful had remained festering. And now there was a spy on the ship.

He leaned back into his chair, thinking hard. Ten days to Target One. Ten days before they encountered the aliens...if they didn't encounter them beforehand. And then...who knew what would happen when they tried to communicate?

133

"This," Doctor Russell explained, "is an all-spectrum disease carrier."

Ted eyed the sealed test tube with a jaundiced eye. It didn't look very safe to him.

"I was under the impression," he said, "that all such research was banned."

"That's true," Doctor Russell agreed, as he put the test tube down on the desk. "However, we are allowed to conduct research into *cures* for genetically-modified diseases – and the only way to do that is to study techniques for modifying the diseases ourselves. Normally, such research takes place in sealed facilities without any chance of the disease escaping into the general population."

Ted scowled. He hated to admit it, but Doctor Russell had a point. It was easy to find sophisticated medical equipment these days and, despite international treaties, terrorists would be very tempted to create viruses that would slaughter everyone who hadn't been immunised ahead of time. There were no shortages of rumours about terrorist groups – and nations – that had tried to do just that, despite the risks. No matter how much care the experts took, diseases could mutate at a terrifying speed.

"In this case," Doctor Russell continued, "the alien biology is so different from our own that there is literally *no* danger of the disease spreading to humanity. That allows us to widen the scope of the disease considerably, to the point where it can infect creatures from the same genetic heritage as the aliens themselves. This will serve as an infection vector that will slash straight through the alien civilisation."

"You've invented a form of Bird Flu that infects everything," he said. He honestly couldn't understand why the Doctor was so pleased with his accomplishments. "All we'd have to do is bio-bomb an alien planet and wait for them all to die."

"Precisely," Doctor Russell said. "And the standard treaties have been set aside, owing to the war."

Ted made a face. If it had been just Britain researching the concept, it might have been possible to keep a lid on it. But the Government had insisted on sharing the research project – and the guilt – with the rest of the spacefaring powers. Now, it almost seemed as though they were competing to build the most horrendous biological weapon possible. The aliens would be in deep shit if the weapon was introduced to any world they occupied.

He shook his head in dismay. Delivering the weapon would be easy enough, with a little work. A missile warhead could be reconfigured to serve as a bioweapon delivery system, plunging through a planet's atmosphere and releasing its cargo before it hit the ground. Or a stealth missile could be used to sneak through planetary defences, posing as nothing more than a tiny meteor. The aliens wouldn't stand a chance.

But it won't get them all, he thought. *Those left behind will want a little revenge.*

"This might work if the aliens were intent on genocide," he said, "but so far we don't have any evidence the aliens are interested in outright extermination of humanity."

"They might be saving the extermination until after they've won the war," Doctor Russell pointed out. "If Hitler had saved the Holocaust until after his victory, I suspect a great many people would view him more favourably, even though he would still be the same complete manic he always was."

"True," Ted agreed. The weapon on the desk could exterminate the aliens – or serve as an incentive to make peace. "A stay-behind team could deploy the weapon if Earth and the rest of the settled worlds were to be destroyed."

"Indeed they could," Doctor Russell said. He smiled, clearly proud of himself. "We believe the weapon will spread rapidly, but it won't become lethal for several months. There will be enough time for it to spread through alien-held space."

Ted snorted. The problem with any form of biological warfare was that the weapons tended to mutate when released into the natural world. And the researchers were dealing with a completely alien biology, no matter how much they claimed to understand what they were doing. It was quite possible the disease would be instantly lethal, fail completely or be defeated by something the aliens had invented for their own medical care. If there were humans trying to improve the basic human form, why wouldn't there be aliens trying to do the same?

And if the disease acted so rapidly it slaughtered an entire planet without going any further, it would be blindingly obvious to the aliens that it had been an attempt at genocide.

"I want you to keep all your research carefully sealed, Doctor," Ted ordered. The researchers were already largely isolated, but they were allowed to talk to the ambassadors and their aides. As if the thought had worked a magic spell, he saw one of the aides appear at the hatch and start walking purposefully towards him. "And do *not* talk about it outside the cleared circle."

"I have every confidence in my security precautions," Doctor Russell protested. "I am no stranger to classified work…"

"Then do as I tell you," Ted ordered, shortly. He turned to face Ambassador Melbourne's aide. "I suggest we take this conversation outside."

The young man - Antony DuBois, if Ted recalled correctly – looked irked, but obeyed. Ted wasn't too surprised. He hadn't met many such aides during his time on *Ark Royal*, something that hadn't prepared him for meeting them after his promotion. The aides all seemed to think they had the clearances enjoyed by their political masters *and* that they had a right to know everything. In some cases, they might have had a point. This, Ted decided as he walked the younger man outside, wasn't one of them.

DuBois turned to face him as soon as the hatch was closed. He was a short man, wearing a formal suit despite special permission to wear shipsuits or modified uniforms. His hair was perfectly coiffed, which suggested a streak of vanity or insecurity. Ted had no time to wonder which, not when he had a flotilla to command and a security crisis on his hands.

"The Ambassador's cabin, Admiral, is much too small," DuBois said. "We need to move him to a bigger one."

Ted kept his expression blank with an effort. Aides derived their status from their superiors. A slight, however unintentional, to one of the ambassadors was a slight to their aides. But under the circumstances, the Ambassador himself had not complained. Had he wanted his aide to do the complaining for him or was his aide trying to do what he thought was best?

"The Ambassador has one of the largest sets of quarters on the ship," Ted said. It was true; there were only two bigger suites on the ship and both of them were occupied. "He also only has to bunk down with his aides."

"It isn't suitable," DuBois insisted. "He needs to make a show to the aliens."

"I don't think the aliens will notice if he shares a cabin or has a palace to himself," Ted snapped, too tired to deal with the situation any further. "I suggest, Mr. DuBois, that you resign yourself to sharing those quarters until we make contact with the aliens."

He turned and strode down the corridor, into the next section. Inside, the air was warm and moist, the temperature a reminder of the alien holding facility on the other side of the moon. Ted had visited, twice, since they'd brought the alien captives back to Earth, but they'd been as uncommunicative as ever. He pushed the thought to one side as he stepped through the second hatch and into Doctor McDonald's working space.

"Doctor McDonald," he said, feeling sweat trickling down the back of his uniform jacket. It was too hot to wear a formal uniform. "I was hoping you'd have time for a proper chat."

Polly McDonald looked up at him. She was wearing a halter top and a pair of shorts that were so tight Ted couldn't help wondering if they were painted onto her skin. He had to remind himself, sharply, that she was young enough to be his daughter as she waved him to a chair and reached for a bottle of water. Ted took it gratefully.

"I'm sorry about the weather, Admiral," she said. "If I am to meet the aliens in their natural habitat, or at least on the shores of their worlds, I need to stay used to their preferred conditions."

Ted hesitated, then removed his jacket and folded it over his lap. "Talking to the aliens is of prime importance, Doctor," he said. "Can you talk to them?"

"Please, call me Polly," Doctor McDonald said. She smiled. "I think talking to them without a voder is going to be damn near impossible; they might be able to hear us, but we can't hear them speaking. Still, we have recordings from the alien cities your people observed and I'm fairly certain we can produce something the aliens can hear."

Ted nodded. "Didn't you try it on the alien captives?"

"Most of them were non-committal," Polly admitted. "Their behaviour is odd, Admiral, at least by our standards. Sometimes they're willing to try to communicate, at other times they seem to be sulking like children, even amongst themselves. We've tried to record their conversations, but we got nothing useful."

"Nothing at all?" Ted asked. "Are we missing something?"

"It's possible," Polly agreed. "The aliens might combine sign language with their high-pitched voices, but I don't see how they developed without some form of non-visual communication. All we hear from them is that they're repeating the same sounds over and over again."

"They could be saying something we can't hear," Ted mused.

"We might not be able to hear it," Polly said. "But the monitors should be able to pick out pitches and changes in tone…even if *we* can't hear it with our merely human ears. There doesn't seem to be enough shift to suggest they're actually talking. It's more like they're rehashing the same statements over and over again."

She frowned. "I keep thinking of some of the weirder proposals on the fringes of science," she added. "The aliens might have been deliberately modified to have a considerable level of intelligence, but a very limited amount of free will."

Ted blinked. "Is that even possible?"

"In theory," Polly said. "You could program limiters into the brain, perhaps ones making it impossible to tell the difference between someone's own desires and orders from someone else. Or you could undermine their sense of self until it simply doesn't exist. In practice…it has never been tried, officially. It would break the conventions on designing a humanoid slave race."

"And *unofficially*?" Ted asked. "Weren't there people who wanted to try?"

"It got shut down before it ever got off the ground floor," Polly said. "Too many people reacted to the concept with absolute revulsion. But I'm starting to think the aliens need to work in groups to reach their full potential."

"They also fly starfighters," Ted pointed out. "I don't care how advanced their technology is, Doctor, but they couldn't fit more than two or three aliens into those cockpits."

Polly smirked. "Even if they were prepared to be very friendly?"

Ted flushed, remembering a rite of passage for junior lieutenants. He'd been told to find out how many lieutenants he could fit into a standard shuttle. Unfortunately, there simply hadn't been enough lieutenants on the ship to fill the shuttlecraft. It had turned out, afterwards, that he'd been meant to fill in the spaces with locals, prostitutes from the nearest brothel. They'd called it an exercise in thinking outside the box. *Ted* considered it an exercise in pointless hazing.

"I don't think they'd actually get any flying done," he said. "I don't think they need to be in groups to think."

"Maybe they can't react to situations outside their orders," Polly said. "I've seen academics, really clever men and women, have problems thinking when they're forced to focus on something outside their subject. They have panic attacks and start trying to escape..."

"I've had officers who had the same problem," Ted said. "They just can't think when something happens outside their orders."

He took a breath. "Do you think we can actually...make contact with the aliens?"

"I think we can build up a communications algorithm," Polly said. "They may well have done their own research into communicating with us. In that case, we will have to match our efforts with theirs and see what happens. But if we can't establish any meaningful dialogue..."

Ted nodded. If the aliens couldn't be talked out of fighting, there would be no choice, but to fight the war to the bitter end. He thought of the test tube Doctor Russell had showed him and went cold. Were the aliens building their own biological weapons program? There were thousands of people with enhanced immune systems these days, mainly in the military, but would they survive whatever the aliens might use to exterminate the human race?

"Do the best you can," he said, standing. His shirt was soaked with sweat. He'd need to shower and change before he went on duty in the CIC. "And let me know if you have any brainwaves that will make contacting them easier."

"Of course, Admiral," Polly said. She looked down at the table for a long moment, then looked up and met his eyes. "I don't think they're an evil race."

"I agree," Ted said. The aliens had passed up countless opportunities for brute slaughter until they'd attacked Earth. Had they actually *meant* to devastate humanity's homeworld? "But they've done a *lot* of damage, Doctor. Even if we do manage to talk to them, coming to a peace agreement isn't going to be easy."

He nodded to her, then strode out of the hatch and walked back to his office. Even now, crawling through a potentially hostile star system, there was no shortage of work to do.

And besides, it distracted him from his growing concerns.

CHAPTER
SEVENTEEN

Kurt felt oddly numb over the days following their joint confession. On one hand, his duties to the starfighter pilots under his command were blurred with reporting to the Marines and going through every last detail of their affair; on the other hand, he kept expecting the blackmailers to make contact and nothing happened. He programmed his terminal to alert him the moment any message arrived, then did his best to put it out of his mind. It didn't work.

He missed Rose, more than he cared to admit. It wasn't just the sex; it was being with her, sharing ideas for how best to deploy their starfighters in combat. But they'd been banned from being together alone and it was hard to get someone else to supervise them. All they could do was keep busy, keep the new trainees working hard to build up their skills and try not to think about the future. Whatever happened, Kurt knew, his career was definitely at an end.

"All clear," the XO said, once *Ark Royal* passed through yet another tramline. "Starfighter pilots may return to their quarters."

Kurt nodded and climbed out of his starfighter. One squadron would remain on Quick Reaction Alert at all times, just in case they encountered the aliens, but the remaining pilots would either go to the simulators or their bunks. Most of the trainees were looking tired and worn these days; if it had been possible, Kurt would have forced them all to take a week's rest. But he knew that it wouldn't be possible until the end of the mission.

He sighed as he looked at the young men and women. Most of them were definitely going to wind up dead.

"Concentrate on your attack formations," he ordered, addressing one group. They'd be going straight to the simulators. "You're not random enough. The aliens will rip you to shreds when you enter attack range."

"I'll put them through the wringer," Wing Commander Falcone assured him. He looked ridiculously young for his rank, but at least he had experience. He'd been nothing more than a newly-trained pilot during Operation Nelson. "And then make sure they get some damn sleep."

"Proper sleep," Kurt ordered. "Sleep machines tend to catch up with you, sooner or later."

He watched them go, then turned and hurried back to his office. The Marines would probably want to talk to him again soon enough and he wanted a nap before they arrived, if only to prevent himself from falling asleep in the middle of the interrogation. They just went over the same questions again and again. Kurt suspected they were trying to catch him in a lie, something that infuriated him more than he cared to say. But he knew they had no reason to trust him. They knew how badly he'd compromised himself.

His office was monitored now, of course. Kurt wasn't sure if it was to make sure he wasn't making love to Rose or to catch anyone trying to leave messages for him, but it was something else he hated, no matter how much he understood. He stepped through the hatch and half-stumbled towards the desk, fighting down the yawn that threatened to burst from his mouth. The lack of sleep was starting to catch up with him.

And a new message was blinking on his terminal.

He stared, suddenly shocked into action. It *was* from the address he'd been given...and he should have been alerted. When he looked down at the terminal on his belt, he saw nothing...but they'd been on tactical alert. Nothing short of a Priority One message would have been forwarded to him. He cursed violently, then opened the message. It was nothing more than a handful of sentences strung together, seemingly at random. But he knew it was the message's arrival that was the *true* notification.

Bracing himself, he stood and strode through the hatch, heading up towards the observation blister. It was late at night, by shipboard time, which probably meant it would be in use by a pair of *legitimate* lovers. The hidden sign indicating occupancy was there, warning him not to enter the compartment. But he had a feeling it was actually there to keep people out until he'd picked up his orders. Cursing again, he walked through the hatch and into the observation blister. It was empty.

Puzzled, he looked around. There was a datachip lying on one of the benches, under the stars. He picked it up and examined it, but saw nothing that separated it from the hundreds of thousands of datachips used throughout the ship. It looked to be a design used by both civilian and military personnel. No one would think twice if they saw it, he realised, silently saluting the blackmailers. And, without the correct access codes, they wouldn't be able to use it.

He popped the chip into his terminal. There was a brief moment of nothing, then the terminal demanded a biometric scan. Kurt swore under his breath, then pressed his fingertip against the reader, wondering just where the blackmailers had obtained his biometric details. They were kept under tight security at Nelson Base, as far as he knew. Fingerprints were one thing, but access to a person's genetic code – which would be possible, if they'd accessed his fingerprint records – was potentially disastrous. Someone could force-grow a clone of someone important and use the clone's DNA to access classified data.

Or perhaps they just took my fingerprints from Luna City, he thought. He had been too distraught to think about the mug of tea he'd drunk. Fred could have arranged for it to be picked up and then delivered to one of his associates. *Now, let's see...*

The files on the datapad unlocked, one by one. Three of them were text files, the fourth was an executable program. He opened the first text file and read it, quickly. It consisted of nothing more than instructions, which he had apparently twenty-four hours to follow or else. They didn't go into details, but it didn't matter. He knew what 'or else' meant.

He sighed. He'd have to take the terminal to the Marines and hope they knew what to do with it. And that the blackmailers didn't notice what he'd done.

———

"They want *what?*" Ted asked.

"Access codes," Major Parnell said. His technicians had been examining the datachip since the CAG had brought it to them. "They want *his* access codes, but also access codes belonging to the XO and the Captain. And they want him to upload the program on the datachip into the main computer."

Ted shook his head, firmly. *Ark Royal* was less dependent on automation than the modern carriers, but they didn't dare risk losing the main computer. It was bad enough that the system was a patchwork of ancient Royal Navy gear merged with Russian, Chinese and French systems. He'd had nightmares about it coming apart at the seams ever since the aliens had proven their ability to shoot through the hull. They'd built as much redundancy into the system as they could, but he knew it wouldn't be enough.

Fitzwilliam had another question. "What does the program actually do?"

"It's a virus," Parnell said. "It won't do anything until it receives the signal. When it does, it will hack its way into the ship's datanet and take control, locking us all out. Or it would, according to the techs, if we were a normal ship. The virus wasn't designed with our systems in mind."

Ted's eyes narrowed. "Are you sure of that?"

"The techs think our systems won't be able to support the virus when it goes active," Parnell said. "But I'd prefer not to test it."

"Me neither," Ted said. He shared a glance with Fitzwilliam. "What about the original message, the one alerting Schneider to pick up the chip?"

"Apparently, it was sent from one of the terminals on the lower decks," Parnell said. "The system was accessed using a standard dockyard access code, not a crewman's personal login. It could be any of the dockyard workers who sent the message."

"Or someone pinched their code and used it," Ted said. Normally, dockyard codes were purged from the system as soon as the ship left the shipyard. This time, with dockyard workers still onboard, the codes had been left in place. "They all use the same one, don't they?"

Parnell nodded.

"We're looking through footage now, sir," he said. "But we may be unable to locate the person responsible. Too many people pass through the lower decks."

"Of course they do," Fitzwilliam agreed. "Haven't you been urging the ambassadors and their staffs to take some exercise?"

Ted tapped the desk, shortly. "What could they do with personal access codes," he mused. "And how could they expect Schneider to obtain them?"

"Someone with enough experience at manipulating a computer could probably pull someone else's access code out of the system," Parnell said. "It's a persistent headache on the ground, sir. Terrorists and insurgents often try to fight smarter, as well as harder, and there's always some idiot who leaves their access codes unsecured. Once they're in the system, they can create dummy login details for themselves and slip in and out at will."

He shook his head. "And anyone onboard ship will be already inside the outermost firewall," he added. "The system won't see anything Schneider does as an attempt to force access from outside the hull."

Ted nodded. One of the Admiralty's persistent nightmares, ever since computers had become utterly indispensable to operating starships, was someone hacking into the Royal Navy's datanet and crashing the entire system, leaving the fleet helpless. The fear was so prevalent that hundreds of precautions had been taken, from isolating each starship to hardwiring certain safeguards into their computer networks. But, during wartime, isolating starships from the datanets prevented them from working together smoothly. No one, it seemed, had seriously considered all-out war with an alien race.

But they might be able to break into our systems, he thought, morbidly. *We broke into theirs and they have a head start.*

"Right," he said. "We can't take the risk of uploading the program."

"It might be workable," Parnell said. "We could disable it first..."

"Too risky," Fitzwilliam said.

Ted nodded in agreement.

"Captain, Admiral, we don't know who left the chip in the observation blister," Parnell said. "And Schneider has been ordered to forward the access details to a specific location within our system, not return to the blister. It's within the entertainment subsection…"

"Where everyone and his aunt goes when they're not on duty," Ted groaned. *Ark Royal* carried millions upon millions of movie files, music tracks and VR simulations to entertain her crew when they had some downtime. *That* part of the network was hard to patrol, let alone to secure. If the files were isolated in a specific location, it was unlikely they'd be discovered by the wrong person. "Can't we track down the user?"

"We can flag the file so we're beeped if it's accessed," Parnell said. "The only question is what we actually give them?"

Fitzwilliam eyed him, suspiciously. "What would you *like* to give them?"

"Access codes that can be cancelled, if necessary," Parnell said. "Look, they *don't* seem to be familiar with our computer systems. Their virus might have failed even if Schneider uploaded it for them. We give them a set of access codes that look modern, but have to be approved and authorised by us before they do anything. At the very least, we'd be able to track down whoever was using them."

"True," Ted said. "But why do they want the codes?"

"Sabotage," Parnell guessed. "Other than that, I can't imagine what they might have in mind. Unless they *are* working for the aliens, of course."

Ted gritted his teeth. "If the aliens could talk to us well enough to tell spies what to do," he said, "why couldn't they talk peace without…"

He waved a hand at the bulkhead. "Surely, they must realise the war hasn't gone as well as might be expected."

"Insufficient data," Parnell said.

"There is another possibility," Fitzwilliam said, suddenly. "One of the Ambassadors is planning something."

Ted gave him a sharp look. "They *know* just how bad things are," he said. "They wouldn't try to rock the boat, would they?"

"My family does a little diplomatic work," Fitzwilliam said. It wasn't common for him to talk about his family, not since his failed attempt to take command of *Ark Royal*. "A great deal of diplomacy, particularly between the major powers, consists of maintaining the status quo rather than one nation attempting to best another nation. That's why we ended up with agreements not to build large numbers of mass drivers and not to fight each other in the Solar System.

"But this is different. This is something completely outside our previous context.

"It's quite possible that one of the Ambassadors has secret orders to try to wring some additional advantage for his own country out of the peace talks," he added. "Or…"

He broke off and swore. "It's the Russians."

Ted blinked. "How can you be sure?"

"If necessary, the Ambassadors have orders to cede space the aliens already hold in exchange for peace," Fitzwilliam said. "Give us ten years of breathing space and we might be able to…*renegotiate* the agreement. No one really *wants* to surrender human-settled systems, but we might not have a choice. And that would include the surrender of New Russia."

"The Russians would be furious," Ted said, very slowly. "But would they want to prolong the war in hopes of liberating their world?"

"They'd be dependent on *us* to liberate their world," Parnell added. "They're down to their last carrier, I believe, and only a handful of frigates. There would be no liberation unless we or one of the other spacefaring powers did the heavy lifting."

"And someone might well have started to pressure the Russians into making concessions while they're down," Fitzwilliam said. "The Russians have suffered the worst of any of the spacefaring powers. Someone else might have decided to take advantage of their weakness."

Ted frowned, more perturbed than he cared to admit. "Have *we* taken advantage of their weakness?"

"Not as far as I know," Fitzwilliam said. "But if the war ended with a return to the *status quo…*"

He allowed his voice to trail off suggestively. Ted barely heard him. If there was a spacefaring power that had good reason to hate the aliens, it was the Russians. Even if the war ended tomorrow on decent terms the Russians would still need decades to rebuilt their lost military and economic strength. And New Russia sat on a handful of tramlines, tramlines the other spacefaring powers would want to use. It was quite possible the Russians feared losing everything in the wake of a peace agreement that left the aliens in control of New Russia...or losing influence and power even if they *did* recover New Russia.

And there was a team of Russian observers on the ship.

"Watch the Russians," he ordered, "but don't take your eyes off anyone else."

Parnell smiled. "We'll try, sir," he said. "But the diplomats are very good at checking their cabins for bugs. I think we'll have to watch from a distance."

He shrugged. "With your permission," he added, "we will provide dummy access codes to the CAG. He can send them to the blackmailers and...hopefully, they'll use them. And then we will know who they are."

"And then we can remove them," Fitzwilliam said. "Five days to Target One, Admiral. And we still don't have any idea what the Russians – or whoever the blackmailers actually are – *want.*"

Ted nodded. The blackmailers had played a card when they'd forced Schneider to work for them under threat of exposure. They wouldn't have shown their hand unless they had something in mind for him, some way to use him for best advantage. And that meant they intended to use him soon, or they wouldn't have run the risk of exposing themselves. And that meant...

He shook his head. "Give me a nice naval battle any day," he said. He looked at Parnell. "Give them the dummy codes, but make damn certain we can override them if necessary. I don't want them to be in any position to harm this ship. If the techs think we can let them think the virus is in place when it isn't, do it. If not, Schneider will have to tell them that he doesn't have access permission to upload anything to the main command network. He certainly *shouldn't* have that permission."

"Aye, Admiral," Parnell said.

"There is an alternative," Fitzwilliam mused. "We pretend to discover the affair and put both Schneider and Labara in the brig. Or claim we caught him trying to upload the virus. They'd pull in their horns and pray to escape discovery, instead of causing further trouble. Then we can honour the agreement with the...*happy couple* at a later date."

"We might not learn precisely what the blackmailers had in mind," Parnell pointed out. "Or just who they were. We have suspicions, Captain. Nothing more."

"No proof of anything, beyond attempted blackmail," Ted agreed.

He glared down at the deck. Naval combat was understandable. The enemy wanted to kill him and he wanted to kill the enemy. But this counter-intelligence work was like shooting at shadows, with the added disadvantage that some of the shadows might shoot back. And that shooting the wrong shadow might be disastrous. Accusing the Russians – or anyone else – of involvement in the affair would not go down well without very real proof.

And the only way to get that proof was to let the blackmailers proceed, praying all the time they could keep them from doing any real damage.

"Shit," he muttered. "They must have been out of their minds."

CHAPTER
EIGHTEEN

Ted felt the tension rising throughout the CIC as *War Hog* made her first transit into Target One. The aliens had been surprisingly – and suspiciously – absent during the last few star systems, but he had no doubt they would encounter the enemy in Target One. It was, after all, a major alien settlement, even without the orbital facilities they'd smashed to rubble during their last visit. And besides, there were several tramlines leading in and out of the system. The aliens would hardly leave it undefended.

A green icon popped back into life on the display and he sighed, minutely. The odds against running into an alien battlefleet on the other side were staggeringly high, but the aliens had managed to do things he would have thought were impossible before. He watched as the display updated, revealing a flurry of signals from Target One, but little else. The aliens, it seemed, hadn't invested in repair efforts.

Probably a good idea on their part, he thought. Target One *was* the only major alien world with a confirmed location. It would make a suitable target for any human raiding formation – and taking out repair ships and yards would cost the aliens dearly. They'd probably prefer to end the war before they started rebuilding the system. *But it doesn't really matter.*

"Take us through the tramline," he ordered. "And then launch stealth probes on ballistic trajectories."

"Aye, sir," Janelle said, relaying his orders to the bridge. She sounded harried – and he didn't blame her. As his aide, she'd ended up handling quite a few of the complaints and whining from various ambassadors and their staffs. *And* some clear attempts to get on her good side, on the assumption she would continue to have ties with the Royal Family. "All ships are reporting ready to go."

Ted braced himself. If they were wrong, if an alien fleet was lying in wait, the attack would begin...now. Nothing happened. The seconds ticked away, the display stabilised and started filling up with passive data. No missiles came raging towards them, followed by swarms of angry starfighters. Instead, there was nothing.

"Hold us here," Ted ordered. "Inform me when the probes pick up something – anything – of value."

He settled back in his chair and tried to relax as the probes flew into the system, heading directly towards Target One. They were close to undetectable, he knew; the aliens would have to be very lucky to catch even a *sniff* of their presence. But they also had their limitations. Their passive sensors wouldn't pick up anything that wasn't radiating a signature into space, while the further they moved from their mothership, the greater the time delay.

Space combat, Ted thought, ruefully. *It is both simple and very complex.*

Slowly, data started to appear on the display. The largest gas giant in the system, which had once hosted a number of cloudscoops before Operation Nelson, seemed to be almost deserted. There was only one radio source near the planet, hanging in high orbit. Ted ordered a secondary fight of drones to be launched towards the radio source, then turned his attention back to the main display. It looked as though the aliens had pulled most of the in-system freighters out of the system. The once-thriving system was ruined.

"I'm only picking up a handful of asteroid miners," Janelle said. "Analysis thinks the aliens have largely conceded the system."

"Best not to take that for granted," Ted warned her. "And Target One itself?"

The drones flashed more data back to the ship as they made their way past Target One. A handful of alien ships – five frigates, two freighters and a ship of unknown design – lurked in orbit around the planet, but there didn't seem to have been any attempt to rebuild the facilities that had once made the system an economic powerhouse. The aliens had swept most of the remaining debris out of orbit, probably breaking it up and then shoving it into the planet's atmosphere, yet they hadn't done anything else. Ted nodded in confirmation of his earlier thoughts. The aliens weren't interested in rebuilding yet.

"We can't get a drone any closer without risking detection," Janelle said. "There won't be any data on alien operations on the ground."

Ted nodded, unsurprised. A handful of human soldiers had been stranded, he knew, despite the best efforts of his shuttle pilots. They'd planned to go underground and live off the land until they could be recovered. God alone knew what had happened to them. There was certainly no way he could attempt to recover them, not now. He had no doubt his flotilla could handle the alien ships, but one of them would definitely broadcast an alert and inform their superiors that the humans had returned to Target One.

"I think we will need to sneak around to Tramline Four," he said. The ship from Faction Two had entered the system through Tramline Four. Unless, of course, it was all an elaborate trick. "There's no point in staying here any longer."

"Aye, Admiral," Janelle said. "Do you want to depart at once?"

Ted glanced down at the ship's status display. That irritating harmonic in the drives seemed to have faded away completely. He wasn't fool enough to believe it was gone for good, but it was marginally reassuring. Perhaps the only problem had been that the drives hadn't been put to work properly during the test cycles. Or perhaps he was overlooking a far greater problem.

But there seemed to be no reason to delay. "Set course for Tramline Four on the planned course," he ordered. "Launch probes to scan the space close to the tramline for any unexpected surprises. And remind the crew to stay on full tactical alert."

He'd expected to see more alien activity as they edged their way around the system. A handful of other installations revealed themselves, but far fewer than there had been in the system before his first visit. He felt an odd pang of guilt and had to remind himself, sharply, that Target One had been producing weapons and starships for the aliens to hurl against humanity's defences. If nothing else, the loss of such a large chunk of their productive capability had to make the aliens pause for thought.

And they took heavy losses in the Battle of Earth, he reminded himself. *Maybe they're just as exhausted and battered as we are.*

He recalled, bitterly, the last time they'd passed through Tramline Four. The aliens had ambushed them there, using the gas giants to form limited tramlines that allowed in-system jumping. It had been a clever tactic, he knew, but the humans had escaped…if, of course, the aliens had *intended* to destroy his ships. They might have been more interested in keeping them apart from Faction Two. And Target Two, the star system on the other side of the tramline, had been left completely unscathed. He had no idea if that was a good thing or not.

A red icon flashed into view on the display. "Captain," Janelle said. "A starship just came out of the tramline. She's heading right for us."

Ted swore. Coincidence? Or deliberate malice? But if the aliens had managed to pick up a hint they were there, they'd have sent something heavier than a single destroyer-sized starship. Unless it was armed with something new and utterly destructive…in which case the war was lost anyway.

Or were the aliens intent on making an evasive run to reach Tramline One?

"Captain," Janelle said, as several more icons popped into view, "I'm picking up four more starships in hot pursuit. They're chasing the first starship. It's taking evasive action."

Ted stared, feeling an odd flicker of *Déjà Vu*. The scenario was almost identical to the last time they'd encountered a starship from Faction Two, save that the aliens had no idea the human ships were there. Or *should* have no idea the human ships were there, he reminded himself sternly. And it certainly looked, he saw as he replayed the first starship's arrival through the tramline, as though they'd been running through the Target Two system. No one, human or alien, took the tramlines at a run if they could help it.

He hesitated, thinking fast. It would be simple to evade both sides, with so much space to hide in, then proceed through the tramline behind them. But if the lead ship *was* from Faction Two…he cursed the aliens under his breath, angrily. If he intervened, he would betray his presence and the aliens would start massing their ships against his fleet. And yet, if he did nothing, he might pass up an opportunity to put the aliens in his debt.

"General signal to all ships," he ordered. "Prepare to shed the cloak and attack."

He paused. "And warn Doctor MacDonald that her services will be required," he added. "We need to convince the lead ship not to run."

———

The first few days onboard the alien starship had been boring, Henry had found, despite the thrill of actually being on an *alien* starship. Working the teaching machines with the aliens had been tedious, even though the aliens seemed to pick up more and more human words and concepts the longer they worked at it. One file turned out to be a semi-pornographic introduction to sex, something that puzzled the aliens. Henry still cringed at the memory of one of them asking if humans needed to be *taught* how to produce more humans.

But they don't have sex, he reminded himself. *Maybe they find the entire concept puzzling as hell.*

It was an odd thought, but he contemplated it as he tried to explain other concepts to the aliens. A discussion of hereditary monarchy merely confused them; democracy seemed more understandable, but they didn't grasp the concept of a representative democracy. Their society seemed to allow everyone who had an opinion to state their opinion, then allow it to settle into the majority viewpoint. Henry couldn't help being reminded of datanet chat-rooms, with the added disadvantage that none of the arguments were remotely theoretical.

Sleeping became easier after he managed to convince the aliens to let them have a fan and straps they could use to keep themselves in place. The aliens themselves didn't seem to have problems sleeping in zero-gravity, although Henry wasn't sure why. Maybe there were water currents running through the ship that allowed them to breathe through their gills, without problems, or maybe they just didn't need the same atmospheric mix as humanity. It was impossible to be sure.

"They're learning rapidly," Jill said, "but I don't think they will ever understand us completely."

Henry couldn't disagree. Teaching machines were designed for human children on isolated colonies, bringing them up to standard without needing to import a dedicated teacher. They were actually quite successful, as long as the kids stayed in front of the machine, and the aliens – it seemed – had learned a great deal from them. But they still didn't understand some of the human concepts. A long explanation of why some humans wore skirts and others wore kilts, despite them being essentially the same thing, had puzzled them completely.

"We probably won't understand them completely either," he said. He'd asked for clothes, only to be turned down. There hadn't been any malice in the alien voice, as far as he could tell, or a desire to humiliate the humans; they simply hadn't understood the requirement. "But as long as we can get them to talk to someone with real power, we can hammer out an agreement."

He looked at her as she turned away, pushing herself towards the bed. It had crossed his mind, more than once, to tell the aliens who he was. He'd been told, in no uncertain terms, that he shouldn't disclose his identity if he was ever taken hostage, although he'd pointed out sarcastically that anyone who tried to kidnap him would have a jolly good idea of who he was already. The thought of becoming an alien prisoner had never crossed his mind...

But he'd also been told, time and time again, that he had no true power. He couldn't make promises the British Government would be bound to keep...

The ship shook, violently.

Jill started. "What was *that*?"

"An impact," Henry said. He pressed his fingers against the deck and felt it throbbing. It was impossible to be sure, but it felt like the starship was going to full military power. "I think that's not good."

One of the aliens swung around to face them. "This ship is under attack," it said. The other aliens were already making their way towards the hatch. "Remain here."

As if we could go anywhere else, Henry thought. He thought the ship had jumped through at least two tramlines, but it was impossible to be sure. Besides, as he had no idea of where they'd been held prisoner or how close it was to Target One, trying to estimate the distance they'd covered was a pointless exercise.

Jill looked nervous. "Under attack by whom?"

The alien said nothing. Instead, it just pulled itself out the hatch and vanished.

"Humans or another alien faction," Henry guessed. "Unless there's a third alien race that has just introduced itself to us."

Jill pulled herself to the bed, then reached for one of the straps. "Is that possible?"

Henry shrugged. "We didn't know there was even *one* alien race until a year ago," he said, dryly. "Why can't there be two?"

But somehow it seemed unlikely. The War Faction might be trying to stop them contacting the human race...or they might have run into a patrolling human starship. Either one was bad, but it would be worse if it was a human ship. The aliens might lose faith in their attempt to make peace if they were greeted with a hail of incoming fire. He glared around the bulkhead, wishing for a tactical display, something – anything – to show what was going on outside the hull. But there was nothing.

He pushed himself over to the bed and strapped himself down. There was nothing else he could do, but wait.

"I'm scared," Jill said. She wrapped her arms around him, her bare breasts poking into his chest. "Why...?"

Henry understood. Their lives depended, now, on the aliens destroying the attackers or breaking contact and escaping. There was nothing they could do, one way or the other, to help the aliens or even save their own lives. If the aliens lost, the first they'd know of it would be when the bulkheads disintegrated into fire. By then, it would be far too late for them to do anything more than die.

"Relax," he ordered, firmly. The nasty part of his mind wanted to know if his private vows to Janelle still held good, despite the certainty of death. Jill looked willing enough...angrily, he pushed that thought aside. He was damned if he was going to rut like an animal in the face of imminent death. "Close your eyes and try to relax."

———

James Fitzwilliam sucked in his breath as the five alien ships came into view. It wasn't easy to disagree with the tactical analysis; Contact One was attempting to escape, while Contacts Two through Five were attempting to catch it. Whoever was flying Contact One was an ace helmsman, he had to admit. He was incredibly skilful at keeping the distance open between the five ships, despite the endless barrage of plasma fire. But his luck would run out, sooner or later.

"Lock mass drivers on target," he ordered. He doubted they would score a hit, unless the aliens did something stupid, but it would give the bastards something else to think about apart from Contact One. "Prepare to fire."

"Mass drivers locked, Captain," Farley said. "Starfighters are ready to launch."

James allowed himself a smile. The battle was about to be joined – and there would be no more sneaking about, either with the aliens or the foreign spy on his ship. This time, everything would be simple.

"Spit a copy of their communications package at them, then the instructions," he said, addressing Lieutenant Annie Davidson. The aliens would be sent a set of diagrams, detailing what to do. Everyone swore blind they'd be able to understand what they were being sent, but James had his doubts. The aliens were *alien*. For all they knew, their system would be unable to display the pictures. "And warn our crews to keep a sharp eye on Contact One."

"Aye, Captain," Davidson said.

"Fire," James ordered.

Ark Royal shuddered as her mass drivers fired, launching a stream of projectiles towards the alien ships. A direct hit would be fatal, he knew, although the aliens would have plenty of time to alter course. The projectiles weren't missiles. They'd keep following a strictly ballistic trajectory, missing their targets. And the aliens would definitely know they were there.

"Launch starfighters," he ordered. Contact One was altering course – but was it because they were obeying orders or because they didn't know who the humans were trying to kill? If the aliens had problems telling humans apart, they might assume that humanity had the same problem. And it did. "All batteries, prepare to open fire."

The other alien ships seemed to hesitate, then pressed the attack against Contact One. James frowned; they had to know they were suddenly badly outgunned and they *could* retreat, so why weren't they running? It would be easy for them to evade contact if they reversed course now. One of them…he blinked in disbelief as mass driver projectiles smashed into its hull, shattering it into thousands of pieces of debris. They'd been so focused on their target that they hadn't even *tried* to evade the incoming projectiles.

"Continue firing," he ordered. The aliens clearly didn't want them talking to Contact One. It was worth some risk to attempt to make contact. "And attempt to raise Contact One."

CHAPTER
NINETEEN

"Fall into formation," Kurt ordered, as the starfighters lanced away from the carrier. "And remember to randomise your manoeuvres."

He smiled, despite the risk of imminent death. It had been a long argument to convince the Captain to put him back on the flight roster – and that had been before he'd made a full confession – but it had been worth it. Here, he could pretend to be a simple pilot, rather than a man caught at the centre of a byzantine plot. And besides, he didn't want to leave his largely untrained pilots at the mercy of the aliens. They needed someone experienced to lead the way.

"Launch missiles from the outside edge of the envelope," he reminded them, designating targets for the starfighters and bombers. "Then close in and strafe their hulls."

He smirked at the thought. If there was one thing the aliens were probably regretting, it was teaching humanity how to produce their own plasma weapons. Once, humanity's starfighters wouldn't have been a serious threat to the alien ships. Now, even a single starfighter could do a great deal of damage. The aliens had good reason to curse themselves for not armouring their own ships against weapons they *knew* perfectly well existed.

But then their carriers would move like wallowing pigs, he thought. He could see the alien logic, even though he disagreed with it. *And they'd be sitting ducks for mass drivers.*

He eyed Contact One warily as his starfighters flashed past it, but the alien craft did nothing suspicious. Kurt continued to mutter advice and reassurance to his pilots, even though most of them had mastered the basic simulations. But a real battle could be dangerously unpredictable. At least the aliens didn't have starfighters of their own…

"Break and attack," he ordered. The alien sensors swept over the fighters, preparing to open fire. "I say again, break and attack."

He yanked his fighter into a crazy corkscrew as he flew into engagement range, followed by the remaining starfighters. Contact Three opened fire, filling space with deadly plasma bolts that chased the starfighters as they closed in on their target. It wasn't fair, part of Kurt's mind noted. Too many human starfighter pilots had died at the Battle of New Russia because they hadn't had the slightest idea of what they were facing. Now…they knew and they still lost pilots every time they faced the aliens.

"Fire," he snapped. The missile launched from his starfighter and zoomed towards the alien ship. One by one, the other starfighters opened fire, their missiles closing in on their targets. The alien ship switched its fire to the missiles, allowing the starfighters to get close enough to read the alien writing on the hull. Kurt smiled, nastily, and opened fire. Streaks of brilliant plasma burned through the alien hull and slammed deep into the ship's innards.

They seem to be less explosive than carriers, he thought, as he yanked his starfighter away a second before a bolt of plasma would have ended his life. *Maybe they have fewer stockpiles of fuel and weapons.*

It didn't matter. The alien craft exploded into a hail of plasma, the blast wiping out two of the pilots who had strayed too close to their target. Kurt heard a gasp from one of the other pilots, another trainee. Clearly, she hadn't taken the warnings about how many of them were going to die to heart. He pulled his attention away from her – Rose would talk to her later, assuming they both survived – and checked the overall situation. Contacts Two, Three and Four were gone. Contact Five was breaking off and hightailing it back towards the tramline.

"Engage and destroy," Kurt ordered, savagely. It felt *good* to lash out and destroy something, even if it was nothing more than an alien starship.

He tried to imagine the aliens wearing Fred's face and felt a rush of blood-lust that shocked even him If this was his last chance to fly a starfighter, he was damned if he was wasting it. "I say again, engage and destroy."

―――――

"The last enemy ship is retreating," Janelle reported. "But she won't make it to the tramline before our starfighters get her."

"It won't matter," Ted said. It would be roughly two hours before the forces orbiting Target One picked up any signals the aliens might have sent, but there was no way he could get to them before they realised the humans were in their star system. Maybe the aliens hadn't sent any signals…he shook his head. Long-range passive sensors would certainly pick up *something*. "But order them to take her out if they can."

He watched, feeling the old helplessness again, as the starfighters closed in on their target. The aliens fought savagely, but hopelessly, refusing to give in right to the last. Ted silently saluted the aliens as their starship died, then turned his attention back to Contact One. She was sitting there, following her orders, and waiting. Was he looking at the first step towards ending the war or a Trojan Horse? Might the aliens have deliberately intended to drive Contact One into their arms?

But that would require far too much to go right for them, he thought, grimly. *They're powerful, but they're not gods.*

"Inform Doctor MacDonald that she can begin transmitting her contact sequences now," Ted ordered. The first attempts to use the First Contact packages to address the aliens had failed, but the aliens had clearly sent back one of their own during the first abortive attempt at communication. Maybe this time it would work better. "Then recall the starfighters, apart from the CSP. I want to be ready if Contact One so much as twitches in our direction."

He looked down at the display, thinking dark thoughts. The alien ship-killer plasma cannon only worked at relatively short range – and Contact One was definitely outside the minimal range for effective use. But there were other weapons, missiles and mass drives in particular, that could do very real damage. The paranoid part of his mind was insisting that they made their way to a safer distance, despite the risks of losing the first real chance to communicate with the aliens. It was the safe thing to do.

"Aye, Admiral," Janelle said. "Doctor MacDonald is sending her signals now."

Ted nodded. Everyone had assumed that mathematics would be universal – but then, everyone had assumed that any alien race would be peaceful, or at least make some attempt to communicate before opening fire. It struck him as odd, given the number of berserkers or downright *alien* aliens in science-fiction, perhaps a legacy of a more idealistic time. But it didn't really matter. All that mattered was making contact now.

"I think they're transmitting signals back," Janelle said. "Steams of numbers and…"

She broke off. "Admiral," she said, her voice shaking, "I think you're going to want to see this."

————

Henry had been lost in prayers when the shaking had finally come to an end. It was impossible, as always, to see outside the bulkheads, but he assumed the aliens had managed to destroy or lose their enemies. The only alternative was that the aliens had been forced to surrender and they were about to be handed over to another alien faction. And then one of the aliens slithered back into the cell.

"Observe," it said. A holographic image appeared in the cell. "A ship."

"*Ark Royal*," Henry said, shocked. There could be no mistake. The giant carrier was unique. He'd seen images of planned future carriers, craft that would – once again – incorporate heavy armour into their designs, but none of them had looked like the Old Lady. She was a relic of a bygone age in too many ways. "You made contact!"

"They are sending us numbers," the alien said. As always, it's voice was atonal, but Henry thought he detected a hint of humour in its face. "We will send them you."

Henry hesitated. Naked and wet, soaked in sweat, he knew he would hardly make the best impression. But there was no choice. Whatever had happened outside the bulkheads, it had clearly resulted in the best possible outcome. The aliens had made contact with humanity!

"Yes," he said. "But how?"

The alien strode over to the bulkhead and pressed one leathery hand against the metal, pulling it away to reveal a hidden compartment. Henry was unwillingly impressed. There were secret compartments and passageways throughout Buckingham Palace – he and Elizabeth had made a game of finding them – but he hadn't had the slightest idea the compartment was there. Inside, there was a human communication system that looked several years out of date.

They must have taken it from Heinlein, he thought. *Or from Vera Cruz.*

"You'd better get out of the pickup," he said to Jill. "School kids are going to be watching this moment for centuries to come."

Jill snorted, but obeyed. Henry adjusted his position so the camera was pointed at his face, then keyed the switch. There was a long pause, then he saw a response. Admiral Smith's face was staring back at him. He looked as though he'd seen a ghost.

He must have thought I was dead, Henry thought, ruefully. It was vanishingly rare for anyone to survive a starfighter accident, let alone a direct hit. There wouldn't have been any time, he suspected, to puzzle through the records and determine what had happened to his starfighter. They would have concluded he'd been killed by the aliens...

"Admiral," he said. He couldn't resist. "Reports of my death have been greatly exaggerated."

———

Ted had known the aliens had taken prisoners. *Ark Royal* had rescued a number of them at Alien-1, drugged victims of the alien attacks on various colonies. But he'd never dared hope that Prince Henry had been taken prisoner. The reports had stated his plasma chambers had lost containment. Even if he'd survived that, he would be stranded in interstellar space, well away from any hope of rescue.

But the aliens had picked him up.

"So it would seem," Ted said, feeling his heartbeat slowly returning to normal. Reports of Prince Henry's death had *definitely* been greatly exaggerated. He cast a look at Janelle, who seemed to have paled alarmingly. It had to be worse for her. "Are you safe?"

"Everything is just peachy," Prince Henry said. "We're both safe and well, sir, but I have a vitally important report to make to you. This whole war is a mistake."

Just peachy, Ted thought. The old code for starfighter pilots, informing their superiors that they weren't under any form of duress. Although *that*, he knew, might well mean nothing when the aliens were involved. They'd have plenty of opportunity to experiment with brainwashing humans.

"I'm glad to see you alive," he said, sincerely. There would be time to evaluate his claim the war had been a mistake afterwards. "How do your… new friends wish to proceed."

He recoiled slightly as an alien stepped into the pickup's range. It was far from the first time he'd seen an alien, but he couldn't help thinking that this one was far more dangerous than the captives – or the dead bodies that had been fished out of the wreckage, months ago. Up close, it seemed to be breathing heavily…and it was floating. There was no gravity in the alien ship.

Is that how they produce better drives? He asked himself. *They don't bother with internal gravity?*

"Send. Shuttle." The alien said. The voice was atonal. Clearly, Polly MacDonald hadn't been the only one trying to break the communications barrier. "We. Will. Come."

"We're picking up a set of images," Janelle said. Her voice had steadied, somehow. "They're showing us where to dock the shuttle."

Ted looked at the diagrams, then nodded. "Tell the shuttle to launch, but remind the Marines to use full biohazard protocols," he ordered. He looked back at the screen. "…Henry, you will have to be checked thoroughly, as will your guests. Can you explain it to them?"

"I can try," Henry said. He had shown no visible reaction to hearing Janelle's voice. "I understand protocols, sir. I'll try to explain it to them."

"Good," Ted said. "The shuttle will be with you in" – he glanced at the display – "ten minutes. I look forward to seeing you again."

But it won't stop us poking and prodding at you until we're sure you're not under outside influence, he thought as the channel closed. *And we may never be entirely sure...*

He looked over at Janelle. "You can't see Henry until the doctors have checked him thoroughly," he said. "But you can watch, if you like, and meet him afterwards. I think you both deserve a chance to meet and talk."

Janelle looked at him doubtfully. "But what if he doesn't..."

She broke off. Ted snorted, inwardly. The CIC of a carrier in the middle of a hostile star system was no place for a discussion about someone's relationship. There was quite enough of that *already*. But she deserved something more.

"I think you'd be best finding out now," Ted said, quietly. He understood. Janelle had been shocked, badly, to learn who Charles Augustus really was. It had ruined her life and damaged her prospects without the consolation of having him in her life. And now...Ted knew he wouldn't have been so concerned if it had been anyone else dating her. "And then you will *know*."

"Yes, sir," Janelle said. "And thank you."

Ted watched her leave the compartment, then keyed his console. "Captain, we will need to put some distance between ourselves and Target One," he said. "Plan out a course through Tramline Four as soon as possible."

"Aye, sir," Fitzwilliam said.

———

Henry wasn't sure what he'd expected from *Ark Royal*. He *hadn't* expected a heavily-modified Marine shuttle, let alone armoured marines who had invited the two humans and seven aliens into the shuttle in a manner that could hardly be considered diplomatic. The aliens seemed to take it in their stride, but Henry was annoyed and Jill seemed openly worried. What if the aliens decided to be insulted later?

But they showed no sign of reaction as the shuttle powered its way back towards the carrier, even when the Marines started scanning them for unpleasant surprises. The small bags of equipment the aliens had brought with them were inspected carefully, with each of them checked thoroughly before being returned to the aliens. None of it seemed dangerous, Henry decided, although the Marines appeared doubtful. But they were unwilling to cause a diplomatic incident by confiscating it.

His tension grew as they approached the carrier, only to be directed to an airlock instead of the shuttlebay. The Marines watched them carefully as the hatch sealed, then pointed towards the airlock. Outside, there were a small team of medical officers in biohazard gear, eying them warily. A pair of trolleys were already waiting for them.

"Go to the docs," the Marines ordered. "We'll take care of the aliens."

"Don't say please and thank you," Henry said. "Be blunt – and keep them together."

The Marine nodded. Henry nodded back, then climbed onto one of the stretchers. Jill climbed onto the other one and lay down, allowing the medics to push them into the biohazard room. Henry sighed inwardly as the doctors started taking blood samples, washing their skin with various chemicals and poking and prodding everywhere. It felt worse than the medical exam he'd undergone during basic training, what felt like years ago. The pilots had joked it was an endurance test rather than a genuine medical inspection.

"You don't seem to have any immediate physical problems," Doctor Jeanette Hastings said. "But you do seem to have some malnutrition, Your Highness. I think whatever they were feeding you wasn't quite right for human consumption."

"I never had my period after the first couple of months," Jill said. "Did they do something to me?"

"I suspect they fed you something that was a natural contraceptive," Doctor Hastings said, turning to face her. "Your malnutrition is considerably more advanced. I'm going to advise the Captain to let me keep you in here for observation and a structured course of treatment."

She frowned. "They also stung you," she added, turning back to face Henry. "There were a couple of surveillance devices stuck to your skin, both firmly fixed down. They could track you wherever you went, at the very least. The devices might also have been audio-visual receptors."

Henry winced. Privacy was always a joke these days when the government *really* wanted to keep an eye on someone. Everyone was guilty of something…and, in his case, the media often tried to sting him with nanotech bugs too. It was something he hated, yet another reason for just walking away from the monarchy. At least the aliens hadn't been interested in his sexual habits. He'd say that much for them.

"Take them off me," he said.

"Already done," Hastings assured him. She stepped backwards. "The Admiral has requested your presence at a briefing in fifty minutes. I would advise you to dress, get something to eat and report back here afterwards. I'll be making up some tailored slop for you too."

"Thank you, Doctor," Henry said. He swung his legs over the side of the stretcher and stood. "Am I all right?"

"If there was a concern, Your Highness, you would not be let out of this compartment," Hastings said, shortly. "Now *go*. I believe someone wants to see you."

Henry gave her a sharp look, then pulled on a clean uniform – they hadn't given him a starfighter pilot's uniform – and stepped out of the hatch. Outside, he stopped dead as he realised just who was waiting for him. Janelle was standing there, staring at him.

And then, before he could react, she slapped him across the face.

"That," she said, "was for letting me think you were dead."

CHAPTER

TWENTY

Henry held Janelle tightly, feeling her heartbeat thumping against his chest.

"You should have told me who you were," she said. "I could have handled it."

"I'm sorry," Henry said. If they'd believed him dead...she would have had her life turned upside down. He cursed himself, angrily. "Do you hate me now?"

"No. Yes. I don't know," Janelle said. "Why didn't you tell me?"

"I wanted to be normal," Henry said. He hesitated, then half-pulled her into a private compartment. Long habits of avoiding the media had taught him to seek privacy whenever and wherever he could. "And I wanted to have a normal relationship too."

He rubbed his cheek where she'd slapped him. In all honestly, he knew he'd deserved it – and worse. The Admiral had been right. Making love to someone outside Sin City risked that person's future, no matter who or what she was. He'd been a selfish bastard, guided by his prick...and the fact he actually *liked* her made it worse. He really should have known better.

You did know better, his conscience pointed out. *You just didn't care.*

"You could have had one with me anyway," Janelle snapped. "I thought you were dead and..."

She broke off as he hugged her again. "I'm sorry," Henry said, and meant it. "I..."

"Have a lot of explaining to do," Janelle said. She pushed him into a chair, then marched over to a food dispenser. "And apparently you have to do some eating too."

She shook her head, rubbing her eyes. "I thought you were dead," she said. "Everyone thought you were dead. What happened?"

"I ejected from my fighter moments before it blew," Henry said. He'd wondered why no one had thought he might be alive, but if they'd known the plasma chambers had been about to explode they might have thought he was certainly dead. "The aliens picked me up and took me to one of their worlds."

"How nice of them," Janelle said. She produced a plate of stew from the dispenser and passed it to him, followed by a mug of hot tea. "I think you'd better eat before you go to the briefing."

Henry smiled as he smelled the stew. It wasn't much – naval rations rarely were – but compared to the tasteless food the aliens had fed them it was delicious. The tea was just as good, sweetened the way he liked it. His mother would have a fit if she saw how he'd forgotten the endless etiquette lessons she'd drummed into his head, but he found it hard to care. He practically inhaled the food and drink.

Janelle sat facing him, her dark eyes anxious. Henry felt another twinge of guilt and silently cursed himself under his breath. She had to have her doubts about him now, both because he'd hidden his identity from her and because he'd seemingly died, leaving her at the mercy of the media. Henry had no doubt at all of what the media would do to someone as newsworthy as his lover. She'd have her life dissected, anything interesting or scandalous would be broadcast to the world and she would never have a private moment again. And it was all his fault.

He searched for words, but none came. He'd acted badly, worse than badly. It would have been more honest to exploit her or even to enter into a loveless relationship. Instead, they'd both cared about one another – and that was the worst of it. They couldn't simply let go.

"They asked if I was pregnant," Janelle said, suddenly. "They thought I might be carrying your child."

Henry swallowed. It was impossible, he knew. Like all crewmen, he had a contraceptive implant – and besides, the Admiralty would never have let her return to space if she'd been pregnant. Technically, it counted as rendering one's self unfit for duty. But in her case...they might have skipped the court martial. The child would have been of Royal Blood.

He felt another pang. If she *had* been pregnant, it would definitely have ruined her life.

"They do that," he said, shortly. *Thank God* the media was largely banned from Sin City – and that he'd been Charles Augustus, while he'd been there. "It's part of my life."

"I understand," Janelle said. She took a breath. "I mean I understand *you*."

She met his eyes. "I do understand why you concealed your identity," she said. "But I don't know if I forgive you for it. It was bad enough mourning your death."

The worst of all possible worlds, Henry thought. Janelle would have been mourning him, their relationship ended by his death...and yet she would still have been wrapped up in the affairs of the Royal Family. She would be nothing to them, completely valueless, and yet she would never have been able to escape.

"I understand," he said. "And if you don't want to see me again..."

Saying the words cost him more than he cared to admit. Janelle had liked him for *him*, not for being born a powerless prince, someone in line to be the figurehead of the British Government. They'd become friends and then lovers without the Royal Family casting a long shadow over their relationship. But, in the end, he understood. Anyone who joined the Royal Family, even if they were terrible gold diggers, bit off more than they could chew.

"We could go elsewhere," he said. There *was* precedent – and besides, they'd already adapted well to his supposed death. He wondered, absently, if he could convince the Admiral not to name him on the report, before deciding it was impossible. "Take up residence on Britannia or even one of the other worlds..."

"You'd be giving up everything," Janelle pointed out. "Your family, your life..."

Henry shrugged. He loved his parents and sister, but he hated what the monarchy had made them become. They were actors who could never really stop acting, out of fear the audience would lose interest and go away. Or, perhaps, men and women under constant observation, knowing all too well that anything they did would be used in evidence against them. There were criminals under less strict monitoring than the Royal Family.

And he'd never felt freer than when he'd been Charles Augustus, a simple starfighter pilot without ties to anyone of importance. He'd been chewed out at the Academy and loved it, put in a starfighter cockpit and told to risk his own life...he was better off, he knew, without the monarchy. And there was no force that could keep him in Buckingham Palace if he chose to leave.

"I'd be making a new life," he said. "Will you come with me?"

Janelle hesitated. "I'll think about it," she said. She rubbed the table gently. "but it will have to wait until the end of the war."

Henry nodded. The war wasn't over yet.

He returned his plate and mug to the dispenser, then reached for her and gave her another hug. She hugged him back, gently, but there was a curious reserve in her eyes. Henry fretted for a long moment, then realised she'd already mourned him once. Part of her had to wonder, even if she never admitted it to herself, if he would leave her again.

But it was an accident, he told himself, angrily. *I didn't mean to lose control of my containment chambers...*

Janelle let go of him, then led him through the corridors towards the briefing room. Everyone they met seemed to stop and stare at him; rumour, it seemed, had spread through the ship faster than the speed of light. Henry cringed inwardly as a number of crewmen saluted, even though they had no obligation to salute a simple Flying Officer. It was clear he would never have a chance to live a normal life on *Ark Royal*, not now. And it was unlikely he'd be assigned to another carrier.

"The BBN did a special on your life," Janelle muttered, as they passed through a set of airlocks. "Someone on the ship told them about us. I don't know who."

"We'll find out," Henry promised. The thought of horsewhipping the bastard was delightful. There was always *someone* ready to betray the royals for thirty pieces of silver or, more practically, twenty minutes of fame. "What did the special have to say?"

"It said you were very patriotic," Janelle said. "They made a big deal out of you giving up your title to fight beside the common man."

Henry sighed. The PR staff at Buckingham Palace had wanted him to go into the navy publically, without using a false identity. They'd been more fixated on the idea of being able to prove the Royal Family was sharing the risks faced by common-born pilots, officers and crewmen than on whatever suited Henry personally. Using a false name made it impossible to claim Henry was taking risks. But if he had used his real name, he wouldn't have been assigned to a front-line squadron.

Or they would have treated me like a Prince, he thought, bitterly.

He came to attention as the airlock opened, revealing the conference room. Admiral Smith rose to his feet to greet them, followed by two officers and a civilian Henry didn't recognise. There was no sign of the Captain, he noted, which made a great deal of sense. If Henry had been brainwashed into killing the Admiral, Captain Fitzwilliam would take over command of the flotilla. But he hadn't been brainwashed...

Oh, really? Part of his mind asked. *And how would you know?*

"Admiral," he said, saluting. "Thank you for coming here."

Admiral Smith returned the salute. "It's clear that your country owes you a massive debt," he said, simply. "You said the war was a mistake, correct?"

"Yes, sir," Henry said. Prince or not, he was damned if he was allowing his military formality to slip now. "A tragic accident."

He took the seat the Admiral offered to him – Janelle sat next to him – and braced himself. "It's difficult to be entirely sure of what they're telling us or vice versa," he said. "But Jill – the girl who came with me – was a witness to First Contact. The Heinlein Colonists, sir, settled a world the aliens had already settled. But neither side realised it until they ran into one another by accident."

"They prefer to live under the water," the civilian said. "I assume the aliens didn't send any ships to their colony prior to First Contact."

Henry blinked at her. She wore shorts and a halter top that were so tight he could see her nipples, almost as if she'd had her clothes painted on. He forced himself to look away, suddenly very aware of Janelle's presence beside him. He'd spent weeks, perhaps months, with Jill, he told himself. It should be easy to avoid staring at a very out of place civilian.

"One of the aliens encountered a pair of humans in shallow waters," Henry said. "The humans panicked, assuming the newcomer was an undiscovered sea monster, and shot the alien. Their report wasn't believed until the aliens attacked the colony in retaliation. Most of the colonists died in the ensuring battle, but a handful of prisoners were distributed among various alien factions. Jill...thinks she might be the only one still alive."

The Admiral winced. "The aliens didn't do anything to mark their colony?"

"Not as far as Jill knew," Henry said. "The planet appeared deserted when the Heinlein Colonists arrived."

"Odd," the Admiral said. "Even our newly-settled worlds have at least one satellite in orbit."

"Yes, sir," Henry said. "But would the aliens need them while they're building an underwater colony?"

There might have been other signs the colonists had overlooked, he knew. The aliens had presumably introduced plants and animals from their homeworld to Heinlein – and their biochemistry wouldn't have matched the local biology. But there had been no reason to run any tests, not if the colonists had believed the planet to be completely undiscovered. All they'd really had to do was ensure the local biochemistry was compatible with humanity or make sure their people knew not to eat it.

"So they believed us to be hostile," the Admiral said, "and struck first?"

"One of the alien factions believed that to be the case," Henry said. "The other aliens call them the War Faction. Sir...the aliens don't think like us. I don't think the War Faction is capable of considering any alternatives. They're...I think they build up their factions around ideology and political concepts. They don't tend to let in other ideas."

"How very human," the Admiral observed.

"It's more like a datanet chat forum," Henry said. "I *think*. They chatter and chatter until the group only consists of aliens who agree with the group, with everyone else excluded from the consensus and sent off to find another group. My *guess*, sir, is that this worked reasonably well when they were all on one world. But when they went into space, the factions effectively became echo chambers. There was no room for new ideas."

"Like some of the asteroid colonies," Janelle said, suddenly. "My Grandfather's colony was based around a specific religious group."

"That would make sense," the civilian said, slowly. "The alien prisoners might be trying to convince each other of their respective ideologies, then sulking when they don't get anywhere. They're just saying the same thing over and over again."

Henry nodded. Humanity had been moving towards a cultural union, some claimed, when space travel and interstellar settlement had become commonplace. These days, there were worlds that attempted to build and maintain a national character – or a religious harmony – that had never really existed on Earth. There had always been ideas creeping in from outside the cultural consensus. But an isolated settlement might be able to maintain a cultural stasis that would endure for thousands of years.

He shivered, remembering some of the debates over religious-themed asteroids. Was it right to allow disparate groups to settle their own asteroids, keeping their people isolated from any outside influences? And then there had been the inevitable accusations of racism and attacks on religious liberty...

"So the War Faction determined we were a threat and took steps to deal with us," the Admiral mused. "And the other factions did...what?"

Henry hesitated. "I *think*, sir, that the other factions were partly convinced," he said. "*We* might not be too happy if the situation was reversed and they landed on one of our worlds. But once the war started going badly – and we didn't act like monsters – the other factions started having second thoughts. They wanted to at least *try* to talk to us."

"Good God," the Admiral said. "And the War Faction tried to stop them – twice, now."

"Yes, sir," Henry said.

The civilian leaned forward. "I'm going to have to go through everything you saw very carefully, Your Highness," she said. "Hopefully, we can actually *talk* to the aliens you brought with you."

"They're Ambassadors," Henry said. Or he thought they were. The concept hadn't been easy to discuss. "But I'm not entirely sure which factions they represent."

"I assume they didn't show you anything militarily useful," the Admiral stated.

"No," Henry confirmed. The aliens hadn't shown him anything he could use against them, except – perhaps – what he'd learned of their culture. "I have no idea where they held us – or even how long it was since the battle."

"Two months," the Admiral said.

Henry shook his head in disbelief. It had felt longer. Much longer.

The Admiral cleared his throat. "We also need to move from this location," he added. "By now, the aliens on Target One will be aware of our presence. They will probably start screaming for help."

"Yes, sir," Henry said. "I believe the aliens will accompany us, if necessary."

The Admiral looked down at the table. "I'd prefer to head further into alien space," he said. slowly. "I don't think anyone would thank us for bringing an alien ship home."

"They did on your first mission," Henry pointed out. But there was something odd about the way the Admiral spoke, as if he was contemplating something he didn't want to think about. "But I think the aliens will be happy to escort you elsewhere."

"No doubt," the civilian said. "I believe the other factions will be just as monomaniacal as the War Faction, just focused on different issues. A faction that wants peace will be quite likely to do whatever it takes to *get* peace."

Henry considered it, briefly. There were no shortage of diplomats who were willing to make whatever concessions seemed necessary to get the other side to sign on the dotted line, even though the concessions were dangerously one-sided. Diplomats hated to admit they'd failed, even when their negotiating partners were intractable. But he hadn't seen that sort of insane single-mindedness from his captors, although he had to admit it was hard to be sure. The aliens hadn't tried to actually *negotiate* with him.

Will they offer us concessions to keep us talking to them, he asked himself, *or will they demand them from us to satisfy the other factions?*

"Let us hope so," the Admiral said. He looked at Henry. "Janelle will escort you to your new quarters, Your Highness. I'm afraid I can't put you back on the flight roster right now."

"No, sir," Henry said, reluctantly. It had been foolish, but part of him had dared to hope he could pass the diplomacy to the Admiral and return to a cockpit. "Will I be able to speak to some of the other flyers?"

"Not all survived," Janelle said, very quietly. "Most of the pilots you knew were transferred elsewhere, in the wake of the Battle of Earth."

Henry started. "They attacked *Earth*?"

"Yes," the Admiral said. "And that will make peace negotiations very difficult."

CHAPTER
TWENTY ONE

Ted had never taken part in high-level diplomatic meetings before the war. Afterwards, when he'd been promoted to Admiral, most of his meetings had been little more than formalities, setting the seal on matters discussed and agreed by lower-ranking diplomats. He hadn't regretted it. Diplomats could spend hours discussing something of minor importance, laying the groundwork for later – more serious – discussions, while military officers had little time to debate their decisions. Being a commanding officer of a starship was much simpler.

But this was different.

He watched through the monitors as human and alien diplomats met for the first time. None of the humans looked particularly comfortable, although that might have been because of the alien environmental requirements rather than coming face to face with the aliens themselves. Ted had a hunch the aliens were just as uncomfortable as their human counterparts, just for different reasons. They'd probably prefer to be under the water, rather than half-sitting, half-standing in atmosphere, no matter how hot and moist the atmosphere was.

"It's working better than I hoped," Polly said, from where she was standing beside him. "It will be a long time before we have perfect translators, but between us we've managed to close the gap to the point we can actually *talk* to them and vice versa."

Ted nodded. The diplomats were talking in what amounted to baby talk and the aliens were doing it right back, often using computer displays to draw out what they meant, but it seemed to be working. There was no time to use fancy words, let alone draw up an elaborate treaty, not when time was steadily ticking away. Who knew when the War Faction would send more ships into the system?

He looked at Polly. "Are you sure this is reliable?"

"We did a lot of work, they did a lot of work…I think this is the best we can do, for the moment," Polly confessed. "I've been working with a couple of aliens on building up a shared system, but that's been going slowly. Their computer designs aren't that different from ours, Admiral, yet some of the underlying programs and operating systems are very different. The techs think the aliens don't have any concept of a decentralised computer system, let alone a secure database."

"They must have *something* for classified information," Ted objected. He looked back towards the diplomats – and, standing at the other side of the compartment, the observers. Several of them were Russians. "Or don't they even have a concept of classified data?"

"Unknown," Polly said. "But they may not have anything of the sort, Admiral. They don't think the way we do."

Ted frowned. It was true enough that governments had a habit of trying to classify data that could be embarrassing or cost them the next election, but it was also true that quite a bit of data was classified for extremely good reasons. The bioweapon formula, he knew, would be buried in the vaults once the war was over, particularly if it was never used. It would only upset people to learn how close the taboo on engineered bioweapons had come to being broken – and by world governments, at that.

But the aliens, it seemed, didn't understand the idea behind classifying or otherwise restricting data.

"I think they're coming to a break," Polly observed. "They're leaving the compartment."

Ted nodded. The human observers were leaving through one set of hatches, the aliens were leaving through the other, which lead to a compartment specifically designed for their comfort. It had taken a considerable amount of engineering to make it possible, but it had been done. The aliens hadn't complained once, although they hadn't thanked the humans either. Ted suspected, from reading Prince Henry's report, that they didn't have social graces in the same way the humans had them. Maybe politeness, too, was a foreign concept.

He turned as Ambassador Melbourne strode into the compartment, already removing his sweaty jacket. Ted concealed his amusement with an effort. The aliens wouldn't notice if the human negotiators turned up wearing nothing, but their birthday suits. On the other hand, he did understand their problem. Recordings of the first talks between humans and aliens were likely to be studied for countless years…and no one would want to see them stark naked when they reviewed the data. But they could easily have worn swimsuits.

"Ambassador," he said. "I trust that talks were productive?"

"I believe so," Melbourne said. He jerked a head towards the hatch leading into a private compartment. "It took quite some time before we managed to smooth out communications, though. We haven't done anything quite like this since Cortes encountered the Aztecs."

"And this would be worse," Ted said, as he led the way into the private compartment. Inside, there was nothing more than a pair of chairs and an empty desk. "Cortes would have been able to understand the Aztecs being human…"

"Cortes also had a handful of people who spoke both tongues," Melbourne interrupted. He sat down, rubbing his white shirt. The sweat had stained it badly. "We have computers that may not be translating properly and some very different ideas about how the universe works."

He shrugged. "Every so often, they have to check with their fellows on their ship," he added, dryly. "I think we're actually dealing with three separate alien factions, not one. Luckily, it allows us a chance to chat with our advisors too."

"Good," Ted said, impatiently. "What have they said to us?"

"First, they'd like to escort us to one of their worlds," Melbourne said. "From what we think we've drawn from them, this will be a chance to talk to several other factions and hopefully convince them to support peace terms. There will also be an opportunity to get to know them better, I believe. Young Henry believes there is little point in hosting a cultural exchange, but I beg to differ."

Ted rather suspected Henry had a point. The aliens were *alien*. They wouldn't understand the great classics of human society, not when there were disparate human groups that didn't understand one another either. And *they* shared the same biology as the rest of the human race. The aliens were nothing like humanity.

"Second, we have discussed potential peace terms," Melbourne continued. "The aliens themselves weren't agreed on what they wanted from us. I believe that one faction wishes to return to the pre-war situation, while the other two wanted to end the war, but keep the worlds and systems they took from us."

"That won't please the Russians," Ted said. He scowled, inwardly. The Marines were overstretched keeping an eye on both the Russians *and* the alien diplomats. "Do they have a reason for that?"

"I believe they think it will serve as a bribe to convince several other factions to throw their weight behind peace," Melbourne said. "But it's difficult to be sure, Admiral."

"So it would seem," Ted said.

He thought he understood. The alien factions, like most of humanity, probably hadn't seen much wrong with a short victorious war. Wars only tended to become massively unpopular when countless soldiers were dying and the war seemed unwinnable. If *Ark Royal* had been scrapped, the aliens would probably be occupying Earth and congratulating themselves on the success of their strategy by now. Instead, they'd been forced to sit back and think carefully about their future.

And they'll want to see something for all the blood and treasure they spilled, he thought, morbidly. *Even if it is just a handful of worlds along the border.*

The Ambassador shrugged. "But we haven't agreed on anything definite yet," he warned. "I *think* they've extended a safe conduct to us, but I don't know if we can count on it."

"I'll discuss it with my officers," Ted assured him. "Where do they want us to go?"

"They gave us a starchart," Melbourne said. "It's not too far from where we believed Faction Two to be based."

"How lucky for us," Ted said, dryly. He turned to the hatch. "I'll discuss it with my officers, Ambassador, then get back to you."

He paused. "Do they want you to visit their ship?"

"It's a possibility," Melbourne said. "Do *you* want to visit?"

"Maybe in peacetime," Ted said.

It was tempting, but he knew better. Fitzwilliam would *sit* on him if he tried to visit the alien ship during wartime. He wondered briefly if he could come up with an excuse to send the CAG there – it would give him a semi-legitimate excuse to avoid his blackmailers – but he knew it wouldn't pass muster. The Commander Air Group was no ambassador. Sending him to the alien ship made about as much sense as sending the Captain down to an unexplored planet.

"Keep talking to them," he said, as he stepped back into the main compartment. "But don't give away too much too soon."

Behind him, he heard Melbourne snort.

———

"Are we sure," James asked, "that these coordinates are correct?"

"We checked them against the tramlines, sir," Lieutenant Commander Daniel Lightbridge said. The helmsman looked nervous, yet eager. "There's no doubt about where we're heading."

James frowned. He understood, as much as anyone else, why it was important to make peace with the aliens. But, at the same time, he disliked the idea of heading further into unexplored space at alien behest. It would be easy for the aliens – or one of their factions – to set an ambush that would cripple or destroy *Ark Royal*.

"I don't see that we have any choice," the Admiral said. "This will put us very near one of the alien worlds."

The bioweapon, James thought. It wouldn't take long, according to the techs, to prep a deployment system. The aliens would regret stabbing a knife in the Old Lady's back, he knew, if they ever realised the connection. Their sensor networks weren't good enough to pick up a stealth missile penetrating their defences. *If we have to use it, we'll be in an excellent place to deploy it for best effect.*

"But it will also risk the flotilla," he pointed out. It was his job to play Cassandra. "Even if this faction means well, Admiral, others are outright hostile. We could be flying right into a trap."

"That would always be a risk," the Admiral countered. "They tried to ambush us last time we were here, Captain."

James nodded. "But this time it will be easier for them to set a trap," he said. "If they knew we were coming…"

He scowled. If the aliens had detected them while they were trying to sneak through the backdoor to Target One, they might have planned a trap – or even a holding mission to keep the Old Lady where she was while the aliens gathered the forces to destroy her. Or was he just being paranoid? It was clear the aliens had treated the human captives relatively well, certainly by human standards, and – unknowingly – they'd returned Prince Henry to his people. James had to admire the Prince for how well he'd handled his situation. He'd done very well.

But had the aliens brainwashed him?

It was a constant worry whenever someone had spent a long time in captivity. Human minds, struggling to defend themselves, started empathising with their captors, even to the point of joining them. Stockholm Syndrome didn't just make hostages untrustworthy as rescue forces stormed terrorist lairs. It kept abused partners and children with their abusers, convincing them they deserved their treatment…and that was without drugs or direct mental manipulation warping their judgement. James had few illusions. Given enough time, there wasn't anyone, no matter how loyal or patriotic, who couldn't be turned into a dagger aimed at his own country. It had happened before and it would no doubt happen again.

The doctor saw no signs of tampering, he thought, *and could the aliens really do a perfect job of it? They've only had a handful of years to study living humans…*

He shook his head. There was no way to know. It was just another uncertainty in a mission that had too many of them already.

"We have to take the risk," the Admiral said. "I'd be happy holding the talks somewhere neutral, but we don't seem to have that option. Instead…"

He cleared his throat. "We will pass through the tramline here," he said, tapping the display. "The aliens will be asked to stay with us until we pass through, just in case. We don't want our course to be predicable."

"It will be," James said, bluntly. He understood the Admiral's concern – and he trusted his judgement – but far too much could go wrong. "We won't be remotely stealthy if we have an alien ship escorting us."

"I know," the Admiral said. He looked down at the table. "I want to detach *Holmes* from the flotilla. She is to make her way back to Earth, under very tight stealth, carrying a complete copy of our translation algorithms, reports and whatever else can be copied over. If the doctors agree, she is to take Miss Pearlman too. I think it would be better for her to be returned to Earth."

James frowned. "You don't want to send the Prince back too?"

"I think we will need him in the future," the Admiral said. "And he *is* a trained starfighter pilot, if we dare clear him for duty. Miss Pearlman is none of those things."

James considered it. It was quite likely the King would be furious at hearing his son had been recovered, but not sent back to Earth at once. The political questions that everyone had thought had died with the Prince would be reopened, starting with the old issue of just who would succeed the Throne. But he understood the Admiral's decision. Prince Henry could still be useful.

"Miss Pearlman might be helpful," he pointed out. "Or do you think she can't be any more informative?"

"We don't seem to need her any longer," the Admiral said. "And she needs better treatment than we can supply onboard the ship. She's on the verge of collapse, James. The aliens didn't realise it, we think, but they were slowly starving her to death. She needs specialised treatment on Earth."

"Don't let the doctors hear you say that," James said, dryly. "But I understand. Besides, she might just be the last heir to the Heinlein Foundation's Trust."

"If they let her claim it," the Admiral mused. He shook his head. "Prepare your ship for departure, Captain. And pray that this isn't all an elaborate trick."

James looked up at the starchart. The spider's web of tramlines shone through alien space, showing a handful of potential hub systems for the alien civilisation. One of them, he was sure, was the alien homeworld. But it was impossible to be sure which one. The aliens, apparently, had flatly declined to discuss the location of their homeworld with their human counterparts. Under the circumstances, James knew, it was very hard to blame them.

They attacked our homeworld, he thought, sourly. *Why wouldn't we attack theirs?*

He thought of the bioweapon and went cold.

———

"Jill's going back to Earth?"

"Yes," Janelle said. There was an odd note to her voice. "Will you miss her?"

Henry sat upright. Of course...Janelle would have seen Jill, naked as the day she was born, accompanying him back to *Ark Royal*. Perhaps she'd wondered what they'd done together, when there had been no hope of getting back to Earth. Or perhaps she was simply concerned...

"I'm glad she's getting treatment," he said. The thought of slowly wasting away was horrific, but it would have happened if they hadn't returned to the Old Lady. "We never felt anything badly wrong."

"The doctors think you might have been fed painkillers as well," Janelle said. "We know they drug some of their captives. They could just have been experimenting with the dose."

Henry winced. "Didn't the blood tests come up negative?"

"They didn't find anything we recognised," Janelle confirmed. "But they might well have missed something, if it had time to filter out of your bloodstream."

"Never mind," Henry said, sharply. He shook his head. They'd allowed him to watch the negotiations through the monitors, but not to actually take part. "Are we going further into alien space now?"

"So it would seem," Janelle said, slowly. "How do you feel about that?"

"I...don't care where I go, as long as I go with you," Henry said. It had been a famous line from one of the romantic movies Elizabeth had loved to watch, before she'd realised just how many frogs she would have to kiss before she found her Prince Charming. "I..."

He ducked as Janelle picked up a terminal and waved it at him threateningly. She wasn't the sort of person to be impressed by romantic platitudes.

"I don't know how I feel," he admitted, instead. "I want to get it over with, Janelle, but I also don't want to go home."

Janelle patted his shoulder, then kissed his forehead.

"You probably should record a message for your family," she said. "I believe everyone else in the crew will be doing the same."

Henry sighed. Part of him was still insanely tempted to try to convince the Admiral to leave him out of his report. But it wasn't even remotely possible.

"I will," he said, reluctantly. What did one say to a family that had burned a casket, then mourned him? Had they mourned publically, knowing the media would crucify them if they didn't, or had they tried to keep their grief to themselves? Had they felt grief at all? Or had Elizabeth envied him for escaping the media? "But I honestly don't know what I'm going to tell them."

"Well," Jasmine said. "Did you miss them?"

"Of course," Henry said, offended.

"Then start by telling them that," Janelle said, practically. "And then tell them just how much you've achieved over the last couple of months."

"I can't," Henry said. He shook his head in bitter dismay. "The message won't stay private, you see."

CHAPTER
TWENTY TWO

"Local space seems clear, sir," Flight Lieutenant Pixie Raga said.

"Glad to hear it," Kurt said, trying to keep the exasperation out of his voice. Flying long-range patrol was always tricky, even without the constant threat of alien attack. *He* knew, even if his wingman didn't, just how unlikely it was they would stumble across anything dangerous. Their presence was more inclined to ensure that any aliens intent on sneaking closer had second thoughts. "But you don't need to keep repeating it again and again."

He sighed. "Just keep one eye on your sensors and the other on your communications panel," he added, "and everything should be fine."

"Yes, sir," Pixie said.

Kurt rolled his eyes. Pixie had been born on Luna and had the fairy-like build of a fifth-generation Luna citizen. If she hadn't worked out end-lessly from the moment she grew old enough to know what she wanted to do, she would have had real problems surviving on *Ark Royal*, let alone Earth. There were genetic treatments for problems caused by being born in a low-gravity field, but her parents had clearly refused to use them. Perhaps they'd just liked the thought of their daughter living up to her name.

The alien system was oddly disappointing. He would almost have wel-comed a swarm of alien fighters, backed up by a pair of carriers, knowing it would distract him from his worries about the future. Instead, the alien settlers had completely ignored them, not even broadcasting towards the alien ship pacing the human flotilla. Kurt wasn't sure if they were trying to stay out of the fighting or if they simply didn't care. If scuttlebutt was correct, and the aliens organised themselves by political attitudes, logically there had to be some aliens who were completely indifferent to the war.

There are peaceniks back on Earth who think the war will ignore them if they ignore it, he thought, sardonically. A number had probably been drowned when tidal waves had battered the British coastline and swept inland. *I wonder how many of them are in refugee camps right now?*

The thought made him grit his teeth. He'd recorded a message for Penny and Percy – and Gayle, although she wasn't related to him – yet he hadn't dared say anything that might end up being used against him. He *had* written a message, which he'd placed in storage, but he had no idea *what* would happen to it. The post-return investigation would probably take the message and use it in evidence against him. And Rose.

He sighed. Rose was busy working the pilots though *yet* another simulation, instead of being with him. He missed her dreadfully, a dull ache in his heart that refused to settle, even though he knew they couldn't be together until after they were discharged from the Navy. Or was he being silly, he kept asking himself in his darker moments. Rose was fifteen years younger than he, after all. Would they stay together in peacetime? Would she be happy being mother to his children? Percy wasn't *that* much younger than Rose…

His console bleeped. "We're reaching the edge of our range," he said, keying the channel open. "Reverse course; sweep back towards the Old Lady."

"Aye, sir," Pixie said. She flipped her craft over – showing off a little – and drove back towards the carrier. "We have more than enough power left in the cells."

Kurt rolled his eyes. Technically, she was right. Practically, it was asking for trouble.

"And what would you do," he asked sweetly, "if you had to hold position outside the carrier with your power fast running dry?"

He went on before she could try to answer. "You need to keep a reserve at all times," he added. "Expect the unexpected. Something will happen to fuck up all your planning and then you'll be glad to have the reserve."

She said nothing as they flew back towards the carrier, passing two more starfighters on patrol as they closed in on the giant ship. Kurt felt an odd sensation in his gut as they looped around and approached the landing deck; part of him was glad to be back onboard, part of him knew the blackmailers could have sent him another message. They hadn't sent him anything else since he'd done the first set of work for them, but he had a feeling time was running out again. They'd made contact with the aliens, after all.

He dropped his craft neatly to the deck and watched, nervously, as Pixie came in to land. It was always hair-raising watching a new pilot try to land and it still worried him, even after making the pilots practice again and again in simulations. But Pixie managed a perfect landing and scrambled out of her starfighter, hastily running towards the washroom. Kurt smirked as he watched her run. Clearly, she had yet to realise the importance to limiting her liquid intake before boarding her starfighter.

Not that anyone wants to mess around with the bags, he thought, as he scrambled out of his own craft. *Everyone remembers what happened to that idiot from the very first flight of starfighters.*

"Commander," a voice said, as he reached the hatch. He looked up to see Major Parnell. "If you will come with me…?"

Kurt scowled inwardly as they walked through a series of corridors and entered Marine Country. "Don't you worry about us being seen together?"

Parnell shrugged. "The aliens being onboard has given us an excuse to run multiple searches for bugs," he said. "We found quite a few, scattered randomly around the ship. Officially, we're blaming them on the reporters who infested the ship during our first cruise."

"Oh," Kurt said. He had no doubt that reporters would use bugs if they thought they could get away with it, but there *were* such things as privacy laws. Not, he suspected, that reporters thought they applied to them. But using them on a military warship was asking to spend the rest of the cruise in the brig. "And has it worked?"

"The blackmailers haven't contacted us to complain," Parnell said, dryly. He mimicked an upper-class accent. "Dashed unsporting of them, don't you think?"

"Yes," Kurt muttered.

They walked into the interrogation chamber and sat down. "We have monitored the access codes you sent them," Parnell said. "There has been no attempt to use them for anything."

Kurt let out a long breath. "Why not?"

"I have no idea," Parnell said. "But they haven't blown your cover, so I'd say they're waiting for the best opportunity to use them. Which may be quite soon. My men are overstretched right now."

"Or they might be playing the long game," Kurt said.

"I doubt it," Parnell said. He sighed. "Blackmail is a complicated tactic to use, Commander, and it can backfire easily. Normally, the blackmailers would work carefully to help you dig a deeper and deeper hole for yourself by supplying them with harmless pieces of information...until the point they were not so harmless. It makes it impossible for you to go to your superiors and confess because, even if they were sympathetic about the blackmail or considered it unimportant, your later betrayals would be much harder to avoid taking into account."

"I'd be hopelessly compromised," Kurt said, slowly.

"Precisely," Parnell said. "Honey traps are far from uncommon in the espionage world. I was on deployment to the embassy in China once and you'd be astonished how many Chinese girls thought a Royal Marine was hotter than hell. None of them were *really* keen on us, of course; they just wanted to get into our communication terminals."

"And did you keep them in your pants?" Kurt asked. "Or what?"

"We were warned not to fraternise," Parnell said. "Which isn't actually *easy* if you happen to be young, stupid and confident that no one will ever find out."

He shrugged. "I never heard anything from any of those girls," he added, "but a couple of more senior diplomats received copies of interesting pictures and a note saying they could spy for the Chinese or their wives would be sent other copies. I think one of them sent a note back thanking them for the pictures and asking for more."

"Hah," Kurt said.

"Point is, you have to lure someone into betrayal," Parnell said. "But in this case they pushed you into an outright betrayal far too quickly. And *that* implies they have a real time problem on their hands. Whatever they want to do, Commander, they want to do it quickly."

"I gave them the codes," Kurt said. "What else do they want from me?"

"Good question," Parnell said. "And once you find out, you need to inform me at once."

"I will," Kurt promised. He wanted to ask if he could talk to Rose, but he didn't dare. "And thank you."

Parnell met his eyes, evenly. "For what?"

"For being understanding…"

"I know, better than you, just how stupid people can be when faced with the threat of death," Parnell said. "I also know that you left yourself vulnerable after the threat of death was removed – and you wouldn't have come forward if you hadn't been urged to confess. Your carelessness got you into this mess, Commander. If you weren't vitally important, if we didn't need as many pilots as we could muster, I would have urged the Admiral to send you back to Earth on *Holmes*. Your conduct has been disgraceful."

"I know, sir," Kurt said.

"You also cheated on your wife and risked your children's futures," Parnell continued. "I know a little about the vetting process, Commander. A family history of adultery would prevent them from taking up any post that required a full security clearance. If the media got hold of it, and they would, because they think you're a hero, they'd have to tolerate questions being asked in inconvenient places. Their lives would be ruined."

He took a long breath. "Frankly, my advice would be to do as you're told until we get back to Earth, then take your discharge, change your name and go elsewhere," he concluded. "If your kids – and Rose – want to go with you, you can take them – or let them go, if they don't want to have anything to do with you. Your weakness will cost them dear in the future."

Kurt clenched his fists, feeling anger spilling up within him. He wanted to throw a punch at the younger man with the older eyes, even though he knew it would be suicidal. And yet he knew Parnell was right. He *had* acted badly.

"Yes, sir," he grated, finally.

"Good," Parnell said. "And one other thing?"

Kurt leaned forward, curiously.

"Watch your back," Parnell said. "They've used you, Commander. They may now seek to discard you."

"I know," Kurt said. "But would they discard me if they thought they might still have a use for me?"

"Probably not," Parnell said. "But as we don't know quite what they want, it's hard to know just when you'd outlive your usefulness to them."

———

"Still nothing from them," Parnell concluded. "The blackmailers are biding their time."

"I see," Ted said. "And we still don't know what they want."

He looked down at the surveillance reports. The Russians – and the other foreigners on the ship – weren't doing anything particularly suspicious. As far as the Marines could tell, the Russians were observing the negotiations and discussing the results amongst themselves in their cabins. But it was impossible to be sure. The Russians had swept their cabin for bugs the first day they arrived and repeated the process every few hours.

"They may have orders to act only if certain conditions are met," Parnell said. "I've had missions like that in the past, sir. Once we slipped fifty miles into hostile country, only to withdraw five days later as silently as we came."

"If that's the case," Ted said, "what conditions will activate their orders?"

Parnell shrugged. "Impossible to say, sir," he said. "Unless we want to try to take them now…"

Ted cursed under his breath. If they had proof – clear proof – that it was the Russians, they could have rounded them all up and locked them in a sealed hold until the ship returned to Earth. But now, without clear proof, it would cause a major diplomatic incident at a time the human race could hardly afford it. The alliance against the aliens was fragile enough, after the Battle of Earth, without him adding to the tensions threatening to rip it apart. He doubted the Prime Minister would thank him for starting a second war.

"We can't," he said. He paused. "Can we arrange a…fake accident for our CAG? Something we can use as an excuse to put him in sickbay for a few weeks?"

"Of course we can, sir," Parnell said. "But that would also deprive you of his services over the forthcoming weeks."

"True," Ted agreed. No matter how he looked at the situation, he saw no way to do anything, but wait for the enemy to make their move. And with aliens on his ship, another alien starship keeping them close company and a prince who might have been placed under alien control, there were just too many variables for him to keep juggling safely. *"Bollocks!"*

He looked up at the display. The alien starship was holding position on one edge of the flotilla, out of plasma weapons range – he hoped. If the aliens intended an elaborate trick…he shook his head. Unlike some human planners he could mention, the aliens didn't seem intent on devising the most complicated plans possible, simply because they could. It would have been far easier to simply shadow *Ark Royal* until a fleet was massed to smash her into rubble. *And* they'd have the advantage of knowing just where the carrier was going and what it would encounter.

"Yes, sir," Parnell said. "I felt safer on Target One, *knowing* the enemy were just lurking below the waves."

Ted had to smile. "We'll reach the destination the aliens have selected within nine days," he said. The potential consequences nagged at his mind. If his calculations were correct, the War Faction would have time to prepare a warm welcome. And then there were the Russians…if it *was* the Russians. His head hurt just trying to keep track of the different factions, human and alien, involved in the war. "And then we will see."

"Aye, sir," Parnell said.

He paused. "With your permission," he added, "I'd like to run a series of counter-boarding drills for the Marines. It would mean sealing off several decks, but…"

Ted's eyes narrowed. "Why…?"

"We need the practice," Parnell said. "The aliens who boarded the ship didn't know where to go, I think; they had to make guesses about where to send their forces. And besides, we're better soldiers than them, I think. They're just not designed for fighting on dry land."

Ted nodded. "I'd hate to fight them in the water, though," he said. "Even Mermen wouldn't be able to match them."

"True," Parnell agreed. "I'd not expect anyone, even an SBS operative, to be able to keep up with them in the water, certainly not without specialist equipment. The aliens could simply out-swim them."

He paused. "Do you realise the aliens must know our biological requirements very well?"

"They had captives," Ted said. "I assume they must have dissected dead bodies too…"

"As far as we can tell, they provided their captives with a proper atmosphere," Parnell said. "They didn't have any trace of anything, but a standard air mix in their bloodstream. And yet they managed to avoid the bends completely, sir. They couldn't have been more than a few metres below the water."

"They might have discovered the hard way how fragile we can be," Ted said. Several alien captives had died in captivity, for reasons no human had been able to understand. Theories ranged from being lonely – which made more sense now – to simply lacking a trace element they needed to eat. But then, surely, *all* of the alien captives would have died. "Or maybe they were just careful."

"Maybe," Parnell said. "But both captives thought they might be much further below the water than they were."

He shrugged. "A mystery we may solve when we talk properly," he said. "Sir…"

Ted looked up, sharply.

"Get some sleep," Parnell said, bluntly. "You look like shit."

"Thank you," Ted said. He had just too many pieces of paperwork to do. And then he had reports to read, review and sign. It never seemed to end. "But I don't have time…"

"You need to be alert," Parnell pointed out. He took a long breath. "Do what I was told to do on my first deployment as a Junior Lt."

"And what was?"

Parnell smiled. "Leave the paperwork until we started home," he said. "If you die on deployment, I was told, they won't hire a medium to force you to finish it."

"That wouldn't be the strangest thing the government has invested in," Ted said. "But I'll do as you suggest."

He waited until Parnell had left, then walked over to the sofa and lay down. There was no point in going back to his quarters, not now. Besides, his quarters just felt odd these days, even though he wasn't sharing them with one of the ambassadors or another outsider. And he would be closer to the CIC.

Sleep didn't come easy, despite his exhaustion. He was almost tempted to order a sedative, but knew he shouldn't. He'd be asleep, dead to the world, if something happened. It wasn't something he could do without clearing it with both Captain Fitzwilliam and his XO – and perhaps the ship's doctor. Sighing, he eventually fell into a fitful sleep.

He was awakened, what felt like seconds later, by the howling of the GQ alarm.

CHAPTER
TWENTY THREE

"All right," James said, as he took his command chair. "What do we have?"

"Incoming enemy starfighters," Farley said. Red icons appeared on the display, so close together that they threatened to blur into a shapeless mass. "I count nineteen of them, perhaps more. They're flying in very close formation."

"Prepare to launch ready starfighters," James ordered. He glanced at the link to the CIC, but Admiral Smith hadn't linked in yet. "And stand by point defence."

He gritted his teeth as a nasty thought struck him. "Get a line down to the diplomats," he added. Once, they had been able to assume that all alien contacts were hostile. They couldn't do that now. "Ask them to talk to the aliens and confirm the newcomers are hostile."

"Aye, sir," Davidson said.

James nodded, then glanced at the display. Nineteen starfighters…so where was their carrier? Long-range sensors showed nothing. The carrier could be under stealth, but it would still have to be somewhere close by… unless, of course, the aliens had managed to extend their endurance. But there were hard limits, even for them.

"Enemy starfighters are reducing speed," Farley said, suddenly. "They're angling away from us."

James frowned. What the hell were they doing? If they'd hoped to get into attack range before he managed to launch his remaining starfighters – which was the only tactic he thought made sense – they should be charging in to attack, not angling away. Or had they suddenly changed their mind for some reason? It would be unlike the aliens, but they *had* to have taken a beating in the recent battles too.

"CAG reports all starfighters ready to launch," Davidson reported. "The diplomats have not yet replied."

"Tell them it's urgent," James snarled. Diplomats! They could talk all day about non-essentials before approaching the really serious matters. But he didn't have time for arguments over the shape of the conference table or how many assistants and aides each ambassador would be allowed. "We need an answer before the newcomers enter engagement range."

He cursed under his breath. Standing pre-war orders forbade him to open fire until the enemy opened fire or if he had a *very* good reason to believe there was an immediate threat to his command. It was easier to patch up a diplomatic misunderstanding if there were no casualties on either side. Now, he had clearance to engage the aliens wherever he found them, but good reason to think he should exercise a little caution. They were already at war with one alien faction. The others should be kept neutral, at the very least.

"Captain," Farley said, softly. "The CAG is requesting orders."

"Launch two squadrons of starfighters, then move the CSP into intercept position," James ordered. He would almost have been happier with a swarm of enemy starfighters bearing down on his ship. At least he would have had good reason to assume hostile intent. "And hold the remaining starfighters at readiness."

The red icons flickered in and out of existence as they moved around the edge of the flotilla's sensor perimeter. James frowned, wondering if the aliens were just trying to force the humans to exhaust themselves. He couldn't ignore the enemy starfighters, but he couldn't deploy too many of his own away from the ship. It could all be a costly diversion. Having his pilots flying constantly would drain them as surely as anything else.

"Launch four ballistic probes, backtracked along the alien course," he ordered. "If there is a carrier out there, I want to find it."

"Aye, sir," Farley said. There was a long pause as he worked his console. "Probes deployed, sir; I say again, probes deployed."

"Good, James said.

He nodded, tersely. Sensor stealth and even cloaking devices had their weaknesses. If the alien carrier was doing anything other than pretending to be a hole in space there was a very good chance the probes would pick up at least a sniff of its location. And then…he scowled as he realised the diplomats had still not replied to his messages. There was no way to know if the enemy starfighters were friendly, neutral or actively hostile. The only evidence he had that pointed to anything other than hostility was the simple fact they were holding outside attack range rather than closing in to engage the carrier.

"The diplomats say the aliens insist the starfighters aren't theirs," Davidson said, suddenly. "They're hostile."

"Good to know," James said, dryly. The War Faction had shown its willingness to kill members of other factions before. Humanity would regard that as an act of war, but the aliens seemed to think differently. Or, he wondered inwardly, perhaps they had problems understanding the other factions. "Warn all starfighters that they are cleared to engage, if the aliens enter attack range."

Long minutes ticked by. The aliens held their position, neither moving closer nor moving away. James had never been a starfighter pilot – his family had flatly forbidden him to attempt to enter the Academy – but he was familiar with their logistic requirements. It was a rare starfighter that could handle more than an hour or two of flying time without needing its life support packs replaced. The alien starfighters seemed to have similar limitations.

So why aren't they attacking? He asked himself. *Or doing something other than poking at the edge of our sensor network?*

"Launch a recon shell of drones," he ordered, slowly. It was possible the aliens were trying to divert his attention from something else, sneaking up on the other side of the flotilla. Or, perhaps, that the Peace Faction's starship was a Trojan Horse. "I want to know if anything is trying to sneak up behind us."

The Admiral's face appeared in the display. James felt his eyes narrow in concern. The Admiral looked haggard, utterly exhausted. It wasn't uncommon for Admiral Smith to work long hours and not get enough sleep – James had known him long enough to be certain there were fewer more dedicated officers in the Royal Navy – but they couldn't afford it. He made a mental note to suggest the Admiral return to bed, then leaned forward. There was no way the Admiral would go to bed now.

"Admiral," he said. "The aliens appear to be trying to make us jumpy."

"And succeeding magnificently," Admiral Smith said. "Tactical analysis?"

"They're trying to wear us down," James said, bluntly. "By now, they must have a pretty good idea of the limits of our technology."

"And starfighter designs," the Admiral agreed. "They'll have captured some models at New Russia, if nowhere else. Withhold the remaining starfighter squadrons for the nonce, I think."

"Aye, Admiral," James said. "But we'll have to rotate the CSP back through the ship in" – he checked his display – "twenty minutes."

"Which raises the question," the Admiral mused. "Do they *know* that we will have reduced fighter coverage then or have they just managed to get lucky?"

James frowned. There might have been spies on *Ark Royal* – he was grimly aware he didn't have enough Marines to cover them all – but it was unlikely in the extreme that any of the spies were working for the aliens. It was hard enough communicating with a faction of aliens that actually *wanted* to talk. Somehow, he found it hard to imagine the aliens successfully comprehending the value of human sexual indiscretions and then using one such incident as a blackmail tool. Unless they'd found a human traitor...an Arnold, a Petain, a Witherspoon...

But there was another option.

"They could have spies on the Peace Faction's ship," he said, slowly. "Or maybe they've just been shadowing us since the first battle and have just decided to up the tension a little."

"It's a possibility," the Admiral said. "Polly thinks it's unlikely – the aliens are a consensual species, apparently – but we have to bear the possibility in mind."

Polly, James thought, with some private amusement. He'd nagged Uncle Winchester to find Admiral Smith a bride – the aristocracy had survived by co-opting commoners with remarkable talents or well-earned fame – but maybe it wouldn't be necessary. But then, Polly MacDonald was young enough to be the Admiral's daughter. It was unlikely the Admiral saw her as anything other than a substitute child. Come to think of it, he'd treated many of his younger crewmen as sons and daughters too.

He pushed the thought aside as nothing more than a pointless distraction. "They will have had time to alert their superiors that we made contact with the Peace Faction," he said, instead. "They might be trying to force us to compromise ourselves in front of the other factions."

"It looks that way," the Admiral agreed. "Order your pilots to hold the line, Captain. There's no way we can do anything else until they close in to attack."

"Aye, sir," James said. "Assuming they do, of course."

He sighed. No military force could remain at full alert indefinitely, no matter what the politicians and armchair admirals thought. Given near-constant alerts, his crews would start to be worn down until they were falling asleep at their consoles. If he knew, beyond a doubt, that the aliens weren't going to attack, he would have sent half of his crew back to bed. But there was no way he could take it for granted.

"And they'll know precisely where we intend to pass through the next tramline," he said. There were two more jumps between their current position and the alien-selected destination and they knew nothing about the next system. The War Faction could be plotting an ambush and there would be no way to be sure until they jumped through the tramline. "They could use that against us."

"Yes," the Admiral agreed, flatly. "We have to get rid of our unwanted shadows."

"And find their carrier," James agreed. He looked down at the display. The drones hadn't found anything, which worried him. Either the alien starfighters had radically extended endurance or the aliens had managed to improve their terrifyingly good stealth systems still further. Neither one boded well for the war. "It could be far too close to us for comfort."

"Unless they've built an escort carrier design of their own," the Admiral suggested. "That could be why they launched so *few* starfighters at us."

James sucked in his breath sharply. The Admiral was right. If the aliens had copied one human idea, why couldn't they copy others? They'd lost enough carriers in the war to be dangerously short of launching plat-forms...he hoped. The alien diplomats had refused to go into hard details about just how much firepower the War Faction had at its disposal. He couldn't blame them, as the negotiations might break down violently, but it was irritating.

They'd want an escort carrier design for the same reason we wanted one, he thought. *Additional starfighter launching platforms.*

He contemplated it as the alien icons moved in and out of sensor range. Escort carriers were nothing more than modified freighters, with a launching bay and additional life support shoehorned into the design. If they hadn't been so modular, rebuilding them would have been a major headache for the shipyards. As it was, they were fragile ships, barely able to stand up to a glancing blow from alien weapons. But then, a hail of plasma fire could burn a fleet of modern carriers to debris.

And if they're feeling the pinch too, he told himself, *they might have sent an escort carrier out here as a diversion.*

"I think we need to rotate crews, Admiral," he said. He paused. "And you should get some sleep."

"So should you," the Admiral said. He looked irked. James guessed that Janelle had been nagging him to sleep too. It was her job, although it took considerable bravery to tell an Admiral when he was doing some-thing stupid. "I'll sleep when things settle down."

"Captain," Farley said suddenly, "the drones are showing no further alien starfighters beyond the force we already detected."

"Interesting," James mused.

He studied the display for a long moment. He'd wondered if the aliens were trying to deceive him into believing they'd only launched a couple of squadrons of starfighters, while keeping the remainder of their force just out of sensor range, but it seemed otherwise. The upper estimate for how many starfighters there *were* in the alien force was twenty-five. Intelligence's best guess for how many starfighters an alien carrier could launch was one hundred, a fair match for humanity's modern carriers. And that suggested there was no full-sized fleet carrier within the system, just an escort...unless, of course, the aliens were playing games. *He* hadn't launched his full complement of fighters either.

He took a breath. "Launch a third squadron of starfighters, then cycle the CSP back through the landing bay," he ordered. There was still time on their life support packs, but he wanted to run them through replenishment as quickly as possible. "Once they're ready to launch, hold them in the bay."

"Aye, sir," Farley said.

James turned his attention back to the Admiral. "With your permission, Admiral, I intend to step down the alert to the point we can send some of the crews to bed," he said. "We should be able to see an attack coming in time to get the remaining starfighters launched and bring the ship back to full alert."

"Wait until the CSP has been replenished," the Admiral said. "That would be the worst moment for them to launch an attack."

James had his doubts. He had thirty-six starfighters covering the flotilla already, with two more squadrons ready to launch at a moment's notice. The aliens were badly outnumbered – and they had to know it. And that meant they should be reluctant to do anything that would bring them up against superior force. But if they were willing to fire on their own people, he asked himself, would they be willing to attack even when they were hopelessly outgunned?

"Admiral," he said slowly, keying the channel so only the two of them could hear, "if we knew the Russians were escorting an alien flotilla though their territory, would we consider attacking it anyway?"

The Admiral frowned. "Probably not," he said. "But it would depend on just how badly the Russians were skirting the treaties."

James nodded. There were treaties governing humanity's wars, with the most important one being a ban on fighting within the Sol System itself, but no one really expected the treaties to last for long if two major interstellar powers went to war. Back when it had seemed likely America would go to war with China, if he recalled correctly, there had been a great deal of debate over just what the Royal Navy should do if either of the nations used British-controlled tramlines. And *that* had assumed the Royal Navy didn't join the Americans in war.

But if the Russians were escorting an alien fleet through their space… how would the rest of the human race react? Was it a form of armed neutrality or deliberate treason against humanity? If the War Faction's monomaniacal approach to the war led them to view the other alien factions as treasonous, would they see themselves justified in attacking the other factions? There was no way to know.

We'd see it as treason, he thought, morbidly. *We'd react very badly to a human nation aiding the aliens we saw as deadly enemies. And the aliens aren't even capable of responding to different ideas, or even the concept we might not be beyond salvation...*

"I think we must assume the War Faction will attack the other factions," he said, slowly. "An alien civil war might be at hand."

"That would depend on just how much firepower the disparate alien factions control," the Admiral pointed out. "It could be a very short civil war."

"If the War Faction controls all the ships," James agreed. "We might have to defend the other alien factions against their enemies."

"With only a handful of ships," the Admiral said. "And we need to lose our shadows as quickly as possible."

He paused. "I think I've had an idea," he added. "But it will have to wait long enough for the aliens to get bored themselves."

"Understood, Admiral," James said. "All we can do now is wait."

He settled back in his command chair and watched, grimly, as the CSP returned to the landing bay. Somewhat to his surprise, the alien starfighters made no attempt to lunge towards the carrier and attack. Instead, they just watched, dancing at the very edge of sensor range. They were distracting, he had to admit, but he was damned if he was allowing them to distract him *too* far. If someone was trying to sneak up on them...

"Stand down one third of the crew," he ordered, once the CSP had completed its replenishment cycle. "Tell them to get some rest in the sleep machines, if available."

"Aye, sir," Commander Williams said. "But if we have to wake them early..."

"I know," James said. Sleep machines worked well – very well. But if someone happened to be woken up too early they'd have terrible headaches. "If worst comes to worst, we will leave them in the machines until they complete their cycle."

"Aye, sir," Commander Williams said, again. "And will you be resting too?"

James shook his head. "Not yet," he said, firmly. He would have to pass the bridge to her sooner or later, perhaps while having a quick nap himself in his office. But he wasn't going to do that until the Admiral's plan was ready to go. "Catch a nap yourself, if you can. You'll have to take command soon enough."

He told himself to relax, but it wasn't easy. He'd been a naval officer long enough to know just how quickly a situation could move from controllable to utterly disastrous – and the aliens were deliberately trying to wear the crew down. It suggested they had more in mind than merely annoying the human flotilla…

…And he wanted to be ready for it when they finally sprang their surprise.

CHAPTER
TWENTY FOUR

"This is a bold plan," Kurt observed.

"But workable," Rose said. "Or it would be, if we were confident in our pilots."

Kurt studied her for a long moment. She looked…less stressed than himself, although he knew *she* wasn't waiting nervously for another message from the blackmailers. Their silence bothered him more than he cared to admit. He wanted, desperately, to just have it come to an end, but he knew he had to wait. There was nothing else he could do.

And he wanted to take her back to his office and screw her senseless. He couldn't do that either.

"I think they should be capable of doing it," Kurt said. "The only problem will be keeping the aliens from realising what we're doing until then."

He paused as the pilots slowly filtered into the briefing compartment. Most of them looked tired, their edges already dulled by the constant alert. Four hours had passed since the alien starfighters had first shown themselves and nothing had changed, save for the pilots out covering the carrier against a sudden attack. If the aliens had wanted to wear down the human fleet, Kurt had to admit, it was working magnificently. And it wasn't costing them anything more than a handful of exhausted pilots.

Unless they have managed to extend their fighter range significantly, he thought. *We still haven't found their damn carrier.*

"All right, listen up," he said, eying the pilots critically. As always, they seemed uncomfortably young and slapdash to be military officers. At some point, he told himself, they were probably going to have to discuss how best to wear a uniform with the survivors. "This is going to take some damn fancy flying."

He ran through the briefing quickly, then studied them all carefully. "If you fuck this up, you will end up dead," he said. The pilots sobered. Three of their friends were already dead, their bodies utterly beyond recovery. "If any of you want to back out, now is the time."

No one said a word.

"Good," Kurt said. "Man your planes!"

He turned back to look at Rose. "Watch our backs, ok?"

Rose nodded. "Of course," she said, primly. "Isn't that my job?"

———

"They're still probing the edge of our sensor range," Janelle said.

"Good," Ted said. His one worry had been that the aliens would change their tactics before the humans were ready to launch their own operation. "Is *Blackburn* in position?"

"Aye, Admiral," Janelle said. "And the remaining squadrons are launching now."

Ted nodded. "Order the pilots to execute the first stage in" – he glanced at the display – "five minutes."

He leaned back in his chair and waited while the seconds ticked away. Timing was everything, all the more so as no one was quite sure just how capable the alien sensors actually were. They were good, according to the analysts, but *how* good? The only real data he had came from how the aliens had reacted to the ECM drones. They'd rarely been fooled for long, yet they *had* been fooled.

"Admiral," Janelle said. "The first stage is commencing…now."

Ted watched, dispassionately, as three squadrons of starfighters suddenly spun around and charged right at the alien starfighters, their sensors rapidly hunting for targets. The aliens started, then fell into a series of evasive manoeuvres that suggested they were unwilling to risk an engagement at such long odds. Ted hoped that was a good sign. If the aliens were feeling sensitive to potential losses, he thought, they were clearly worn down by the fighting too.

"They're moving back out of range," Janelle reported. "The starfighters are pushing them back."

"Good," Ted said. "Execute Phase Two."

―――

"All right," Kurt said, as he watched his comrades charging the alien starfighters. "Follow my lead."

HMS *Blackburn* was ugly enough to make *Ark Royal* look pretty – and indeed, the ancient carrier had a stubborn grace that the heavily-modified freighter couldn't match. She was nothing more than two hundred meters of blocky shapeless hull, studded with a handful of sensor blisters and weapons. Her true striking power came in the two squadrons of starfighters she carried to support *Ark Royal*. Kurt had barely a handful of seconds to admire the escort carrier before his starfighter latched onto her hull.

"Sound off," he ordered, as the remaining pilots docked. He listened as, one by one, they confirmed they were docked to the ship's hull. "And now we wait. Maintain radio silence."

He sucked in his breath. If they were lucky, if everything had gone according to plan, the aliens wouldn't have seen them docking with the escort carrier. They'd see the carrier as carrying nothing more than its onboard fighters, half of which were currently taking part in the attempt to force the alien starfighters to fight. And that was what the Admiral was counting on.

His starfighter shivered, slightly, as *Blackburn* fell out of formation and headed towards the rear of the flotilla. A frigate moved towards it, then apparently changed its mind – or had it changed by the Admiral. Kurt hoped the aliens believed *Blackburn* to be heading back to Earth, back down the series of tramlines. They had to view the carrier as a tempting target, he knew. *He* would certainly have considered it a prime target…

And now we wait, he thought, as the carrier kept moving. *And pray.*

―――

"The aliens have broken contact," Janelle reported. "Our starfighters are requesting orders."

"Tell them to return to the flotilla," Ted ordered. The aliens would have a free shot at *Blackburn* – or so it would seem. But what if they refused to take the bait? "And then tell *Blackburn* to continue with her operation until Simon Says otherwise."

"Aye, sir," Janelle said. There was a long pause as the starfighters rocketed back towards the carrier. "The aliens are filtering back again."

And what, Ted asked his unknown counterpart silently, *are you thinking? Are you interested in taking a free shot at a makeshift carrier or are you more concerned with monitoring the flotilla?*

"I'm picking up nineteen alien fighters watching us, but a number seem to be headed towards *Blackburn*," Janelle said, carefully. "I can't get a precise figure on just how many of them there are, sir."

"Then launch two more probes towards their point of origin," Ted ordered. He cursed under his breath. The beancounters would make a terrible fuss when they realised just how many probes he'd fired off in less than a day. But it was easier to replace probes, no matter how expensive they were, than pilots. "They *have* to have a carrier nearby."

He glanced at the ship's status board and cursed again. The crew were well-trained and *very* experienced, after two deep-penetration missions into alien space, but it was clear that tiredness was already beginning to bite. Captain Fitzwilliam was rotating crew through sleep machines as much as possible, yet they didn't dare reduce their number of active crew-members below a certain level. It would end badly.

We need to slap them back, he thought. *And convince them to keep their distance.*

———

Twenty-two fighters, Kurt thought, as the alien starfighters flashed towards *Blackburn*. It was clear they intended to blow the escort carrier away in the first attack, then return to harassing *Ark Royal*. But they were in for a nasty surprise, he told himself firmly. If they kept coming in at that speed, they wouldn't be able to escape before his pilots tore into them.

He counted down the seconds, then triggered his starfighter's drives, pushing the ship away from the escort carrier. The aliens seemed to flinch as the remainder of his squadron followed him, but it was definitely too late to escape. Space filled with plasma bursts as the humans opened fire, lashing the aliens back from the carrier and blowing seven alien craft out of space before they even had a chance to fire back. And then the aliens returned fire.

"Keep evading," he snapped, throwing radio silence to the winds. There was no point in trying to hide any longer. "Don't give them a chance to draw a bead on you!"

His starfighter spun, then blew another alien fighter into vapour. But the aliens had recovered now and picked off two human fighters in quick succession. Kurt cursed under his breath, knowing that losses would be fairly even from this point until the inexperience of his pilots made itself felt. An alien pilot drew a bead on him, then lost contact as another human pilot blew him into dust. And then the aliens were suddenly retreating at high speed, leaving the humans behind.

Odd, Kurt thought. *They must be closer to their sources of replenishment than us.*

He scowled at the thought. It would take weeks to get replacement starfighters to *Ark Royal*, assuming the Royal Navy or anyone else had starfighters to send. He assumed the aliens had bases far closer to the flotilla; hell, they might well have some starfighters assigned to Target One or Target Two they could call on. But instead...the aliens were definitely worried about losses. It was interesting, to say the least, and indicative of something. He just wished he knew what.

"Simon Says *Blackburn* is to return to the flotilla," the Admiral ordered. "I say again, Simon Says *Blackburn* is to return to the flotilla."

Kurt nodded. Simon Says was an old trick, one used when there was a good chance the enemy was listening in on allied communications. Using it against the aliens seemed pointless, if only because the aliens couldn't understand human words. But the diplomats *had* been making progress, he reminded himself. The hostile aliens might have made *more* progress if they'd had human prisoners to work with, just like Prince Henry. And they might have been less reluctant to use torture to force the prisoners to talk.

He set his starfighter to return to *Ark Royal* and concentrated on monitoring the remainder of the battle. It looked as though the aliens had fallen back completely, but it was difficult to be sure. They might just have other ships shadowing the carrier...

"Await orders," a new voice said, as they returned to the flotilla. "We may have found something interesting."

"Understood," Kurt said. The enemy carrier? Or what? "We will hold position and wait."

————

Ted leaned forward, fascinated despite himself. "What the hell is that?"

"The analysts think it's an in-flight refuelling craft," Janelle said. "The pre-space militaries used to use something like it for jet fighters. I don't think anyone ever considered using it for starfighters, not until now."

"Clever," Ted said. "Very clever."

He shook his head in amused disbelief. The alien craft wasn't much larger than a standard shuttle, which was partly why it hadn't been detected until one of the probes had gotten lucky. But it was clearly capable of carrying enough power cells and life support packs to allow the alien starfighters to recycle and return to the battle without needing to go through a massive carrier. He had to admire the ingenuity of the concept. The aliens had developed a way of deploying starfighters away from planetary bases without a carrier.

But it was also an opportunity. No matter how fast they flew, the alien starfighters were more than nine hours from the closest inhabited world in the system. Without that tanker, he told himself, they would never get home.

"Pass the word to the starfighters," he ordered. "I want that thing taken out."

"Aye, sir," Janelle said.

————

Kurt lifted his eyebrows in surprise as his orders popped up on the display. The aliens had come up with something new – no, not entirely *new*, but certainly a new adaption of an older concept. And if it could be taken out, the battle might be won without further ado. He relayed his orders to the rest of the squadron, then yanked his starfighter around and raced towards the alien tanker. The remaining pilots followed in his wake.

"Switch to random fire," he ordered, as the alien starfighters rose up to bar his way. The tanker didn't seem to be anything like as manoeuvrable as an assault shuttle, let alone a starfighter. It's only real defence was remaining undetected. "Don't let them lure you into a dogfight."

A quick glance at the scope told him that two pilots had ignored his orders, but the remainder held firm behind him as they blasted through the alien formation and closed in rapidly on the tanker. It tried to alter course, then open fire with weapons of its own, but it was futile. Kurt pushed down on the trigger and watched with unholy glee as the tanker exploded into a colossal fireball, which faded rapidly in the inky darkness of space. Behind him, the aliens reversed course and threw themselves back towards the carrier. They had to know they didn't have a hope of survival, he realised, so they were determined to inflict what damage they could in their remaining hour of life.

"Pursuit course," he ordered. He wasn't *that* worried about the Old Lady, but the frigates and escort carriers were at serious risk. As, he reminded himself sharply, was the alien starship from the Peace Faction. "Take the bastards out!"

But he already knew it might be too late.

———

"Enemy starfighters closing on attack vector," Farley reported. "CSP is moving to engage."

"Activate point defence," James ordered, sharply. The aliens looked more intent on ramming his ship than trying to strafe her with plasma fire. But then, they had good reason to know that strafing *Ark Royal* was a waste of time. Unless they blew off her weapons

210

and sensor blisters...he shook his head. There was no time to waste thinking about the potential dangers. "And fire as soon as the aliens come into range."

The alien craft swooped down on *Ark Royal*, then scattered. Three plunged directly towards the carrier, two picked off before they could slam into the hull; the third rammed the hull directly, only to inflict nothing more than a scar. The remaining starfighters headed towards the smaller ships, despite the growing hail of point defence. One of them slammed into *Bolton* and the escort carrier vanished in a tearing explosion. The final alien starfighters changed course and headed towards the fleet transport. But it was too late. The CSP overwhelmed and destroyed them short of their target.

"HMS *Bolton* confirmed destroyed," Farley said, quietly. "No lifepods; I say again, no lifepods."

James winced. He'd seen too many people die since the war had begun. Very few of them had had a chance to escape into the lifepods before their ships exploded. Prince Henry had really been incredibly lucky. But at least *Bolton* was replaceable. She'd only carried fifty crewmen, not counting her pilots. The Royal Navy had had a dozen more conversions under way when the flotilla had departed the Sol System.

"Launch a final shell of recon drones, then stand down," he ordered. "Recall all but one of the starfighter squadrons; designate the remaining squadron as CSP. Recycle one squadron to replace the CSP as soon as possible."

"Aye, sir," Farley said.

James let out a long breath. "Commander Williams, you have the bridge," he said. "Inform me if anything changes."

"Aye, Captain," Commander Williams said. "I have the bridge."

James nodded, then strode towards the hatch to his office. He needed a rest, urgently. And so did the Admiral. But nagging the Admiral wasn't his job.

But you should ask him to rest anyway, he thought, as he stepped through the hatch. *He needs his sleep too.*

———

"It does look as though the War Faction has determined that the other factions are committing treason," Ambassador Melbourne said. "What else explains attacks that will widen the war?"

Henry shrugged. Ambassador Melbourne wasn't as bad as some of the ambassadors he'd had to deal with, thankfully. But then, the Ambassador knew Henry had done a considerable amount of legwork in organising the first true diplomatic meeting between humans and aliens. He wasn't just a useless Prince to the Ambassador.

"So it would seem," he said. He paused. "You know, I never thought to ask. What do they call themselves?"

"Something we cannot even *begin* to pronounce," Ambassador Melbourne told him. "We did ask them, but we don't have a proper translation for the answer. We're still arguing if we should call them something in Latin, perhaps 'intelligent fishes.'"

Henry shrugged, again. He knew no Latin.

"But others think that would be offensive," Ambassador Melbourne added. "They don't seem to think the way we do, but they might object to being called fishes."

"They have more in common with frogs," Henry said. "But I suppose the French would be pissed if we called them frogs."

Ambassador Melbourne nodded, bluntly.

"I think you didn't come here to talk to me about naming conventions," he said, shortly. "It is nice to talk to you, Your Highness, but I don't have time for a long chat. What do you want?"

You to be polite, Henry thought, although it was hard to blame the Ambassador. Henry *had* interrupted a meeting with the Ambassador's aides, just to make his request. As reasonable as the Ambassador was, interrupting him could not have gone down well.

"I believe you will have packed a few hampers," he said, remembering his first diplomatic mission. "Please can I borrow one?"

Ambassador Melbourne's eyes narrowed. "Can I ask why?"

"I'd prefer not," Henry said. "But I would be prepared to offer my endorsement in the future."

The Ambassador studied him for a long moment. Henry was powerless, formally, and he would have little power even if he took the Throne.

But he would have a great deal of informal influence, if he saw fit to use it properly. The Ambassador would be able to call in the debt one day.

"Very well," Ambassador Melbourne said, finally. "But I would advise you to be careful."

"I'm always careful," Henry lied. "Have it delivered to my cabin at the end of the day."

CHAPTER
TWENTY FIVE

It had been years since Henry had seen a full-sized hamper, even one designed for a handful of people rather than a full diplomatic party. Setting it up on his own had been a headache, but it wasn't as though he was short of time. His only real official duty was monitoring the diplomatic talks and offering his insights, such as they were. Trained researchers seemed to have already moved ahead, thanks to computer assistance, of where he'd been when they'd returned to the Old Lady.

He looked up as he heard the door chime. "Come," he called. "It's open."

The hatch hissed open, revealing Janelle. She started into the room... and then stopped and stared in disbelief. Henry had set up the table with knives, forks, plates and glasses from the hamper, each one worth more than a midshipwoman would see in a year. The cold meats and bread in the centre of the table, surrounded by sauces and spices, were just the icing on the cake.

"...Henry?"

Henry rose to his feet, suddenly very nervous. It had seemed a good idea, even a great idea, when he'd first had it, but now...he honestly wasn't sure if it had been a good idea after all. They'd first met and courted in the heat of battle, with the certainty of death hanging over their heads, and now...she'd thought him dead and a liar and...what if she laughed in his face or slapped him again?

"I thought we needed a proper dinner," he said. He waved a hand to indicate the table and the glowing candles he'd placed around the compartment. "What do you think?"

Janelle stared at him, then shook her head in amused disbelief. "Where did you get the food?"

"There's always a diplomatic hamper or two dozen wherever the diplomats go," Henry said, as he motioned for her to take one of the seats. "They always have the best food, intended for the diplomat and his counterpart to share while bonding – or perhaps doing some secret negotiation. I just asked for one."

Janelle sat down. "And you want to share it with me?"

Henry swallowed. This wasn't going according to plan.

"I wanted us to have a proper dinner," he said. "And a proper chat. We haven't really had time for it since we reunited, have we?"

"No," Janelle said. He could see the doubt in her eyes warring with something else. Guilt, perhaps. There wasn't much food on the table, but it was of higher quality than anything else on the ship. The mess served slop by comparison. "Henry…"

"Please, eat," Henry said. He took a piece of bread, buttered it expertly, then reached for a chunk of chicken. "This is all going to a good cause."

Janelle hesitated, then took a piece of bread for herself. They munched in companionable silence for several minutes, trying out the different slices of chicken, pork and beef with their respective toppings. It *was* a very diplomatic meal, Henry knew, as he swallowed a piece of beef with horseradish sauce. The diners could take whatever they wanted, add whatever seasoning they wanted to try and eat. There would be no row over badly chosen dishes.

He put down his final piece of bread with some satisfaction, then poured them both a glass of rose water. It had been a surprise to discover that there was no alcohol in the hamper, but perhaps that was for the best. Alcohol might have made them both act badly.

"There's rarely very much in these hampers," he explained, as she took her glass. "The idea is to show off the very top-class foods, rather than try to negotiate when the other side is stuffed to bursting. It isn't an easy balance to strike."

He sat back in his chair and looked at her. She was stunning, as always, but there was a harder edge around her now. Loving him, losing him... and discovering that her life was no longer her own had to have left scars. Henry cursed himself under his breath, then leaned forward. He wanted – he needed – to make her understand.

"I fell in love with you," he said. It was so hard to find the right words. "I wanted to enjoy being with someone who wanted me for myself."

"And so you did," Janelle said. Her voice was very even, but he thought he heard a quaver in her tone. "But I never expected to discover you were hiding a dark secret."

"I know," Henry said. Most boys would have concealed a past girl-friend or an unwholesome relationship, perhaps an experiment with homosexuality. *He'd* concealed a connection to the Royal Family. "I should have told you from the start."

"But you couldn't," Janelle said. "You had no way of knowing what I would do with it."

"No," Henry said. He swallowed, again. Other royals had been betrayed through trusting in the wrong person. "You might have wanted to become a Princess or you might have contacted the media or..."

"I understand," Janelle said, tonelessly.

"I was going to tell you," Henry said, remembering the Admiral chewing him out for selfishness. "I told myself that I would confess the truth on the voyage back to Earth and if you decided you didn't want to be part of the Royal Family – or even have a relationship with someone in the family – we would separate and no one would be any the wiser."

"That would not have happened," Janelle pointed out. "*Someone* saw fit to contact the media about me after your name was revealed."

"I know," Henry said. He felt so *useless*. "I couldn't keep that from happening."

"Of course not," Janelle said, bitterly. "You were dead – *presumed* dead."

She half-rose to her feet, glaring at him. "Do you know what I went through because of you?"

"...*Yes*," Henry said. He didn't know the specifics, but he could guess. The media would have sifted through her life, looking for scandal to tantalise and thrill the masses. Even after Earth itself had been attacked, he knew, nothing would have changed. They'd tell themselves that they were distracting the people from their woes. "And I didn't mean it to happen."

"But it did," Janelle said. She slapped the table, tears visible in her eyes. "They had people harassing my parents, for crying out loud! My parents!"

Henry almost pointed out that he had reporters harassing *his* parents too, but somehow managed to hold his tongue. It wouldn't have helped. His father had been born in a glass house, knowing – all too well – that anything he did would be used against him. And his mother, born to minor nobility, had had far more privacy until she'd married King Charles and discovered the truth behind the royal household. Janelle hadn't even had *that* degree of scrutiny before she'd become his lover.

"Tell me," she said. "Does it end? Does it ever end?"

"No," Henry said.

He took a breath. "I don't intend to stay," he said. "When we get back to Earth, Janelle, I intend to abdicate my position. I won't be Prince Henry any longer."

Janelle managed a weak smile. "I think they know about Charles Augustus by now," she said. "Call yourself John Smith this time."

"Perhaps," Henry said. "It was foolish of me to hope I could honour my family's wishes and have a normal life. I can go elsewhere and I will. There are quite a few asteroid colonies where my privacy would be respected. I can go there and live a blameless life."

Janelle frowned. "And would you be happy there?"

"I would be," Henry said, "if you came with me."

He took a breath. "I love you," he said, simply. "You're smart, sensible and pretty and…I love you."

Janelle leaned forward. "How do you know you love me?"

She held up a hand before he could say a word. "I researched your family history," she said, softly. "Almost every marriage your family entered into when both partners were young ended badly. They either separated or stayed in relationships that were effectively warzones. There was no way they could have a long relationship as an unmarried couple."

Henry winced. His parents – and Royal PR officers – would have vetted any girlfriend he'd met outside Buckingham Palace. Some of them had been deliberately pointed at him, he suspected; they'd seemed to know who he was, even without being told. Others had been reluctant to enter into the full glow of the media spotlights. He could hardly blame them, he knew; a single night spent with one of the girls could have ruined her life. And how could he blame Janelle for feeling the same way.

"We don't have to marry," he said, softly. "We could go to one of the asteroids together and set up a home there. If we can't endure one another..."

Janelle hesitated. "I wanted to stay with the Old Lady," she said. "But that might not be possible now, Henry."

Henry nodded, cursing himself once again. If Janelle became the Princess Consort, even unofficially because they weren't married, the Admiralty would probably insist on transferring her somewhere safer. Henry, now his identity was no longer a secret, would probably be transferred elsewhere too. Hell, the bastards could even justify it without reaching for torturous logic. Henry knew, without false modesty, that he'd learned a great deal from his career as a starfighter pilot. The Academy would probably be happy to have him teaching the newer recruits.

And reporters are banned from the Academy, he thought. *I could be safe there. We could be safe there.*

"We could go to the Academy," he said. "I could teach; you could... teach too."

Janelle snorted. "How to catch a Prince in ten easy lessons?"

"Charge though the nose for them," Henry advised. "They won't last long."

Janelle started to pace the room. "I don't know how I feel," she admitted. "I fell in love with Charles Augustus..."

"Who is me," Henry said.

"...And discovering I was also dating Prince Henry was shocking," Janelle said. "I already mourned you once."

"I believe there's a tradition that if someone is reported dead, falsely, they are guaranteed a long life," Henry said. It was one of the pieces of trivia he'd been forced to remember for some diplomatic meeting or another. "I can't remember where it comes from, but..."

"This isn't funny," Janelle snapped, whirling around to face him. "My life turned upside down."

"I know," Henry confessed. He rose to his feet, then walked over to the sofa and sat down. "I didn't intend to cause you any problems."

"But you did," Janelle said. She sat down next to him. "And now we have to deal with the consequences."

Henry hesitated, then wrapped an arm around her shoulder. She relaxed into his touch, minutely. He felt an odd surge of relief – she still cared for him – which he pushed aside, mercilessly. He'd managed to get into trouble, before, by misreading a girl's body language. It was the last thing he wanted to do now.

"Yes, we do," he said. "This is a Morton's Fork, Janelle. Whatever choice we make, there will be pain. Lots of pain."

He sighed. If they married and remained as part of the Royal Family they would have no privacy. If they remained lovers they would have no privacy. If they broke up they would *still* have no privacy. Janelle would be considered a helpless victim by some parts of the media, a jezebel-like bitch by others…and everything in between. The only halfway reasonable solution was to walk away from the Royal Family completely.

It wouldn't be easy, he knew. He did have his training, which would buy his way onto one of the independent asteroids, but it would be a far from easy life. And Janelle, too, would have to work for a living. She wouldn't have the gilded cage she would have if she lived in Buckingham Palace. But then, he knew she didn't *want* the cage. If she had, she would have taken him back at once.

"Then we live together elsewhere," Janelle said, firmly. "Are you really prepared to do that for me?"

"Yes," Henry said, with utter certainty. He'd died once – or at least he'd been reported dead. Reading his obituaries had been eye-opening. He'd always known the media was two-faced, but switching between endless praise – as if he'd been a Mary Sue – and savage condemnation had surprised even him. And none of them had talked about what he'd been like as a person. "I will not remain at their mercy any longer."

He shrugged. "I can write to my parents and Elizabeth," he added. "That's what happened before to Prince George. He might no longer be part of the Royal Family, but he could still contact his family."

"If you're sure," Janelle said. "I'm sorry."

Henry stared at her. "*You're* sorry?"

Janelle looked back, her eyes bright with tears. "I loved you, then I mourned you and then I cursed you because of the damage you did to my life," she said. "And now here I am, wanting you, pushing you into abandoning your birthright because it's the only way you can have me. I'm a bitch and yet I can't go to the other side…"

Henry reached for Janelle, pulled her to him and kissed her, hard. She kissed him back, her hands reaching around to stroke his back. Henry felt the kiss grow longer and longer, then his hands were suddenly working at her uniform, pulling it away from her body. It was suddenly very hard to undress without tearing something…

Afterwards, they lay together on the deck, holding each other tightly. Henry kissed her, allowing his mouth to trace the edges of her face, one of his hands stroking her breast gently. She moaned, a deep sound, then reached down to stroke him in return. They were both interrupted, moments later, by the sound of the buzzer.

"Duty calls," Janelle said, as she reached for her wristcom. "I'm back on duty in an hour."

"Bugger," Henry said. Several viler words came to mind, but he held them back. Had they ever had a chance to just lie together and cuddle? It wasn't very manly – he still cringed at some of what he'd been told, at school, was proper manly behaviour – yet it felt good. And it definitely felt better than a loveless coupling with a prostitute. "Want to shower together?"

Janelle smiled, then winked at him. "Why not?"

Henry pulled himself to his feet, then followed her into the washroom. It was barely large enough for two bodies, but he didn't mind as he splashed soap on his hands and started to wash her breasts. Her nipples hardened as he stroked them, then she pushed his hands away reluctantly. Henry knew she had a point – she did have to go on duty – but he couldn't help feeling disappointed. His body was intent on telling him just how long it had been since he'd slept with her, prior to his capture.

"Don't tell the Admiral about our decision," he said. Now he'd made the decision, he felt curiously free. He had a long way to go before he could separate himself from the monarchy for good, but he felt better for knowing what he was going to do. "He might be obliged to tell someone."

Janelle frowned. "Who?"

She stepped out of the shower and rapidly began to dry herself. Henry forced himself to look away as her bare body winked at him, then concentrated on washing himself clean. In hindsight, it would probably have been better to ask her to bring spare clothes to his quarters before she came, but he couldn't have done that. She might have snapped at him for presumption.

He sighed as he took a towel and scrubbed himself dry, then walked out into the main room, where Janelle was buttoning up her uniform. She looked remarkably presentable, he decided, although the grin on her face was quite alarming. Henry hesitated, then told her to concentrate on appearing normal. *Everyone* would know what had happened if she walked out of his cabin with that grin.

"Bastard," Janelle said, without heat. She made a show of eying his face. "And what about *your* grin? You're smirking like a cat in heat."

"I have to clear away the mess," Henry said. He looked down at the remains of the hamper. They hadn't even managed to get to the chocolate cheesecake...he shrugged, then transferred it to the fridge. It could be devoured later. He had a sudden vision of licking it off her breasts and had to fight to keep calm. "And then review more and more boring diplomatic stuff."

Janelle smiled. "Have you thought about requesting assignment to the embassy, once one is set up on the alien homeworld?"

"The government wouldn't let me, I suspect," Henry admitted. The thought was tempting, but there were too many objections. He'd have to remain Prince Henry, for a start. "They're very keen to keep the Royal Family away from power. Too many people remember King Charles I."

"He was centuries ago," Janelle protested. "I thought most people remembered Charles III."

Henry shrugged. Charles III had been unlucky enough to be monarch during the Troubles. He hadn't been malicious, but there had been too many politicians eager to divert blame onto the monarch's shoulders. Charles's reputation had never really recovered. His namesake, however, had plotted to destroy Parliament and wage war on his own people. Henry would have liked him more if he'd slaughtered reporters by the bucket load. Instead, he'd started a civil war and then lost, losing his head in the process.

"Aristocrats have long memories," he said, instead. "They need to think long-term if they have any hope of surviving at all."

CHAPTER
TWENTY SIX

"I think we definitely have company," Farley said. "But she's being very careful to stay out of sensor range."

James cursed. The alien contact had appeared shortly after they'd crossed the tramline into the second-to-last system and maintained its position since then. There was no way to tell if it was a carrier or something smaller – although he suspected it was no bigger than a frigate – but it was keeping a solid lock on the flotilla's position. They couldn't run and they couldn't hide.

"Keep an eye on it," he ordered. He briefly considered several tactics for forcing the enemy starship to fall back or engage his forces, but nothing would work unless the aliens chose to cooperate. "And keep running through the drones."

"Aye, Captain," Farley said. "Local space appears clear."

James nodded, impatiently. The system was barren, with nothing more interesting than a handful of comets and a tiny asteroid field. He'd wondered, privately, if the aliens had blown up a dwarf planet to make it easier to mine, but the concept seemed somewhat inefficient. There was no shortage of resources for the aliens to use in nearby systems. Instead, it looked as though the aliens used the system as a transfer point and nothing else.

He settled back in his command chair, watching the ship's status display. The course they were taking towards the other tramline was a least-time course, set by their alien companion, something that bothered him more than he cared to admit. It would be easy for the aliens to set up an ambush. Hell, the tanker-supported attack on the flotilla could have been intended to distract them long enough for the aliens to put their fleet together. They couldn't have expected a handful of fighters to do more than scratch the Old Lady's paint.

But they did kill Bolton, he thought. The escort carrier was a very minor ship, compared to the giant fleet carriers, but losing her launching platform would hurt. They could have rotated their starfighters through her recycling system if necessary. *It wasn't a total loss.*

The hours ticked by slowly, with no sign of anything from the shadowing alien craft. It was odd, but in a way James was almost pleased to see it. If the War Faction felt the urge to keep a sharp eye on the flotilla, he told himself, it suggested the Peace Faction wasn't planning an elaborate double-cross. He was still mulling over the different possibilities – and the reports from the diplomats – as *Ark Royal* approached the second tramline.

He keyed his console. "Admiral," he said, "I'd like to alter course."

It might be worthless, he knew. The aliens had a tactical speed advantage – and they might well have a stealthed ship monitoring the tramline in position to jump through and arrange for any waiting ambushers to change position. But it had to be done. If the aliens were friendly, they'd understand. And if they weren't, it would give the Old Lady her best chance of punching her way through the ambush or escaping back into the barren system.

"See to it," the Admiral ordered. He looked well-rested, for once. "But don't go too far from our current course."

James nodded and issued orders. *Ark Royal* altered course slightly, angling towards the tramline at an angle that would change their exit coordinate significantly. Moments later, *War Hog* moved ahead of the flotilla, intent on jumping through the tramline first. If she didn't return…James cursed under his breath. It had all been simpler when they'd thought there was one alien faction and *all* aliens were hostile. Now…

"*War Hog* has jumped, sir," Farley reported.

"Good," James said, silently counting down the seconds. If the frigate had run into a hot reception, he knew, she might have been blown apart before she could jump out again. This time, an ambush would have been all too easy. "And our friend?"

"Holding position, as always," Farley said. "I don't think they did more than match our course and speed."

James sighed. The alien diplomats seemed to have much less freedom than their human counterparts. Every hour, they sent back countless terabytes of data to their starship, detailing the talks with the humans and requesting instructions. The researchers had sworn the aliens probably never did anything individually, but their discussions seemed more than a little excessive. But then, if the aliens on the ship represented several different factions, it was quite likely the diplomats themselves couldn't form a consensus. They needed to talk to their faction-mates.

We need to work out some proper terminology for this, James thought, ruefully. The diplomats had urged the researchers not to place any simple words on the alien concepts, pointing out that the words could lead to misunderstandings. But humanity wasn't entirely used to a concept of nationhood where nationality could be switched at the drop of a hat. *And then see if we can emulate anything of theirs that's worth copying.*

An icon flashed back into life on the display. "Captain, *War Hog* has returned," Farley reported. "She's transmitting now."

James switched his attention to the secondary display as it started to fill with data. Local space was seemingly clear, but the system itself was clearly heavily industrialised. The frigate's passive sensors had detected energy signatures all over the system, suggesting an industrial base on the same level as Target One – or Earth. Hundreds of spacecraft made their way through the system, thousands of settlements could been seen in the asteroids and planetary orbits. It was a staggering display of alien industrial might.

And if they'd been united against us, he thought morbidly, *they would probably have won the war by now.*

"Admiral," he said, formally. "It looks as though we can enter the system."

"It does," Admiral Smith said. There didn't seem to be anyone waiting in ambush. "Take us through the tramline."

"All ahead full," James ordered. "Take us into the system."

He braced himself, instinctively, as the carrier slid towards the tramline and vanished from the barren system, only to reappear, nanoseconds later, in the alien system. The display flickered, then lit up with the live feed from the starship's passive sensors. If anything, the frigate's preliminary scans had underestimated the sheer size and power of the alien system.

"I'm picking up cloudscoops, mining stations, industrial nodes..." Farley's voice trailed off. "Sir, if my observations are accurate, this system has a considerably greater industrial potential than Earth."

James sucked in his breath sharply. Earth's high orbitals had been colonised for over two hundred years, allowing humanity to move its industrial base from the surface of its homeworld to orbit. And then there were the settlements on the moon and the outer planets, the mining stations in the asteroids and the gas giants, the countless installations built by the spacefaring nations...all of the economic predictions suggested that Earth would be the centre of the human sphere for hundreds of years to come. None of the settled worlds had anything like the same level of industry.

But the alien system was clearly older and far better developed.

He eyed the display, thoughtfully. "Is this their actual homeworld?"

"...Unknown," Farley said. "One of the worlds is definitely within the life-bearing zone, and it is clearly heavily industrialised, but there's no way to tell if it's their actual homeworld."

He paused. "It may be settled by multiple factions, though," he added. "The analysts will have to check, sir, but I think their industrial base is actually quite inefficient for its size."

James frowned, stroking his chin. The same could be said of Earth's industrial base. Twenty-two nations, of varying size and power, had established industrial nodes, mining stations and other off-world facilities. Even with the threat of interstellar war against a ruthless alien race, few nations had been willing to combine their industrial bases with those of their rivals. But then, the duplication of facilities had probably worked out in humanity's favour, in the long run. They weren't completely without a vitally important facility.

But if the aliens were showing the same pattern...did it mean that the system was ruled by a collective of factions, rather than just one? Or were they completely misinterpreting the data? There was no way to know.

"Keep monitoring the system," he ordered, finally. "Can you pick up any defensive installations?"

"No, sir," Farley said. "There's a number of starships passing through the system, without trying to hide themselves, but I can't get accurate data at this distance."

"True," James agreed. They were over twenty light minutes from the life-bearing world. The data they picked up would be out of date by the time they received it. "Inform me the moment anything changes."

"We could launch probes," Farley offered. "A ballistic probe would be almost completely undetectable."

James hesitated. It was a tempting thought; they *needed* tactical data, particularly if they had to attack the system at a later date. But he knew the aliens might take it badly if they detected the probe – and he'd learned the hard way not to take anything for granted where alien technology was concerned. They *might* get lucky, after all, and it would be potentially disastrous.

It was easier sneaking up on Target One, he thought. *There, we knew we were going to hit the system. Now...*

"No," he said, out loud. "Passive sensors only."

He paused. "And our shadow?"

"Still with us," Farley said. "They came through the tramline just after we made transit. I don't think they changed course and speed at all."

"Keep an eye on him too," James ordered. He settled back in his command chair, forcing himself to relax. "And tell the CAG that two starfighter squadrons can stand down. The remainder are to remain on alert."

"Aye, sir," Farley said.

———

Ted had rarely been intimidated in his life. As a young officer, he'd been too stupid to be intimidated; as an older drunkard, he'd been too drunk to be intimidated. But he felt intimidated, more than he cared to admit, as the alien system slowly revealed its secrets. It was growing alarmingly clear that the aliens had a far greater industrial base than humanity had realised.

Then they should have been able to deploy a much larger fleet, he thought, slowly. *Did they only start building up a military after they encountered us at Heinlein?*

But it didn't seem too likely. The Royal Navy – and the other spacefaring navies – had spent near two hundred years learning what worked and didn't work when it came to interstellar war. There had been no shortage of mistakes over the years, as well as ideas that had come before or after their time. *Ark Royal* herself was an example of an idea that hadn't quite worked out quickly enough to suit the planners. He found it impossible to believe that the aliens had only started to build their military machine after Heinlein. A fleet as large as the one humanity had observed would take decades to build.

We built up a war fleet too, he thought, remembering his history lessons. Early concepts of the demilitarisation of space hadn't lasted, not when there was something in orbit worth protecting. Early tin-can spacecraft had given way to larger, more powerful starships, with each spacefaring power seeking ways to outdo its rivals. Then they'd produced starfighters and carriers and fast frigates…there had been no real way to halt the development of military starships. No spacefaring power would consider calling a halt when their rivals would take advantage of the opportunity to leap ahead of them.

And yet, there had been no real threat…

The thought bothered him. Had the aliens believed that there *would* be a threat, one day? The diplomats had asked and the aliens had claimed that humanity was the first intelligent race they had encountered, but it was hard to be sure. They might be lying – or there might be a translation problem. But would they have built up all the firepower they'd used against humanity if they hadn't seen a need for it?

Perhaps they were fighting each other, he thought, dryly. *Humans didn't know about aliens until Vera Cruz and we still built up a shitload of firepower.*

"Admiral," Janelle said, "we're picking up a signal from the alien ship. They're requesting we approach the life-bearing world and enter high orbit. They actually sent very detailed diagrams."

Ted wasn't surprised. If *he'd* been in charge of planetary security, *he* would have been very reluctant to allow a warship like *Ark Royal* anywhere near the planet without making damn sure she was harmless. And none of the aliens would *ever* mistake *Ark Royal* for harmless.

"Follow their instructions," he said. "And watch for any signs of trouble."

But the closer they came to the planet, he knew, the more damage they could do if the aliens decided to turn hostile. He could fire missiles towards the planet – or mass driver projectiles, inflicting horrendous damage. Even without the bioweapon, he could make the aliens pay an immense price for any treachery. And yet…he knew losing the Old Lady would be disastrous for humanity. *Ark Royal* had come to symbolise humanity's only hope of victory.

He watched, grimly, as more and more icons appeared in the display. The planet was heavily defended, with nine orbital battlestations and countless starfighters zipping to and fro, making no attempt to disguise the fact they were watching the humans with eagle eyes. There were fewer warships than he had expected; the largest one, holding station several hundred thousand kilometres from the planet, was a battlecruiser comparable to the ship *Ark Royal* had captured, months ago. He couldn't see any carriers at all.

They could be under stealth, he told himself, *or perhaps they're elsewhere. Or maybe they don't exist.*

He'd been forced to become more familiar with productive figures during the run-up to Operation Nelson than he'd ever wished to be. Producing starfighters in vast numbers was relatively simple. They weren't that complex, he knew; the real problem was producing starfighter pilots who could last longer than thirty minutes against the aliens. But the real bottleneck lay in producing carriers. Part of the reason modern carriers were so frail was that the designers had cut the armour back to the bare minimum. A carrier like *Ark Royal* could take upwards of two to three years to build.

Was it possible, he asked himself, that the aliens had worked their carrier force to the bone?

Wishful thinking, he thought, coldly. *You don't know anything of the sort.*

"We're entering orbit now," Janelle said, breaking into his thoughts. "They're inviting us to send a party down to the surface."

She paused. "And they're inviting you to join them."

Ted was seriously tempted. He'd never set foot on an alien world; hell, this was the first semi-friendly visit *any* human had made to an alien world. The Marines had raided alien worlds before, but that had been far from friendly. And yet he knew he couldn't risk leaving his command or falling into unfriendly hands.

"Tell them that I respectfully decline," he said. "No, tell the diplomats to decline for me."

"Aye, sir," Janelle said. "The analysts are sending you their preliminary report now."

Ted glanced down at his console. The alien world – the analysts had dubbed it Atlantis – was almost completely drenched in water. There were no ice caps – or, if there had been, they'd melted long ago. Judging from the report, the aliens had deliberately created a greenhouse effect to heat the world to the standards they considered acceptable. Somehow, they'd managed to avoid the runaway effect that had made Venus so unsuitable for immediate settlement.

But we're working on terraforming the world now, he thought. *The aliens have just done the same as ourselves.*

"It'll be like walking into a sauna down there," he said, gazing down at the orbital images. It was painfully obvious that once-great continents had vanished below the waves. Alien settlements, placed in shallow waters, could be seen everywhere. "Make sure the shuttle pilots are aware of local conditions."

"Aye, sir," Janelle said.

Ted turned his attention back to the tactical display. The aliens, either out of consideration or paranoia, had cleared orbital space around the flotilla, but he was far too aware that it was purely nominal. Ground-based weapons or starship-launched missiles could reach the flotilla within seconds. Ideally, he would have preferred to keep his distance from the planet, but the aliens had ensured it wasn't an option. He couldn't tell if they were trying to be welcoming or planning a sneak attack when he was looking the other way.

"Admiral," Janelle said suddenly, "our shadow has revealed himself."

"I see," Ted said, as a light cruiser materialised some distance from *Ark Royal.* "And what does *he* want?"

"Unknown," Janelle said. There was a long pause as she worked her console, accessing the live feed from the ship's passive sensors. "But he's exchanging signals with the orbital defences. They're not even trying to hide the signals."

"Odd," Ted commented. Any amount of information could be sent via laser, with no one outside anyway the wiser. "Do they want us to know what they're saying?"

"I don't think we can break the code," Janelle said. "Even if they *think* they're sending it in clear..."

Ted shrugged. "Keep an eye on him," he ordered, slowly. There was nothing else they could do, unless they opened fire and restarted the war. "And let me know if he does anything worrying."

He settled back in his command chair. Everything rested on the talks. Everything.

And if they didn't work, he reminded himself grimly, he would have to deploy the bioweapon. No matter the claims the designers made, Ted doubted it would be completely effective. And the aliens would know that humanity had attempted genocide. The war would become utterly merciless. Humanity's worlds would burn when the aliens struck back, exterminating large parts of the human race. And the survivors would find it impossible to rebuild their society.

Feeling sick, Ted forced himself to wait. There was nothing else he could do.

CHAPTER
TWENTY SEVEN

"Well," Ambassador Melbourne said, "is this better than flying a starfighter?"

Henry shook his head as the shuttle bounced through the planet's atmosphere. It was impossible to fly a starfighter within a planetary atmosphere, thankfully, because he had a feeling it would be just as bad if he'd tried. The shuttle shook so violently as it descended that he felt sick, so sick that only bloody-mindedness was keeping him from throwing up everything he'd eaten over the last few days. Several of the Ambassadors and their aides had lost that battle and were vomiting into paper bags.

"No," he said. The shuttle plunged, so sharply that he had the unnerving sensation that it was about to crash, then steadied. Outside, lightning flashed against the portholes. "In a starfighter, no one can smell vomit."

The Ambassador chuckled as the shuttle rocked again, then shuddered so violently that Henry thought it had rammed another shuttle in midflight. He braced himself, trying hard to breathe through his mouth, as the shuttle lowered itself the final few metres, then hit the ground with a terrifying *bang*. The deck rocked so violently that, for a long moment, he was honestly not sure it was over.

"Well," the Ambassador said. "See if I use this airline in future."

Henry chuckled as he undid his buckle and stood. His legs felt unsteady as he staggered towards the hatch, which was being opened by two armed Marines. The shuttle's display panel beside the hatch showed an alarming number of red lights, suggesting that the flight through the planet's atmosphere had been more hazardous than he'd realised. Whatever the aliens had done to terraform – *alien*-form – the planet had royally screwed up the planet's weather system. The flight had been thoroughly unsafe.

Maybe they did it on purpose, he thought, as the hatch opened. *They wanted to discourage visitors.*

The planet's atmosphere smelt warm and mushy, almost like one of the few surviving tropical rainforests. Rain poured from high overhead, the raindrops falling so heavily that Henry was half-convinced that someone was pouring water on them from above. It was very hard to see past a few metres, but he was almost grateful. The ground below the shuttle might have been made of concrete – and slightly slanted to allow water to run down towards the ocean – yet it didn't look particularly safe.

He stepped out of the shuttle and smiled as he felt the rain pounding down, drenching his uniform within seconds. Behind him, the ambassadors slowly righted themselves, their aides working desperately to change their clothes before they caused a diplomatic incident by turning up smelling of vomit. Henry had no idea if the aliens had a sense of smell – he'd certainly never thought to ask – but they probably had a point. There was nothing to be gained by taking unnecessary risks.

"Here, Your Highness," one of the Marines said. "You'll need this."

Henry sighed – everyone called him by his title or honorific now – and took the proffered umbrella, unfurling it above his head. He suddenly felt hotter as the rain started splashing off the fabric instead of his uniform, but fought the reaction down. Moments later, he started as a handful of aliens emerged from the mist and stopped at the edge of the landing pad. They seemed in no particular hurry.

"Out you come," he called into the shuttle. "They're waiting for us."

The Ambassadors staggered out of the shuttle, followed by their aides. Some of them looked so thoroughly traumatized by the flight that their legs were still wobbly, despite having had a few moments to recover and change their clothes. The aliens made no comment, merely waited until the humans had joined them, then motioned for the humans to follow their path through the rain. Henry hesitated, then took the lead. He *was* the only person who had spent time on an alien world before.

It grew easier to see as the rainfall slowly abated, but not to walk. Off the landing pad, they found themselves squelching through muddy paths that seemed to be on the verge of turning into swamps. Henry managed to keep his footing, but others were not so lucky. They slipped and stumbled as they slowly made their way down the path towards the ocean. And, piece by piece, the alien city came into view.

Henry sucked in his breath, unwillingly impressed. The city seemed to be set within the water, almost like a fairytale castle. And yet, it was covered with aliens, just like the city he'd seen before. They lay on the sloped rooftops like seals on ice floes, watching the humans through large unblinking eyes. Henry forced himself to walk onwards, despite their silent observation. Behind him, the Ambassadors fell silent as they followed their escort into a large building. Inside, it was surprisingly cool. Henry found himself shivering at once.

"They've prepared it for us," Ambassador Melbourne noted. "They're *trying* to be welcoming."

He was right, Henry realised, although by any normal human standard the alien negotiation chamber was ridiculous. The humans had been assigned chairs that looked to have been designed for children, while the aliens themselves lounged in a swimming pool that would keep their skins hydrated. Maybe they'd cooled the air to make their guests feel more at home, he considered, although it was impossible to tell for sure. One smaller pool, crammed with strange fish, might have been intended as a buffet.

They told us to bring our own food, he thought, recalling the hampers that had been packed on the shuttle. *It might have been dangerous for us to eat their food.*

There was a splash as one of the escorts entered the swimming pool and vanished beneath the water. Henry looked into the murky depths and realised that the swimming pool was linked to the ocean – and the thousands of aliens gathering outside. Some of them had different coloured skin, he saw, as they pressed against the glass and peered into the negotiation chamber. Was that a reflection of their faction, he asked himself, or merely nothing more than a slight biological difference? There was no way to know.

He added it to the list of questions to ask when the aliens were more inclined to talk about their biology, then stepped backwards as a handful of aliens entered the pool. Several rose to the surface and eyed the humans with their massive eyes, others remained below the waters, as if they didn't want to be seen. Henry wondered if they were other negotiators or if they were something different. Perhaps the surfaced aliens each represented a different faction and the ones lurking below the waves were their aides or supporters. But there were more alien representatives than human ambassadors.

They must have mistaken the aides for additional ambassadors, he thought, slowly. *Or perhaps they just don't care about who has the most aides and other assistants. We would, because we often mistake perception for reality. But the aliens might have different ideas of how to proceed. They might not give a damn if we want to send a hundred aides and they want to send none...*

The lead alien waved one slimy hand. "We greet you," it said. As always, the voice was produced by a voder and seemed completely atonal. "You are welcome to our" – there was a gap, as if the translator couldn't find a suitable word – "and we will talk to you."

"We thank you," Ambassador Melbourne said. He was keeping it as simple as possible, hoping to avoid translation problems. "We will talk to you."

There was a long pause. Henry realised, slowly, that the aliens were discussing how to proceed amongst themselves, even though it was rude. But he'd already reasoned out that human concepts of polite or rude behaviour meant nothing to the aliens. They probably wouldn't notice if one of the diplomats picked his nose or scratched his ass at the negotiation table.

"You settled a world we had already settled," the alien said. There was no emotion in its voice, even though a human would be screaming accusations. "And one of your people killed one of our people."

"That is correct," Ambassador Melbourne said. "However, we were unaware of your presence, let alone your claim on Heinlein."

And you did nothing to mark your presence, Henry thought. The Heinlein settlers would never have landed if there had been anything to suggest the presence of intelligent life forms on the planet below. *Why didn't you put a satellite in orbit to tell us you were there?*

He shook his head. The aliens had been as surprised to encounter humanity as humans had been to encounter them. There probably hadn't seemed any *reason* to put a satellite in orbit or place a permanent guardship in the system. They'd just assumed the colony could grow normally and settle the surface area when they had finally built up a large population. Given how they bred, it was quite likely the alien population would have expanded faster than any comparable human population.

And there's another problem, he thought. *Will they simply out-breed us in future?*

"Our people did not realise that you were an intelligent race," Ambassador Melbourne said, drawing Henry's attention back to his words. "The death of one of your people was a tragic accident. Your response was equally tragic."

"That is correct," the alien said.

Henry frowned. Several of the underwater aliens didn't seem inclined to agree. One of them pulled the designated speaker under the water, where he was promptly surrounded by several other aliens who seemed to be making a point. The discussion – if discussion it was – lasted several minutes before the designated speaker returned to the surface. Clearly, Henry decided, whatever the underwater aliens had wanted to say had been too important to risk saying out loud, even when they had good reason to believe their words would be inaudible to human ears.

But we are recording everything, Henry thought. *They might have a point.*

"We believed your people to be intent on taking our world," the speaker said. "Your greeting was…unfriendly."

"Yes, it was," Ambassador Melbourne said. "But you managed to surprise two immature youths of our race. The tragedy might well have been inevitable."

"And you are older and wiser," the alien stated. Or was it a question? Henry couldn't tell, despite having seen the aliens far longer than any other human save Jill. "We believed your settlement of our space meant inevitable war."

"We had no knowledge of your presence," Ambassador Melbourne countered. "The settlers who first encountered you moved far beyond our settled sphere."

"That is correct," the alien said. "But there would have been contact eventually."

He was right, Henry knew. Heinlein might not have had any orbital presence, but it wouldn't have been long before a human ship sighted an alien ship in deep space. It might have gone better that way, he thought. There would have been a chance to use the First Contact package in the spirit of actually opening communication, rather than avoiding a war. And then they could have agreed to share the border worlds.

"Your race settles worlds quickly," the alien said. "The War Faction believed that war was inevitable. Can you argue otherwise?"

Ambassador Melbourne smiled, although it was unlikely the aliens understood the expression or the emotion behind it. "Does the War Faction speak for all of your people?"

"No," the alien stated.

"The colonists who made contact with you do not speak for all of us," Ambassador Melbourne said. "Had we known you were settled on that world, we would have either conceded it to you or come to an agreement about sharing settlement rights. Instead of attempting to talk, your War Faction started a war."

"Had they attempted to talk," the alien pointed out, "you would have known to prepare for war."

He was right, Henry knew. If humanity had *known* there was a potential alien threat, the last two years would have been spent building up the various spacefaring navies, developing new weapons and plotting tactics, rather than minor scrabbling between human powers.

"But that is the crux of the issue," Ambassador Melbourne said. "You never gave us a chance to discuss peace."

Which makes perfect sense for the War Faction, Henry thought. *If you believe war to be inevitable, and you literally cannot admit anything to the contrary, what's the point in abandoning the advantage of surprise?*

"None of us *knew* about the first encounter," the Ambassador pressed. "How could we have decided on peace or war?"

He took a breath. "You have factions of your own," he said. "Why did you assume we didn't have factions too?"

Henry rather suspected he understood. Humans tended to think in terms of 'us' and 'them.' And humans were always more sensitive to differences within 'us' rather than differences within 'them.' 'Us' might have dozens of subunits; 'them' was always one vast hive mind, utterly united in intent and purpose. The idea that there might be as many differences among 'them' as there were among 'us' was hard to grasp. And the aliens might have their own blind spots when it came to other forms of life.

"Mistakes were made," the alien conceded. "We talk now. But War Faction must be convinced to end the war."

"We propose a return to the pre-war situation," Ambassador Melbourne said. "If there are worlds along the border that have been settled by both of us, we can agree to share. You can have the oceans, we will have the land. Worlds settled by one race will remain the property of that race."

Henry wondered, briefly, just who would get the better part of that deal. There were only a couple of worlds with more land surface than oceans. But, at the same time, the aliens needed land to build their technology, just like humans. Their colonies on any shared worlds might not be able to develop past a certain point.

"There will need to be some surface habitation," the alien stated. "And there will be…"

He was tugged back under the water for another discussion. This time, several other aliens swam into the pool and joined the argument. Henry watched them swimming around in a complicated dance and wondered, suddenly, if the aliens ever considered swimming an art form. There was far more elegance in their movements below the waters than he'd ever realised. It was almost beautiful.

This time, a different alien rose to the surface. "There are settlements on worlds we took from you," it said. "Those settlement factions are to remain in place."

The Russians will love that, Henry thought, grimly. *So will the other occupied worlds.*

He blinked as the alien was yanked back below the waves before Ambassador Melbourne could formulate an answer. Henry glanced at the ambassadors, saw them muttering amongst themselves, then looked back at the water. This time, the swimming dance seemed almost ominous. It was difficult to tell the aliens apart, but it looked as though several factions were having second thoughts about the settlement rights.

Finally, a third alien – he thought – rose to the surface. "We have yet to agree amongst ourselves," it said. "But settlements must be protected."

"We can wait for you to determine what you want," Ambassador Melbourne offered. "Do you have suitable quarters for us?"

"Yes," the alien said. It must have sent a silent signal, for several aliens entered the room from the rear. "We will resume discussions in five of your hours."

Ambassador Melbourne offered no objection. Instead, he followed the aliens out of the building and back into the jungle. A handful of pre-fabricated buildings sat there, clearly of human design. The words on the side, in Spanish, suggested they'd been taken from Vera Cruz. Inside, the aliens had done their best to set everything up for their human guests, right down to food and water supplies. Henry had to admit they hadn't done a bad job, although it looked faintly odd. They hadn't quite known what they were doing.

"Check the water and food before you use any of it," he ordered one of the Marines. "And then scan for bugs…no, scan for bugs first."

He waited until the Marines pronounced the building clean, then sat down. "Do you think we made progress?"

"It's uncommon to have an opposing negotiator revising his demands as he goes along," Ambassador Melbourne said. "But in this case it may not be surprising. The aliens clearly don't think like us."

Henry nodded. "Just keep focused on the issue at hand," he advised. The aliens seemed to appreciate simplicity. "And hope the factions that want peace out-mass the factions that want war."

"And what happens," the Chinese Ambassador asked, "if the War Faction decides to continue the war on its own?"

"Let us hope the aliens have more sense," Ambassador Melbourne said, after an uncomfortable moment. If some of the reports from Earth were accurate, several human nations wanted to leave the war – and would have done so, if the aliens had offered them a way out. "And that we manage to convince them that the war will end in mutual disaster."

Henry sighed – humans rarely showed sense – and then walked into one of the back bedrooms. He'd promised Janelle he'd call her from the surface...and besides, he had a report to write. He might not have been an accredited diplomat, but he did have considerable experience with the aliens. And besides...he *wanted* to do something with his life before he left the family for good.

He smiled, remembering their last night together. It had been great, even though she'd been worried sick about him. And how could he blame her?

Just flying down to the surface was hair-raising, he thought. Several of the Ambassadors had been so unwell they hadn't said a word during the first meeting. *Who needs the aliens to kill us? Their planet does a damn fine job of it.*

CHAPTER
TWENTY EIGHT

Ted rose to his feet as Ambassador Melbourne was escorted into his cabin, after – according to the Marines – having a long shower and a change of clothes in his quarters. It was hard to blame him. The people down on the surface had compared the alien world to a tropical rainforest, with worse weather and better company. At least the aliens weren't trying to play games with the human representatives, the ambassadors had noted. They seemed to be playing it fair.

"Ambassador," he said. "Welcome back."

"I don't think they chose such an uncomfortable world on purpose, but it would have been very cunning if they had," Ambassador Melbourne said. "I haven't had such an unpleasant time since the last meeting in Arabia. At least this place doesn't have flies."

"That's one thing," Ted said. The biochemists had claimed the alien world was more or less habitable for humans, but he doubted many would want to settle there permanently. Both the weather and geology were completely screwed up by human standards. "And how are the talks?"

"I swear the aliens keep changing their demands to suit themselves," Ambassador Melbourne said. "They don't even let us answer before they alter them. It's weird."

He shrugged. "I know diplomats who just demand more and more," he added, "but the aliens sometimes demand more and sometimes demand less. It makes absolutely no sense."

"Their factions must keep arguing over just what they want from us," Ted said. Over the last four days, countless starships had passed through the system. He assumed they were transmitting messages from other alien factions. "What *do* they want?"

Ambassador Melbourne sighed. "The War Faction seems to need placating," he said. "The aliens want to keep their gains, including New Russia. In exchange for this, they will agree to peace – and that human settlers will be allowed to manage their own affairs. Or leave, if that's what they want to do. But the aliens want to keep the worlds themselves."

"Putting them in position to launch a second war on favourable terms if the peace breaks down," Ted said, slowly. New Russia was only two jumps from Earth. "And it lets the War Faction claim victory."

"We believe so," Ambassador Melbourne said. "It's what they want from us, Admiral. The occupied worlds may be the price for peace."

"Crap," Ted said. It was unlikely such a dishonourable peace would go down well with the British public – and the Russians would go ballistic. "Anything else?"

"No reparations from either side," Ambassador Melbourne said. "We won't help them rebuild Target One; they won't help us rebuild Earth. We're to share a handful of worlds along the border, but not Heinlein. That's to remain part of the War Faction's domain. One system, probably New Russia, is to be designated a meeting place for future discussions – they won't try to expand any further in our direction in exchange for us doing the same."

He sighed, again. "They weren't willing to discuss trade at the moment," he added. "I think they want to settle the war before discussing anything else."

"Wise of them," Ted said. "Do you have authority to make such an agreement?"

"More or less," Ambassador Melbourne said.

Ted's eyes narrowed. "More or less?"

"The Russians probably won't accept it," Ambassador Melbourne pointed out. "Several of the other occupied worlds have founders who won't be pleased either. But they won't be able to stop it, I think, without our support. And that support won't materialise."

Ted studied him for a long moment. "You're talking about betraying our allies," he said.

"You knew it was a possibility," Ambassador Melbourne reminded him. He shook his head. "Admiral...can we win the war?"

"I don't know," Ted confessed. The sheer level of alien industry in the system was staggeringly high. Given time, the aliens could simply out-produce humanity and win the war easily. And there was no way to change that without a few years of peace to rebuild from the war. "It seems unlikely."

"Without the...special weapon, it does," Ambassador Melbourne agreed. "I have discussed the matter extensively with the other ambassadors. We have agreed to accept the terms the aliens have proposed. The Russians will be compensated with settlement rights to another world on the other side of the human sphere and we will assist them in transferring the population of New Russia to New Russia The Second. We'll do the same for the other occupied worlds."

He paused. "Although I don't think that Mulligan's population would honestly notice if the aliens claimed their skies."

Ted nodded. Mulligan's population largely consisted of men and women who wanted to return to the days before industry. They'd largely been ignored by the aliens after their system had been occupied, according to the recon flights. They simply didn't have anything the aliens wanted, nor were they a threat. It was easy to imagine them just continuing to exist, largely unaware of the outside universe, while the aliens settled their seabed.

But what if the aliens start melting the icecaps, he thought. *They could drown the human settlers without even noticing what they'd done.*

"No," he said, slowly. "So...you intend to accept those terms?"

"Unless the aliens change them," Ambassador Melbourne said. "Again."

He snorted, rudely. "I am nervous about pushing the matter too far," he admitted. "A human diplomat would start with outrageous demands, then allow them to be pared down to something more acceptable. As long as his core demands were met, anything else would be gravy. But I don't think the aliens use the same tactic. I have the feeling that they're discussing it more intensely among themselves than we are...and that their faction consensus keeps shifting depending on who holds the upper hand at the moment. Trying to pare their demands down too far might shift the balance in favour of the War Faction."

Ted groaned. "you're trying to influence alien politics?"

Ambassador Melbourne gave him a surprised look. "You're an Admiral," he said. "Don't you know how much time and effort smaller nations put in to influencing British politics?"

"No," Ted said.

"The Americans used to get it worse," Ambassador Melbourne added. "Now...the smaller nations have nothing we want, so we force them to work hard for our favour."

"Politics," Ted said.

"Politics," Ambassador Melbourne agreed. "In this case, we don't want the aliens to get buyer's remorse shortly after making the deal with us. So...we offer them excellent terms and hope they're not greedier than the average human despot."

"How very reassuring," Ted said. He paused as a nasty thought struck him. "Have you discussed this with the observers?"

"Not yet, but we're going to need some of them to sign off on it," Ambassador Melbourne said. "Practically speaking, if America, France, China and us agree, the peace treaty will go through. However, it could lead to some very nasty diplomatic arguments."

"Or outright war," Ted warned. "The Russians will feel they've been sold out."

"We have contingency plans," Ambassador Melbourne said, confidently. "The Russians will be given plenty of compensation."

Ted had his doubts. The Russians had spent nearly eighty years and a substantial chunk of their GNP on turning New Russia into a going concern. Before the war, they'd even established a formidable industrial base in the system, although it didn't compare to Earth's or Target One. From a strictly unemotional point of view, the compensation might be sufficient, particularly given that they would have to invest in a great deal of rebuilding in any case. But he had the feeling the Russians would not be keen to simply abandon New Russia. It was part of their motherland now.

But what can they do about it? He asked himself. *They can't continue the war alone...*

"I hope the aliens keep the treaty," he said. He read Prince Henry's notes. The man had the makings of a worthwhile naval strategist, if he was allowed to remain in the military. "If they plan to buy a few years of peace before restarting the war...well, New Russia is only a handful of hops from Earth."

"Give us a few years and we will have plenty of nasty surprises ready for them," Ambassador Melbourne said, confidently. "And we will have time to prepare more defences around Earth and the other settled worlds."

"True," Ted agreed, reluctantly. "But I still think we need to be careful."

Ambassador Melbourne rose to his feet. "I need to get a nap, then discuss matters with the observers in the morning," he said. "Thank you for your time, Admiral."

Ted watched him walk through the hatch, then keyed his console. "Major Parnell, Captain Fitzwilliam, report to my office," he ordered. "Immediately."

The Marine must have run, Ted decided, as Major Parnell entered the office, barely five minutes after Ted had called him. Or perhaps he'd been somewhere nearer Officer Country than he'd been prepared to admit. Half of the Marines *were* keeping an eye on the alien diplomats and the Russians, after all. Ted rather wished he'd been able to draw more Marines from Earth before departing the planet.

"You wanted to see me, sir?"

"Yes, Major," Ted said. Captain Fitzwilliam joined them a moment later. "The Russians are about to be sold out."

He explained, bluntly. "We can expect a violent reaction," he concluded. "I want you and your men to be on alert."

"We should call a security drill," Parnell suggested. "We've been calling them at random during the trip, so they shouldn't trigger any alarms."

"Not here," Ted said. They were orbiting an alien world. A single mistake could accidentally restart the war. "But I want you to secure the ship as much as possible without sounding the alert. We need to be ready if the shit hits the fan."

"Risky," Fitzwilliam said. "The last thing we want is the aliens mistaking our internal problems for a planned attack."

Ted nodded. "But we have no choice," he said. "We *cannot* risk restarting the war."

Parnell frowned. "Admiral, with all due respect, we could secure the Russians now," he said, simply. "There would be no problem in taking and holding them as prisoners until we returned to Earth."

"But then there would be a diplomatic headache," Ted pointed out, flatly. "They'd claim their diplomatic immunity was violated. Unless we had a suitable excuse it could be used against us."

"The safety of the ship is at stake," Fitzwilliam said.

"*I know that*," Ted snapped. He took a breath, calming himself. "Captain, these are very delicate diplomatic negotiations. We don't dare risk an incident that can be used as an excuse to undermine them."

"I don't like it," Fitzwilliam confessed. "This seems far too much like we're baiting the Russians, trying to tempt them into revealing their hand."

Ted knew he had a point. From a dispassionate point of view, allowing the Russians to prove their hostile intent would make it easier to convince the diplomats on Earth to disregard the Russian objections. But it was also risky. The Russians would do *something* to upset the negotiations, he suspected, unless they intended to try to muster support on Earth. But what?

"We may not have a choice," Ted said. "There's just too much at stake."

"I hope you're right," Parnell said. He pulled himself to attention. "And we have a couple of platoons of Marines down on the surface. We're undermanned, sir."

Ted nodded, bitterly.

"Deputise crewmen, if necessary," he said. They'd planned counterboarding operations, with armed crewmen serving as first responders. "But make sure they're well-briefed."

"Aye, sir," Parnell said. "It will be a nightmare."

He paused. "Can I at least wipe the codes from the system? If they attempt to use them, Admiral, we'd know."

"Do it," Fitzwilliam urged.

"Please," Ted agreed. "And be ready for anything."

"Aye, sir," Parnell said.

He saluted, then left the office.

"I'm not happy about this, Admiral," Fitzwilliam said, flatly. "This is *my* ship. The final word on decisions concerning her safety is mine."

Ted glared at him, then lowered his eyes. He *wasn't* commander of *Ark Royal* any longer, no matter how much he might miss the days when he was her master. It was Fitzwilliam who commanded now, he knew, and Ted had stamped on his toes quite badly. But most Admirals wouldn't have merely moved up in rank while staying on the same ship. They would have transferred to another ship, just to break the emotional ties between them and their previous command. Ted hadn't done that, not when *Ark Royal* was the only effective fleet carrier in human service. He'd stayed on his former command.

"I know, Captain," he said. "And I am sorry."

"There are too many things at stake here, Admiral," Fitzwilliam added. "I think you need to be more careful about balancing them. That's why you have subordinates."

"*Yes*, Captain," Ted snapped.

He sighed. "See to your ship, Captain," he ordered. "And pray that we manage to get through the next few days alive."

Captain Fitzwilliam turned and left. The stress was getting to him, Ted saw, but it was getting to all of them. Fighting the war had been much simpler, even when he'd been trying to balance competing national imperatives – and egos – during Operation Nelson. Now, the slightest mistake could prove disastrous.

When we get home, I'll transfer my flag, he thought. *Or take that desk job, if the war comes to an end. They won't let me command another fleet.*

It wasn't a comforting thought. He was growing too old to command a fleet, particularly without the seasoning the more conventional officers had had. And yet he would regret returning to Earth and spending the rest of his days there. Shaking his head, Ted returned to his paperwork – and his silent prayers. One tiny mistake…and all hell could break loose.

———

Years ago, Odette Roma had made one tiny, but fatal mistake. She'd developed a gambling habit, one that had threatened to consume her life. Her salary as a Personal Assistant in the French Ministry of Foreign Affairs and International Development – the Diplomatic Service – hadn't been anything like enough to cover her losses. She'd faced utter ruin when someone had arrived to offer to pay her debts, in exchange for tiny pieces of intelligence from her work.

There had been no choice, she told herself. If she admitted her gambling losses to her superiors, they would brand her a security risk and transfer her somewhere less prestigious, if they didn't simply fire her and make sure she was blacklisted everywhere in Europe. But if she took the money, she would be able to cover her debts...and she wouldn't have to give out much intelligence. Her contact swore he worked for a corporation. She wasn't exactly committing *treason* if she was merely helping a French corporation, was she?

But she knew better now, after five years of sending pieces of ever more sensitive information to her contact. She wasn't working for a corporation, but a foreign power – and she was hopelessly compromised. If the truth ever came out, she would never see the light of day again. She'd be buried in an asteroid penal colony and carefully interrogated by the *Direction centrale du renseignement intérieur* until they knew everything she'd told her contact – and then shot her for high treason. Odette had considered suicide and she'd considered making a clean breast of it, but she'd known it would be the end. How could she face her family and co-workers once they knew what she'd done?

She looked down at the datapad in front of her. Ambassador Pierre Gasconne was a fat overweight tub of lard with wandering hands – she'd been ordered to do whatever it took to ensure she was attached to the Ambassador when he departed Earth - but she had to admit he was a skilled diplomat. France wouldn't do *too* badly out of the treaty the ambassadors had hammered out, even if it was very far from perfect. But other powers would be far worse off.

Her instructions were clear. If she learned anything about the planned treaty, anything at all, she was to copy it to an address on the diplomatic datanet. She knew better than to try to trace it back to her contact. In truth, she wasn't entirely sure who she was working for. But there was no choice. If she failed them, she knew, her career would be utterly destroyed.

Carefully, she copied the data from the pad into one of the spare terminals, then transmitted it to the address she'd been given. Moments later, the terminal automatically wiped itself blank, erasing all traces of the message. It was a standard security precaution when travelling on an insecure starship. Who knew who might raid her cabin when she was eating in the mess? But it hardly mattered. She knew the message was on its way to her contact...

Shaking her head, she sat down at the table and started to work through the proposed treaty, line by line. It was her job, after all. And her contact evidently didn't mean France any harm – or so she told herself. They could have used the intelligence she'd sent them against France quite easily, if that had been what they'd had in mind. Instead, they'd done almost nothing as far as she could tell. Perhaps it wasn't such a bad bargain after all. Perhaps she was even helping France by sending her contact intelligence...

Or perhaps she was just deluding herself.

She'd never be allowed to quit, she knew. Her contact wouldn't let her resign or vanish into the underworld. Resigning without his permission would be repaid by betrayal. Her reputation would be destroyed, her life shattered and she would never see the outside world again. No, she had no choice. She had to do whatever they wanted her to do.

What other choice did she have?

CHAPTER
TWENTY NINE

One of the lessons of Russian history, Peter Golovanov had been told, was that weakness invited betrayal and attack. The Russians had looked weak in 1941 and paid the price when Hitler's forces had stormed across the border, leaving a trail of wreckage in their wake; they'd looked weak in 1991 and had been forced to watch, helplessly, as Western political unions moved eastwards towards Moscow. Despite persistent financial problems, the Russian Government had poured money into becoming a spacefaring power, struggling desperately to keep up with the other spacefaring nations. One of the *other* lessons of Russian history was that the only way to earn respect was through military power.

But that power was gone now, he knew.

The Russian Government had invested far more of its capital in New Russia than anyone outside the country realised. In the long term, they'd planned, the vast majority of the ethnic Russian population would move to New Russia, which would become a new homeland free of the curses of the past. But New Russia was gone now – and with it the results of years of investment. The only thing preventing a general economic crash that would have wiped out the Russian economy once and for all were the infusions of liquid wealth from the other spacefaring nations – and those, he had been told, would not last. Russia could not afford to lose New Russia. There was just no way they could develop another world with the resources they had on hand. Nor could they afford to build up the military strength needed to recover the planet on their own.

He looked down at the draft treaty and swore, under his breath. The Russian Government had refused to send an Ambassador to the meeting, knowing it would force them to either concede New Russia permanently or break ranks with the other spacefaring powers. They'd made their feelings clear, Peter had been told. But it was also clear that they were about to be betrayed. The other colonies were minor investments, a few billion American dollars worth of infrastructure…but New Russia was different. There was nothing that could compensate the Russian Government for what it had lost in the war.

And his orders were clear. In the event of a betrayal, he and his team were to launch a final attack on the aliens. They knew it was likely suicide, but they would carry out their orders without fail. The price for being what they were, cybernetic infiltrators, was being programmed to obey orders, provided they came from the correct authority. He could alter his tactics to suit himself, but not disobey outright.

It could cost the human race everything, he knew, but he understood. The Russian Government would never accept permanent subordination – and that was what they would be facing, if the treaty was passed without further argument. At best, there would be decades before they could count themselves as a first-rank spacefaring power; at worst, the chaos on the Russian border would sweep northwards and eventually overwhelm civilisation. He thought of the barbarity of the Central Asians and shuddered. Better to die hacking and slashing at the aliens then be condemned to a slow lingering death.

He rose for his feet, then reached for the communicator. It was fortunate that the British had respected diplomatic immunity, for he'd been able to bring a considerable amount of equipment onto the ship with only a handful of cursory scans. Avoiding detection had been relatively simple. All he needed to do now was start the operation and hope everything went according to plan.

And if it doesn't, he thought, *at least we'll show them that Russian interests always have to be taken into account.*

There were people, including some of her co-workers, who would have considered Galina Bezukladnikov a monster. She had no conscience. Indeed, any traces of conscience had been carefully edited out of her by the procedures that had cleared her to work in the Russian Biological Warfare Centre years ago. She'd gone into the operating room a bright young woman with a boyfriend and a loving family; she'd left a scientist so dedicated to scientific research that she'd ended her relationship with her boyfriend and moved everything she wanted to keep into the complex. But there hadn't been much she'd wanted to keep. Her old life no longer really existed, even in her own mind.

The challenge of creating a bioweapon designed to attack the aliens had been thrilling, about the only thing that did thrill her these days. She'd worked hard as part of the joint research team, often pushing the limits much further than they'd considered possible. But then, she had no moral or ethical doubts about her work. It was merely a scientific puzzle that had to be solved, like some of the other riddles she'd tried to solve over the years. The Russian Government wanted a disease that would attack everyone who wasn't of Slavic descent; Galina had worked on the program, heedless of the dangers. It was just another job for her, after they'd tampered with her mind. She didn't even care that they'd harvested eggs and raw genetic material from her body in hopes of producing the next generation of scientists.

She glanced down at her wristcom as the message arrived, then carefully removed the device and dropped it on her desk. The holographic representation of the bioweapon flickered, then vanished as she cancelled the display. It was a beautiful piece of work – pride in their creation was almost all the emotion she was allowed – but there was no time to become lost in admiration. All that mattered was that there was no need to try to build safeguards into its genetic structure. It would burn its way through the alien biochemistry like a forest fire, with no hope of a cure being discovered in time to save the aliens from certain death.

Opening her secure drawer, she removed a case and opened it, revealing a pair of stunners and one full-sized pistol. Keeping them hidden had been a challenge, but every scientist had their own personal workspace and no one else was allowed to use it. Galina would have rolled her eyes, if she'd been able to care enough to sneer. She had spent months taking time off her work to learn how to shoot properly, even though it wasn't her strong point. But then, she was already inside the defences. No one else could get into the biological warfare laboratory without permission.

She hefted one of the stunners, then walked around her desk and through the hatch. Outside, four technicians – all British – sat at their desks, refining future versions of the bioweapon in the event it became necessary. Galina lifted the stunner, then opened fire, zapping all four of them before they even knew they were under attack. She watched them fall off their chairs and hit the deck, then walked dispassionately around the compartment until she reached the hatch to Doctor Russell's office. He was fond of her, she knew; his eyes followed her sometimes, just like some of her superiors back on Russia. But she had no feelings about his attentions, one way or the other. All that mattered was her work.

The hatch hissed open and she stepped through, drawing the pistol from her belt. It looked much more intimidating, she'd been told, than the stunners, even though she didn't dare actually kill him until her mission was complete. Doctor Russell looked up at her and smiled in welcome, an expression that vanished the moment he saw the pistol in her hand. She pointed the weapon at his head and motioned for him to stand.

"Galina," he said, shocked. "What are you doing?"

"Stand," Galina ordered. "Do *not* attempt to sound the alert."

She motioned for him to stand against the bulkhead, then pressed the weapon into his back as she searched him roughly, removing his wrist-com, terminal and collection of pens and pieces of paper. He'd always been scribbling down notes as they'd talked their way through the development process, something Galina had always found inefficient. If the Russian Government hadn't needed the British DNA samples to construct the bioweapon, she was sure, they would have developed one of their own far faster. And they wouldn't have needed such a complex plot to actually *deploy* the damned thing. But the British had managed to keep firm control over the living aliens...

"Come with me," she ordered. "And keep your hands on your head."

He was shaking as he walked back out of the cabin and into the research chamber. Galina noted his terrified movements with some irritation, although part of her mind was pleased. If he was scared, unlike her or anyone else with her conditioning, it was much less likely he'd try something heroic. He almost stopped dead when he saw the stunned technicians, gaping at them as if he thought they were dead. Galina almost rolled her eyes in annoyance. She'd seen co-workers die slowly, a moment's carelessness costing them their lives. There was no point in whining over stunned co-workers when they could easily be dead.

"Galina," Russell said, "why are you doing this?"

Galina prodded him with the barrel of the gun, forcing him towards the large sealed hatch that led into the bioweapon vault. If she could have opened it without Russell, she would have stunned or killed him and opened the hatch herself, but the safety precautions insisted they needed two people to open the hatch. A normal human would have cursed. She just took it in his stride.

"I won't open the hatch," Russell said. He stopped, trying to look stubborn despite his obvious fear. "The bioweapon…"

Galina pointed the gun at his leg and fired, once. Russell screamed in pain as the bullet shattered his bone, sending him falling to the deck. Pain – real physical pain – had never been part of his life. It hadn't really been part of Galina's either, she had to admit, but she'd had her pain sensitivity modified too. Pain was nothing more than a distraction from her duty.

"If you refuse to cooperate, I will shoot you again, then leave you to bleed out on the deck," she hissed. "And then my comrades will do truly awful things to the other technicians."

Russell stared at her, his eyes wild. Galina sighed, pulled him to his feet and dragged him over to the hatch, leaving a trail of blood on the deck. Russell didn't even try to struggle as she pushed his palm against the sensor, which accepted his code. She added her own code a moment later, opening the first hatch. Inside, a keyboard glowed in the semi-darkness.

"Enter your code," she ordered. She hauled him up and held him in front of the keyboard. Behind them, the outer hatch slid closed. "Enter your code or the pain will become a great deal worse."

"Fuck…" Russell said. "I…"

Galina slapped him. She didn't have time to let him go into shock. Perhaps she should just have twisted his arm instead, but that would have meant letting go of the gun. Russell stared at her, his eyes clearing, then looked at the panel. They didn't have long before the security systems realised that no secondary code had been entered and sounded the alert, then put the entire complex into lockdown. It would be disastrous.

Russell weakly reached out and input his code. Galina didn't pray, but she braced herself to kill him and then herself if he inputted the wrong code. If the system locked down, they would both be trapped until the entire complex was reopened by the Royal Marines. They'd find the stunned bodies and know that something had gone badly wrong. But the secondary hatch clicked open, revealing a waft of cold air. Inside, the bio-weapon was waiting.

She dropped Russell to the deck and strode over to the first set of vials. It was a truly brilliant weapon in its own right, she knew, although she also knew that anyone with a conscience would consider it thoroughly horrific. Deployment wouldn't be a problem, not as long as they had a shuttle and the correct ID codes. And it was completely harmless to human life. She could smash a dozen vials on Earth and nothing would happen. Unless, of course, the aliens took the planet and turned it into a colony.

This will ensure we never lose our worlds, she thought. The bioweapon would slaughter any alien or alien-derived lifeform that set foot on an infected world. *And the aliens will know to leave us alone in future.*

Galina pocketed four of the vials, then took one last look at Russell. He was clutching his leg, completely unaware of the outside world. She considered killing him for a long moment, then dismissed the thought as pointless. Instead, she walked back out of the hatch and closed it behind her. The chamber would remain sealed until someone opened it, but she was fairly sure he would survive. And if he didn't…his work was already done. She didn't give a damn about his future.

She strode through the outer chamber and then through the decon-tamination compartment, without bothering with the procedure. It was useless, she knew; they were hardly working with anything that could harm humanity. And besides, the alien diplomats on the ship shouldn't know anything about what was happening in the lab. If they did come to visit, they'd wind up being used as test subjects. It felt odd not to have live test subjects – she'd used political prisoners and other undesirables in

Russia – but the computer simulations were excellent. The bioweapon was completely lethal – and completely incurable. Or so they hoped.

Dropping her lab coat in a rack, she pulled on a tunic and settled back to wait. It wouldn't be long now.

———

The interior of *Ark Royal* was confusing as hell, but Peter had one advantage the British might not realise he possessed. It hadn't been *that* long since a team of Russian commandos had deployed on the ship and they'd taken the opportunity to map the ancient craft's interior as thoroughly as possible. Some details were lacking – the commandos hadn't been allowed anywhere near the bridge or main engineering – but it was complete enough for him to mentally fill in the blanks. And besides, as an observer, he had been given a tour of the ship along with the ambassadors.

He glanced into a compartment and smiled as he saw a junior crewman inside, folding clothing. It was one of the details of military life civilians never considered; *someone* had to wash the uniforms and do the ship's laundry, after all. Peter slipped inside, came up behind the crewman before he had a change to blink and snapped his neck effortlessly. The crewman let out a groan and collapsed like a sack of potatoes. Peter hastily undid his uniform jacket and trousers, removing them from the corpse, then pulled them onto his own body. A quick glance in the mirror revealed that he looked like a sloppy but passable crewman. His nametag read BUCKLEY.

Picking up the laundry basket and positioning it to cover the nametag, he walked out of the compartment and headed up towards Officer Country, passing several other crewmen on the way. Hardly anyone paid attention to him, which wasn't surprising. No one ever noticed the help, he knew; the FSB had always learned more from janitors or maids than it had from higher-profile spies. It was astonishing what people would say when they considered themselves alone, as if their servants were far from human. He passed through the hatch into Officer Country, then paused and checked his watch. He was five minutes ahead of schedule…

He hesitated. Timing was everything; it wouldn't be long before their actions were very noticeable, no matter how much they sneaked around. And then all hell would break loose. The ship would go into lockdown, the Royal Marines would search the interior inch by inch for the Russians and they'd be wiped out. Eventually. They could do a great deal of damage before they died, he knew, but destroying the carrier had never been part of the plan. The human race was going to need *Ark Royal*.

He pushed the thought aside. There was no time for woolgathering.

Can't afford to waste time here, he thought, as he strode towards the Captain's cabin. *I'd be noticed and ordered to go find something else to do.*

He stopped outside the solid hatch, then keyed the switch.

———

James had been reading the latest tactical report on the system when the hatch opened. It didn't sit well with him to consider ending the war on such poor terms, but he was starting to think the human race didn't have a choice. The aliens might well have a larger industrial base than humanity and, if they did, the war would be ended when they drowned humanity in carriers, starfighters and other warships. If the aliens hadn't been so diverse themselves, he suspected, the war would have been lost by now. Instead, they had a chance for peace.

The Russians will be furious, he thought. *But what choice do we have?*

Uncle Winchester would probably be relieved, he considered. And so would most of the British population. They needed time to rebuild, to establish more colonies and learn the lessons of the war. Then, perhaps, they could renegotiate the terms of the treaty. Or find other ways to work with the aliens. If both sides had learned a great deal from merely fighting each other, who knew what they could discover in peacetime?

The hatch bleeped. James frowned, then called "Open."

He looked up, surprised, as a crewman stepped into his cabin, carrying a laundry basket. But his steward handled his laundry…and the crewman was wearing a very ill-fitting uniform and…

It was too late. He saw the gun in the man's hand an instant before the intruder fired.

CHAPTER
THIRTY

"Major," the tech snapped. "Someone attempted to use the codes!"

Major Charles Parnell swore. He'd hoped to have more time to get his forces organised before the shit hit the fan. As it was, he was still badly undermanned and he'd barely managed to get a handful of armed crewmen rounded up to reinforce the Marines. Against alien boarders it might not have been a problem, but against humans it was just *asking* for a friendly fire incident. *That* was the last thing they needed.

"Shit," he said. "What did they try to do?"

"I'm not sure," the tech said. "I think they tested the codes and discovered they weren't responsive."

Charles thought, fast. "Declare a security alert," he ordered. "And put the entire ship into lockdown. No one goes anywhere without the right authorisation."

"Aye, sir," the tech said.

"Then call the deployed platoons," Charles added. "They are to move in and secure the diplomatic zone. Treat the diplomats gently, but firmly."

He looked down at the display as the ship's alarms started to howl. There were seven Russians on the ship – eight, if one counted the researcher assigned to the bioweapon…he swore, violently, as he realised what the Russians might have in mind. The bioweapon was humanity's ace in the hole, the secret weapon that could be used to threaten the aliens with utter catastrophe if they didn't agree to reasonable peace terms. And the Russians had been very involved with producing and testing the weapon.

You fucking idiot, he told himself. *How the hell did you miss that?*

"Redeploy Platoon Two," he ordered. Armed and armoured, Platoon One should have no problem handling unarmed diplomats. "They are to secure the biological research laboratory and put it into complete lockdown. I want every one of those damn scientists accounted for."

———

Peter muttered a curse under his breath as the alarms started to howl, an automated voice informing the crew that a full internal lockdown was now in effect. He'd assumed they wouldn't remain undetected indefinitely, but the British had caught on faster than he'd expected. They must have been watching their computer network for signs of trouble, he thought, as he knelt down next to the badly wounded Captain. Or perhaps the virus had triggered a security alert. Using it had always been chancy.

"Hold still," he muttered, as he produced the monofilament knife and held it against the Captain's palm. "This will probably hurt."

He sliced into the palm, digging through blood and gore for the implant. It was tiny, no larger than a penny, but it was the key to the operation. He pulled it free and pressed it against his own hand, making sure it was still covered in the Captain's blood. As long as it thought it was still working for its rightful owner, using it shouldn't trigger alarms. Peter straightened up, pointed his gun at the Captain's forehead, then decided against it. There was no point in wasting more bullets. The Captain would bleed to death if he didn't get medical assistance quickly, in any case.

Straightening up, he walked out of the hatch and walked down the corridor. The hatch at the far end was sealed, unsurprisingly, but he pushed the stolen implant against the sensor and it hissed open on command. The Captain had full authority on his ship, even to override a lockdown if necessary. Smiling to himself, Peter kept walking. The countdown was moving faster now.

———

259

"Admiral, they attempted to use the codes," Parnell reported. "The entire ship is in lockdown."

He hesitated. "And they may be going for the bioweapon."

Ted swore. He'd missed the bioweapon…but it made sense. If the Russians wanted to upset the peace terms, using the bioweapon would work perfectly. Either the aliens would be exterminated or the war would resume, more ruthless than ever before. And now his ship was under threat…

"Sweep up the diplomats," he ordered. "And then secure the entire ship."

"I've already got a team heading to the bioweapon lab," Parnell said. "But the security systems there may have been compromised. There's a Russian researcher as part of the team."

"They can't be compromised without two researchers," Ted said. He'd checked the security precautions himself. "One person can't override them alone."

Parnell snorted. "They've used blackmail, sir," he said. "They could have someone else compromised…or they could just force someone to open the hatches at pistol point. Not everyone has enough courage to refuse."

Ted went cold. "Lockdown the entire ship," he ordered. "Everything has to be completely secured."

———

Polly MacDonald barely heard the alarm as she sat, wearing nothing apart from a pair of bikini panties, in front of a handful of aliens. The heat and moisture in the air made wearing anything else inadvisable, although she still felt embarrassed to show herself to anyone human. She doubted the aliens knew or cared that she was practically naked. Indeed, they were naked themselves.

She smiled, remembering some of the more absurd suggestions for what the aliens wanted from the war. Women was one of them; the theorists, who had watched too many stupid movies for their own good, had speculated that the aliens wanted to crossbreed with humans to produce a superior form of life. Given that alien and human DNA were completely different – that had been established right from the moment the first alien bodies had been recovered – it was clear that it was biologically impossible. But that hadn't stopped an increasing number of silly stories – *I Married An Alien* was the tamest she'd seen – spreading through the datanet.

"We talk to solve problems," the alien said. It's companions said nothing audible to human ears, but the sensors picked up their words. "We discuss every last detail before we proceed."

That, Polly decided, might explain the somewhat scatterbrained approach the aliens had taken to diplomatic meetings. Instead of deciding what they wanted beforehand, the aliens had changed their minds several times, probably because their internal consensus had kept shifting from one point to another. On one hand, she could see the value of having the most comprehensive consensus possible; on the other, she could easily see it causing another war in the future. To humans, it suggested that they weren't serious about negotiating.

She looked up, sharply, as the hatch hissed open. It wasn't locked – the crew didn't want to convince the alien guests that they were actually prisoners – but Polly had thought there was an understanding that she wouldn't be interrupted unless she called for help. The last time someone had entered the chamber she'd covered her breasts – and then had to explain her reflexive motion to the aliens. It had been an embarrassing and completely pointless conversation.

The man who had entered the chamber was carrying a large gun in one hand and a box in the other. Polly opened her mouth, but he shot the lead alien before she could say a word. She gasped in horror, which only succeeded in drawing his attention to her. His eyes were cold and utterly dispassionate as he looked her over, then returned to shooting aliens. The aliens themselves either tried to swim away – a hopeless task – or lunged forward. Polly, frozen to the spot, could only watch in helpless disbelief as the aliens were slaughtered.

And then the man pointed his gun at her. Polly watched him, too shocked to feel anything, as he studied her, then turned and walked away. She started to shake the moment the hatch closed behind him, clutching at one of the alien bodies. It felt leathery against her bare skin…

Gathering herself, she reached for her communicator and hit the emergency alarm. But no one came.

———

"Security alert," the tech said. "The alien diplomatic lounge."

Charles nodded, grimly. There were meant to be several Marines keeping an eye on the aliens, but he'd withdrawn most of them to prepare to swoop down and seize the Russians before they could act. His mistake, he cursed himself, silently promising his dead men that he would avenge them. They'd clearly underestimated the Russian capacity for deception – or skill at hiding their talents. If they'd done so well, they were commandos or other special operatives. The Russians were masters at producing unstoppable men.

And they were clearly trying to sow as much confusion as possible.

"Move the reinforcements to secure the bridge and the other priority-one locations," he ordered. "And tell the team heading towards the biological lab that they're to haul ass."

The tech nodded once. "Aye, sir," he said.

Charles ground his teeth in frustration. The Russians had been tipped off in advance, he knew, which meant there was *another* spy on board. Probably someone assigned to the diplomatic sector, he guessed, and probably one of the diplomatic assistants. They'd have the access to see the treaty, even if it wasn't shared with the observers just yet. One of them had sent the data to the Russians and triggered their operation.

And there were too many problems and he couldn't react to them all with the forces he had on hand.

"Sir, Midshipwoman Jenkins just raised the alarm," the tech said. "The Captain's been shot!"

Another diversion, Parnell asked himself, *or something more sinister*?

"Tell her to do what she can for him," Parnell ordered. Under lockdown, the bridge crew wouldn't be allowed to leave the bridge, even for a piss. Jenkins – he vaguely remembered her as a young officer, still wet behind the ears – would need help as quickly as possible. "And order a medical team to get to Officer Country as quickly as possible."

He cursed, wishing he was out there with his men. It had been *so* much simpler on Target One. There, they'd known the enemy and how to engage him. Here…he wasn't even sure where the enemy were or how many of them there were, save that they were on the ship. It would take far too long to sweep the entire hull, sealing corridors, passageways and maintenance tubes off as they moved. But what other choice did he have?

"Start working through the sealed compartments," he ordered, bluntly. "I want their inhabitants to sound off, then remain where they are. It should shorten our search time."

"Aye, sir," the tech said.

Parnell rubbed his shaved head. This was *not* going to be easy.

———

They hadn't realised he'd injured – perhaps killed – the Captain, Peter decided, as he made his way through a series of sealed hatches. A handful of crewmen, trapped in sealed corridors, stared at him in disbelief, too stunned to do anything before he stunned them and kept moving. There was no point in trying to use the intership cars. The Royal Marines would have deactivated them as soon as the lockdown began and using the Captain's override would certainly trigger alarms. And then they'd check with the Captain and redirect the intership car somewhere they could hold it until the time came to take him prisoner.

He slipped through another set of doors and smiled as he walked towards the biological research centre. Doctor Galina Bezukladnikov was standing in front of the hatch, her face utterly expressionless. She was beautiful, in a way, with long blonde hair and a perfect patrician face, but also dead to the world. Peter had heard rumours that women like her, reprogrammed to meet the state's requirements, were sometimes used to service the high-ranking officials in the Kremlin. Why not? A programmed woman – or man, if the official's tastes ran that way – would be calm, obedient and utterly discreet. Unless the FSB had done the reprogramming…

You couldn't trust anyone in Russia completely, Peter knew, if you wanted to work in government. Trust was a dangerous liability.

"These are the vials," Galina said. Her voice was as flat and cold as her eyes. "One vial, released onto the planet's atmosphere, will be sufficient. Tests have proven that the world has been adapted for alien life forms, thus they share the same biochemistry. It will spread rapidly through the planet's ecological system."

"Good," Peter said. He'd used bioweapons before on a mission that had never been revealed to anyone outside the Kremlin. "How long before the disease takes effect?"

"One month," Galina informed him. "There will be ample time for it to spread undetected."

Peter took the vials and pocketed them. "Stay here," he ordered. Galina was important enough not to risk, but he had a feeling the British wouldn't be interested in taking prisoners after their Captain had been killed. "Wipe the databanks completely, make sure there's no hope of a cure, then hold out as long as you can."

He turned, then started to make his way back down the corridor. It wouldn't be long before the Royal Marines arrived, even though they'd have to check every compartment they passed for hostiles. His remaining forces, scattered through the ship, would be doing what they could to keep the British busy. But without access to the Captain's ID codes, they'd have real problems getting beyond a few compartments...

Shaking his head, he forced himself to run. Time was definitely not on his side.

———

"One of the Russians attacked Main Engineering," Sergeant Potter reported. "We killed him as he broke through the hatch, sir."

"Good," Charles said. Eight Russians on the ship; two dead. That left six. At least two more of them were launching other divisions, forcing him to divert his forces to deal with them. "Keep the compartment sealed, then wait."

He cursed under his breath. Surprise attacks were always treacherous; there were always moments when the entire situation seemed utterly beyond repair, as if chaos had swept up and taken over the world. It took years of training and experience to look beyond the chaos, to realise that the smoke and noise was no substitute for firepower and solid protections, but he had enough experience to handle it. Or so he told himself.

"Keep sweeping forward," he ordered. He clicked a switch and displayed a holographic diagram of the carrier's interior. Entire sections had been sealed and deemed cleared, for the moment. The crew trapped inside them would be unable to help or hinder the Royal Marines as they swept the remainder of the ship. But what did the Russians have in mind?"

His communicator buzzed. "Major, this is Hawthorne," a voice said.

"Go ahead," Charles said.

"We had to break into the biological compartment," Hawthorne reported. "The Russian woman fired on us, so we ended up stunning her. I think the entire compartment has been thoroughly trashed. The consoles look like they'd detonated their self-destruct charges."

"Secure the woman; take no chances," Charles ordered. He'd seen enough female special operatives to know that they could be deadlier than their male counterparts. Men tended to underestimate women, particularly if they wore revealing clothes and simpered at all the right moments. The file said that Doctor Galina Bezukladnikov was a harmless biological researcher, but the Russians had lied before. They certainly hadn't declared the presence of their commandos attached to the observation team. "And then…"

He broke off. "What happened to the other researchers?"

"Four of them are stunned," Hawthorne said. "The others are presumably in their own quarters…"

There was a pause. "There's a bloody trail leading to the inner vault," he added. "I think someone used his ID to break into the chamber, then left him there."

"Get the other researchers up and force them to open the chamber," Charles ordered, although he knew it might already be too late. The Russians had had one of their people on the research team. They could have killed the other researchers already. "And have a medical team standing by."

He thought fast. The Russians had abandoned their mole, which meant…they'd already taken the bioweapon. But where were they taking it?

They'd want to deploy it, he thought. *They'd need to go to the shuttlebay and take a shuttle.*

"Redeploy Platoon Four," he ordered. The closest shuttlebay to the biological warfare compartment was quite some distance, but a trained commando could cover it in minutes. "They are to seal the shuttlebay completely, then deactivate the shuttles."

He paused. "And pass the word to the other shuttlebays," he added. There was always a maintenance crew assigned to each shuttlebay, even during lockdown. "They are to shut down their shuttlecraft completely."

———

"The Captain was shot," Doctor Hastings reported. "Admiral, they also hacked his implant out of his palm."

Ted cursed. "Pass the word to the Marines," he said. He had to admire the idea, even though he would have dismissed it if someone had suggested it to him. The lockdown, designed to keep the Russians from running amok, actually worked in their *favour*. His forces had to clear each compartment and reopen the hatches before making progress. "And then lock out the Captain's command overrides."

"It can't be done," Janelle reminded him. "The Captain's overrides are hardwired into the system."

Ted cursed, understanding – finally – why the Russians had wanted the access codes. If they'd had the codes they could have crashed the entire datanet – and then used the Captain's ID to bring it back up, selectively locking out the Royal Marines and the remainder of the ship's crew. The Old Lady's internal security precautions would have been turned against her legitimate owners.

"Then track his ID codes," Ted ordered. "They'll need to use them if they want to get anywhere."

But where were they going? The shuttlebays were sealed. There was no other way off the ship, was there?

He smirked in honest admiration. Oh yes there was. And the Russians were devious bastards for thinking so far ahead. Their first blackmail victim had been the CAG, after all, someone who could give them the access they needed.

"Redeploy the Marines," he ordered. "Tell them to secure the starfighter launch tubes."

CHAPTER
THIRTY ONE

"You know," Rose said, "we should have a lockdown more often."

Kurt snorted. The moment they'd heard the alarms, they'd jumped into Kurt's office before the hatch sealed, trapping them in the compartment. Alone, they hadn't wasted time; they'd stripped, made love and then dressed again before the alert could come to an end. It was in direct breach of the Admiral's orders, but after so long he found it hard to care.

"I think we probably shouldn't," he said. There had been no call for starfighter pilots since they'd entered orbit, but he'd kept his crews on alert anyway. Who knew when the shit would hit the fan? "What happens if we come under attack now?"

Rose shrugged. "Do you have any idea what this is?"

"No," Kurt answered. But the sinking feeling in his chest suggested one possible answer, no matter how much he tried to avoid it. The Russians were finally making their move. "It could be anything…"

The hatch, which had been locked, hissed open. Kurt started, half-expecting to see Marines and a pissed-off Admiral, then stared as he saw two men wearing ill-fitting uniforms. One of them was pointing a gun at him; the other was carrying a large roll of duct tape. He stared, then climbed to his feet as one of the intruders motioned with the gun.

"Get over against the wall," he ordered, in a thinly-accented voice. "Girl; lie down on the ground, face down. Put your hands behind your back."

Kurt glared at him, but saw no alternative. As soon as he was away from Rose, the man with the duct tape knelt down and used the tape to tie her hands behind her. Moments later, he'd wrapped her ankles together, then used a final piece of tape to cover her mouth. Her angry eyes glared daggers at the man as he searched her, removed anything that could possibly be used as a weapon, then rolled her into the corner. She was so tightly wrapped she could barely move.

"You're going to come with us," the leader said. He met Kurt's eyes. "And if you don't cooperate, we'll be forced to hurt your girlfriend."

The blackmailers, Kurt thought, numbly. He offered no resistance as he was searched, then his hands bound behind his back with tape. One of the blackmailers pointed him towards the hatch, the other dropped a black object next to Rose and then checked the remainder of the office before following Kurt and his captor out into the corridor. Kurt wanted to ask what the object had been, but neither of the men looked communicative. He barely had a chance to throw Rose a helpless look before the hatch hissed closed, blocking his view of her angry face. She hated being helpless more than anything else.

I'm sorry, he thought.

Outside, there was a body lying on the deck. Kurt barely had time to realise that it had been stunned before the blackmailers pushed him down the corridor, heading for the starfighter launch bay. During lockdown, Kurt knew, it would be almost deserted apart from the starfighter pilots in the launch tubes. They wouldn't be able to leave until the alert came to an end.

He braced himself, then opened his mouth. "What…what are you doing?"

"We're getting off this ship," one of the men said. The other one merely grunted, then elbowed Kurt in the back, hard. "And you're going to help us launch a starfighter."

Kurt stared at him. "Are you mad?"

"You can open the emergency hatch," the man said. "And you will. Or your girlfriend will die and your reputation will be ruined."

"You're not with her," Kurt said. "I…"

The man produced a small terminal. "We left a bomb next to her," he said, darkly. "One push of this button" – he pointed – "will detonate it and she will die. I suggest you behave yourself and the two of you will come out alive."

Kurt thought desperately as they stepped into the launch bay. They had to be mad...unless they really did intend to blow the emergency hatches. But opening them would require the Captain's override codes and he doubted the blackmailers had them. And even if they did succeed, where would they go? The aliens were the only other force in the system. Had they been working for the aliens all along? Or had a stealthed warship followed them all the way from the solar system? It didn't seem likely.

"There's nowhere to go," he pleaded. "You could surrender now and you'd live..."

"Be quiet," the leader ordered. "Ah. Four empty Spitfires."

Kurt followed his gaze. There were eight Spitfires in the launch tubes now, with pilots utterly aware of what was happening behind them. He wanted to do something, anything, but what could he do? There was nothing...he had no weapon, his hands were bound and they were trapped. All he could do was wait and pray the Marines arrived in time to save the day.

"Go to the switchboard," the leader ordered. He removed something small and dark from his palm and passed it to his companion. "Open the emergency hatch."

Kurt stared, just before the second blackmailer grabbed his ear and yanked him towards the switchboard. It wasn't meant to be used at all, nothing more than a relic of the Old Lady's early days, when they'd worried about the ship's datanet being so badly damaged that starfighters would have to be launched and recovered manually. They couldn't even use it without the Captain's overrides. But the blackmailers didn't seem to notice – or care. The leader climbed into the nearest Spitfire and started the engines.

"Do not do anything stupid," the second blackmailer said, as he cut Kurt's hands free, then pressed his palm against the sensor. The console unlocked. "Open the emergency hatch."

"As you wish," Kurt said. How had they managed to unlock the console? How had they managed to get the Captain's overrides? It was vaguely possible they had something that could be used to access Russian-designed computer cores, but the system in front of him was British. Outdated, sure, but still secure. "If that's what you want."

He noted the position of the breath mask, then pushed hard down on the emergency hatch system. The blackmailers hadn't realised, he saw, that the entire compartment would vent into space the moment the emergency hatches blew free. He grabbed for a mask a second later, then hung on for dear life as the atmosphere vented into open space. The second blackmailer grabbed for him, but Kurt kicked him in the face and watched him plummet helplessly out into space. He pressed the mask against his face, feeling it seal to his skin, then took a deep breath as the last of the atmosphere vanished. And then he turned, just in time to see the stolen starfighter vanish through the hatch.

Damn it, he thought, as gravity reasserted itself, His exposed skin started to hurt as the cold of space seeped in. *What now?*

Desperately, he ran over to the nearest starfighter and scrambled into the cockpit. There was a very welcome hiss as atmosphere flooded into the craft, allowing him to tear off the mask and reach for the communications system. God alone knew what had happened, but he needed to report back to the Marines and ask for instructions. He couldn't help a surge of brutally-powerful guilt. Was all this the result of his dalliance with Rose?

He keyed the system, searching for a channel. But it was nearly five minutes before his call was patched through to the CIC – and then to the Admiral.

"Admiral," he said. "The blackmailer took one of the starfighters."

"Shit," the Admiral said. There was a pause. "Can you get after him?"

"Yes," Kurt said. He brought the starfighter's drives and weapons up to full readiness. "But why...?"

The Admiral laughed, bitterly. "There's a bioweapon on that ship, Commander," he said, shortly. "They have to be stopped before it can be deployed."

Kurt nodded, then triggered the starfighter's engines and powered the craft through the hatch and out into space. The blackmailers had done a very good job of confusing everyone, he had to admit. It would be difficult to launch the ready starfighters or get the remaining pilots into space before the aliens reacted, perhaps assuming the humans intended to launch a sneak attack on their world. And yet...how did they plan to deploy the bioweapon? He recalled everything he'd seen or heard since the blackmailers had captured him, but there had been nothing to suggest they'd armed the starfighter with anything capable of deploying the bioweapon. The craft didn't even carry any missiles...

"Admiral," he said slowly, "how can he deploy the weapon?"

"They can drop into the planet's atmosphere," the Admiral said. "The damn thing might even survive a gentle re-entry."

But they can't fly into the atmosphere, Kurt thought. The starfighter would break up and fall to the surface if someone was idiotic enough to try. But if the pilot didn't mind committing suicide, the bioweapon might just float down to the surface anyway...if it survived the heat of re-entry. Would it? Kurt recalled some accidents during the early days of spaceflight, where genetic material *had* made it down to the surface. The early days of science-fiction had included hundreds of diseases from outer space...

And there was no way to be sure the bioweapon wouldn't survive the fall.

"Understood, Admiral," he said. "I'm on my way."

———

"We have all but one of the Russians accounted for, Admiral," Parnell reported. "The last one was just killed attempting to break into the armoury."

Ted nodded, shortly. "Good," he said. "And Commander Labara?"

"We found her tied and gagged with duct tape, but she's alive," Parnell assured him. "They actually left a remote grenade beside her, probably to keep her quiet. We deactivated the device and threw it out into space."

He paused. "She wants to speak with you, Admiral."

"She'll have to wait," Ted said. He needed to speak with Rose Labara too, but later, when he'd had a chance to think through what had happened. "There's too much to do."

He sighed. Five Russians dead on *Ark Royal*, one more in custody, one blown into space and one on a starfighter heading towards the planet.

One Russian agent who could still pull the whole thing off, if he got close enough to the world. In hindsight, it had been terrifyingly obvious what the Russians had in mind. But he'd been so horrified by the bioweapon's mere existence, to say nothing of its prospective results, that he hadn't even considered the possibility. Did the Russians intend to provoke an unwinnable war or were they intent on ending the war by exterminating the aliens completely?

The thought made him shudder. *He'd* come to view the aliens as intelligent beings in their own right. He would have felt the same way if he'd faced Russians or Chinese in combat, even though he would have fought them with the same effort he'd brought to fighting the aliens. Fighting them, defeating them in battle, was one thing, but committing genocide was quite another. There was no way he would have bombarded civilian populations…

And so it had been unthinkable that anyone *would*. He'd been so adamant that the aliens were alien, and had to be treated with great care, that he hadn't been thinking about the Russians as anything other than fellow humans. And it had been a wise thing to think, particularly during Operation Nelson. He couldn't afford to think of the foreign ships under his flag as anything but human.

But the Russians had been prepared to slaughter uncounted billions of aliens. He'd seen reports of endless skirmishes along the Russian southern borders, where civilisation broke down and tribal warfare was epidemic. The Russians had responded with staggering force, calling down targeted fire from orbit and blasting entire villages to rubble. Why would they *not* slaughter the aliens? They weren't even *human*.

He turned his gaze to the status display. Repair crews were working frantically, but it would be hours before the Old Lady was ready to launch starfighters again. If the aliens attacked now, the carrier would be thoroughly screwed. So far, the aliens seemed bemused, rather than hostile. That would change, he knew, if they ever worked out what had actually happened…was still happening. There was nothing he could do, any longer, to influence events. All he could do was pray.

And watch, helplessly, as two starfighters battled for the future of humanity.

———

Peter spared a moment to think of Ivan as the starfighter raced towards the planet, sacrificing any form of stealth for speed. They had been friends and comrades for a long time, well before the aliens had made their presence felt. But now Ivan was dead...they'd always known they would die together, but it was still a shock.

He pushed the thought away as he watched the alien defences. So far, they hadn't reacted to his presence, as far as he could tell. It was quite likely the aliens were monitoring events closely, unsure of just how best to respond. If they waited long enough, he told himself firmly, they'd lose everything before they made up their minds what to do. And even if they didn't...he remembered the briefing papers and smiled. It was quite possible the aliens would smash his starfighter and the bioweapon would still survive. Unless the designers had been blowing smoke again, he knew...

They used to promise us the superman, he thought, feeling an odd calmness settling over his mind now he knew he was going to die. *And how many men died, mutilated savagely, before they mastered enhancements?*

He pushed the thought aside as the console sounded an alert. Someone was on his tail.

———

The blackmailer was a pilot, Kurt noted, but he was not an *experienced* pilot. Spitfires had quite a bit in common with Russian-designed *Grigorovich* starfighters, yet there were some modifications that had been added to the later generations of Spitfires the blackmailer didn't seem to know existed. For one thing, it was possible to boost the drive if the pilot didn't mind the risk of burning out his compensators. Kurt pushed his drives as hard as he dared, knowing he had to catch up with the enemy before it was too late.

He sucked in a breath as the alien world came into view, a blue orb hanging against the infinite darkness of space. It was astonishing just how little land surface there was on the planet, most of it subject to truly horrible weather. The aliens, utterly unconcerned about the mainland, probably didn't care about the rain. Or thunder and lightning...

The starfighter ahead of him lunged forward, then altered course lightly. Kurt recognised it as an attempt to hit the atmosphere at an angle, the only – theoretical – way a starfighter could enter the atmosphere safely. But it wouldn't be easy to actually land on the water, let alone the mainland. Kurt cursed and removed the safeties from his weapons, then locked onto the starfighter and opened fire. There could be no risk of allowing the starfighter, even as a piece of wreckage, to enter the planet's atmosphere.

He frowned as the blackmailer spun the craft through a crazy series of loops, then came up shooting.. Kurt evaded with ease, but he could tell that the enemy pilot was determined to go through with his mad plan. As soon as Kurt had altered course enough to throw off his aim, the pilot had altered course and started to move back towards the planet. And every time he did it, Kurt suspected, he'd get closer and closer to his goal. Completing his mission would be much simpler if he didn't intend to survive afterwards.

And he didn't dare risk blowing up the enemy starfighter in the planet's atmosphere…

This is all my fault, he thought, and drove the starfighter forward. One hand reached for containment chamber controls and started to remove the safeguards, one by one. *I'm sorry…*

"Admiral," he said. "Please tell my children – and everyone else – that I love them."

He cursed under his breath as he closed the channel. There had been no time to say goodbye to Rose. She'd have to make do with the letter he'd written for her and stored in his private database. Penny and Percy would have their own letters; he hoped – prayed – that the Captain would take care of them, even after Kurt's death. And Molly…where *was* Molly now? Dead…or in the arms of someone who could make her happy? Oddly, he felt no hatred or anger any longer, not now he was about to die. She deserved what happiness she could find in life.

I'm sorry, he thought, and rammed the starfighter forward.

————

Peter watched, grimly, as the enemy starfighter closed in. The pilot was no longer firing, which was odd…and worrying. If the starfighter had been blown to rubble, there was a possibility the bioweapon would survive. But if the pilot wasn't shooting any longer…it suggested he knew what he was dealing with. Did he have another way to deal with the bioweapon?

He swung his starfighter around, then gasped in horror as the enemy flyer roared towards him at terrifying speed. An experienced pilot might have managed to evade, but by the time he yanked his starfighter away it was already too late.

You can ram if you like, he thought, in the last seconds. *The bioweapon might survive…*

———

Kurt timed it perfectly. The containment chambers, already overloading, exploded microseconds before his starfighter crashed into the enemy starfighter. There was a blaze of light and heat, then nothing.

And both starfighters were utterly vaporised by the blast.

CHAPTER
THIRTY TWO

"Well, Captain," Doctor Hastings said. "How are you feeling?"

James scowled at her. "Like I've been shot," he said. His palm ached terribly. "What happened to me?"

"You were shot," Doctor Hastings said. She ignored his glare with practiced ease. "You took three bullets to the chest, Captain. Frankly, you're damn lucky to have survived long enough to reach sickbay. You've got the constitution of a horse."

"I must have bonded with them," James muttered. He'd always enjoyed riding as a child, even though Aunt Cecilia had watched him like a hawk every time he dared to ride one of her precious horses. "And my hand?"

"They cut your ID implant right out of your hand," the Doctor said. "And then they used it to open hatches throughout the ship. Good thing there weren't more of them or they might have managed to overwhelm the crew and take the Old Lady for themselves."

James swore, feeling his head threatening to explode. The Russians had clearly managed to put their plan into action, despite their best precautions. In hindsight, they should have grabbed the Russians from the start and thrown them into the brig, despite the diplomatic nightmare it would have caused. But they hadn't and he'd been shot and...

He shook his head. "The ship," he asked, urgently. "What happened to her?"

"Intact and operational," Doctor Hastings said. She took a breath. "The Admiral wishes to speak with you as soon as possible. I'd prefer to put you back under, Captain, but if you feel up to talking to him…"

"Please," James said. "Call him."

The Admiral arrived two minutes later, looking tired and worn. James reminded himself that Admiral Smith had been the commanding officer of *Ark Royal* for years before his promotion, long enough to hold the ship firmly in his heart. Seeing her…*violated* in such a manner, through the darkest treachery, had to hurt. They hadn't reacted so badly to the aliens who'd boarded the ship during Operation Nelson, but they'd been known enemies. The Russians, on the other hand, had pretended to be allies.

"Captain," the Admiral said. "It's good to see you awake."

There had been a time, James recalled, when the Admiral would probably have been glad to have him out of the way. The older and more mature officer he'd become cringed at the memory of just what sort of fool he'd been as a young man. But now…the Admiral genuinely regretted his injuries. James felt a pang of bittersweet affection for the older man as the Admiral sat down next to the bed.

"Thank you, sir," he said. He looked down at the bandages covering his chest. "What's our current status?"

"I'd tell you not to worry, but it would be pointless," the Admiral said, ruefully. "The ship is safe, for the moment. Commander Williams has taken over command and is supervising the effort to clear up the mess. Right now, we have thirty-two dead crewmen and fifty-seven injured, but no serious long-term damage to the Old Lady herself."

James winced. Those crewmen had died under his command. He'd lost officers and crewmen before, during Operation Nelson, but it still *stung*. And all the worse, he reflected, for the treachery the Russians had used. Losing people to the aliens didn't hurt so badly, somehow. He had *known* the aliens would do their best to kill him and his subordinates.

"What we *do* have is a diplomatic nightmare," the Admiral continued. "The aliens want answers and, so far, we don't know what to tell them."

"The truth," James suggested. "They have factions of their own. I think they'd understand if we explained that one of *our* factions tried to do something stupid."

"The bioweapon came very close to being deployed," the Admiral said. "If they find out what the Russians tried to do…"

James smirked. "Tell them something along the same lines, but not too horrific," he suggested. "The Russians might have wanted to drop a dirty bomb into the planet's atmosphere instead."

"Or even kill our diplomats on the surface," the Admiral said. He sighed. "The Russians killed *their* diplomats too. We're working on coming up with *some* sort of explanation, but it's going slowly. They're not going to be pleased about losing their people to a faction fight among humans."

"And killing ambassadors is practically a declaration of war," James said.

"Merciless war," the Admiral agreed. "We need to keep a sharp eye on the other diplomats too – the *human* diplomats. God knows if *they* have plots of their own up their sleeves."

"True," James agreed.

"I don't understand it," the Admiral confessed. "What the hell were they thinking?"

"They thought they couldn't lose," James speculated. He felt very tired, suddenly. His chest ached with sudden pain. "It's the aristocratic delusion. You're born to power, you understand power…and you don't really think you *can* lose. You sport and play with your victims, convinced that – if they bit back – you could handle it. That they would suffer far worse than you."

He sighed. "But you never really believe there might be someone more powerful than yourself out there."

"No," the Admiral agreed.

"We'll have to do something in response," James continued. "The Russians cannot be allowed to get away with attempted genocide and trying to restart the war."

"No," the Admiral agreed. "But that, I suspect, will be up to the diplomats."

He stood. "I'd advise you to sleep, Captain," he said. His face twitched into a grin, clearly remember James urging *him* to rest. "You may have to go home the express route."

James looked down at his chest and shuddered. "I hope not, sir," he said, although he knew it wouldn't be the Admiral's decision. "I can't leave the ship."

"She's in good hands," the Admiral assured him. "Rest now."

He strode out of the room. James sighed and lay back on the bed, trying not to give in to the wave of bitterness and anger that threatened to overcome him. He'd need months, if not years, to recover from his wounds and there was no way the Admiralty would leave *Ark Royal* without a formal commanding officer for that long. They'd probably promote Commander Williams to Captain when the ship returned to Earth. There might be another carrier command in his future, he knew, but it wouldn't be *Ark Royal*.

Maybe it will be one of the new carriers, he thought. Uncle Winchester *had* offered him a post on the design crews, pointing out that they needed officers with genuine experience to help them avoid old mistakes. No one had built a carrier like *Ark Royal* for sixty years. But he'd refused the offer at the time, intending to remain in command of the Old Lady. Now...now he might not have a choice. He wouldn't be seeing action again anytime soon.

"Lie still, Captain," the Doctor advised.

James started. He hadn't even heard her walking up to the bed.

"I need a status report," James said. "Can you ask Anderson to send someone to brief me..."

The doctor pushed something against his neck. James had barely a moment to recognise it as an injector before his head started to spin. Moments later, he was completely unconscious.

———

"She's a normal human, for a given value of *normal*," Parnell said, as Ted entered the brig. Doctor Galina Bezukladnikov sat on a chair in the cell, her arms cuffed behind her back. "But her companions were all augmented cyborgs."

Ted cursed. No wonder they had caused so much havoc.

"And we missed it," he said. "How did we miss it?"

"We didn't do any deep scans," Parnell said. "They didn't *look* like normal cyborgs, not like the ones we landed on New Russia. As long as we didn't scan them thoroughly, they could pass for normal without fear of detection. The implants must have been completely stepped down until they went active, sir. We didn't have a clue they might have any form of enhanced abilities."

"Clearly our security precautions need to be revised," Ted muttered. The Admiralty would probably have a great many scathing things to say about the whole affair. He had a feeling the post-battle assessment would be unfriendly, if only to ensure that other commanding officers didn't repeat their mistakes. "Next time, we'd better take the liner with us instead of housing the diplomats on the ship."

"Yes, sir," Parnell said. He nodded towards the girl in the cell. "Someone did some fiddling with her brain, Admiral. Doctor Bezukladnikov may not be completely human."

"Shit," Ted said. "Has she said anything?"

"Nothing," Parnell said. We scanned her body thoroughly, Admiral, once we took her into custody. There were a handful of oddities, but nothing that would allow her to break out of the cell and cause havoc. Her ultimate disposition might depend on what happens when we return home."

Ted nodded. The Russians would probably claim their agents had gone rogue. In their place, he would have had a contingency plan for outright failure. The agents had had families on New Russia, they'd planned their operation without consulting their superiors, no one on Earth had known what they'd had in mind, etc, etc. They wouldn't be believed, Ted was sure, but it was quite possible the government would snatch at their excuses as a fig leaf to justify taking no direct action. The human race couldn't afford an internal struggle, not now.

But they attempted to commit genocide on a terrifying scale, he thought, bitterly. *The Holocaust was nothing compared to what the Russians had in mind.*

He shuddered. As far as anyone could tell, the bioweapon had been completely vaporised when the two starfighters died. It certainly *should* have been vaporised, Ted knew, although the remaining researchers had been unwilling to commit themselves to any definite statements. They'd hemmed and hawed before admitting that they'd designed the bioweapon for maximum survivability. In the end, Ted knew, they'd just have to pray the bioweapon had been destroyed and no tiny fragments would make it through the planet's atmosphere and down to the ground. If they did…

They must have been out of their minds, he thought. Humans tracked disease outbreaks with suspicious eyes, knowing just what an unscrupulous medical researcher could do with a lab and bad intentions. *There's no way such an outbreak could be regarded as anything natural, not when it was targeted on the entire biosphere. They'd know we intended to commit genocide…*

…And if the war continues, we might have to do it again.

Parnell coughed. "Admiral?"

Ted hesitated, replaying their conversation in his mind. "Keep her here, for the moment," he ordered. "We'll take her back to Earth and hand her over to the intelligence officers there. I doubt the Russians will complain about us holding her, under the circumstances."

"Others will complain," Parnell said. He snorted. "I don't think the remaining researchers have quite realised that she betrayed them. They want her back."

"Ignore them," Ted ordered. "Keep her in the cell."

Parnell saluted. Ted nodded, then turned and walked out of the brig, heading down towards Pilot Country. The pilots, according to Commander Williams, had been badly shocked to lose Kurt Schneider, even though he'd died heroically. Ted understood. Whatever his faults, and he'd had many, Kurt Schneider had been a good commanding officer, very much a father to the young men under his command. There had been older units, built from officers and men over years, that hadn't survived the loss of a beloved commanding officer. Or even *any* commanding officer.

And how, he asked himself, *would Ark Royal react to losing a Captain?*

He pushed the thought aside as he stopped in front of the CAG's office, then keyed the switch to open the hatch. Inside, Commander Rose Labara sat at her former lover's desk, staring down at the latest readiness reports. Doctor Hastings had warned that Commander Labara was physically healthy, after the Marines had recovered her from the office, but mentally unstable. She should have been placed on medical leave – and would have been, Ted knew, if he'd had any replacement for her. The only person who could take her place was Prince Henry and he didn't have anything like as much experience.

"Commander," he said.

Rose Labara started, then rose to her feet. "Admiral," she said. Her face was stained with tears. The uniform she wore was crumpled, making her look sloppy or – worse – careless. "I'm sorry, I…"

"Don't worry about it," Ted said. He'd never been one for military formalities. "Everyone needs time to mourn."

She would have been discharged after the return to Earth, he knew, and spent the rest of her life with her lover, if fate hadn't intervened. Ted couldn't help wondering just how long their relationship would have lasted when one of the partners was far older than the other one. It was no solid basis for a relationship. And they would have given up their careers for each other…

Would there have come a time, Ted asked silently, *when you cursed him for surrendering to your charms and taking you in his arms?*

He pushed the thought aside, annoyed. "I am sorry for your loss," he said. "I believe he was a good man, merely…misguided."

"Thank you, Admiral," Rose said, tartly. "Will you write that on the memorial stone after the end of the war?"

"I think so," the Admiral said. He paused. "We recovered a handful of datachips from the Russians, Commander, including one that held recordings of your…*activities*. I doubt they're the only ones they have, but I don't think they're likely to release the recordings now that Commander Schneider is dead. Even if they did…"

He shrugged. "He died well, Commander," he added, "even though the truth will probably never be told. There will be an investigation, but your career should be safe."

Rose shook her head. "I showed poor judgement during wartime," she said. "How *could* my career be safe?"

"You also showed good judgement when you were confronted by blackmailers and threatened with exposure," Ted pointed out. "I believe it was you, Commander, who insisted that Schneider bring his problem to my attention. Everyone makes mistakes – and your mistake was pretty damn stupid – but you also managed to deal with the consequences despite the threat of exposure."

"And now Kurt is dead," Rose said. She looked down at the desk, shaking her head helplessly. "What will become of his children?"

"I think they will be fine," Ted said. He frowned at her doubtful expression. "They will have to come to terms with losing a father, of course, but they won't suffer because of his mistake."

"I hope you're right, sir," Rose said. "What will happen now?"

Ted studied her for a long moment. Starfighter pilots lived fast and burned out early, unless they saw the writing on the wall and transferred to other duties before it was too late. The certainty of death or the loss of everything that made life worthwhile had eventually driven her into her lover's arms. And now...

He sighed Rose's life had changed over the course of the mission, confronting her with the prospect of losing her career...and then losing a lover. At least they hadn't broken up, the romantic in Ted thought, even though he knew it was absurd. She'd merely watched him being marched off to his death instead. There was no way that wouldn't leave a scar.

"You will resume your duties," he ordered, reluctantly. He'd have to recall Prince Henry from the surface too, just to have someone who could take her place, if necessary. "If we manage to get back to Earth without further ado, you will be able to make some judgements and decisions about your future then. I would advise you to consider a permanent transfer to the Academy" – *if they'll take you*, his thought added silently – "or another division."

She didn't argue. She didn't even look angry at his suggestion. And *that* was worrying.

"Yes, sir," she said, instead. "Will there be a service for him?"

"There will," Ted said. He paused, then leaned forward. "Commander... the starfighter pilots on this ship have never lost a commander before now. You will need to work with them, to keep them busy...they can't be allowed to brood. And I can't allow you to brood either."

"I understand, sir," Rose said. She looked up, meeting his eyes. "What will you tell his children?"

"That their father died bravely," Ted said. It wasn't, technically, his job to write the letter to the next-of-kin, but he might make an exception in this case. "I wasn't planning to go into details."

"Yes, sir," Rose said. "Thank you, sir."

Ted was tempted to ask what, if anything, Commander Schneider's children had known of the affair, but he held his tongue. Instead, he took one final look at her, then started to walk towards the hatch. And then he turned back.

"Get a shower, Commander, then dress in a clean uniform and get out there," he ordered. "I wish I had time to let you rest, but I have none. The war may not be over."

"Aye, sir," Rose said. She stood, reluctantly. "I'll do my duty."

"*That* has never been in doubt," Ted said.

He smiled, humourlessly. The investigators might disagree, but *he* hadn't been able to find any signs that Kurt Schneider had pulled strings on his lover's behalf. Rose hadn't been promoted at his command. She'd earned her rank, as far as Ted could tell. But then, almost all of the survivors of their first mission had been promoted. Rose was merely one of a handful who had stayed with *Ark Royal*.

"I know it isn't easy to lose a loved one," he added. Others might be able to visit a counsellor, but how could Rose when her affair had been thoroughly illicit? "If you need to talk, Commander, you may talk to me."

He nodded to her, then turned and strode out of the hatch.

CHAPTER
THIRTY THREE

"Do you think," Henry asked as he stumbled down the muddy path, "that they do this on purpose?"

"I think they're just as uncomfortable as we are," Ambassador Melbourne said. "Just for different reasons."

Henry snorted, rudely. The alien mainland was a rainforest, the trees pressing so close to the diplomatic chambers that the only way anyone could walk was through the paths the aliens had cut through the foliage with fusion torches. The whole island was infested with insects, which buzzed endlessly in the background, and spider-like creatures that showed no fear of humanity. Their bites weren't poisonous, thankfully, but they tended to itch terribly until one of the medics found a treatment that worked. Even so, he reflected as sweat dripped off his bare back, he would be glad to return to orbit. There were certain people who should never be allowed to wear swimsuits or bathing costumes.

Least of all diplomats, he thought, sourly. The thought of turning up to a diplomatic meeting on Earth clad in a swimsuit or bikini was absurd, but it made sense on the alien world. Few of the diplomats could wear suits and ties for long in the heat, even if they weren't ruined to exposure to sweat and water. But it didn't make them look any more attractive. Some of them really needed to cover up.

He kept his opinion to himself as the jungle came to an end, revealing a path leading down to the water's edge. This time, the aliens hadn't invited them to a city, but to a lagoon that reminded him of Jill's description of

First Contact. Hundreds of aliens were swimming in the water, surfacing briefly like dolphins at play before diving back under the waves. Henry checked he still had his mask on his belt as Ambassador Melbourne led the way down to the water, stopping just on the edge of the beach. The aliens made gestures that needed no translation.

Come on in, Henry thought, feeling a sudden spurt of affection for the playful creatures. *The water's fine.*

He walked into the water until it was waist deep, then halted as the aliens surged around him, swimming alarmingly close with no regard for his personal space. But then, they were an intensely social race, he reminded himself. They probably had no conception of personal space, let alone any of the problems that had caused humanity to invent the concept in the first place. He forced himself to keep his face impassive as the smell of so many aliens in close proximity grew stronger. Did the aliens, he wondered absently, find humanity as smelly as humans found them?

The aliens scattered, suddenly, as five more aliens surfaced and swam towards the two humans in a calm, measured fashion that Henry found somewhat ominous. He'd seen the aliens practically dancing through the water, moving in a manner that reminded him of penguins at the zoo, but now they seemed frighteningly serious. He shivered, despite the warm water, as he recalled the events in orbit. The report hadn't been as clear as he would have wished – it was clear the writer feared the aliens might try to intercept the transmission – yet it had been thoroughly alarming. An attack on the alien-settled world had been narrowly averted.

It could restart the war, Henry thought. They hadn't even come to a final agreement before the Russians had tried to restart the war. They might not even have fared too badly in the final settlement, given the way the aliens kept changing their demands. But it hardly mattered now. *We might be back at war within the week.*

"We greet you," the lead alien said. As always, the voice was chillingly atonal, betraying no trace of emotion. "There was fighting in our system between humans. Explain."

Ambassador Melbourne splashed forward through the water until he could look the alien right in the eye. Henry silently admired his pluck. As much as he'd seen of the aliens since his capture, he still found it hard to look right into their oversized eyes. They were very far from human, he knew, and the sense of inhuman intelligence looking back at him was chilling. The aliens simply didn't *think* like humans.

"One of our factions objected to the peace terms," the Ambassador said. They'd agreed, previously, that they would tell some of the truth if the aliens asked. No one had expected they wouldn't be concerned about the incident, even if it had taken them two days to agree to call the humans for an interview. "They attempted to take control of our ship and attack your world. We stopped them."

The aliens, as one, ducked below the waves. Henry silently counted nearly ten minutes before their heads broke the surface again. This time, he was almost sure, it was a different alien facing the human ambassadors. But, as always, it was very hard to be *certain*.

"You have factions of your own?" The alien asked. "What do they stand for?"

Henry and Ambassador Melbourne exchanged glances. How did one explain the concept of *nations* and *nationality* to a race that possessed neither. The alien factions were based around ideas and concepts, not birthplace. It was true, Henry suspected, that someone born into a faction would always remain *part* of the faction to some extent, but their opinions might change as they grew older. Or when they were exposed to new ideas.

"Our factions are based on birthplace," Ambassador Melbourne said, finally. It was as good an explanation as any, under the circumstances. "This faction disliked the idea of surrendering New Russia to you."

The aliens ducked back under the surface. This time, they returned within moments.

"This issue must be debated," the lead alien said. "We will call you when a consensus has been reached."

That sounded more than a little ominous, Henry decided, as the aliens dropped back under the waves and vanished. Even the more playful aliens they'd encountered at the start had disappeared below the water. He stared over the surface for a long moment, wondering just how many aliens there were under the sea, then turned and made his way out of the water and up onto the beach. Ambassador Melbourne followed him a moment later.

"Creepy," the Ambassador commented, suddenly.

Henry followed his gaze *Something* was moving along the beach. For a moment, he thought it was an optical illusion, a mirage caused by the heat and water droplets in the air, for it looked like a beach towel crawling over the sand. And then he saw that it was made of hundreds of thousands of spiders, making their way in unison towards the water. A shiver ran down his spine as he stared at them in disbelief. There was nothing like that on Earth.

"Another form of alien intelligence," the Ambassador mused. He didn't seem scared, merely curious. "Do you think they might become intelligent, one day?"

"Would we even recognise them as intelligent?" Henry asked. He'd read novels where the enemy were intelligent spiders – or creatures so alien that any form of communication was completely impossible. "Would they recognise us as anything more than a food source?"

The Ambassador shrugged. "I've negotiated with religious fanatics who think we have no right to exist," he said, as he turned and walked back to the path. "They're always difficult to do more than threaten, then carry out the threats if they refuse to listen to reason. Spider-aliens might not be too difficult after dealing with fanatics."

He didn't say anything else until they were back in the diplomatic compound and one of the Marines had swept the compartment for bugs. The aliens had been remarkably considerate about not trying to bug the diplomats, Henry had seen, although he had a private suspicion that nothing ever remained secret among the aliens for long. There were just too many aliens changing their allegiance from one faction to another without anyone trying to stop them. He had a feeling the aliens had no concept of a security clearance either.

Maybe it works for them, he thought. He couldn't deny that the aliens had built their own spacefaring empire, fully humanity's equal. *But it wouldn't work for us.*

"The aliens may find the idea of one of our factions attacking them worrying," the Ambassador said. "Or they may feel that the peace treaty wouldn't be kept."

Henry understood. If the Russians had tried to attack the aliens, what was to stop them from trying again and again. And what would the aliens do then? Restart the war? Or demand that the rest of humanity prevent the Russians from launching further attacks, something that might prove impossible without war? Hell, given time, the aliens might use the situation to their own advantage. A humanity permanently at war with itself wouldn't be able to prevent the aliens from quietly settling vast tracts of interstellar real estate.

Unless there are other aliens out there, he thought. If there was one alien race, there would be others…and they might be even more alien or less friendly than the first race humanity had encountered. *Who knows what's beyond the next star?*

"So we need to convince them otherwise," the American said. He looked askance at Henry for a long moment, then gazed back at Ambassador Melbourne. "How do we do that?"

"I don't know," Ambassador Melbourne said. "I just don't know."

Midshipwoman Hawking entered, looking far better than the Ambassadors in a one-peace swimsuit that kept her reasonably decent, but left little to the imagination. No one batted an eyelid, Henry noted with droll amusement. Wearing swimsuits everywhere had once been embarrassing or exciting. Now, everyone was used to showing so much flesh. He couldn't help wondering what would happen when the diplomats tried to return to Earth. Would they insist on breaking diplomatic convention by wearing comfortable clothes to meetings?

"Your Highness," she said. "Admiral Smith has requested that you return to *Ark Royal*."

Ordered, Henry translated, mentally. If there was one person on the ship who wasn't impressed with his title, it was the Admiral. He wondered, briefly, if the Admiral wanted to discuss the negotiations with him personally, then dismissed the thought. If Admiral Smith had wanted to hear anything from the horse's mouth he would have called Ambassador Melbourne directly.

"I'll catch the next shuttle," he said. "Or does the Admiral want me at once?"

He sighed, inwardly. There was one flight a day to and from orbit, in a shuttle designed for high-intensity operations. It was still, according to the handful of people who had travelled from the surface to orbit and back again, a nightmare out of the days before antigravity systems. Flights to space hadn't been so rough since humanity had started probing beyond the planet's atmosphere. Henry knew, without false modesty, that he was a brave man, but he still found the idea of being at the mercy of the planet's weather terrifying.

If we get out of the war alive, he told himself firmly, *we* will *go live on an asteroid.*

"As soon as possible," Hawking said. "One of the shuttles was held for you."

"Must be something important," Ambassador Melbourne said. "I'll record a brief report for the Admiral on chip and you can take it with you."

"Yes, sir," Henry said.

The flight back up to the carrier was, if anything, worse than the flight down to the surface, even though there was a lesser risk of falling out of the sky. Henry hadn't come so close to throwing up since his first ride on the high-intensity simulator at the Academy, months – it felt like years – ago. They'd been testing his limits, he recalled, and just about every-one had thrown up, eventually. Henry had been told, afterwards, that he hadn't even come close to setting a record for endurance. By the time the shuttle landed in the carrier's shuttlebay, he felt the urge to kiss the deck as soon as he staggered out of the ship.

"Henry," Janelle said. "How are you feeling?"

Henry smiled at her, then felt his legs buckle. "Tell me," he said, as he steadied himself by leaning against the shuttle's hull. "Are we engaged in combat operations or is it just me?"

"It's just you," Janelle told him. "The Old Lady moves like a wallowing pig."

Henry nodded, wordlessly. The carrier wouldn't shudder and jump like a shuttlecraft, not unless someone did something stupid like trying to take the carrier into a planetary atmosphere – and even the Old Lady's mighty drives wouldn't be enough to save the crew from the stupidity of whoever took the plunge. Henry had a sudden vision of the carrier plummeting to the surface like an asteroid and hitting the ground hard enough to permanently damage the planet's ecosystem. No wonder so many people had worried about the asteroids orbiting Earth, he thought, as he managed to force himself to stand upright. It could have been disastrous if one fell out of orbit.

And then the aliens attacked, he thought, *and those asteroids weren't targeted. And the aliens still killed billions of people.*

Janelle led him through the ship's corridors, quietly filling him in on what had happened over the last few days. Henry listened in growing disbelief; he'd known it was bad, but he hadn't realised just *how* bad. He had no idea what the Russians had thought they were doing – stealing a starfighter seemed like pointless evil – but they had to have had *something* in mind or the effort would have been utterly wasted, along with their lives. But what?

Maybe they just thought that firing on the alien fortresses would be enough to restart the war, he thought. It still seemed like a pointless waste. *But wouldn't the aliens have realised that one starfighter couldn't do enough damage to serve as a declaration of war?*

He pushed the thought aside as they stepped into the Admiral's office. Admiral Smith looked tired, as if he needed to sleep desperately. It might well be the case, Henry knew, remembering the times he'd had trouble sleeping. He certainly hadn't slept very well when he'd been an alien prisoner, even though he'd been fairly certain he wouldn't be physically harmed. The thought of waking up to find an alien looming over him had kept him on his toes.

"Admiral," he said.

"Welcome back," the Admiral answered. He *sounded* as tired as he looked. "Commander Schneider is dead."

Henry winced. He'd *known* Commander Schneider from back when he'd been Charles Augustus. The CAG had been a good man, by his standards; he'd taught Henry a great deal more than he cared to admit. And he hadn't tried to fawn on the prospective Heir to the Throne, even after he'd learned the truth. That, if nothing else, marked him out as someone Henry could like. And he *had* liked Schneider...

"I'm sorry," he said, sincerely. He'd hoped to catch up with Schneider, but he'd always been busy, even when Henry had been pacing his cabin with nothing to do beyond reading pointless reports. "He deserved better."

"Yes. Yes, he did," the Admiral mused. "And so did the Captain."

Henry swallowed. Captain Fitzwilliam was a good man too, even if he had chewed Henry out once or twice. But Henry had to admit he'd deserved the row.

He shook his head, running one hand through short white hair. Henry couldn't help wondering if the Admiral had grown older over the last few weeks, for his hair seemed whiter than before. Years ago, his father had told him that every senior politician went grey very quickly – and used hair dye or more complex surgery to make it seem like they were still youthful. Personally, Henry rather preferred the older look. It suggested the Admiral took his responsibilities seriously.

"But I don't have time to commiserate," the Admiral continued. "I'm recalling you to active service – Rose Labara is being bumped up to CAG, with you as her second. I expect you to get along with her, despite your identity becoming common knowledge. There isn't time for anything else."

"No, sir," Henry said, firmly. The thought of getting back in a cockpit was intoxicating. "I'll be happy to serve in any capacity."

The Admiral's lips twitched. "You might regret saying that," he said. There was no humour in his voice. "I need you to take up your new role at once, so I'm giving you a brevet promotion to Commander. It may not last past our return to Earth, but you'll need it for the position."

"Yes, sir," Henry said. Once, the promotion would have thrilled him. Now, he knew it was something he wouldn't have had without special circumstances. And if he *was* allowed to keep it, everyone would know he'd been favoured…and why. "I won't let you down."

"Good," the Admiral said. "Go."

Outside, he hugged Janelle tightly. "You could have told me," he whispered. "I wouldn't have let on…"

"I thought it would be better left as a surprise," Janelle said. She walked beside him as they made their way to the hatch. "There's one other point the Admiral might not have mentioned, Henry. Commander Labara was very upset when the CAG died. *Very* upset."

Henry hesitated. "Were they…?"

"I believe so," Janelle said. She paused. "That is *not* common knowledge, Henry, and you must not spread it any further. But if she allows her grief to distract her…"

Henry winced. How could *he* complain about someone having an affair with one of their shipmates? But any relationship between a senior and a junior was always bad for discipline, if only because of fears of favouritism. And yet…one of the lovers was dead. It no longer mattered.

"I'll keep an eye on her," he promised. "And wish me luck."

He sighed. They'd be going into the simulators as soon as he entered the compartment. But then, what *else* could they do?

CHAPTER
THIRTY FOUR

"Admiral," Janelle said, suddenly. "Long-range scans are picking up fifteen starships entering the system from Tramline Three and advancing on the planet."

Ted frowned. Five days had passed since the aliens had informed the humans that the issue of human factions would need to be debated. Five days, during which he'd waited, feeling ice prickling down the back of his spine. Five days…

He'd forced himself to do the paperwork, to read up on all the reports and pray the aliens listened to reason. But if they worked out what had *really* happened, they'd be furious and almost certainly go back to war. Humanity wouldn't react very well to attempted genocide either.

"I see," he said. He forced a calmness into his voice he didn't feel. "Time to orbit?"

"Thirty-seven minutes," Janelle said. "They're really pushing their drives."

And they came out of the tramline as close to the planet as possible, Ted thought. There were human researchers who believed it might be possible to fiddle with the exit coordinate, but nothing had actually been proven. *They must be in a hurry.*

"Bring the flotilla to combat stations, covertly," he ordered. Thankfully, they'd researched the tricky condition during the journey to the alien world. His crew would be as ready as possible, without alerting the aliens that something was wrong. "And then signal the Ambassador. I want him to ask the aliens what's happening."

He settled back in his chair and forced himself to wait. There had been no shortage of starships making their way in and out of the system since they'd arrived, but most of them had been civilian or commercial designs. None of them had shown the urge to push themselves forward so hard there was a very real chance of burning out the drives. But the newcomers were trying hard to reach the planet, as if they were racing against an invisible deadline. Did the aliens have politicians who knew nothing of the realities of space travel, he asked himself, or was something more sinister afoot?

"The Ambassador states that he's heard nothing, but he is going to ask for a meeting," Janelle reported. "There's nothing wrong where they are, apparently."

"Noted," Ted said, eying the status board. One by one, departments and compartments all over the ship were checking in, reporting themselves at battle readiness. The only thing they didn't have was powered up weapons. Starfighters were hanging in the launch bay, ready to engage the enemy if necessary. Ted would have preferred to launch them at once, but it might have seemed a hostile act. Instead, all he could do was wait. "Let me know the moment they respond."

The alien craft blazed closer, angling their approach so they were plunging straight towards the planet. Ted studied the mass readings thoughtfully, silently concluding that the aliens had ten frigates, four middle-sized starships and one larger craft of unknown design. It didn't seem large enough to be a carrier, but that meant nothing. Even the bulk freighters the Royal Navy had converted into escort carriers held two squadrons of starfighters apiece, giving them a nasty sting.

"One of the probes picked up a great deal of chatter between the planet and the incoming ships," Janelle said, suddenly. "They're talking past each other."

Ted frowned. One of the more annoying aspects of the speed-of-light limit was that even radio signals suffered from incessant time delay. It was quite possible to send a message to a starship five light minutes away, then have to wait ten minutes – at least – for a reply. In some ways, it was a blessing – he hated to think what the Admiralty would do if they could issue orders in real time – but it was also irritating. One person could send another message while waiting for the answer to the first one, confusing both sides. It was considered preferable to send compressed messages rather than risk a misunderstanding that could cost lives.

But the aliens, it seemed, were ignoring the problem. Instead, they were talking…no one could have a conversation like that, Ted was sure. They were dictating to each other, issuing orders and perhaps even threats, without even waiting for the other side to reply. The thought worried him more than he cared to admit. If the Russians had been prepared to upset one set of negotiations in hopes of ending the war on their terms, what might the alien War Faction be prepared to do?

"Admiral," Janelle said, "the alien defence grid is coming to life."

Ted swallowed a curse. The aliens might have given the flotilla some space, but he was too old an officer not to know that the distance between the carrier and the alien defences was meaningless. A safe distance would have been much further from the planet. Now…he found himself unsure what to do. If he brought his ships to full alert, he might panic the alien defences…and if he didn't, he risked being taken by surprise if the alien newcomers proved to be hostile.

"Activate our defence grid, but hold starfighters in their tubes," he ordered, finally. He would have preferred to avoid using starfighters anyway – the squadrons still hadn't shook themselves down properly – but he might not have a choice. "And…"

"Admiral, I have Ambassador Melbourne for you," Janelle said. "Do you want me to put him through?"

"Yes," Ted said. He keyed his console. "Ambassador?"

"The War Faction is making its move," Ambassador Melbourne said, without preamble. "It thinks we cannot be trusted at all, Admiral, and the Russian actions just prove we cannot even honour our commitments to protect their diplomats. They're choosing to override the other factions and launch an attack on us."

Ted cursed out loud. "And what are the other factions saying?"

"They're still arguing," Ambassador Melbourne said. "I don't think outright defiance of the factional consensus has ever been a problem for them before."

Something else we taught them, Ted thought. *The Russians acted alone. Why not the War Faction?*

He paused. *But they did attempt to prevent the Peace Faction from making contact...*

"Please inform them that I intend to take all necessary measures to protect my ships," Ted said, shortly. "And ask them to keep their ships out of the engagement if the shit hits the fan."

"Understood," Ambassador Melbourne said.

Ted tapped his console. "Commander, move us away from the planet, then launch starfighters," he ordered. He had no idea how the remaining factions would react to humans killing aliens anywhere near one of their worlds, even though the War Faction had started the engagement. "Warn all ships that they are to only engage hostile targets."

"Aye, sir," Commander Williams said. She sounded rather more than a little dubious. In the middle of a high-speed engagement, separating friend and foe could become a little tricky. "I think some of them might be more hostile than others."

"I know," Ted said. If the War Faction wanted total war, how many other factions wanted a limited war, or a territory grab, or anything else between a war of annihilation and peace? "The sooner we put some distance between us and them, the better."

He watched, grimly, as the flotilla moved away from the planet. Long minutes ticked by, then the War Faction starships altered course, aiming to intercept the human ships. Ted gritted his teeth, wondering if he dared fire first. What would the fence-sittings take as a hostile act? Or use as an excuse to come down against humanity? The war had been a great deal simpler before the humans realised there was a way to *talk* to their enemies.

But we were also losing, he thought, gloomily. *If we can get some of the alien factions on our side, we might have a chance to survive.*

"Captain," Janelle said. "All starfighters have launched; I say again, all starfighters have launched."

"Order them all to fall into CSP formation," Ted ordered. On the display, blue icons fanned out around *Ark Royal*. Ted traced their patterns with his eye for a long moment, hoping that Prince Henry and the other young pilots survived, then turned his attention back to the overall situation. "And launch a ballistic probe towards the enemy starships."

"Aye, Admiral," Janelle said. She paused. "We only have a couple of probes left."

"We won't have any if we lose this battle," Ted said. The beancounters would definitely throw a fit when they found out how many probes he'd expended, but he found it rather had to care. "Launch the probe, then put the results on the main display."

"Aye, Admiral," Janelle said.

"And send a signal," Ted added. The researchers – he thought of Polly and felt an odd pang - thought the aliens responded better to bluntness than diplomatic weasel words. "Tell them to break off or we'll open fire."

"Aye, Admiral," Janelle said. There was a long pause. The seconds ticked past the moment the aliens could have responded and retreated into the distance. "No response, sir."

"Shit," Ted muttered. He'd hoped they could communicate now, but the War Faction clearly wasn't interested in talking – or anything, beyond victory or defeat. The other aliens were doing nothing, but watching. "Show me the live feed from the probe."

He sucked in his breath as he saw the enemy fleet. On one hand, it was weaker than he'd expected, unless the War Faction had invented a brand new weapon. The Royal Navy had come up with quite a few weapons that could end the war if they were ever put into production and deployed and the aliens, he had to admit, were revoltingly ingenious. But on the other hand, he'd expected the aliens to commit a much larger force against *Ark Royal*. If there was anyone who had good reason to know how tough the ancient carrier was, it was the War Faction.

"Admiral," Janelle said. Her voice was calm, but there was a hint of alarm running through her words. "The enemy are launching starfighters."

Ted nodded. So the fifteenth ship was a carrier, then. Larger than an escort carrier, according to the probe, but nowhere near as big as a modern carrier or *Ark Royal*. Four squadrons of starfighters zoomed out into space, then hurled themselves towards *Ark Royal's* covering fighters. They seemed remarkably confident that the carrier's fighters couldn't leave their posts and engage the enemy starships.

And they might be right, Ted conceded, reluctantly. He wouldn't have hesitated to take the risk of thinning his fighter cover with a veteran crew, but *Ark Royal's* pilots were too green to be fully trusted. *And yet it might not matter.*

"Alter course, bring the mass drivers to bear on their ships," he ordered. It was time to try something new. "I want to execute a full scattershot in" – he checked his console – "five minutes."

Janelle looked up from her console, frowning. "Admiral," she said carefully, "it is unlikely that will affect the enemy starfighters."

"It doesn't have to," Ted said. One of the major downsides of mass drivers was that smaller ships could dodge their projectiles, if they had time to react. It would be a great deal harder for them to avoid the tiny scattershot projectiles. Even if they missed completely, the aliens would have a nasty fright. "Aim for the ships, then prepare to fire."

"Aye, Admiral," Janelle said. "Weapons locked on target."

Ted nodded, then diverted his attention to the display monitoring the alien world. So far, nothing seemed to have happened, one way or the other. Their defence grid was armed, sweeping space with active sensors, but they weren't launching fighters or missiles at either side in the coming battle. Ted gritted his teeth, understanding far too well why the aliens would prefer to stay out of the fight. *They* didn't seem too concerned about the prospect of the War Faction living up to its name.

They're not human, he reminded himself, savagely. There wasn't a human power that had survived the Troubles that would allow the murder of its ambassadors to pass without making more than a minor complaint. Ted had been expecting a diplomatic offensive, perhaps even a demand that the sole surviving Russian was handed over for punishment, but nothing had happened. The aliens, it seemed, considered their ambassadors expendable.

It might make sense, he told himself. The aliens *believed* in consensual thinking. Sending ambassadors to a foreign power might risk losing the ambassadors to that power, if the ambassadors were talked into accepting a different point of view. And the aliens bred so rapidly that child mortality had to be terrifyingly high. The aliens weren't evil or malicious, even to their own kind, but they were disconcertingly lax in places. They had an oddly uncaring attitude to their own lives that worried him. It wasn't that they were prepared to throw away their lives just for a tactical advantage, more that they simply didn't worry if they lived or died.

He shook his head, pushing the thought aside with an effort.

"Order the starfighters that they are to engage when the enemy craft cross the red line," he ordered, "assuming the aliens don't open fire first."

He drew it out on the display. "We can't hold fire past that point," he added. "If they're coming that close they mean business."

It wasn't a pleasant thought. The aliens might not have any concept of personal space, according to the ambassadorial reports, but they knew better than to deliberately court a collision. Two starships ramming each other would have been disastrous, as would ramming a starfighter into a modern carrier. But then, it wouldn't have mattered if one starfighter had rammed *Ark Royal*. The armoured carrier would just have shrugged off the impact and kept firing.

"Aye, sir," Janelle said. She paused. "They will cross the red line in two minutes."

Ted nodded and braced himself.

———

"Engage as soon as they cross the red line," Commander Rose Labara said. "I say again, engage as soon as they cross the red line."

Henry nodded to himself, keeping a watchful eye on Rose's fighter. He remembered her as a combative pilot, one of the ones who would start a fight merely if someone looked at them the wrong way. In hindsight, she was just the sort of personality type to start a fling with her superior officer, believing it would be meaningless. The certainty of death, sooner rather than later, would merely have added spice to the relationship.

But she'd clearly felt *something* for her former commanding officer, Henry had to admit, although it surprised him. Starfighter pilots weren't the type to settle down, at least until they'd sown their oats and completed their time in the cockpit. The lives they led told against it, he'd learned very quickly. It was easier to find a prostitute in Sin City or a companion in Luna City than try to balance married life with a carrier where one could die at any moment. And he was sure Rose had done just that in her earlier days...

And now she was in mourning. And leading her pilots out to do battle with the aliens.

Henry sighed and redirected his attention towards the oncoming storm. For once, humanity had the numbers advantage, although he knew that meant nothing. The pilots Rose had had to take in hand simply lacked the polish of Academy graduates; Henry had been astonished, envious and terrified when he'd realised they hadn't even passed the final exams. Five days of heavy exercising in the simulators had convinced him that the raw material was there, but the discipline was lacking. They would get there, given time. But he suspected time was about to run out.

He scowled. The alien tactics made no sense. It looked as though they were trying to rush the carrier, a pointless exercise if there weren't infinite reserves. Their forces would probably punch through the CSP and strafe the hull – the Admiral's insistence on letting the aliens fire first unless they crossed the red line would make certain of it – but it wouldn't get them anything. Unless they had a nasty surprise up their sleeves...

Which they don't wear, he thought, dryly. *Perhaps they're just so desperate to restart the war that they're trying to goad us into firing on the other factions. But the more distance we put between ourselves and them, the less-likely that is to happen. We're not going to accidentally fire on the good guys...*

"They will cross the red line in thirty seconds," Rose said. Everyone could already see it from their displays. "Lock weapons on target; prepare to engage."

And the game, if game it is, becomes serious, Henry thought. *But what are they doing?*

"Red line in ten seconds," Rose said. "Choose your partners..."

Henry felt his stomach clench. It had been easier before he'd been a captive, he realised, easier to deal out death against a faceless and monstrous enemy. Now...

They want to restart the war, he thought. What were they doing? Were they planning to sacrifice themselves in the hopes of convincing the other factions to rejoin the war or did they merely intend to carry on without their former allies? Did they intend to force the humans into firing first or were they merely taking advantage of the situation to get closer before they opened fire? Or were they planning to break off at the very last minute?

They could have engaged us already, if they'd chosen to open fire, he thought. *We're well inside their engagement range and vice versa.*

And yet they didn't know about the red line. How could they?

But it didn't matter, he told himself, until after the war had been brought to a formal end, when historians from both sides could fight and refight the war at leisure. *They have to be stopped.*

"Enemy craft are launching missiles," Rose said. "All starfighters; engage. I say again; all starfighters, engage."

CHAPTER
THIRTY FIVE

"Enemy craft are launching missiles," Janelle reported.

Ted nodded, unsurprised. Plasma weapons were largely useless against the Old Lady and the War Faction knew it. Using missiles – probably with bomb-pumped laser warheads – was their only hope of inflicting serious damage on the carrier. And they'd managed to launch the missiles from a dangerously close range. He cursed diplomacy under his breath, then keyed a switch.

"Commander Williams, you are authorised to open fire," he said. "Take out as many of those missiles as possible."

He forced himself to watch calmly as *Ark Royal's* point defence weapons opened fire. Humanity had improved the system enormously since the start of the war, adding plasma weapons and rail guns to the ancient systems that had once been designed to counter older threats, but he knew the targeting was far from precise. Several of the alien missiles vanished as the point defence picked them off, others fell to the starfighters as they opened fire on the alien ships, yet a handful made it into engagement range and detonated. The ancient carrier rocked violently as bomb-pumped lasers stabbed into her guts.

"Four direct hits," Janelle reported, as red icons flashed up on the main display. "No serious damage, as far as I can tell, but our armour took a beating."

Ted winced, feeling his ship's pain. "Keep engaging the alien ships," he ordered. Damage control teams were already on their way to the damaged compartments, while the datanet had already adapted to the loss of various communications nodes and other systems destroyed by the blasts, but he knew damage would likely mount up rapidly. "And try to drive the alien ships away from us."

New red icons flashed into view on the display as the alien ships launched a second salvo of missiles. Ted frowned – the aliens had to know ship-launched missiles were hellishly inefficient – then realised the aliens were playing it carefully, rather than coming close enough to allow Ted to pick them off with his mass drivers. It would be a long drawn-out engagement, but the aliens would hold the upper hand. He turned his attention to the targeting systems as the mass drivers continued firing, sending blasts of scattershot towards the alien ships. One of them was hit and blown apart by the impact, the remainder kept evading the incoming projectiles.

He frowned as the missiles closed in on his ship, then redirected part of the CSP to form the first line of defence. The remainder kept dogfighting with the alien fighters, trying to keep them from returning to their mothership or interfering with the point defence systems. Alien missile after alien missile vanished – there was plenty of time to plot targeting solutions as the missiles had been launched from well outside sprint mode range – but there were too many of them to ensure they were *all* destroyed. Ted braced himself for a second attack on his ship, then let out a sigh of relief as three of the four missiles that detonated managed to miss their target. Only one beam stabbed into his ship.

"They've damaged the starboard flight deck," Janelle said. "I'm redirecting damage control teams to that sector."

Ted cursed. The aliens, deliberately or otherwise, had crippled *Ark Royal's* ability to recover her fighters. Cycling the starfighters that required replenishment through the ship was going to take time, placing a colossal strain on his operations. And even though the alien starfighters were being beaten back, counterattacking was going to be a major problem.

"Redirect the bombers and two squadrons of escorting fighters," he ordered. "They are to target and destroy the alien ships."

He gritted his teeth in frustration. Kurt Schneider should never have died. *He* would have handled the matter without Ted's personal intervention. But Commander Labara had to be out there with her ships…Ted cursed under his breath, angrily. If he took up a post at the Admiralty after returning home, if the war came to an end, he was going to make damn sure there would never be another shortage of starfighter pilots.

"Aye, sir," Janelle said. The carrier shuddered again as one of the alien starfighters accidentally crashed into her hull. "Starfighters are being redirected now."

Ted let out a long breath. "Target the alien carrier with scattershot," he ordered. The timing was just about right, assuming the intelligence geeks were correct about just how long the alien fighters could remain active without replenishment. "Then throw two massive barrages at her. Make her run for her life."

Janelle smiled, darkly. "Aye, sir," she said. There was a long pause. "Projectiles away."

The alien formation scattered, their carrier falling back rapidly as she tried to evade. Ted felt a moment of envy – the lighter carrier was far more manoeuvrable than *Ark Royal* – before dismissing it as stupid. The price paid for the ability to alter course sharply was a near-complete lack of armour. One hit from a mass driver and the alien carrier would be blown into dust. It was why modern carriers had thinned out their armour until it was almost non-existent.

But it made sense until we encountered the aliens, Ted thought, morbidly. *Our own attempts to produce plasma weapons failed miserably.*

The alien starfighters – those that had survived – darted back, clearly intent on protecting their carrier. Ted didn't blame them, even though there was a planet and its orbital facilities within easy range. In their shoes, he would have wondered what sort of welcome he'd get from the other factions too. Besides, the carrier was the only ship that could replenish them in time to return to the fight. But it was already too late. The human starfighters were closing in on their targets at terrifying speed.

"The bombers are preparing to engage their targets," Janelle said. She sounded tense, unsurprisingly. Prince Henry was leading the strike. "The aliens are trying to engage them with plasma weapons."

The regulations governing relationships will have to be revised, Ted thought, in a moment of irrelevance. What did it say about the ancient carrier's crew that there had been at least two mission-threatening romances?

He wondered, absently, if there had been others, then pushed the thought aside. *If any of us get home we can worry about it then.*

Two starfighters vanished in puffs of smoke as they fell prey to alien weapons, but the remainder closed in and opened fire, launching their missiles towards the alien ships, then breaking off as the aliens redirected their attention towards the missiles. Nine of twelve missiles were vaporised before they had a chance to detonate, the remainder entered attack range and detonated, savaging the alien ship. It disintegrated, moments later, in a colossal explosion.

"Target destroyed," Janelle said, calmly. "Secondary strike engaging... now."

Ted smirked, ruthlessly. The aliens hadn't brought along anything like enough starfighters to win the engagement, now their first attack on the carrier had been defeated. But the aliens themselves didn't seem to agree. Even as his starfighters were retreating, the aliens were reconcentrating their forces and preparing to continue the fight. Ted eyed the display, concerned. So far, the aliens seemed to have screwed up. And yet he had too much experience to rely on that hopelessly optimistic assumption.

Unless they assumed the other factions would join in, Ted thought. Intelligence's estimates of just how many starfighters could be crammed into the alien fortresses made frightening reading. Target One had been nowhere near so heavily defended. *That would make sense – and explain why they brought only a small amount of firepower to the fight.*

"Continue firing," he ordered, as the aliens started their second offensive. This time, their starfighters were noticeably depleted. Behind them, missiles were launched as the alien ships opened fire. "And try to drive them away from our hull."

"Aye, sir," Janelle said. "I..."

She broke off as the display suddenly flared with ugly red light.

———

These bastards just don't know when to give up, Henry thought, as he dodged a plasma bolt from one of the alien fighters. The aliens had skill, he had to admit, but they didn't have the numbers to win. *They should be running now...*

He broke off as an alert sounded over the emergency channel, then glanced at his display. The other alien factions had finally taken a hand, launching so many starfighters that the human sensors couldn't even begin to count them all. Henry felt absolute despair as a wall of starfighters threw themselves towards the human ships, so many that he knew there was no way they could stop them all, or escape. The ancient carrier and her flotilla were doomed.

"We're picking up a signal," Rose said. She sounded utterly despondent, very different from her normal self. But then, the odds facing them had become utterly impossible. They could trade ten alien starfighters for every human craft and the aliens would still come out ahead. "They're broadcasting to us all..."

Henry keyed a switch. "Stop. Firing," an atonal voice said. "Both. Stop. Firing."

"What?" Henry said. On the display, the original group of alien starfighters were breaking off and putting some distance between themselves and the human ships. "What are they doing?"

"Intervening, it would seem," Rose said. She took a breath. "Did they tell you anything about this on the planet?"

"No," Henry said, flatly. The aliens had been debating the issue, the last he'd heard, although as a starfighter pilot he no longer had access to the diplomats. He'd worried the aliens would see the Russian actions as proof humans were irrationally evil. "But I would suggest doing what they say."

Rose laughed, a little hysterically. "I suppose several thousand starfighters are a strong case for obedience," she said. She cleared her throat. "All ships, fall back to CSP position; I say again, all ships fall back to CSP position."

Henry frowned – Rose hardly sounded commanding – but obeyed, making a mental note to have a private chat with her later. It was probably against regulations to do so...he shook his head. Given that he planned to leave the Royal Navy at the end of the war, it wouldn't matter if she wrote angry remarks in his file – and besides, it was unlikely anyone would take them seriously.

He sighed, inwardly. Had he finally fallen into the trap of using his rank as a weapon?

The wave of alien starfighters kept their distance from *Ark Royal,* but positioned themselves to stand between the human ships and the War Faction's flotilla. Henry watched grimly, wondering if the War Faction's monomania would lead it to open fire on the other aliens, even though they were grossly outgunned. But it seemed not. Instead, the aliens recovered their starfighters and set out for the tramline, exchanging angry messages with their fellows the whole time. Henry would have liked to be able to understand what they were saying. He had a feeling that it would have shown him more of just how the alien society actually worked.

But it wasn't possible. One day, he knew, there would be an automatic translator that would allow translations to be carried out in real time. Until then, all they could do was wait…and pray it wasn't an elaborate trick.

———

"Hold fire," Ted ordered, as the alien starfighters slipped into position. He had to admire their nerve, although the certainty of possessing superior firepower had probably helped the alien decision to cover *Ark Royal.* "Recall one half of the starfighters and get them replenished, then replace the CSP and send them through replenishment."

"Aye, sir," Janelle said.

Ted nodded to himself, then looked back at the display. He'd known absolute despair as the wall of starfighters rushed towards his ships, then a burst of pure relief as the aliens ordered their fellows to stop firing. He couldn't help reflecting on how the aliens had clearly drawn inspiration from humanity's actions. Kurt Schneider's death had definitely not been in vain, not when he'd given his life to save the aliens from the Russians. The aliens had mirrored that action when they'd put themselves between the humans and the War Faction.

But the War Faction's ships were still retreating, broadcasting angry messages towards the alien world. Their homeworld, perhaps? Ted knew there was no way they could be translated properly, leaving him with a disturbing mystery. What, if anything, was the War Faction actually *saying*?

His imagination provided everything from lists of Captain Haddock's favourite insults to promises of revenge at a much later date. But the aliens seemed inclined to just let the War Faction go without taking further action. It couldn't be that serious, could it?

His console buzzed. "Admiral," Commander Williams said, "is it wise to draw down the CSP?"

"I don't think we have a choice," Ted said. "The starfighters do need replenishment – and besides, they have enough firepower to make the issue immaterial. If half of those ships are armed with missiles, they'll take us apart within seconds, no matter how many starfighters we have on CSP."

"Yes, Admiral," Commander Williams said. She sounded annoyed and worried; Ted didn't blame her. With her commanding officer in sick-bay and unlikely to return to duty anytime soon, the responsibility for commanding the ship had fallen on her shoulders. At least she'd had more experience of being the XO than Captain Fitzwilliam, when he'd assumed command. "However, we still don't understand their intentions…"

"I suspect we will find out," Ted said. He smiled. "Personally, I'm inclined to view this as a hopeful gesture. If the other factions are prepared to intervene to help us, we may well have grounds for peace after all."

He sighed inwardly as the connection broke. Despite his optimism, and he *was* optimistic, he knew it wouldn't be that easy. The human race had an agreement that there would be no serious fighting within the Sol System itself. It was quite possible that the aliens had something comparable, something that had forced them to intervene despite preferring not to take a side. But they'd already taken a side, simply by intervening. Somehow, Ted was sure the War Faction wouldn't change its ways because the other factions had disagreed with it.

"Admiral," Janelle said, "I have the basic damage report."

"Show me," Ted ordered.

He studied the display for a long moment, silently blessing the starship's long-dead designers. They'd worked enough redundancy into the carrier that the damaged compartments could simply be sealed off, rather than repaired before they returned to Earth and entered a shipyard. And the launching tubes could be patched up, given enough time. The whole system was designed for quick repair. It was, after all, the most vulnerable place on the ship.

But the real problem lay in the damaged armour. There was enough damage to ensure that the aliens would have several places to shoot at, when they returned to the offensive. They couldn't be patched up in time, not without a shipyard…

"Tell the engineers to do what they can," he said. "Then order the compartments evacuated and sealed. I don't want anyone in them if we have to engage the enemy once again."

"Aye, Admiral," Janelle said.

Ted took a breath as he mentally worked through the list of repairs. They'd loaded additional sheets of more modern armour when they'd crammed the ship before departure, but he knew it wouldn't have the resiliency of the old-style protection. The aliens might realise that the hull wasn't properly patched and target it specifically. It was what Ted would have done in their place. And it would prove hellishly effective.

Bastards, he thought.

"We also fired off half of our mass driver projectiles," Janelle added. "The tactical section is requesting permission to mine a nearby asteroid."

Ted shook his head. He could see their point – mass drivers tended to run through ammunition at terrifying speed – but the aliens might well object to humanity taking some of their patrimony. They could ask, of course, yet he had the feeling the aliens would say no. It would probably be better, from their point of view, to have the Old Lady effectively disarmed.

We wouldn't be too happy about an armed alien ship orbiting Earth, he thought, ruefully. *Why would they be any different?*

"Admiral, Ambassador Melbourne is requesting an immediate meeting," Janelle said, suddenly. "There doesn't seem to be time to bring him back to the ship, so he wants to open a secure channel."

"I'll take it in my office," Ted said, rising to his feet. A request for a secure channel…it had to be bad news. "Inform Commander Williams that she has tactical command; continue to monitor the repairs and inform me if anything requires my attention."

"Aye, sir," Janelle said.

Ted stepped through the hatch into his office, sat down at his desk and pressed his hand against the sensor, allowing the terminal to identify him. The touch reminded him of Captain Fitzwilliam's implant, missing – presumed destroyed – since the destruction of the stolen starfighter. They'd have to produce another implant, Ted knew, for Captain Fitzwilliam or Commander Williams if she assumed permanent command. The medical reports had suggested that would be the case, sooner rather than later. Captain Fitzwilliam was in no state to resume command.

"Ambassador," he said, when Melbourne's face appeared in the small display. "I understand you wished to speak to me?"

"Yes, Admiral," Ambassador Melbourne said. He looked deeply worried. "The aliens just informed me that the War Faction has fragmented. One faction has decided to accept peace, Admiral, but the other faction has no intention of ending the war."

Ted felt ice crawling down the back of his spine. It had happened before, when humans fought humans, that some extremists refused to accept a negotiated peace, even when the peace terms were in their favour. Some of them had even managed to prolong the war until the end was undeniable. And they'd always cost their fellows dearly.

He took a breath. "Admiral," he warned, "they're going to attack *Earth!*"

CHAPTER
THIRTY SIX

James had rarely felt quite so helpless in his entire life. He'd endured his fair share of bumps and bruises as a child, including a fall from a horse that had left one leg broken, but nothing ever quite like this. It had taken hours of arguing to convince Doctor Hastings that he could attend conferences in a wheelchair, then he'd had to endure the indignity of being pushed through the corridors by his steward. The only saving grace was that he wasn't – quite – out of command. It wouldn't last, but for the moment he intended to savour it.

But being in a wheelchair was nothing compared to the thought of what was advancing towards Earth.

"The War Faction has mustered a considerable fleet," Admiral Smith said. His fingers traced the tramlines on the holographic display. "It is their intention to head directly to Earth and end the war by bombarding the planet with radioactive weapons. Earth will be rendered uninhabitable and billions of humans – billions *more* humans – will die."

James took a breath. It hurt even to breathe. "Can't the other factions stop them?"

"Apparently not," Admiral Smith said. "They took heavy losses in the earlier battles too, Captain. They claim they don't have more than a handful of ships available and they're holding them back to defend their worlds against the War Faction."

"Or us, if we retaliate," Farley said. The tactical officer leaned forward. "Some of their factions may want peace, but they might also think that the War Faction succeeding wouldn't actually be a bad thing. Or they may assume we can tell the difference between factions when we counterattack."

"Or they may all be hostile, just disinclined to lift a finger themselves," James said. He'd seen aristocrats watch others self-destruct without doing anything to save their lives, merely because it was more fun to watch than intervene. "Can we stop them?"

"Earth's defences…were badly battered during the previous battle," Admiral Smith said. "If the objective is to get a single radioactive warhead into the planet's atmosphere, Captain, they'll succeed. A stealth missile will accomplish the mission perfectly."

Just like we planned with the bioweapon, James thought. *And we may still deploy the bioweapon in response to the War Faction's attack.*

Admiral Smith leaned forward. "According to the aliens, the War Faction has a base here," he said, tapping one location on the starchart. "You will note that it is some distance from the border, as they suspected there would be further contacts between Heinlein and Vera Cruz and they wanted distance between us and their shipyards. Their fleet is gathered there…"

"We can't get there in time," James said. It would take at least two weeks to get to the alien system, by which time the aliens would have already started off towards Earth. The signal ordering the offensive would probably have *already* reached the system. His chest twanged, painfully. "Admiral…is it hopeless?"

"No," the Admiral said. "I believe there is another possibility. They must assume we will be warned, so they will take the shortest possible route to Earth. In order to do so, they will have to jump through the New Russia system."

He looked from face to face. "We will depart within the hour, along with all but one of our flotilla," he continued. "If we move at considerable speed, we should be able to reach New Russia before the aliens and prepare to make a stand there."

"We will be pushing the drives to the limit," Anderson warned. The Chief Engineer looked exhausted. "If we lost the drive midway to our destination, Admiral, we would be screwed."

"We have to take the risk," Admiral Smith said. "We can try to buy time for Earth to prepare its defences, or even come to our aid. That is *all* we can do."

He rose to his feet. "It has been seventy years since the Old Lady was commissioned into the Royal Navy," he said. "Until this war began she was not tested in combat. But now she has been tested and she has done us proud. She will do us proud once again in this, our final battle."

"If we win this, the war will come to an end," he concluded. "And if we lose, at least we will go down fighting, buying time for Earth."

James felt a surge of pride in his ship as the Admiral paused. It was true, he knew, that *Ark Royal* had never been expected to serve as more than reinforcement to the modern carriers, back before the Battle of New Russia. But since then, the Old Lady had done brilliantly, surviving damage that would have ripped a modern carrier apart. There was very good reason to be proud of her and her crew.

"Captain Fitzwilliam, remain behind," the Admiral ordered. "Everyone else; dismissed."

"Admiral," James said, as soon as they were alone. "I…"

"I'm sending *Standish* back to Earth," the Admiral interrupted. "She will be carrying urgent dispatches for the Admiralty, a copy of the draft treaty and a note of my intentions. I'm also stripping her of most of her experienced crew for the carrier."

"Captain Shawcross will love that," James predicted, sarcastically.

The Admiral smiled, humourlessly. "I'm sending Janelle back too," he said. "And Polly. And a dozen others who are probably more suited to return to Earth. And you."

James stared. "Admiral, this is *my* ship," he said. "I…"

"I need someone who can convince the Admiralty to deploy reinforcements to New Russia," Admiral Smith said. "And you're badly injured, Captain. I could hear you grunting in pain throughout the meeting. You can't stay on the ship."

"I'd throw a tantrum if I thought it would get me anywhere," James said. Cold logic agreed with Admiral Smith; sentiment insisted he should be on the command deck as the Old Lady faced the aliens one final time. "I assume it wouldn't, right?"

"It wouldn't get you anything other than a bad memory," the Admiral said. He took a datachip and pressed it into James's hand. "Get that to the Admiralty, James, and tell them that I will be taking up that desk job after the end of the war."

"That would be a good idea," James agreed, mischievously. "Admiral…"

"And thank you," Admiral Smith said. "For *everything*."

James swallowed, remembering just how far they'd come together.

"You're welcome, Admiral," he said. He managed to get to his feet, then pull off a snappy salute. "I'll see you back on Earth."

But, as he was wheeled through the hatch to catch his shuttle, he had the strangest feeling he would never see the Admiral again.

———

"I wish we had time for…"

Henry shook his head. "I'm sorry," he said, changing his tune. "That makes me sound awfully selfish, doesn't it?"

"You're not the only one," Janelle said. She looked…irked. "I still don't understand why the Admiral is sending me back to Earth."

"Maybe he thinks Captain Fitzwilliam will need help in convincing the Admiralty to act," Henry speculated. "You served as Admiral Smith's aide. Who knows his thinking better than you?"

But he had a different idea. The Admiral might have come to think of Janelle as a daughter, of sorts. He'd been furious when he'd discovered that Henry and Janelle had become lovers, but he'd been more concerned for Janelle than Henry himself. In hindsight, Henry understood just what the Admiral had been feeling. His reported death had caused no shortage of problems for his lover.

And the Admiral may think no one will be coming back from this mission, he thought, morbidly. The odds had never been good, but now they were worse. *He might have wanted to make sure she survived.*

"Here," he said, reaching into his pocket and retrieving a datachip. "If I don't make it back, please will you give this to my family."

Janelle stared down at the chip, then looked up at him. "You'll make it back," she said, firmly. "And you still owe me a homestead on an isolated asteroid."

316

Henry grinned, then swept her into a hug. He wanted – he needed – to hold her as long as possible, before her shuttle departed *Ark Royal*.

"Promise me something," he said, as he held her. "If…if I don't make it, and I might not, don't let the monarchy destroy your life. Stay in the navy or go elsewhere – and change your name. Whatever you do, don't let the monarchy claim you. It will destroy any hope of a normal existence."

"I understand," Janelle said.

She kissed him, her eyes bright with unshed tears, then she turned and practically ran through the hatch. Henry stared at her retreating behind for a long moment, then closed his eyes as the hatch hissed closed. She didn't know it, but he'd changed his will. He *did* have a sizable sum of money in his own name, after all, and if he didn't come home it would go to Janelle, making her a wealthy young woman. She could go to one of the worlds outside the British Commonwealth and make a life for herself, well away from the monarchy.

And goddamned reporters, he thought, sourly. He'd taken a moment to review some of the crap they'd sprouted about him after his death and most of it had been nonsense. Maybe he could sue for libel after he returned to Earth…he shook his head, tiredly. If there was one thing the Royal Family had learned about the parasites who believed they had a right to know everything, it was that squashing one or two of them was pointless. There were always more of the vermin scurrying around.

He sat down and reached for a datapad, forcing himself to concentrate on his duties. There would be time to miss her later, afterwards. And pray they both survived.

———

"*Standish* has departed, sir," Commander Williams said. "She's on her way back to Earth."

"Good," Ted said. He looked up, expecting to see Janelle in her usual place. But she was gone. "Set course for New Russia, Commander, and take us there as fast as possible."

"Aye, sir," Commander Williams said.

Ted sighed, then looked up at the starchart, running through the calculations again and again. It was going to be close, he knew, very close. If they'd screwed up one or more of the assumptions, the aliens might make it through the New Russia system before the Old Lady arrived, forcing them to chase the aliens to Earth. And then...*Standish* would probably reach Earth in time, he hoped, but would it be enough? Earth's defences were weaker than they'd been ever since the human race had started reaching into outer space.

He wanted a drink. He needed a drink. But there was no alcohol on the ship, apart from the illicit still he knew existed *somewhere*. And besides, the last thing anyone needed was a drunken Admiral in command during the climactic battle of his ship's career. They would win, he knew, or die bravely. There was no alternative.

And he'd sent Janelle home.

He wasn't sure *why* he'd done that, although he knew he could easily justify the decision afterwards, if necessary. She was a promising young officer; service on *Ark Royal* as his aide would guarantee her a place at the Admiralty, if she wanted it, or a chance to move to one of the new carriers when they finally entered service. And the Royal Navy *needed* promising young officers. But he knew that wasn't the only reason for his decision.

He reached out and stroked the bulkhead as the ship started to move, heading directly towards the nearest tramline. The aliens had sworn blind that no one would attempt to impede their passage, although Ted had no intention of taking it for granted. *Ark Royal's* course would be easy to predict, once the aliens calculated her destination. If they sent word to the War Faction...

But it wouldn't matter, Ted told himself. The War Faction's fleet *had* to go through New Russia. There was no alternative unless they wanted to add several weeks to their journey, several weeks Earth could use to prepare the defences and get hundreds of thousands of people off the threatened world. The Old Lady would get to New Russia first and confront the aliens. Any other outcome was unthinkable.

He stroked the bulkhead again, feeling a dull *thrumming* flowing through the metal. The Old Lady was cumbersome and inelegant – and ugly as sin – but she was beautiful to him. She had *always* been beautiful, although he could never have expressed the sensation in a manner anyone else could understand. There was a crudeness to her structure, a sense the designers hadn't given a damn about anything beyond functionality…and yet she had a heart and soul that the more modern carriers lacked. He could have retrieved his career, Ted knew, if he'd given up the drink. But he'd chosen to stay on *Ark Royal*, instead of retiring and drinking himself to death.

It had been a strange time, he recalled. His loyal crew had worked to keep the carrier functional, even though few of them had believed the ship would ever return to active service. They'd bought, begged and occasionally stolen components they needed to keep the ship in working order. They'd even allowed schoolchildren to tour the ship in exchange for funds they'd invested to keep the carrier active. Ted had often wondered why the Admiralty had never caught on. But then, the carrier had been out of sight and out of mind.

Until she was needed again, he thought, as his hand slipped away from the bulkhead. *And now they need her more than ever.*

———

"The drives are having real problems, Commander," Anderson said, days later. "We're overstressing both the regular drives and the modified Puller Drive. I think we're at grave risk of losing the latter."

Ted cursed under his breath. Losing the ship's drives would be utterly disastrous, but he didn't dare slow down. There were only a handful of hours before the aliens would pass through New Russia – assuming they had left when he'd calculated they'd get the message – and they had to be there first. He'd given the whole issue of bringing the aliens to battle a great deal of thought, but the only way to force them to engage was to be there first. There was no time for repairs.

"Take us through the tramline as soon as we reach it, then take the Puller Drive down completely," he ordered. They didn't need the alien modifications to get back to Earth, if they'd missed the alien fleet. "But we can't deactivate the other drives."

"So it would seem," Anderson said. The Engineer exchanged glances with Commander Williams. Judging from the way they looked at each other, they'd probably planned the discussion beforehand – and it was not going according to plan. "Admiral…."

"We don't have a choice," Ted said. "If we fail now, we risk everything."

Commander Williams stood upright. "Admiral," she said, "I believe…"

Ted cut her off. "If you want to make a formal protest, Commander, you may do so," he said. "I will note it in my log, which will be submitted before the formal Board of Inquiry into my actions. However, I believe we have no choice, but to take the risk."

Her face twitched with suppressed anger. Ted briefly wondered if he should have sent her back to Earth instead. Commander Williams had been an up-and-coming officer, with a post on a modern carrier, before the aliens had proved that modern carriers were little better than target practice. She wasn't inclined to accept risks Ted knew to be unavoidable. But then, the Old Lady had far more redundancy built into her than a modern carrier.

"I will log a formal protest," she said, finally.

"Noted," Ted said. He wondered if she'd realised that there were only two options; victory or defeat. If they won, the slate would be wiped clean; if they lost, they were screwed anyway. "We have only one more jump to make, Commander. Take up your station and prepare for transit."

"I would prefer to be on the secondary bridge," Commander Williams said. She hesitated. "Have you given any thought to tactical command of the flotilla?"

"Yes," Ted said. He paused. "Why…?"

Commander Williams looked, for a long moment, as if she'd bitten into a lemon. "You have more command experience than myself," she said. "I think you should take command of the ship."

Ted eyed her, surprised. Had Captain Fitzwilliam told her to step aside if they managed to intercept the aliens? Or had she come up with it on her own? Or…

Technically, it was dereliction of duty. But she was right. He *did* have far more command experience with the ancient carrier. And this really wasn't the time to learn.

"Take the secondary bridge, Commander," Ted said, gently. He made a mental note to ensure her career didn't suffer for her decision. "And then prepare for the final transit."

———

The bridge felt almost like home, Ted reflected, as he took the command chair. It wasn't the same being in the CIC, where there was a sense of detachment from the battle. Here, he sat at the nerve centre of his ship.

"Take us through the tramline," he ordered.

He waited. For a moment, there was nothing…and then the universe darkened, as if he were about to sneeze. And then the entire ship shook so violently that he was half-convinced the Old Lady was coming apart at the seams. And then everything snapped back to normal.

"Admiral," Anderson said, "we made it to New Russia, but we lost the Puller Drive. Completely. Even the human-designed systems have burned out."

Ted sucked in his breath, then sighed. Whatever happened, he knew, they would not be leaving the New Russia system. Not now. They were trapped.

"Understood," he said. At least the realspace drive had survived. "Do what you can."

CHAPTER
THIRTY SEVEN

"This is quite a report, Captain," the First Space Lord said.

"Thank you, sir," James said. It had been a nightmarish trip from the alien homeworld – if it was their homeworld - to Earth, pushing the frigate's drives to the limit. "Will you take action?"

"I will have to raise the issue at the Defence Council," the First Space Lord said. He took a breath. "There will be reluctance to send any major forces away from Earth."

James took a breath. "We don't dare risk fighting them in the Sol System," he snapped. "If they want to make Earth uninhabitable…"

The First Space Lord held up a hand. "I understand what's at stake, Captain," he said. "But it will be a joint decision."

"Then blackmail the Russians," James said. "We have evidence they tried to undermine – hell, *destroy* – any chance of a negotiated peace. They killed Royal Navy personnel and blackmailed others. Tell them we won't seek revenge in exchange for their voting alongside us."

"The Russians don't have the clout they had before the war," the First Space Lord pointed out. "Their vote might not be as much help as you're suggesting."

"Then send the remaining fleet alone," James pressed. "Sir…"

"I will deal with the issue," the First Space Lord said. "Now, I suggest you prepare for a major debriefing. I understand you made contact with the aliens…"

"We made contact with the Russian settlements in the asteroid belt," Davidson said. The communications officer looked stressed. "They claim the aliens haven't sent any additional ships into the system."

Ted nodded, relieved. Either they'd beaten the aliens to the system or the aliens had decided to take the long way to Earth. Either way, humanity would have a chance.

"And the ships orbiting the planet itself?"

"They've just been watching and waiting," Davidson said. "The Russians say the aliens haven't even called in orbital strikes."

"They probably don't have any real interest in our settlements," Ted guessed. "And they've shown no interest in us?"

"None," Farley confirmed. "I think they must have detected our arrival, sir, but they haven't left orbit to investigate."

"Good," Ted said. He looked over at Anderson. "How bad is it?"

"The Puller Drive is completely fucked, sir," Anderson said. His voice was calm, too calm. "I believe the realspace drive will hold, for a while, but not for long. We really need a full refit..."

"Which we're not going to get," Ted said. Anderson hadn't said 'I told you so,' but Ted was sure he'd thought it once or twice. It was hard to blame him. One way or the other, *Ark Royal* had come to the end of the line. "Concentrate on strengthening the hull and preparing for engagement."

"Aye, sir," Anderson said. "I have some ideas that might be costly in the long run, but will give us an advantage for the moment."

"Then prepare them," Ted said. "We will assume this is the last battle and ready everything for the fight."

"Aye, sir," Anderson said, again.

"Launch two of our remaining probes to watch the tramlines," Ted ordered. "And then prepare to start Operation Deception. Dismissed."

He watched them go, then sank back in his chair. For better or worse, *Ark Royal* could no longer leave the New Russia system, where she'd fought her second major engagement with the aliens. They were committed, now. Victory or death...but then, the War Faction felt the same way.

They were apt students, Ted thought, with a flicker of amusement. *But then, so were we.*

He rose to his feet and headed for the hatch. Operation Deception – the attempt to convince the aliens that *Ark Royal* had headed towards the tramline to Earth – would start in thirty minutes, allowing him barely enough time to tour his ship. It was tradition, after all, that the Captain would tour the ship before battle. Had he done it before? He couldn't remember.

But we have to pretend to be a hole in space, he thought. The War Faction could not be allowed a chance to avoid engagement. They might want the carrier destroyed, but somehow he suspected they would prefer to head straight for Earth. Even with a fully-working drive, they would have been unable to catch the alien ships. *We need to impale them on our weapons.*

Sighing, he walked through the hatch and down the corridor towards the intership car. He would start with Main Engineering, followed by Tactical and then Sickbay. Doctor Hastings was already preparing for the casualties she would receive, although if the ship were to be destroyed, Ted knew, it would be pointless. But they had to hope for the best, even as they prepared for the worst.

And pray that God remembers us this day, he added silently, *if that we forget him.*

———

Nerves had rarely been a problem for Henry before, he had to admit – at least, not when it came to bearding people more powerful than himself in their lairs. Being a Prince tended to teach *some* lessons, starting with the simple fact that most people considered themselves more important than they really were. And besides, he wasn't blind to the implications of losing the Puller Drive. *Ark Royal* was not going to leave the New Russia system unless a new drive unit could be brought to her…assuming she survived, of course.

He hesitated, then keyed the buzzer. There was a long pause before the hatch hissed open, revealing Rose sitting at her desk, half-asleep. Henry looked around for a bottle of alcohol before realising she was exhausted and depressed, not drunk. Shaking his head, he closed the hatch behind him and locked it, then strode over to face her.

"Wake up," he snapped.

"Piss off," Rose said, without moving. "Go do your damned job."

"Go do yours," Henry said. He hesitated, then walked around the desk and hauled her to her feet. "I understand you're depressed, I understand you're frustrated and pissed and everything else, but you have a god-damned job to do."

He pushed her towards the washroom, exasperated. "You can either undress and shower yourself, or I'll strip you naked and shove you into the water myself," he added. "Your choice."

"Bastard," Rose said. She moved away when he reached for her uniform buckle. "I'll go, I'll go..."

Henry watched her go into the washroom, then sat back and waited for her to emerge. It was nearly twenty minutes before she came out, looking furious. Washing herself would have helped wash away the tiredness as well as everything else. Henry sighed inwardly and braced himself. Her being angry was a good thing.

"You have absolutely no right to treat me like a child," Rose snapped. "I don't believe you were promoted over my head!"

"I will be, if you keep acting like this," Henry said. He understood how she was feeling, but there was no time for any form of compassionate leave. She should have been sent back to Earth with Captain Fitzwilliam. "Commander..."

He took a breath. "We are about to face the worst battle of our career," he said, softly. "It could win or lose us the war. We simply don't have time to fret about our missing loved ones" – he saw her start violently – "or anything else, but fighting and remaining alive. I will not allow you to decline into a wreck when there are pilots who desperately need your leadership."

Rose glared at him. "Do you realise his death was my fault?"

Henry shrugged. Janelle hadn't told him the full story. He'd suspected there was more, but he hadn't wanted to put her in a position where she had to break a confidence or refuse to tell him something. If Rose blamed herself...

"Look," he said. "Did you kill him personally?"

"They took him and he died and I could do *nothing*," Rose snapped. "It was my fault he died."

"I thought the same too, once," Henry said. But it hadn't been *quite* the same. Losing a dog, even a mutt that was effectively a member of the family, wasn't anything like losing a lover. "Commander – Rose – when we get back to Earth, you can mourn him in any way you see fit. But now, we need you in the cockpit, ready to kick some alien ass."

He slapped her on the back, hard enough to sting. "And besides, I think I crossed a line when I threatened to undress you," he added. "You'll need to assume your rank again just to hand out something sufficiently awful as punishment."

Rose smirked. "Booting your ass out the airlock seems about right," she said. Her smile faded quickly. "I've been a fool, Henry."

"You should have seen me as a child," Henry said. "I couldn't get away with nothing."

"A Royal Brat?" Rose asked.

"Worse than that," Henry said. "When I was restrained they said I was a prig; when I threw tantrums, they talked about me being badly brought up. When I did something stupid they made fun of me; when I did something clever they said I must have been coached. When my father let me run wild he was spoiling me rotten; when he gave me a clip around the ear they screamed that he was abusing me. I'm sure there are worse things in life than being a prisoner of the media, but I haven't met them."

Rose smirked, again. "Being an alien prisoner?"

"Oh, no," Henry assured her. "Being an alien prisoner was quite relaxing, actually. They didn't have the slightest idea who I actually was."

"Neither did I, until it was too late," Rose said. She smiled, reluctantly. "Janelle Lopez is a very lucky girl."

"I like to think so," Henry said. He sobered. "We won't be launching any starfighters because the Admiral wants to remain in hiding, but we do have simulations to run. Will you join us in twenty minutes?"

Rose sighed, then nodded. "I'll get a cup of coffee and something to eat," she said. "And…"

She broke off. But Henry understood the unspoken apology.

"If you need anything, afterwards, ask me," he said. "There are places you can go where the media can't follow, if you're careful."

"I may face a Board of Inquiry," Rose said, as she stood. "No, I *will* have to face a Board of Inquiry. But I will have to come to terms with my involvement in the whole affair. There's no point in trying to run."

"I understand, I think," Henry said. He rose, then walked towards the hatch. "I'll see you in twenty minutes."

———

"We've been trying to find ways to board alien ships," Parnell said, as Ted toured Marine Country. "But I don't think they'll let us do it again."

Ted nodded in agreement. The first – and so far the last – successful boarding operation in outer space had been carried out by the marines attached to *Ark Royal* during her first mission. It had only worked, he suspected, because the aliens had never seriously considered the possibility. Normally, boarding a starship without the crew's consent was tricky as hell – and the crew could blow their own ship, if they thought they were in serious danger of losing control. The aliens hadn't rigged their own battlecruiser to self-destruct before it was too late.

But they won't make the same mistake twice, Ted thought. They'd certainly *tried* to board *Ark Royal*, during Operation Nelson, but it hadn't worked. They hadn't tried again, which suggested they'd decided it was futile and given up. *We'd just be sending Marines to their deaths.*

"We are looking at ways to rig plasma cannons to assault shuttles and using them as a last line of defence, or even ramming units, but they won't be a match for starfighters," Parnell added. "They just don't carry enough armour."

"Something to work on in the future," Ted said. Marine Assault Shuttles were tough, but nowhere near as tough as *Ark Royal*. "But set them on automatic. They might soak up some alien fire."

"Aye, sir," Parnell said. "I've assigned the rest of the Bootnecks to damage control duties, for the moment. They'll armour up when the aliens arrive, then be ready to repel borders."

"Just in case," Ted agreed. They couldn't take the alien reluctance to board human ships – in the wake of their failure – for granted. It was quite likely the aliens would consider the ancient carrier a prize worth taking. "And I think…"

He paused as his wristcom bleeped. "Admiral, this is Farley," a voice said. "The probe is picking up starships crossing the tramline – multiple starships."

Ted nodded. "Understood," he said. It would be an hour, at the very least, before they could engage the enemy. "Get me a detailed breakdown of enemy forces as soon as you have it, Commander. I'll be on the bridge in five minutes."

He closed the channel, then looked up at Parnell. "It's been a honour," he said. "And thank you for everything."

"It could be harder," Parnell observed. "There are no friendly aliens mixed in with the hostiles here, are there?"

"No," Ted said. The War Faction had splintered, according to the aliens, until the only ones left were the true fanatics. None of them would have second thoughts now. "Just aliens who want to kill us all."

He nodded to the Marine, then strode out of Marine Country and walked – there was no point in running – up to the command deck. The crewmen he passed nodded to him – salutes were forbidden when the ship was at alert – and smiled, looking confident. Ted knew they'd inherited a tradition of victory, a tradition that had been earned after the Battle of New Russia. Spacers were superstitious and they knew Old Lady had never been defeated, not once. Ted hoped that would hold true one final time.

The bridge was a hive of activity when he stepped through the hatch and paused, studying the red icons on the display. Most of them were standard alien ships, including three carriers, but one of them was unknown… and larger than *Ark Royal*. It seemed to be slower too, he noted, as more and more data scrolled up on the display. The ship's mass had to be comparable to the ancient carrier's immense bulk.

"I think that's a battleship," Commander Williams said, quietly. "They must have decided to rush one into service after they ran into us."

"Or maybe they had plans to turn on the other factions," Ted offered. An armoured battleship…no, a dreadnaught, perhaps even a *superdreadnaught*, would be a formidable opponent against the other alien factions, even now the aliens had put bomb-pumped lasers into service. "If they'd known about the Old Lady, they wouldn't have launched the war without some way to deal with her."

"They could have started work on her after the first battle," Commander Williams offered.

Ted shook his head. It had taken five years to build *Ark Royal*; even now, with the aliens breathing down their necks, the best the designers had managed to do was slim it down to three years. Perhaps a battleship would take less time, but he had his doubts. They'd have started with a completely new design and completed it impossibly quickly, if that was the case.

"Or they refitted a design they already had," he mused. He dismissed the thought a moment later. "How many ships are we looking at?"

"Twenty-two," Farley said. "Fourteen frigates, two cruisers, three carriers, one battlecruiser and one monster…"

"Designate her as the *Monster* class," Ted ordered, calmly. It was a formidable force, easily enough to break through Earth's defences and launch stealth missiles into the planet's atmosphere. And, facing carriers that were lightly armoured, they might even cripple humanity's remaining fleets beyond repair. "Time to intercept."

"They're moving along the projected course, at speed," Farley said. "They'll enter engagement range in fifty-seven minutes."

Ted smiled, then walked over to his chair and sat down. "Continue feeding targeting data to the sensors," he ordered. "The principle target are the carriers, not the superdreadnaught. I want them smashed as soon as we open fire."

Commander Williams gave him an odd look. "You don't want to target the superdreadnaught?"

"No," Ted said. He hesitated, then explained. "The superdreadnaught doesn't carry any starfighters, I assume. Without starfighters, she will be vulnerable to volley-fire from Earth's defences, even if she smashes us into pulp. Even if her armour is as tough as ours, Commander, she will be vulnerable."

He studied the display for a long moment. The aliens might be in a hurry, but they weren't being *too* trusting. They had a CSP fanning out ahead of them, probing for trouble. It was quite likely they'd stumble across the waiting ambush before it was too late to save their fleet from instant annihilation.

"Take aim," he ordered. "If they stumble across us, fire without waiting for orders."

Farley swallowed, nervously "Aye, sir," he said. "Weapons locked on target."

Ted understood. A twitch on Farley's part could start the battle early, sacrificing the advantage they'd risked everything to build. He understood far too well.

He keyed his console as the alien fleet grew closer, opening a channel to the entire ship. "All hands, this is the Admiral," he said. "We are about to engage the enemy one final time. If we win, the war comes to an end. If we lose, the aliens will push past us and attack our homeworld. On us rests the fate of Earth – and all of humanity."

There was a pause as he struggled for words, then fell back on the classics.

"Britain expects that every man will do his duty," he said.

He closed the channel. On the display, the alien ships were drawing closer and closer, their starfighters fanning out ahead of them. It wouldn't be long before they stumbled across the ambush and then all hell would break loose. But it had been long enough.

"Fire," he ordered.

CHAPTER
THIRTY EIGHT

"Projectiles away, sir," Farley said.

"Launch starfighters," Ted snapped. On the display, the alien carriers were starting to launch their own starfighters, despite being caught by surprise. "Launch missiles!"

Ark Royal shivered again as she launched her first barrage of missiles. Ted had few illusions – only a handful of them would survive long enough to detonate – but one or two direct hits would finish any alien starship, apart from the enigmatic superdreadnaught. The craft was heavily armoured, of that he was sure. It simply didn't seem to have the speed of any of the other alien craft.

"Starfighters launched, sir," Farley reported. He swore, barely loudly enough for Ted to hear. "Enemy ships are launching missiles of their own."

They must have the reactions of a Marine, Ted thought, with cold amusement. *They didn't know we were waiting in ambush, but they still had their starfighters ready to launch at a moment's notice.*

"Direct hit," Farley reported. "One of the alien carriers is gone, sir."

Ted nodded. On the display, one of the alien carriers had been shattered into debris by a direct hit. Another was dodging mass drive projectiles, but even its drive was unable to alter course radically enough to save it completely. A direct hit to the rear section smashed its drives and left it completely helpless. Ted was marginally impressed that the remainder of the starship remained intact, despite the damage. A final projectile slammed into the hulk and completed its destruction.

"Target destroyed, sir," Farley reported. There was a hint of heavy satisfaction in his voice. "Their starfighters are motherless now."

"Continue firing," Ted ordered. The mass drivers were running out of ammunition at terrifying speed. There simply hadn't been time to find a suitable asteroid in the New Russia system and reload. "Target the remaining carrier and the superdreadnaught. Destroy them both."

The smaller alien ships picked up speed, advancing towards the Old Lady as they fired missiles towards the flotilla. Ted watched numbly as hundreds of missiles closed in on his ships, most of them picked off by the point defence or the CSP. But the priority – protecting *Ark Royal* – had a cost. Four missiles engaged HMS *Blackburn* and blew the escort carrier into flaming debris.

"*Blackburn* is gone," Farley reported. "No lifepods detected."

Ted nodded. He'd mourn later.

"Continue firing," he ordered. "Move *Wart Hog* into position to provide covering fire."

He scowled, inwardly. The attack on Earth had been gravely weakened by the loss of the carriers, but the aliens could still break through and use a frigate to attack the planet with a radioactive warhead. It was the old nightmare of terrorism on a planetary scale, one that had only grown worse as humanity expanded further into space. They'd hoped the aliens could be deterred from attacks aimed at genocide, but it was unlikely the War Faction gave a damn about their own people. All they wanted was the destruction of the human race.

"Alien starfighters are closing in," Farley reported. "Our own starfighters are moving to cover us."

"Stand by point defence," Ted ordered. "Warn the CSP not to come within plasma range."

"Aye, sir," Farley said.

———

Henry wanted to cheer as two of the alien carriers died in quick succession, but there was no time. The bastards had managed to launch their starfighters quicker than the Old Lady could match, putting over two hundred starfighters into space before they'd been smashed by the mass drivers. Some of the alien craft would have to be pushed back into space, Henry was sure, because their remaining carrier wouldn't have space for them all. But it wouldn't matter.

"Prepare to engage," Rose said. She sounded firmer, much to his relief. "Remember; we have to kill at least four apiece."

She makes it sound easy, Henry thought. He was relieved, more than he cared to admit, that Janelle had been sent back to Earth. The aliens had them badly outnumbered, even though they'd lost their carriers. There was a very strong possibility that none of the human starfighter pilots would survive this day. *But what else can we do?*

The alien starfighters flashed into range, firing madly the moment they had clear shots at the human craft. Henry jinked his starfighter to one side, then fired back, selecting automatic and allowing his targeting systems to do the firing for him as he concentrated on evading incoming fire. Space filled with plasma bolts as both sides converged, the aliens trying to blow their way through the human formation. But the CSP had a plan.

"Bombers are in position," Rose said. "On my mark...*mark!*"

Henry clutched his thrusters and pointed the starfighter away from the alien fighters. The remaining pilots followed, leaving the aliens with a clear path to *Ark Royal*. They'd be indecisive for a long moment, Henry was sure. Did they take the shot at the Old Lady or did they chase the human starfighters? Either one would expose them to human fire. And then the aliens made up their minds. Over a hundred starfighters hit their thrusters and roared towards *Ark Royal*.

"Engage the alien carrier," Rose ordered. "The Old Lady can take care of herself."

———

"Plasma weapons on standby, sir," Farley reported, as the red icons descended on *Ark Royal*. "Targets locked..."

"Fire as soon as they come into range," Ted ordered. "Don't hold back."

The alien starfighters seemed to wobble as they realised just how many plasma cannons had been placed on the carrier's hull. Even *their* carriers couldn't put out so much defensive firepower, not when an exploding cannon could do serious damage to its host. But the human engineers had just fixed the cannons to the hull; if they overloaded and exploded, they'd only scar the carrier's armour. And the sheer weight of firepower they could pump out more than made up for any risk.

Ted smirked, remembering the first time the Royal Navy – and their allies – had tried to attack an alien carrier. They'd been unprepared for plasma weapons back then and the results had been disastrous. Now…

Payback's a bitch, he thought, as dozens of alien starfighters exploded as they tried to weave their way through the hail of fire. A handful of plasma cannons were lost as their containment chambers exploded, but the remainder just kept firing. He couldn't help wondering what it would mean for the long-term development of space warfare technology, assuming they survived the war. Had the starfighter had its day?

A handful of very skilled alien starfighters made it through the point defence and engaged the Old Lady directly, firing plasma weapons into the weapons and sensor blisters covering her hull. Ted had to admire their nerve as they tried to avoid his point defence, while doing their best to cripple the Old Lady and leave her a blind defenceless wreck. One by one, they died, but they did real damage. If they lost more sensors, he noted, targeting their weapons would become impossible.

"Launch our remaining probe," he ordered. "Set it up as a secondary sensor platform, ready to take over if necessary."

It wouldn't work well, he knew, even though active sensors were hardly necessary now that both sides had abandoned stealth. The probe didn't have the sensor capacity of a full-sized carrier, even the ancient *Ark Royal*. But it might be all they had, if the aliens kept pounding on the hull. It looked very much as though the remaining starfighters were nerving themselves up for another round.

"Admiral," Farley said. "We're running out of mass driver projectiles."

Ted muttered a curse under his breath. The aliens had proved alarmingly effective at blocking or destroying the projectiles, now they knew they were under attack. Both of the targeted starships were still intact… and closing in on *Ark Royal*. He didn't want to know what the superdreadnaught used for weapons, but he had the alarming sense they were about to find out. It had launched missiles, he knew, yet he doubted they were *all* the craft carried.

"Continue firing," he ordered. Was there any point in trying to convert scrap metal into projectiles? It was worth a try. "Then have engineering start shoving pieces of scrap into the factory. Tear out anything that isn't absolutely essential."

Farley smirked. "Including the kitchen sink, sir?"

Ted had to smile. "Yes," he said. "Everything."

And then the carrier rocked violently.

––––––

The alien carrier wasn't *that* different from a modern Royal Navy carrier, Henry noted, as the starfighters closed in on their target. She was a long cylinder, with six smaller cylinders surrounding her, each one capable of launching and recovering two squadrons of starfighters or other small craft. The aliens didn't seem to draw any line between fighters and bombers – the Royal Navy had cut down on bombers after developing its own plasma weapons systems – which gave them a flexibility Henry was inclined to envy. But it was also a weakness.

He sucked in his breath as the alien CSP moved to engage, firing as they came. The aliens seemed frantic to keep the humans away from their carrier, which made sense. If they lost the remaining carrier, they'd be unable to recover their starfighters, condemning their pilots to die in the inky darkness of space. Henry felt a moment of...*guilt* – he'd almost died in space – then issued his orders. The human starfighters broke and attacked. One alien starfighter exploded under his fire, another slipped away and rolled, then came back towards him at terrifying speed. Henry had bare seconds to evade before it was too late.

"I can't shake this guy," one of the newer pilots said. "Some help, here?"

Henry nodded, then swooped after the alien pilot. He was good, he noted, but not good enough to chase one human while evading another. Henry would probably have broken off if someone had tried to attack *him* like that, yet the alien pilot hesitated a fraction of a second too long. A direct hit blew his craft into vapour; Henry spun away, then turned just in time to see the bombers make their attack on the carrier. Four bombers died as enemy point defence opened fire; the remainder evaded and launched their missiles, then spun away as the aliens started focusing their attacks on the missiles. Nine missiles died, the remaining two detonated and stabbed beams of deadly light into the alien carrier.

"Aw," Rose said. "She survived."

Henry was marginally impressed. The aliens obviously hadn't had time to coat the ship in any form of heavy armour, certainly nothing comparable to *Ark Royal's* solid state protection, but they *had* managed to add some additional shielding that had improved her chances of surviving a direct hit. One of her launching tubes was gone, along with some of her interior, yet she could still fly and fight.

Rose cleared her throat. "Bombers return for replenishment," she ordered. "Fighters...attack."

The alien starfighters grew more desperate as the human starfighters closed in on their target, one of them even resorting to ramming a human craft in a savage attempt to force it away from the carrier. But it wasn't enough. Henry pressed down on the firing stud as the enemy carrier came into range, sending bolts of superhot plasma burning through her hull and into her vulnerable interior. The other pilots followed, knowing it was only a matter of time before they blew the carrier apart. Behind them, the alien starfighters followed, firing constantly. Two human starfighters died before the alien carrier started to die.

"Break off," Henry snapped, as he saw the first explosion. Several alien craft had died in the Battle of New Russia, when the aliens had introduced humanity to plasma weapons for the first time, as the human carriers had died under their fire. "All ships, break off!"

He yanked his starfighter away from the carrier just in time. A series of explosions tore the ship apart, sending pieces of debris scattering through space. Henry grinned, despite himself, as he saw the alien starfighters suddenly hesitate. Had they had second thoughts, he wondered, now that their mothership was gone. It was a little too late to save their lives, he suspected. They could have tried to surrender, but *Ark Royal* was in no state to recover alien starfighters.

"Scratch one flattop," Rose said. "I say again, scratch one flattop."

She paused. "Target the superdreadnaught," she added. "And the frigates."

"Understood, Commander," Henry said. He cursed as he saw one of the frigates the aliens had configured as an anti-starfighter craft hove into view. There was no point in trying to engage her, not when she could put out more plasma firepower than *Ark Royal* herself. "On my way."

————

"Direct hit, lower decks," Anderson reported. "They targeted the weakened sections of the hull."

Ted nodded, unsurprised. The aliens had managed to slip at least one missile close enough to detonate – and they'd already had a good idea where to aim. Thankfully, they'd stripped as much as they could out of the damaged section, but the aliens had burned through the armour and damaged other parts of the ship. It wasn't a good sign.

"Get the damage control parties to work," he ordered. There would be no time to do anything more than patch up the holes, but it had to be done. "Cover them as best as you can."

He turned his attention back to the main display, just in time to see the alien carrier become a ball of flaming plasma. Many of her starfighters had survived, but their days were now numbered, unless they could land on the superdreadnaught and replenish there. Ted glanced at the constantly updating reports from the analysts and noted they didn't seem to have concluded the superdreadnaught could carry fighters. It certainly hadn't launched them...

So why did they build you? Ted asked, silently. *You're a big target – and you would be dead by now, if we had more projectiles. We didn't build battleships because we knew they were nothing more than easy victims if the enemy used mass drivers. So what were they thinking when they built you?*

"Enemy starfighters are returning to the attack," Farley reported, breaking into Ted's thoughts. "Their frigates are following...and launching additional missiles."

"Clever of them," Ted said. It was; the missiles could do real damage, thus the point defence had to be retargeted on the incoming missiles. But that gave the starfighters a chance to get close and attack the point defence directly, which would cripple the Old Lady's chances of responding to further missile attacks. And the network had already lost several cannons to overloading containment chambers. "Target the missiles, then recall our own starfighters. We're going to need them."

"Aye, sir," Farley said.

Ted nodded, then surveyed the situation. Any halfway rational foe would be breaking off by now, but the War Faction had burned its bridges when it had defied the other alien factions and tried to restart the war. They had nowhere to go; they had to complete their objective of destroying Earth or die trying. And they also wanted to destroy *Ark Royal*. If they'd been human, they might have thought of the carrier as lucky, just like so many other ships named *Ark Royal* throughout the years. They'd throw everything at the carrier in hopes of smashing her, once and for all.

"Alien craft are launching shuttles," Farley added. "And breeching pods."

Ted blinked in shock. *They're trying to board us?*

"Warn the Marines," he ordered. They'd already donned their armour, thankfully, but they'd been reassigned to the damage control teams. "Tell them to prepare to repel boarders."

He looked up at the display. Missiles, starfighters and shuttles were racing towards *Ark Royal*, forcing him to make some desperate decisions. Which threat had to be handled first?

"The starfighters are to go after the shuttles," he ordered. "Point defence is to continue to engage the missiles."

"Aye, sir," Farley said. He paused. "Recommend we set the starfighters as a secondary priority."

"Do it," Ted said. If a point defence weapon didn't have a shot at a missile, it could take a shot at a starfighter. The aliens couldn't be allowed to realise that the starfighters were no longer primary targets. "And..."

Missiles started to vanish, but two got close enough to detonate, stabbing deep into *Ark Royal's* guts. The entire carrier seemed to scream in pain; Ted thought, for one horrified moment, that the compensators had failed completely before rational thought caught up with him. If the compensators had failed, they'd be dead. Red lights flared on the display, showing damage mounting up at terrifying speed...

"We took a major hit," Anderson said. "Fusion Three is gone; datanet nodes #51 to #78 are gone. I have no links at all to section..."

"Patch it up," Ted snapped, cutting him off. There was no time for a detailed damage report, not now. The loss of one of the fusion reactors alone was disastrous. "They're about to land."

"Marines are being deployed now," Farley reported. "But the aliens aren't heading for the gaps in the hull."

They did that before, Ted recalled. The carrier shuddered as another missile slammed into her hull. This time, the warhead was conventional, which puzzled him. It looked as though the aliens had wasted a hit. A nuke would have been largely deflected by the armour, but it would have inflicted some damage...

His thoughts mocked him as the aliens altered course. It looked as if they were being stupid. And yet he knew they were far from stupid. *But it's the only way in...*

He looked up at the display and knew the answer. "They're planning to land on the hull and take our defences apart," he said. Why the hell hadn't they considered it a possibility? "Tell the Marines to get out there, now!"

But he already knew it might be too late.

CHAPTER
THIRTY NINE

Major Charles Parnell gritted his teeth as he led the way through the airlock, knowing all too well that the aliens could be waiting in ambush on the far side. He'd never liked hard-entry operations, where there were only one or two angles of attack and the enemy knew it, and this was worse. An injury that could be handled on the ground would be utterly lethal in space. But no one greeted his Marines with fire as they filed out onto the hull. Instead, there was no sign of the enemy.

"Advance carefully," he ordered. "And watch your backs."

He shivered as he led the advance forward. Flickers of light danced overhead, like twinkling stars, as the aliens pressed the offensive against the carrier. Bolts of lightning – plasma fire – seemed to flare out from the weapons blisters and vanish into the darkness, while shapes moved high over their heads. He thought, for a second, that he caught sight of something moving, only to realise that it was one of the blisters altering its position. The aliens could be anywhere.

Charles kept a careful eye out for the aliens as they snuck forwards. It had been months since he'd walked on the Old Lady's hull, during damage control duties. Fighting in space was very different to fighting on the ground; if they accidentally jumped off the hull they would keep going and be lost in space forever. His boots were magnetically linked to the hull, but it wasn't strong enough to ensure he could never lose touch with the ship. That would have made it impossible to walk.

"Sir," one of his men hissed. There was no need to whisper, but they kept their voices low out of habit. "I see them."

Charles followed his pointing finger and saw the aliens, clustering around one of the larger weapons blisters. They wore heavier suits than anything the Marines wore, but it shouldn't have been surprising. Their environmental requirements were different from humanity's, after all. He used hand-signals to motion his men forward, then lifted his rifle. The real danger of fighting on the ship's hull was accidentally inflicting more damage on an already battered starship. But there was no alternative.

"Fire," he ordered.

A stream of pellets killed five of the aliens before they could react, blowing their bodies away from the ship and out into space. The remainder spun around with surprising speed – Charles couldn't help wondering if they'd been enhanced in some way – and started to return fire with hand-held plasma weapons. *They* didn't seem to care about damaging the ship. Charles cursed the weapons under his breath as he dropped to the hull, then crawled forwards. Months of research had not yet delivered a way to duplicate the alien weapons for humanity, despite their obvious advantages. It was a very minor frustration in the great scheme of things, but it rankled.

He tongued his communicator as the Marines advanced rapidly. "We have engaged the enemy," he said. Another alien shuttle drifted into view, heading towards the hull. One of the Marines launched a handheld missile at it before it could start unloading its boarding party. "Prepare reinforcements at the major airlocks, but do not deploy unless we call for them."

And then he concentrated on sweeping the aliens off his ship's hull.

———

The alien superdreadnaught was armed to the teeth, Henry discovered, as the humans starfighters closed in on their target. She practically bristled with plasma weapons, each one spewing out hundreds of bolts every minute. A dozen human starfighters died as they tried to slip into firing range, the remainder ducking and weaving so wildly that one of them actually slammed into the ship's hull. It absorbed the damage and rumbled on, utterly uncaring.

"Break off," Rose ordered, finally. "She's heading right for the Old Lady."

And she might prove indestructible, Henry thought, as they put some space between themselves and the alien ship. *She has too much firepower for missiles or mass drivers to slip through her defences.*

He fired a shot at an alien starfighter, then rejoined the badly weakened CSP surrounding *Ark Royal*. The aliens were actually landing on the ship's hull, hacking away at her point defence and sensor blisters. He had to admire their dedication; they probably wouldn't survive, but they'd fatally weaken the Old Lady. *Ark Royal* wouldn't be able to retreat any longer…

Up close, it was clear the Old Lady was in serious trouble. One of her starfighter launch bays was wrecked, while atmosphere was venting from her lower hull. Henry couldn't help finding that more ominous than anything else. The Old Lady had plenty of atmosphere – carriers were far larger than any other ship in the fleet – but her inner airlocks should have automatically closed, preventing much of the atmosphere from leaking through the gashes in her hull. If the airlocks had failed, the interior damage had to be severe.

"Shit," Rose said, as a flight of alien starfighters descended on the carrier. "They're going to shoot through the holes. Take them out!"

"Understood," Henry said. The regular squadrons had been shot to pieces. Pilots flew with whoever they could find, no matter what squadron they were assigned to. Many of the survivors were doing well, he noted, or they would be dead by now. There were only thirty-two starfighters left in the fleet. "Moving in…now."

The alien starfighters hung in front of the gash, pouring plasma fire into the Old Lady's interior. Henry had no illusions. They would hit something explosive or important sooner or later, blowing through airlocks and exposing more of the crew to vacuum. He opened fire as soon as he was in position, blowing one of the starfighters into flaming debris. The second starfighter angled away, returning fire in a steady stream of glowing bolts, but the third starfighter hit its drivers and flew right *into* the carrier. Moments later, it slammed into the bulkhead and exploded, violently.

"Incoming missiles," Rose snapped. "Engage them…"

Henry spun his starfighter around, too late. Rose picked off one of the missiles, but the second was far too close to be stopped. And then Rose shoved her starfighter forward and both the missile and her craft vanished in a ball of fire.

"No," Henry said. She couldn't have sacrificed herself like that, not now. There were pilots who needed her. But she had found the death he suspected she'd craved. "I…"

He shook his head. There would be time to mourn later.

"This is Henry," he said, as he yanked his starfighter away from the ship's hull. He'd never quite sorted out the difference between Prince Henry and Charles Augustus. "I am taking command of the starfighter squadrons."

He glanced at the status display and shuddered. Five more pilots had died in the last few minutes. The aliens were regrouping themselves, while the Old Lady's point defence had been critically weakened and the super-dreadnaught was closing in, belching out missiles as if her commander no longer cared about holding back. And maybe he didn't…

"Regroup here," he ordered, silently thanking God that they'd duplicated the alien weapons system. If they'd had to replenish their weapons as well as life-support packs, they would have been wiped out by now. "And prepare to fight to the last."

———

"*War Hog* is gone, sir," Farley reported.

Ted nodded. The aliens had battered *Ark Royal* so badly he could feel his starship dying around him. *War Hog* had seemed to lead a charmed life; she'd been part of Operation Nelson, then Operation Trafalgar, without taking any damage at all. But now she was gone, blown away so completely there was nothing left. There certainly weren't any lifepods drifting through space…

The bastards would probably use them for target practice, he thought, sourly. Surrender wasn't an option. *All we can do is fight.*

He gritted his teeth as he looked down at the mounting damage reports. Entire compartments and sections were unsalvageable, sealed off to prevent the damage from spreading, while over half of the ship-mounted weapons and sensor blisters were gone. If the Marines hadn't been trying to keep the alien boarders from hacking away at the ship's systems they'd *all* be gone by now, leaving the ship blind and defenceless. Fusion Four had followed the previous reactor into death, crippling his ship. If the aliens managed to take out one or two more, he knew, they wouldn't have to take out any more of the weapons. The Old Lady would be defenceless anyway.

"Warn *Doyle* to move into position to cover us," he ordered. The last frigate...she wouldn't last long, but perhaps long enough. "And continue launching missiles and projectiles towards the superdreadnaught."

He took a long breath, tasting smoke in the air. *That* was far from normal. The air circulation system had to be breaking down too. He keyed his console, sending a warning to all hands to keep their breathmasks at hand. If the circulation system was dying, considering just how much damage the ship had taken, the air would rapidly become toxic.

"Aye, sir," Farley said. "But we're not breaking through its defences."

Ted nodded, reluctantly. The alien commander seemed to be mad; he was keeping his ship crawling towards *Ark Royal*, as if he intended to hammer her to pieces at point-blank range. Some alien weapons *did* have very short ranges – the magnetic bottle holding the plasma together rarely lasted long – but it seemed a little extreme. At least there was no sign the aliens had developed mass drivers. Ted couldn't understand the oversight – mass-producing mass drivers was a relatively simple – yet he couldn't help being grateful for it. The Old Lady was in no state to survive a single direct hit.

But perhaps there was method in the alien commander's madness. His ship was intact, no matter how many missiles Ted threw at it. Her designers seemed to have placed a great deal of effort into protecting the ship and Ted had to admit, reluctantly, that they had done a very good job. The ship was almost as tough as *Ark Royal*, perhaps more so. They'd created a war machine intended to take the war to Earth...

Maybe they didn't have it planned before they encountered us for the first time, Ted thought, sourly. *The bastard is practically designed to face Ark Royal.*

His ship shuddered as another alien missile slammed into the hull, thankfully striking a piece of intact armour. If it had gone into the hull before detonating…Ted didn't want to *think* about what would have happened if it had. And the alien starfighters were regrouping…

"Prince Henry has taken command of the starfighters," Farley said. "They're preparing to defend the ship."

Ted nodded. It was futile now, he knew. There was no way any of the starfighters could be recovered and replenished under enemy fire. Prince Henry and his remaining pilots would die in space, alone. They'd create a new legend, he was sure, but they would die. He remembered how some of the PR staff had tried to make a legend out of the Prince's first reported death and shuddered, again. The Monarchy would probably benefit from Prince Henry's death.

"Understood," he said. There was nothing he could do now, but keep fighting. If the enemy commander wanted a close-range engagement, Ted would give it to him. "Helm, point us right at the enemy superdreadnaught."

"Aye, sir," Lightbridge said.

The carrier shook, yet again.

"Damage to rear sectors," Anderson reported, though the intercom. "We've lost rear sensors and point defence. Long-range communications are down."

Ted cursed. The communications didn't matter – there was no one to talk to – but losing the sensors and weapons was disastrous. Once the aliens realised what they'd done, they'd target their missiles through the blind zone and rip the carrier to shreds.

"Take us right towards them," he ordered. If the alien superdreadnaught had one disadvantage, it was that she was almost as cumbersome as *Ark Royal*. "Reroute all spare power to the drives, even life support. I want everything you can give me."

"Aye, sir," Anderson said.

Ted sucked in a breath. "Gentlemen, it's been a honour," he said. "Ramming speed."

"Aye, sir," Lightbridge said.

———

James shuddered, then vomited into a plastic bag as HMS *Formidable* crashed through the tramline and entered the New Russia system. He wasn't the only one in the CIC to lose his lunch, despite having made two more high-speed transits over the last four days. Angrily, he spat into the bag, then dumped it into the recycler and fixed his gaze on the display. It was far too clear that there was already a battle being fought within the system.

He gritted his teeth against the ache in his chest, then straightened up. His uncle and everyone else had advised him not to join the relief force, let alone take command, but he'd insisted. The doctors had stabilised his condition, yet they'd also warned him there would be pain. They'd been right.

But he was damned if he was leaving the Admiral to fight alone for any longer than necessary.

"Launch probes," he ordered, as the passive sensors fought to make sense out of what they were picking up. "And transmit a general signal. Inform Admiral Smith that we are on our way."

"Aye, sir," Lieutenant Benton said.

James nodded. It had taken two days of arguing, pleading and outright blackmail to convince the other interstellar powers to join the relief mission. HMS *Formidable* had been joined by the Russian *Kirov* and the American *George Bush*, as well as a dozen smaller ships. Putting together the mission had been a political nightmare. The Russian commander had strict orders to cooperate, but as he hadn't been told anything about the bioweapon it was clear he thought he was supposed to be obstructionist. And the Americans hadn't been much better.

If we manage to survive this war, James thought, *we'll build up the navy to the point we won't ever need to think about coalition operations again.*

He stared in horror as the display rapidly filled with data. The flotilla was almost gone, save for *Ark Royal* and a single frigate. It was clear the carrier had taken one hell of a battering…and was heading towards the massive alien ship, preparing to ram. James couldn't imagine *anything* standing up to a direct impact from the carrier, no matter how much armour the aliens had bolted onto their ship. But it would almost certainly destroy the Old Lady too…

"Take us towards them, maximum speed," he ordered. "Communications, raise Admiral Smith!"

"No response, sir," Benton said. "I'm not even picking up her IFF. She may have lost communications completely..."

"Then extend the signal," James snapped. On the display, the final frigate's icon winked out of existence. "Contact the starfighters, get them to pass on the message..."

But he already knew it was too late.

———

For a long moment, the battle seemed to come to a halt as the two massive starships advanced towards each other, neither one able or willing to change course. Henry stared in disbelief as the Old Lady inched forward, aiming directly at the alien superdreadnaught. The alien pilots seemed equally stunned, equally unsure what to do. Henry fought for words, for orders, for...*something*, but nothing came to mind. The collision had become inevitable.

"No," he said, as the alien superdreadnaught opened fire. Plasma bolts rained down on *Ark Royal*...and glanced harmlessly off her armour. They'd already crippled her point defence and sensor blisters; no matter how badly they hammered the hull, they simply didn't have the firepower to break through and destroy the ship before it was too late. "No..."

He swore as a new communication icon popped up in front of him. HMS *Formidable*, it stated. For a moment, he thought it was an alien trick; HMS *Formidable* had died at New Russia. But then he remembered the new carriers, the ones that had been on the verge of entering service, and glanced at his rear sensors. Three new carriers had come through the tramline, a wave of starfighters sweeping out in front of them. But he already knew it was too late.

"Fall back on *Formidable*," he ordered. His pilots were alarmingly close to running out of life support. "And remember this day."

———

Ted clutched his command chair as the aliens finally brought their heavy plasma weapons to bear on *Ark Royal*. Damage started to mount up rapidly, but the carrier's armour could handle most of the blasts, deflecting them from her innards. Not, in the end, that it mattered.

You did well, he told himself, silently. His career had stalled after he'd turned to drink – and even the love he'd developed for the Old Lady hadn't kept him out of the bottle. It was only the prospect of actually fighting a war that had caused him to abandon his alcohol, flushing it down the toilet rather than taking the risk of storing it. *And you wouldn't have been suited for a desk job anyway.*

He smiled at the thought, then glanced around the bridge. Consoles were darkening as power failed or internal reporting systems collapsed, but it hardly mattered any longer. They were doomed the moment they struck the alien craft. He searched for the words to tell his crew just how proud he was of them, yet nothing came to mind. But he thought they knew.

Goodbye, he thought, silently. There was no point in trying to evacuate the ship. Even if the lifepods made it away in time, the alien starfighters would pick them off one by one. *I love you all.*

Moments later, the two ships came together and exploded.

―――

His life support unit was flashing red, but Henry ignored his own orders and watched helplessly, forcing himself to bear witness, as *Ark Royal* slammed into the alien ship. For a moment, he thought the carrier would shatter the alien ship but survive herself…and then the first giant explosion billowed through her hull. Moments later, both craft had been smashed by the blasts. Giant pieces of debris blasted out of the fireball and drifted through space.

Henry closed his eyes, silently bidding the ancient carrier farewell. She had been his home – his first true home, where he could be himself. He'd met his friends and lover there…

…And now she was gone.

But she had not died in vain, he told himself. She'd created a legend… and she'd ensured there would be peace. What better legacy could she ask for?

CHAPTER

FORTY

"Well," Uncle Winchester said, "I dare say your old commander would be proud."

"I don't think he would have cared for a state funeral," James said, sourly. Admiral Smith had requested burial in space, according to his will. "But I suppose the politicians must have their chance to pay homage to him."

"Welcome to politics," Uncle Winchester said. He leaned forward. "But I dare say he would have approved."

James had his doubts. The Russians had been blackmailed once – and it had ensured that they had largely escaped consequences for the attempt to use the bioweapon. Officially, rogue agents had carried out the attack on *Ark Royal*, only to be stopped at the last hurdle. The truth would remain buried – forever, if the Russians had their way. It was infuriating to think that the Russians had largely escaped punishment for their actions. The only consolation was the awareness that they wouldn't be paid any compensation by the other powers.

But they may get New Russia back anyway, James thought. The final negotiations with the aliens had hinted that they might abandon New Russia, purely to disarm the remaining elements of the War Faction. At that point…the Russians would reassert their claim to the system and, with so many people on the planet's surface, they'd probably win. *And who knows what will happen then?*

"Perhaps, Uncle," he said, finally. "And what of your plan to leave the system to die?"

"We may send the ships out anyway," Uncle Winchester said. "Who knows *what* we will encounter in the future? It might be a sensible idea to have a hidden colony or two, some distance from the rest of humanity."

"And stake a claim before the official borders wash over the system," James pointed out, snidely. "It might be workable."

"Indeed it might," Uncle Winchester said. "And *congratulations*, Admiral Fitzwilliam."

James sighed. The Admiralty had been coming under fire for failing to dispatch the relief mission in time to save *Ark Royal*. It was irritating – for once, it wasn't the bureaucrats fault – but they'd tried to make up for it by handing promotions out to the survivors like confetti at a wedding. James was now the youngest Admiral in the Royal Navy and charged with taking command of the multinational fleet guarding the border worlds. It wasn't a job he particularly wanted.

"Thank you, Uncle," he said. "And have you made the arrangements I wanted?"

"I have," Uncle Winchester said. "No one could deny you anything, not now. I would suggest you start looking for a wife. Quite a few young ladies were introduced to London during the last season. One of them would be interested."

"No, thank you," James said. "I don't want a young wife."

He scowled. "Did you complete the arrangements *exactly* as specified?"

"Yes," his uncle said. "If there had been a problem, young man, I would have told you."

James nodded. "I think Admiral Smith would have approved of *that*," he said. "And I thank you for your assistance."

He shook his uncle's hand, then walked to the door and headed down the stairs. Outside, rain was lashing down on London, a mocking reminder that the end of the war hadn't brought a return to the days before the war. Even now, millions of civilians squatted in refugee camps, while hundreds of thousands more had been conscripted into labour battalions and sent out to help shore up the defences. It would be years before Britain returned to normal.

Ignoring the water dripping down his uniform, he walked through the half-empty streets until he entered Hyde Park. The refugee camp that had been established there was gone, now; the grass was so sodden with water that it was almost a marsh in its own right. But the government had insisted on placing the memorial there, right in the heart of London. A giant piece of hull metal, scorched and battered by the alien weapon that had blasted it away from *Ark Royal*, sat on the ground, etched with names. They'd wanted to build a whole new Nelson's Column, James knew, for Admiral Smith. And they would, one day.

But this will do, James thought, as he stopped in front of the hull and ran his eyes down the list of names. Three thousand crewmen had died on Operation Trafalgar, starting with a handful of pilots he'd barely known and ending with ADMIRAL THEODORE SMITH. He felt a moment of bitter Survivor's Guilt as he saw other names; Commander Williams, Commander Rose Labara, Commander Kurt Schneider, Major Charles Parnell...

He shook his head. No one knew, outside a handful of government officials, just what had happened to Commander Schneider. The Russians would keep their mouths shut, he knew, if only to avoid a full disclosure of *everything* that had happened on the Old Lady's final mission. His children would never know that some people considered their father a traitor. It would certainly never be allowed to affect their lives.

"I'm sorry, Admiral," he said, looking back at the Admiral's name. "You deserved better."

He carefully unbuckled the Victoria Cross from his uniform and looked down at it. Admiral Smith had wound up with medals from almost every nation on Earth, after *Ark Royal's* first cruise. Now, they were stored in the Imperial War Museum. One day, when the world was normal again, people would flock to see them and hear about the adventures of HMS *Ark Royal*. He wondered, sardonically, if they'd ever learn that the Admiral had beaten the demon drink as well as the aliens. Or would the slate be washed clean?

Carefully, he placed the medal beside the hull fragment, then turned and walked away.

———

"You can't be serious!"

Henry allowed himself a smirk. God! He *hated* Victor Forsyth. The man was a PR hack, dedicated to making the Royal Family look good at all times. He might have been more tolerable if he hadn't also insisted that Henry bow, scrape and grovel whenever there was the slightest hint of controversy. After watching *Ark Royal* die, Henry was damned if he was apologising for anything ever again, no matter who got their panties in a bunch. And he no longer cared about what it did to the Monarchy. It was, after all, nothing less than child abuse to have someone like Forsyth make him feel guilty for everything. Regular beatings would have been kinder.

"I'm very much afraid that I am," he said, dryly. It was wrong of him, but he revelled in Forsyth's shock. "I've already packed my *personal* possessions. And I've also written a speech. Do you like it?"

"You *can't* go up in front of the media and say that," Forsyth objected. "It would do inestimable harm to the country! People's confidence would be shattered..."

Henry waved a hand around to indicate the luxurious room. "I don't think they'd be amused to discover that people like you and I were still living in luxury when half the country is starving," he said. "And let's be honest, shall we? That is *precisely* what we are doing."

He stood. "I've explained everything to my father," he added. "And while he isn't too pleased, he understands. I'll be leaving London tomorrow and I won't return."

Winchester cleared his throat. "Perhaps we could arrange a compromise, Your Highness," he said. "There are ways we can appease both sides of the issue."

"There's no room for compromise," Henry said. He ticked off points on his fingers as he spoke. "I do not want to be part of the Royal Family any longer. I don't want my fiancée or my children to be part of the Royal Family. I..."

"Janelle Lopez has her duties to the Royal Navy," Forsyth said. "She might not be allowed to resign..."

Henry smirked. "You do realise you're talking about a heroine, one of the few people to know Admiral Smith and survive? I dare say the media would be *very* interested if you tried to pressure her."

Forsyth blanched. "But..."

"But what?" Henry demanded. "You kept me here through ties of love and loyalty and patriotism. I still love my family, but I see no reason to surrender the rest of my life to become a figurehead for the government and the country. What could I possibly do to show the people that the Royal Family is part of them that will outshine almost dying in the final battle of the war?"

He snorted. "And stop trying to appeal to my loyalty," he added. "I got sick of it after they took photographs of me on the toilet as a young boy. If it had been anyone else, you assholes, the reporter would have been charged with taking indecent pictures of *children* and slapped in jail. But for me...the bastard got away with it scot free."

Winchester held up his hand. "We would not presume to threaten your future wife," he said, "but the country is not particularly stable at the moment. You leaving now could threaten confidence in the government when we need it to remain stable."

Henry snorted. "At rock bottom?"

"We have a compromise," Winchester said. "There will be an embassy on Atlantis, as I believe the alien homeworld will be designated. You are a naval officer with considerable experience of working with the aliens, as is your future wife. I believe you could be assigned there for the remainder of your term in the military, if not longer. You would have privacy, Your Highness, and you would be well away from Earth."

"And my sister would succeed the throne, if she wants it," Henry said. "Let's face it. She will make a much better figurehead than myself."

He paused. "And what about *my* children?"

"If your sister dies childless," Winchester said, "they would be in line to take the throne..."

"No," Henry said. "My price for doing this is that I and any children I might have are excluded from the succession permanently. If Elizabeth dies childless, there are other potential heirs..."

"And you're the one in first place," Forsyth said.

"And it hardly matters," Henry snapped. "If there was power in the throne, I might take it and use it...and my first decree would be to have you beheaded. But there's no reward for making myself a target for reporters, pollutions – sorry, *politicians* – and everyone with a grudge against Britain."

He took a breath. "You have my terms," he said. "If you can handle them, let me know and I will speak to Janelle about it. If not…bye-bye."

Grinning, he turned and walked out of the room. Maybe it wasn't quite as satisfying as the fantasy he'd had of slowly feeding Forsyth and his ilk into a mincing machine, then feeding their remains to reporters, but it had felt good. And even if he did take the post on Atlantis…

…He would be a long way from any damned reporters.

And that, he knew, was all he really wanted.

———

James hadn't visited his father's study since the day he'd entered the Academy. It had normally been denied to him and his siblings, as his father did most of his work from the manor and flatly barred his children from disturbing him during office hours. The only times he'd visited had been when the servants had wanted to report his conduct to his father, who had always taken a dim view of it.

He looked around the room, marvelling at how little had changed. The walls were covered with bookshelves, the desk – a copy of one in Buckingham Palace – was bare, save for a computer terminal and a piece of paper with a handful of scrawled notes. He was studying the book titles, wondering how many of them his father had actually read, when the door opened, revealing Percy and Penny Schneider. Behind them, Gayle – their nanny, according to Commander Schneider – looked reluctant to enter the room.

"Please, take a seat," he said. "All three of you."

He sighed inwardly as he met their eyes. Percy was clearly trying to be a grown man, suppressing his emotions in public, while Penny and Gayle both looked badly upset. It was hard to blame any of them. Their mother – and Gayle's parents – had vanished in the tidal waves, while their father had died shortly afterwards on active service. And they were far from alone. Hundreds of thousands – perhaps millions – of people remained missing, presumed dead. Or perhaps they'd simply changed their identities and vanished.

"Your father was a very brave man," he said, simply. "He gave his life to save countless others."

He looked at Gayle. "I believe he intended to adopt you, at least until you reached adulthood," he added. "He certainly filed the paperwork to do so before *Ark Royal* left Earth for the final time. I don't think there would have been any major objections. He was a war hero, after all, and already the father of two teenage children."

"Yes, sir," Gayle muttered.

James understood. She'd lost her parents, then her prospective adopter in quick succession. The normal legal headaches to adoption had been removed in the wake of the crisis, but the legal *protections* had also been removed. There had already been incidents, according to the media, when children and teenagers had been adopted by deliberately abusive adults and treated worse than slaves. Gayle had no reason to look forward to a bright future. None of them had, not really.

"It is my intention to adopt you," James said. "All three of you. I believe your father would have wanted me to see you – all three of you – safe."

Percy frowned. "And the price of this?"

"Nothing," James said. He understood. Percy would have been exposed to more darkness in the last few months than he'd seen in his entire previous life. It had matured him, but it had also left him cynical and worn. "Just…try to live up to your father's standards."

Penny sighed. "But here…?"

"For the moment," James said. He looked around the room, trying to understand how it must seem to them. Their parents had never been rich. "There are options, if you don't want to join my extended family. I believe there are asteroid settlements, or farmsteads on Britannia, or…I could probably arrange almost anything for you. But I believe that if you live here, at least until you become legal adults, you'd have the best possible introduction into society."

He took a breath. "I'm expected to report onboard *Formidable* within two weeks," he said. "By then, the diplomatic headaches should have been sorted out and we'll know where the borders actually *are*. I'd prefer you gave me an answer by the end of the week and, until then, you are more than welcome to stay here."

Percy rose to his feet. "Thank you, sir," he said. He was certainly *trying* to be formal. "We will discuss it amongst ourselves and let you know."

James nodded, then watched as they filed out of the room. They'd do well whatever they chose, he was sure. And the aristocracy had thrived when it had finally started integrating talented commoners. Kurt Schneider had died a hero. His children would be sought after for marriages, if they chose to stay. And if they didn't...

He shook his head, then tapped the computer terminal. Uncle Winchester had sent him a detailed set of diagrams for the planned next generation carrier, one built after the lessons of the First Interstellar War were analysed and integrated into the design. She would look like the Old Lady, he knew, although she was also smoother in places, despite the ever-present weapons and sensor blisters. He smiled, then swallowed hard when he saw the nametag on the top of the diagram. HMS *Theodore Smith*.

It was, he decided, precisely what humanity's first interstellar naval hero deserved.

The End

AFTERWORD

Wow. Just wow.

I posted *Ark Royal* on 15ᵗʰ January 2014. By the end of the month, I had sold over 10'000 copies, a success that left me absolutely stunned. I wrote *The Nelson Touch* – Book II – in March and sold 6000 copies in eight days. As of writing, *Ark Royal* has over 1000 reviews and has sold upwards of 65'000 copies. I am astonished and delighted and very – very – proud.

And, when I asked readers to vote for Book III or a spin-off, the majority vote was for Book III. I hope you enjoyed reading it as much as I enjoyed writing it.

When I started to plot out this series, I fixed on two things. First, that I would leave the background history – future history – a little vague. I've seen books suffer from having a detailed history that later proved incorrect or was treated as terrifying by some readers. The Troubles, in particular, were left undefined. I may go back to that era and write a book set there and then, but it will be very different from *Ark Royal* – and intensely political.

The second thing was that I would remember that the officers and crew of *Ark Royal* were *human*.

Times of stress bring out the best in some people and the worst in others. War is very stressful. We can see acts of astonishing heroism like a man throwing himself on a grenade to ensure his comrades survive, mixed with disciplinary problems, prisoner abuse, and an indifferent attitude to local civilians. I wanted to show the crew suffering from stress, fighting to overcome (or not) their demons and, in the end, being *human*. Soldiers, sailors and airmen are not machines. They can and do break under the pressures of war – or make stupid decisions that come back to haunt them.

And now a word about the future.

Ark Royal's story is concluded, along with the war, but there will be many stories to tell set in the post-war universe. I intend to write a second trilogy following a smaller ship patrolling the borders or fighting a minor war with other humans, as well as the planned spin-off covering the Battle of Earth. Please let me know what you would like to see next.

As always, you can follow my work on my blog, post on my forum or simply sign up to my mailing lists for future announcements.

Thank you for reading. If you liked this book, please don't hesitate to leave a review, share the link and tell your friends <grin>.

Christopher G. Nuttall
Edinburgh, 2014

BARBARIANS AT THE GATES
Christopher G. Nuttall

The Federation has endured for hundreds of years, but now it is dying, killed by the corruption and decadence of the Senate and the rising power of military warlords. The shipping lanes are coming apart, the colonists are revolting and outside forces are pressing against undefended borders. Now, as one warlord makes a bid for supreme power, the entire edifice is on the verge of falling apart. Two officers, bearers of a proud military tradition, may be all that stands between the Federation and total destruction.

Admiral Marius Drake has fought for years to defend the Federation against the enigmatic outsiders. Now, he is charged with putting down a rogue warlord who has risen against the Senate and challenged its authority. If he fails, the schism will eventually rip the Federation apart. But with shadowy figures moving in the background, he knows it will not be easy to save the Federation from itself.

Lieutenant Roman Garibaldi, newly-graduated from the Naval Academy, knows no other cause than the Federation. Human unity is a cause worth fighting for. But as he faces the grim reality of interstellar civil war, and the exploitation of humans and aliens underlying the Senate's vast power, he comes to realise that the price of the Federation's survival may be more than anyone can pay.

But with the Senate suspicious of any competent commanding officers, purging the navy on the slightest excuse, their success may condemn them to an inglorious death.

Read the free sample.

CHAPTER ONE

The Luna Academy is the sole source of officers for the Federation Navy. Every year, five thousand young men and women enter the academy; five years later, the survivors are allowed to start the long climb towards command. The rewards are great, but so is the pressure. It is no surprise that the Academy rarely graduates more than a thousand new officers every year.

-An Irreverent Guide to the Federation, 4000 A.D.

Luna Academy, Sol System, 4092

"Cadet Garibaldi," Professor Kratman said, walking through the desks until he was standing right in front of his chosen victim, "I wish you to consider something for the benefit of your fellows. What do the First Battle of Zion, the Battle of Spider Bite and the Battle of Athens all have in common?"

Roman Garibaldi fought hard to keep his expression under control. Professor Kratman wasn't known for suffering fools gladly and the obvious answer—all three battles had been fought in space—was almost certainly not the right one. But then, there might not be a right answer; Kratman was hardly above throwing an unanswerable question at the class. The professor—his face was badly scarred by radiation burns, leading to much speculation outside class—was waiting patiently. Disappointing him was not an option.

Roman considered it briefly, thinking hard. All three battles had been studied extensively during Second Year, right before the cadets had passed their first tests. The three battles were significant—two had marked the start of a war; the third had effectively ended one—but there were hundreds of other such significant battles in the Federation's two thousand year history. He ran his hand through his blond hair and smiled as the answer came to him.

"Sir," he said. "The three battles represent *conceptual* defeats."

"Oh?" Professor Kratman said, peering down at him. "And were the defeats imaginary, then? Were the dead bodies floating in space delusions of an oxygen-starved mind?"

Roman shook his head, ignoring the titters from his classmates. If nothing else, Professor Kratman taught cadets how to think on their feet.

"No, sir," he said. "The defeats represented a failure of imagination by the losing side. They thought they knew everything and allowed themselves to be surprised by the enemy."

"Interesting," Professor Kratman mused. He made a show of stroking his hairless chin. "And would you care to elaborate for the benefit of your fellow cadets?"

"Yes, sir," Roman agreed. It wasn't as if he had a choice. Besides, he was uncomfortably aware that he might just be giving the professor rope to hang him, as Kratman was also known for allowing cadets to trip themselves up in the hopes they would learn from the experience. "Prior to the First Battle of Zion, it was commonly believed that aliens would be peaceful, rather than being just as violent as humanity. When the Zion Defense Force encountered alien starships emerging from a previously undiscovered Asimov Point in the Zion System, they allowed themselves to be suckered into a position that allowed the Snakes to obliterate the entire force with ease. The result of this failure was the occupation of Zion and the First Interstellar War, which served as the catalysts for binding the Federation together."

Of course, he thought as he took a deep breath, *the Inheritance Wars are still a sore subject in the Federation.*

"In the Battle of Spider Bite, the...ah, loyalist commander *knew* that all he was facing were converted freighters and a handful of local defense starships. He charged through the Asimov Point, leading a fleet of battlecruisers and battleships, only to run into an enemy armed with compressed antimatter, a substance that had never before been used in combat. The result was the total obliteration of the Federation force and the Inheritance Wars.

"In the Battle of Athens, the rebel commander *knew* the loyalist forces would have to come through one of the Asimov Points in the system and had drawn up his forces to contest the gateway, as military doctrine demanded after the discovery of the first Asimov Point. The rebels were taken completely by surprise when the loyalists, using the continuous displacement stardrive, bypassed the Asimov Point network and assaulted their positions from the rear. It was the decisive battle of the Inheritance Wars."

Roman braced himself. "In all three battles, one side was presented with something completely outside its context," he concluded. "They suffered from a failure of imagination."

"An interesting viewpoint," the Professor said. He looked around the room. "Would any of you care to comment?"

"I would, sir," Cadet Blake Raistlin said.

Roman rolled his eyes inwardly. Cadet Raistlin was from one of the wealthiest families on Old Earth, with ties that led all the way up to the Grand Senate, and when they'd first met, Raistlin had tried to put the RockRat in his place. He had been astonished to discover that Roman was not only able, but willing to fight back.

But Raistlin had gone on. "How could any of the commanders have predicted that they would be faced with a threat outside their...accepted *context*?"

Professor Kratman, unlike some of the other academic staff, showed no inclinations to play favorites. "Would you care to elaborate, cadet?"

Raistlin shot Roman a mischievous look. "The defenders of Zion expected to face human enemies, not aliens," he said. "Compressed antimatter was only a theory, as was the continuous displacement drive. How could they have prepared to face a threat they didn't even know existed?"

"Interesting point," Professor Kratman mused. He turned and faced Raistlin. "Do you believe that the universe is *fair*, cadet?"

"No, sir," Raistlin said. It was one thing that had been drummed into their heads since they had entered Luna Academy. The universe was *not* fair. It simply didn't care about humans—or aliens. "But you cannot blame a commanding officer for doing everything by The Book and then being defeated by something outside of The Book."

"The Board of Inquiry might disagree with you," Kratman said dryly, referring to the inquiry held whenever a Federation starship was lost on active duty. "Let us consider the situation, just for a moment. Why did the defenders of Zion believe that aliens would be peaceful and friendly? Answer—the general belief at the time, encouraged by the discovery of Graveyard a few years prior to the First Interstellar War, was that a violent and aggressive race would not make it into space. Their logic was fundamentally flawed as *humanity*, a violent and aggressive race, had already made it into space. They thought of humans as being somehow... less than aliens. If we made it through the bottleneck and out into space, why couldn't another violent race? Reasoning from a single example, like Graveyard, produces dubious results, not least because Graveyard might have been the result of an interstellar war."

Roman shivered. A few years after the discovery of the network of Asimov Points—which allowed instant travel between star systems—human explorers had stumbled across a dead world, destroyed by nuclear war. The level of devastation had been so high that no one knew what the inhabitants had called themselves. Their records had been so badly damaged that no one would ever know what had taken place to cause the war, or why it had been fought to such a dark finish.

"The Battle of Spider Bite is also indicative of the dangers of stagnated thinking and unchallenged assumptions," Kratman continued. "The loyalist commander *knew* that the rebels didn't have the firepower to take on his entire fleet. It should have occurred to him that they would not have declared independence and started the war without being sure that they had something that could tip the balance in their favor. And they did—compressed antimatter. The resulting disaster could have been avoided, if only by holding a formation that was more than a premature victory parade.

"The Battle of Athens represents a third such example. After fighting the Inheritance Wars for so long, both sides were looking desperately for a silver bullet that would allow them to end the wars without further loss of life. The rebels were experimenting with automated missiles that would allow them to sweep the Asimov Point without risking ships and lives; it was not a great intellectual leap to wonder if the loyalists were doing the same. Indeed, the rebels had their own gravimetric research program that would have led to the stardrive if the Inheritance Wars hadn't been terminated before they could put it into production. In short, the rebels allowed themselves to be pinned against the Asimov Point by a force that had entered the system from an unsuspected direction, and were obliterated."

He grinned. "Let us consider another two battles, shall we? Cadet Raistlin: what do the pre-space Battle of Midway and the First Battle of Sapphire have in common?"

Roman had to smile as Raistlin blinked in shock. If the Inheritance Wars were still a sore subject, the far more recent Blue Star War was effectively forbidden territory. Cadets were rarely encouraged to study the war, even in the privacy of Luna Academy, while relatively little material on the war had made it out into the civilian sphere. The bare facts, of course, couldn't be covered up, but the precise details? The Federation Navy had restricted the data and covered up the reports, if only to spare the embarrassment. He wondered, absently, how the well-connected Raistlin would answer.

"Sir," Raistlin said. He had clearly decided to plunge for honesty, rather than dissimulation. "Both battles—both defeats—were the result of massive overconfidence."

"A very good answer, cadet," Kratman said sardonically. "An answer that is perfectly accurate, yet devoid of any actual detail. Please, would you elaborate for your fellow cadets?"

"Yes, sir," Raistlin said. Somehow, he managed to regain his balance. "In the Battle of Midway, the Japanese had an overpowering advantage in almost every important category. They should have brushed their American opponents aside and taken Midway, smashing the remaining American carriers at the same time. Instead, their overall commander divided their force and the Americans caught four of their carriers and sank them. The result was the sudden cessation of the Japanese advance.

"The First Battle of Sapphire, likewise, should have been a Federation victory. The fleet sent to secure the blue giant had enough firepower to take on the entire enemy force and crush it, but the commanding officer chose to break his fleet into three smaller forces and launch a simultaneous assault through two Asimov Points, while the third crossed interstellar space. The result of this…ah, poorly devised plan was the destruction of two of the assault forces, because they couldn't actually provide mutual support in their advance."

"And why did that happen, cadet?"

"Because coordinating a battle across interstellar distances is impossible," Raistlin said. "The three assault forces couldn't communicate with one another, while their opponents could use the advantage of the interior position to reinforce their defending forces—effectively smashing the attacking forces one by one."

"In other words, the commanding officer tried to be clever," Kratman said. He smiled, a rather humorless expression. "Being too clever or too dumb can cost you victory, or worse."

The Professor walked back to the front of the room and smiled at the cadets, this time with a hint of warmth. "There is actually a second point that both battles have in common. Both have been studied by military strategists—the latter battle with rather less enthusiasm, I should add—and extensively wargamed. Would you like to guess at the results?"

He paused, but no one took the bait. After a long moment, he went on.

"The conclusion, in both battles, was that the side that lost should have won. Overconfidence led to disaster—or, as Admiral Vane put it during the First Interstellar War, war is a democracy. The enemy has a vote."

He paused. "You have a question, Cadet Goldsmith?"

"Yes, sir," Cadet Karen Goldsmith said, and nodded.

Roman listened with interest. She rarely spoke, but when she did, she was always worth listening to. Besides, with long red hair and a remarkable smile, she was easy on the eyes as well.

"As I understand it," Goldsmith said, "in both wars it was primarily a matter of production. The resources available to the Americans and to the Federation far outstripped those available to their enemies. Once the victors had mobilized for war, their victory was certain. If that is the case, why were the battles so important?"

"*If* that is the case, cadet?" Kratman asked dryly.

Goldsmith flushed, but said nothing. History, Military Strategy and Moral Philosophy was not a class to be unsure of one's grounds.

"In one sense, you are quite right," the Professor said. "The sheer weight of firepower and material available to the victors ensured that they would be victorious. In a different sense, you are wrong; firepower and material alone does not win wars. Wars are fought—and thought—by intelligent beings. You might as well ask why the losers chose to fight at all."

He smiled. "In war, there are far more factors than just the material and armament. Is one side really committed to the war? If not, will they fight to the finish or will they abandon the war when the cost in men and material grows too high? The Japanese calculated that the Americans lacked the will to continue the war to the bitter end—oh yes, they knew about the disparity in long-term power. But America's short-term weakness did not lead to long-term weakness or defeat, not least because the Japanese lacked the firepower to capture or destroy America's industry.

"In the Blue Star War, the shock of the defeat forced the Federation Navy to clean house, while the political leaders who got the Federation into the war found themselves purged or marginalized. The defeat provoked fury among the high and mighty, who put aside their political struggles to unite and see the war through to victory. You may wish to consider what might have happened if the Senate hadn't been so unified. The Blue Star War might have been abandoned and the Federation's prestige would have been severely dented."

Roman considered the scenario as the Professor summed up his final lecture, outlining its relevance to the cadets and the Federation Navy. The reason the Outsiders were pushing so hard along the Rim—where the Federation's writ barely ran and outlaws and pirates hid themselves from Federation justice—was that the Federation Navy wasn't showing the will to either protect the human population or hunt down the pirates and the aliens who were supporting them. He recalled, bitterly, how his parents had died. After that, he had thrown himself into his studies and eventually won a coveted scholarship to Luna Academy. And if he earned a First in the exams, he would be on the short list to command his own ship.

"I was on the *Matterhorn*," the Professor concluded.

Roman blinked in surprise. The *Matterhorn* was a legend, one of the most famous ships in the fleet. The superdreadnaught had led the assault force into Sapphire and right into the ambush that had shattered the attacking force. The *Matterhorn* had been the only starship to survive, her CO somehow managing to get his wounded and bleeding starship back through the Asimov Point, losing over two-thirds of his crew in the brief encounter. He found himself looking at Kratman with new respect. All of the Academy's staff were supposed to have combat experience, but real combat experience was rare in the Federation Navy. The Blue Star War, the last significant conflict, was over sixty years ago.

"It was a nightmare," Kratman said. "We flew right into a trap and were lucky to survive. Others—people I had known since I was a cadet—didn't survive. You all have survived five years of the Academy, but your experience of the real universe is limited. And yet, if you pass the final exams, you will be on the track to command and, eventually, the Admiralty. If you survive…"

───────

By long tradition—Luna Academy had been founded in 2161—the cadets were granted a free period after every class. It hadn't taken long for Roman—and the other survivors of five years of brutal winnowing—to realize that falling for the temptations of Luna City was a good way to lose one's place in the Academy. The cadets, after their first year, were expected to discipline themselves. Very few wasted their time partying when they had to study.

Roman nodded to Raistlin as the class broke up, some heading for the library and others for the simulators, where they would study the battles the Professor had outlined. A handful, who had been ordered to undergo extra EVA training or additional duties, looked downcast. Raistlin nodded back—despite his origins, he wasn't actually stupid—and made a show of walking in the opposite direction. Picking fights outside class was another good way to lose one's place.

"So," Cadet Sultana Narayanan said, "how much trouble do you think the Professor is going to get into?"

Roman shrugged. "None, I suspect," he said. The Blue Star War might have been forbidden territory, but studying the war was vital, if only to avoid making the same mistakes again. "I think there are times when he says things just to see how we will react."

It made, he decided, a certain kind of sense. The cadets who bought the official line hook, line and sinker wouldn't be showing the mental agility needed to command starships in battle. Besides, they were—or they would be, once they graduated—Federation Navy officers. They *needed* to think for themselves.

"Or maybe he wanted to tell us something without saying it outright," he added. "Something we had to pick out for ourselves."

"Maybe," Sultana said. It was rare for her to talk to anyone outside classes, but in some ways they were both loners. Sultana had left her homeworld under a cloud and Roman was a RockRat, part of an asteroid-dwelling society that rarely interacted with the rest of humanity. "Do you think that…?"

At that moment, the emergency alarm went off. "ALL CADETS REPORT TO SAFE LOCKS," the intercom bellowed. "I SAY AGAIN, ALL CADETS REPORT TO SAFE LOCKS! THIS IS NOT A DRILL!"

Roman and Sultana exchanged glances—the emergency alarms were never sounded, outside scheduled drills—and then started to run. A Safe Lock was never far away.

CHAPTER TWO

The Senate, as laid down in the Federation Constitution, is restricted to only one thousand members—not counting the Grand Senators, who hold their positions until resignation or death. It should not be surprising, therefore, that representing the entirety of the Federation becomes a problem, or that there is a growing disconnect between the Senate and those they represent.
-An Irreverent Guide to the Federation, 4000 A.D.

Senate Hall, Earth, Sol System, 4092

"The Senate Committee on Outsider Incursions is now called to order," the Speaker said. "As per the Senate Security Act of 3702, I declare the room sealed."

Vice Admiral Marius Drake nodded impatiently. It had been a year since he had been recalled to Earth for "consultations," and ten years since he had been assigned to the Rim and ordered to hunt down and destroy the Outsiders. But the mission had not been successful, as the Outsiders were good at hiding from the Federation Navy—they'd had plenty of practice—and the Senate hadn't given him either the authority or resources to provide escorts to protect merchant shipping.

But as bad as that was, it was nothing compared to the last year's worth of inactivity on Earth—a complete and utter waste of his time. At first, the Admiralty had refused to admit that there *was* a problem with the Outsiders. And then everything had got worse once the politicians had become involved.

Politics was at the root of everything, these days.

Marius straightened his dress uniform as the room slowly came to order. At ninety-one years of age, he still looked young and handsome, thanks to the longevity treatments made available to promising young Federation Navy officers. His short, dark hair contrasted oddly with the gold dress uniform, to say nothing of the cape some sadist had designed for the Federation's naval officers to wear. Marius had no idea who had designed the cape, or why, but the uniform made him feel ridiculous. At least he'd honestly earned the medals on his chest. Perhaps the Senators would look at the medals and realize that he knew what he was talking about, unlike their paid military experts. It was astonishing how experts always provided advice that led directly to whatever their clients wanted to do.

Of course, that kind of wishful thinking was what had started the Blue Star War in the first place.

The Senate Hall was massive, holding not only the Grand Chamber— where all one thousand Senators and the Grand Senators passed laws that affected the entire Federation—but also hundreds of secure rooms for more private meetings. The chamber the Committee had reserved for its own use was small by the standards of the Grand Chamber, but it was still remarkably luxurious. No expense had been spared, not in the computer systems, nor the paintings that hung on the wall, or even the obsequious servants offering coffee or tea on demand to the Senators.

Marius had been brought up to believe that using human labor was a sign of decadence. In an age where robots were common, human servants were there merely to illustrate how important their masters considered themselves to be.

He looked up at the Senators and winced inwardly. They didn't look happy. Grand Senator The Honorable Carlton Brockington, Leader of the Conservative Faction, had somehow secured the chair for his own party. He was older than Marius and he hadn't aged anything like as well, unless Brockington was for some reason deliberately displaying his age. Fashions, for everything from clothing to faces and bodily shape, changed so rapidly on Earth that Marius, who had spent most of his life in interstellar space, had no hope of following them.

Grand Senator Alison Wallisch, Leader of the Socialist Faction, sat next to him, her blue eyes flickering from person to person. Her improbably beautiful heart-shaped face, surrounded by a mass of blonde curls, concealed a devious mind and—like all Senators—a certain ruthlessness and willingness to throw a friend out of the airlock if the friend threatened her power. Four of the other Senators were non-factors, brought in to bolster the two main factions, but Senator Chang Li, Representative from Nova Athena, and Grand Senator Rupert McGillivray were different. Despite himself, Marius, who followed politics closely, couldn't understand why either of them were on this Committee. Chang Li was from the Outer Rim and had no effective power base to speak of. And as for McGillivray...

"Vice Admiral," Brockington said in a cold, accusatory tone. "You have failed to defeat the Outsiders and restore peace and prosperity to the Rim. And now you come before us and ask for extra resources. Why should we assign additional starships and manpower to your command?"

Marius kept his expression blank, drawing on years of experience since graduating from Luna Academy. "The level of forces assigned to my command, Your Excellency, is insufficient for the task at hand," he said as calmly as he could. "If you want results, you need to assign me additional ships."

The senators murmured audibly, possibly talking to their staff members via communications implant. Of course, using such implants in public was impolite, but who would dare tell that to the Senators? Everyone else pretended not to notice, but Marius would remember the slight.

"You have been assigned over three hundred starships," Brockington said after a long pause. "Why is that insufficient?"

"Your Excellency, my area of responsibility covers over five *thousand* light years and four hundred inhabited planetary systems," Marius said. "The odds against me managing to place a single unit in a star system that is about to be attacked by pirates are astronomical. I cannot provide reliable protection for merchant shipping, let alone hunt down the various pirate bases, which are utterly impossible to detect in such a vast area of space. Furthermore, I have been denied the authority to insist on convoys being formed and escorted. Governor Barany has flatly refused my requests to institute even a limited convoy system, which my advisors have estimated would cut our losses by over a third."

He thought rapidly. *Should he bring up the other matter? If ONI was right, Governor Barany was actually taking money from the pirates. And that couldn't be allowed.*

"Worse, there is evidence to suggest that there are at least three unknown alien races in the Beyond, races that are aware of our existence and are actually providing help and support to the pirates. They may well have absorbed human technology, in direct violation of Directive 001. When I brought this to the governor's attention, he refused to grant permission to launch survey missions, let alone punitive raids against the unknown aliens. Instead, he promised to send the question to the Senate. I received no response by the time I was recalled."

It took everything he had to keep the anger out of his voice, but he managed it.

"The pirates have graduated from pest to serious annoyance," he continued after a beat. "They started by raiding freighters; now, they're raiding entire *planets* and carting off vast numbers of humans to use as slaves. We captured a pirate ship three years ago that carried nothing but human females, who were apparently destined for prostitution or slavery. The settlers out there are paying the pirates to leave them alone, giving them money or women in exchange for peace."

Marius hoped the Senators understood just how wrong that was, but worse was yet to come.

"And that's not all, as those settlers who refuse to cooperate often *die*, Your Excellency. This is most likely why pirates have destroyed at least four colonies down to the last man, woman and child."

There was an uneasy pause, as several of the Senators busied themselves with their terminals rather than look at Marius or their fellows.

"How many do you believe died in the last ten years?" Senator Chang Li asked. "How many humans have died because we didn't protect them?"

Marius considered her for a long moment. Back when the Federation was formed, the older planets had insisted they be allowed to represent their daughter colonies in the Senate, something that had dovetailed nicely with the limit on how many Senators could be voted into office. In practice, it ensured that the out-worlds, the ones at most risk from the pirates, had no voice in government. Senator Chang Li was only the third colonist to serve as a Senator, and she was isolated. The Senators had become aristocrats in all but name.

"The Rim records are of limited value," Marius admitted. "However, the best estimate I can give you is that over seventy *million* humans have been killed by the pirates, or carted off to serve as slaves, or have scattered and are hiding from both us and the pirates. The situation is intolerable."

"It is we who decide what is intolerable," Grand Senator Alison Wallisch said. Her voice was very cold. "I have here, in my implant, a communication from the governor. He states that Vice Admiral Drake has been unwilling to cooperate with the governor or local governments." She smiled thinly. "Perhaps you would care to explain why you showed so little respect for properly constituted authority, admiral?"

This time, it was harder to hide the rage.

"With all due respect, Senator, I discovered very quickly that sharing my operational plans with the governor meant that they were shared with the pirates," Marius told her. "I told the governor about a planned ambush; the pirates somehow avoided it. I told him that I planned a raid on a pirate base; the base was empty when I got there and rigged to blow with antimatter. I told him to keep the information in confidence and not to share it with anyone, not even his wife, yet somehow the information got out."

"Governor Barany is a man of the highest reputation," Alison said. "How dare you accuse him of...supplying information to the pirates?"

"The evidence is in his bank accounts," Marius said, throwing his last card onto the table. "He has a whole series of payments with no discernible source and..."

"Impossible," Alison said. She turned to her fellow Senators. "The admiral is attempting to excuse his own failures by blaming the governor! I move that we consider this in closed session."

There was a brief moment of silent communication. "I disagree," Chang Li said. Her almond eyes sought out Marius. "We need to send more starships into the sector to protect the population."

"At a colossal cost," one of the Conservative Senators pointed out. "Deploying an entire fleet into the Rim would strain our logistics quite badly and—"

"There are human lives at stake," Marius snapped, unable to control himself any longer. "Right now, *billions* of human lives are at risk of being kidnapped, killed, or simply wiped from existence. And here you are, worrying about cost!"

There was a long pause.

"I think, admiral, that you had better withdraw," Brockington said. "We will inform you of our decision in due course."

———

"The governor is one of her men, of course."

Marius didn't turn as the Grand Senator came up behind him. Instead, he stared out of the massive window, looking down towards the towers of Federation City. Centuries ago, the city had been built to serve as a home for the Federation's Government, back after the First Interstellar War had taught the human race the value of unity. Now, it was just like any other city on Earth: massive towers, teeming slums and a monstrous overpopulation problem. The punishment for any crime, these days, was deportation, yet it was never enough to keep pace with the growing population. Sooner or later, the teeming mass of humanity was going to rise up and drag the entire planet down into a nightmare.

"You spoke truth to power," Grand Senator Rupert McGillivray said dryly. "What makes you think that that will go unpunished?"

Marius turned. McGillivray was old, perhaps the oldest man in the Federation. His white hair and short, white beard were an affectation—he could have altered it at will—but the slow motion of his walk and the way his body shook told the true story. Traditionally, a Grand Senator who reached such an age—his detractors claimed he was senile—should resign, but McGillivray had held onto his chair. As the last of the Imperialist Faction—the faction that had provoked the Blue Star War—he was effectively impossible to dislodge.

"I like to think that the government would do the right thing," Marius said honestly. "Didn't they see the records from hijacked ships and ruined planets?"

"Of course they did," McGillivray said. "What makes you think they care? Everyone in the Senate is focused on keeping and expanding their power bases. Dead colonials along the Rim don't vote; wealthy citizens in the Core Worlds do so, frequently. Pleasing them is far more important than trying to stop the pirates."

He shrugged as he took one of the seats that allowed him to stare out over Federation City. The sun was setting in the distance.

"Admiral, no one of your high position can afford to be ignorant of politics," McGillivray said. "I know; you reached your position through merit and you deserve it, but merit alone isn't enough these days. There's a total deadlock in the Senate and no one is going to go out on a limb and suggest that sending a few hundred additional units out to the Rim might be a good idea, even with a clear and present threat to the entire Federation."

Marius nodded dismally. "But they're playing fast and loose with the security of the entire *Federation*," he repeated with emphasis. "How long is it going to be before we face an even greater threat?"

McGillivray smiled. "Are the new aliens a danger to the Federation?"

"I don't know," Marius admitted. "The Senate banned us from sending survey missions out to their space; hell, we know very little about them. The real danger is that they will get organized as a unit if we give them time, perhaps allying with the pirates and rebels. They have to know, by now, what life as an alien in the Federation is like."

The thought was a bitter one. The First Interstellar War had left a legacy of xenophobia running through the Federation. No alien race could be permitted to threaten humanity ever again. Aliens were second-class citizens even on their own homeworlds, denied weapons or access to spaceflight. They were banned from Earth and the Core Worlds, while the out-worlds often used aliens as a source of cheap labor. Marius had no more love for the aliens than the average human, yet even he was prepared to admit that no rational alien race would want to join the Federation.

Of course, the Blue Star War had made it clear what would happen to any race that *refused* to cooperate.

"True," McGillivray agreed after a pause. He leaned forward, assuming a lecturing pose. "The Conservatives want to keep things as they are, because they're effectively in charge of half the galaxy. They're allied with most of the big interstellar corporations because the corporations want to keep the laws and procedures they already have…"

"Keeping them on top," Marius put in.

"Precisely," McGillivray said. "The Socialists are trying to challenge this by distributing federal largesse to the population of the Core Worlds, the planets that can make or break Senators. In theory, they can effectively buy votes because they promise to keep the money flowing. In practice, what they're actually doing is damaging the tax base; the big corporations have the legal framework to escape taxation, or they're moving operations out to the out-worlds. So the Socialists raise taxes on smaller businesses and individuals, which makes their continued survival impossible, which means they're actually expanding the pool of needy people who need federal support to survive. Worse, because most of the Core Worlds are actually significant, raising taxes there is politically dangerous, so they start taxing the out-worlds, which causes massive resentment and a black market.

"Back when we had the Imperialist Faction, all three were balanced, but now..." He shook his head. "My family was there when the Constitution was first written," he said slowly. "And now I may live long enough to see the Federation tear itself apart."

Marius blinked. "Surely it's not that serious..."

"Oh, yes it is," McGillivray insisted. "You remember how reluctant they were to send ships to the Rim? They've been cutting the military to the bone in order to fund their pet projects; they've been cutting back on everything. The Survey Service has effectively been disbanded. The Asimov Point Monitoring Service has been placed on indefinite hold. They've even been skimping on ICN funding for the Rim and..."

Marius held up a hand, as etiquette demanded. A message had just downloaded into his implants. "They want me to head back to the Admiralty," he said flatly. He would have time to think about McGillivray's words on the way. "Thank you..."

"Thank *you*," McGillivray said. He winked. "It's astonishing how few people pay attention to me these days."

———

Admiralty House—the headquarters of the Federation Navy—was on the other side of the continent from Federation City. No one knew, now, why it had been built there, but it was tradition and, as such, could not be interfered with by mere mortals. Marius had his own theory; the Snakes, the first alien race humanity had encountered, had bombarded planetary defense centers with abandon, ignoring the danger to civilian populations. Building the HQ so far from the civilian population might just save civilian lives if the enemy took the high orbitals and chose to bombard the planet before invading.

The shuttle raced towards the city at several times the speed of sound. It was a sign of haste that the Admiralty had assigned his transport to the first available craft, rather than wait for an aircar. Someone in the Senate must have lit a fire under someone's ass. Marius didn't mind. The shuttle might be disarmed, but it felt more…natural than a luxury aircar. Sitting behind the pilot gave him time to rest. There was no point in trying to think, not after hearing from both the Senate and Grand Senator McGillivray. He'd find out what was waiting for him when he landed.

He looked up sharply as an alarm shrilled. It was the planetary defense alarm, an alarm that was never used, even in drills. The Solar System wasn't under attack—was it?

A moment later, the looming shape of Admiralty House—coming into view in the distance—vanished in a flash of blinding light.

CHAPTER THREE

As the homeworld of humanity, Earth is the single most heavily defended world in recorded history. Only a madman would try to breach the defenses and claim Earth for his own—or so we are told. History is all about people doing the unexpected and, one day, Earth's defenses may be challenged from an unsuspected direction.

-An Irreverent Guide to the Federation, 4000 A.D.

Near-Earth Orbit, Sol System, 4092

Although he was on the command deck, Commander Jacob Fallon had been slacking off when the attack began. In theory, he was currently in command of Earth Defense Station Three. The truth was that command networks and override protocols linked all of the defense stations—and automated orbital weapons platforms—into a single, coherent whole. With Commodore Peking on Earth Defense Station One for a conference with Port Admiral Gordon, the commander of Earth's defense network and the Home Fleet, the crew of EDS3 had been relaxing. Nothing had threatened Earth since the First Interstellar War, centuries ago, and few members of the crew expected anything ever would.

Fallon came to his feet as alarms shrieked, dropping his small—and, technically, illegal—data terminal on the deck as the main display wall lit up with red icons. He'd never seen anything like it outside of drills, and even then the drills hadn't been too intense; after all, everyone *knew* that attackers could not reach Earth without fighting their way through half the Federation. There would be plenty of time to reconfigure defenses and reallocate resources to deal with any new threats.

Or so they had believed.

The main display zeroed in on a single, expanding red icon, flashing to yellow as it faded away. Where EDS1 had been, hanging over Earth like a protective shroud, there was nothing more than an expanding cloud of debris and superheated plasma. A second icon—confirming the detection of a nuclear detonation on Earth's surface—almost passed unnoticed.

Jacob was too astonished to speak, even as the alarms yammered and trained personnel struggled to respond to the completely unanticipated situation. What the hell was going on? All drills were scripted and announced in advance. It couldn't be a drill, but it couldn't be real...could it?

"Bring the station to red alert," he ordered his crew. *If that wasn't the most unnecessary order in the history of the Federation Navy,* he thought, considering the alert had automatically sounded. "Get me..."

He broke off as new red icons flared into existence. *Starfighters!* Someone had launched starfighters?

It seemed impossible, but someone *had*. They were attacking Earth's network of defensive installations. Jacob just stared, unable to speak or even think. The Earth Defense Stations were not only four times as massive as the largest superdreadnaughts or assault carriers, they carried far more missile launchers, starfighters, and armor, if only because they didn't need to fill their internal compartments with drive units and emergency supplies. Who would dare attack such massive formations?

"Launch our starfighters," he ordered, trying to sound as calm as he possibly could. He fell back on basic tactics, information he'd learned at the academy and then allowed to slip out of his head, because there was nothing else to do. The hostile starfighters had to be hunted down and destroyed before they caused more damage.

Except...where had they come from? No one could have slipped a fleet of assault carriers near Earth without being detected, even if their cloaking systems were superior to those of the Federation Navy. He couldn't even see who they should be engaging! And he didn't know who—or what—was in command. The entire datanet seemed to be stuttering...

Marius held on to his seat for dear life, struggling to comprehend what had just happened as the shuttle tumbled end-over-end. The internal compensations struggled to keep everyone alive as the shuttle was tossed through the air; it felt as if the hand of God had touched the shuttle.

There was no time for panic. Someone had nuked Navy HQ. There was no other explanation. An antimatter bomb, even an old-style antimatter device, would have wiped out the entire continent and he would be dead. The shuttle he was in would have been swatted like a bug.

He tried to access the emergency channels through his implant as the pilot finally managed to steady the craft, but there was no response. He had no way to tell if the blast was disrupting communications—although that should have been impossible, given the sheer level of redundancy built into Earth's network—or if someone was deliberately jamming communications.

The shuttle had stabilized, allowing him to look towards Navy HQ. Marius shuddered as an ominous mushroom cloud rose into the air, tinged with flickers of fire and shadow. No one had used a nuclear weapon on Earth's surface since the Age of Unrest. Only seven nukes had ever been used at all, even during the darkest days of the Third World War.

But then, by that point the winners had learned how to bombard targets from orbit and obliterate their enemies with nice clean kinetic strikes.

"We're alive," the pilot said in relief. "Sir…"

"The system is under attack," Marius said. "Hold your position while I try to find out who's in charge."

He linked his implant into the shuttle's communications nodes. Much to his relief, that allowed him to slip through the disruption and into the emergency network. It was already overloading because of calls from the surrounding area and would probably collapse. Linking into the military channels was harder—it needed his ID codes to gain access—and it seemed impossible to find a superior officer.

If Navy HQ had been hit, the enemy—whoever they were—had decapitated the Federation Navy. Home Fleet's commanding officers would be dead. He knew that, but he still held out hope that someone, anyone, might outrank him and be able to tell him what was going on.

The datanet should have linked him instantly to the senior surviving officer within range. Instead, it took minutes to sort through the conflicting tidal waves of data and finally locate the senior officer. Marius shivered again as he realized that the senior officer in the system—at least the senior officer plugged into the datanet—was a mere commander.

Dear God, how high had the casualties been? What had happened onboard EDS1 to slaughter the defenders of Earth?

"Sir, EDS1 is gone," the pilot said, answering his unspoken question. He'd been flicking through what remained of the flight control network. "The station has been completely destroyed."

Marius cursed. The attack was internal, then; there was no way to smuggle a nuke or an antimatter bomb onto a defense station without help. It had to have been an internal detonation. Nothing else, not even a bombardment with compressed antimatter, would have obliterated the station so quickly. He accessed the network again and swore, angrily. EDS2 had gone silent. The senior officer was still a mere commander.

"This is Vice Admiral Drake," he said as he linked into the communications network. "Here are my ID codes and command authority. I suggest that you verify them, then open a secure link."

There was a long pause.

"Admiral, I'm Commander Jacob Fallon, in command of EDS3," Commander Fallon said. He sounded as if he were on the verge of coming apart, either through shock or relief. No one had expected an attack on Earth, let alone what had to be an internal rebellion. "Thank God you're alive!"

Commander Fallon sounded relieved to discover that someone was senior to him and could therefore take charge. Marius accessed his implants, briefly skimming through Fallon's file. It was not a distinguished one.

"Just so," Marius growled. He would have to work with Fallon, no matter his limited experience. "We're still alive and I, for one, intend to stay that way. You have my command codes. Declare a Case Omega and run through the network, then let me know if there is anyone senior to me..."

"But sir," Fallon protested. "I don't have the authority to declare Case Omega."

"You're in command of a battlestation," Marius snapped. "You have the authority! Now, get in touch with the network and find out who's in charge."

He disconnected from the network and looked over at the pilot. "Set course for EDS3," he ordered. Fallon sounded as if he was on the verge of panic, which meant—if nothing else—Marius had to be on the scene to relieve him, if necessary. "Call up a flight of starfighters for escort and get them to fly top cover."

His implant buzzed as Fallon contacted him. "I ran a Case Omega, sir," he said. "You're the senior surviving officer within the Earth-Luna Sphere."

Marius nodded. The attack had clearly been carefully planned. Had they held off for another few minutes, he would have been in Navy HQ when it was destroyed. But if he'd maintained his original plans, he'd have been there at least ten minutes sooner. Which meant that if Senator McGillivray hadn't wanted to talk with him, Marius himself would already be dead.

The attackers, whoever they were, had planned to decapitate the defenses and they'd come alarmingly close to success. Their tactics showed a chilling level of ruthlessness. Breaking the taboo on using weapons of mass destruction on inhabited planets showed a single-minded determination to succeed, if only because of what the Federation would do to them if it won the war.

"Right," he said. "I am assuming command of the defenses of Earth. Give me a situation report, now."

"Sir, the datanet has been crippled," Fallon said. "I barely know anything…"

"Then give me what you have," Marius said patiently, checking the shuttle's ETA at the station. "What do you know about what's going on?"

"Ah…EDS1 has been destroyed, sir," Fallon said. "I have dispatched SAR gunboats and shuttles, but they don't hold out much hope of finding survivors. EDS2, EDS7 and EDS9 are non-responsive; they're intact, yet they're not linked into the command network and are refusing to respond to hails. I don't know their exact status. And there are dozens of enemy starfighters flying around, engaging the defenses."

Marius scowled. Starfighters needed a base—either a starship or a station—to operate. Their life support packs wouldn't last indefinitely, which meant that someone had to have launched them. But from where?

He glanced at the holographic near-orbit display as the shuttle rose out of the atmosphere and considered it. The starfighters could have come from the silent battlestations, yet if that was the case, there should be more of them. And then the treacherous commanders would have had to convince the fighter jocks to support them, too…no, it wasn't possible to form a conspiracy of that magnitude without Federation Intelligence or ONI getting wind of it beforehand.

He looked at the display again, and knew the answer.

"There are too many freighters in orbit—breaking orbit now," he said slowly. Converting freighters into makeshift carriers was an old trick. And now that the fighting had begun, hundreds of innocent civilian craft were breaking orbit and fleeing, unaware that some of their comrades were actually enemy starships. "Ten gets you twenty that at least one of them is working for the enemy…"

He frowned. "I want a general broadcast," he ordered. "All civilian ships within the Earth-Luna Sphere are to cancel their drives and prepare to be boarded. Any that refuse to stop will be fired upon and destroyed."

Fallon sounded shocked. "But, sir…"

Marius ignored the protest and drove onwards. "Have you re-established the command datanet yet?"

"No, sir," Fallon said. "The coordinating systems were mounted on EDS1, and were destroyed by the blast that took out the station."

And it never occurred to you to try to work around the problem? Marius thought, wondering what connections Fallon must have such that he had avoided being sent somewhere harmless, perhaps an asteroid mining station.

"I see," he said as coldly as he could. "Your station may not have been designed to serve as a command station, but the computers will be able to handle it for at least a few hours. And by then, we will either have won or lost the coming battle. Reboot the system and prepare for operations."

"Sir, the manual clearly states…"

"*Fuck the manual,*" Marius swore at him. "This is war! Doing what the enemy expects us to do is a certain way to wind up dead, with the enemy laughing at us. Now, forget the manual and reboot the fucking system, right fucking now!"

"Sir, our escort has arrived," the pilot interrupted. "We should be on the station in ten minutes, unless we hit unexpected trouble."

Marius nodded absently, thinking hard. He'd warned the Senate about the dangers of largely unknown alien races, but he knew that no alien race could have launched such a devastating and precise attack. The level of access the unknown attackers had demonstrated they had internal help, which meant that whoever was behind the attack was trying for a coup, rather than destruction for the sake of destruction. Destroying Earth would have been easy—a single antimatter bomb would depopulate the planet—but anyone who wanted to replace the Federation with his own rule would need Earth's legitimacy.

And that suggested there had to be a second level to the plan. Destroying EDS1 and Navy HQ would cause confusion, but the disarray wouldn't last. Even if Marius hadn't stepped up to the plate, *someone* would have taken command sooner or later. There had to be an incoming enemy fleet heading towards Earth, having somehow been smuggled into the system. That, at least, was no longer impossible. The stardrive had seen to that.

"Ah, the network is up and running," Fallon said. He sounded relieved. Marius wondered how he would cope in a battle where multiple antimatter detonations would disrupt the network effortlessly. Coordinating a fleet in combat wasn't easy. "The three silent stations are continuing to refuse to respond."

Treachery or equipment malfunction? Marius thought. There was no way to know for sure.

"Link into Marine HQ at Camp Heinlein," he ordered. Unless the Marines had been hit as well, Major General Tobias Vaughn would still be alive. And Vaughn, who had once been the senior Marine on Marius's first command, was one of his closest friends. "Inform the Major General that I want armed Marines in the air and heading for the three stations. Once they board, they are to secure the stations and confirm their status, then prepare to start searching the civilian ships. If they meet with resistance, they are authorized to use deadly force."

"Yes, sir," Fallon said. At least he'd learned to take orders without objecting. "Ah, four bulk freighters are continuing to accelerate away from Earth, heading towards the Dead End."

Marius smiled, feeling the old excitement shimmering through his mind. The Sol System possessed two Asimov Points, but one of them—the Dead End—led only to a single useless star system, without even a handful of asteroids to arouse the interest of the RockRats. The Dead End was defended, of course, yet it was simply not as important as the Gateway, the second Asimov Point within the system. And there was no logical reason for anyone to want to go there, unless they had something illegal in mind. And *that*, to his mind, effectively confirmed their guilt. Converting a bulk freighter to a starfighter carrier was easy.

"Order the starfighters to intercept and move up gunboats in support," Marius ordered calmly. "If the bulk freighters refuse to surrender and hold position, the pilots are authorized to open fire. No further warnings."

Fallon clearly swallowed an objection. "Yes, sir," he replied. "I shall pass your orders on to the pilots."

Marius nodded. In five minutes, he would be aboard the station and ready to take command of defensive operations. But where was the enemy fleet? Their commander would have to strike a balance between secrecy and the need to strike hard before the defenders reorganized.

How close…?

—

"We should do something," Raistlin protested. "We shouldn't stay here."

Roman couldn't disagree. For cadets, spending any time in the Safe Locks was a foretaste of hell. They were armored rooms, isolated from Luna Academy's life support system and, in theory, anyone inside could survive a disaster that took out the remainder of the academy. Now, with over seventy cadets from all five years crammed inside this one, tiny room, it felt claustrophobic.

"And what, pray tell, do you think you could do?" Proctor Amanda Wallace demanded. She was tall and, to the cadets, a force of nature. The proctors didn't teach, not formally; they supervised the cadets and, when necessary, provided discipline. "Do you think we could take *Emprise* and *Enigma* out into battle?"

Raistlin flushed red, while a handful of cadets tittered. *Emprise* and *Enigma* were the two old starships that had been assigned to the academy for training purposes, but they were *far* from state-of-the-art. Roman, and every other cadet, even those who had no intention of going into

Engineering, had spent months crawling over the two ships, eventually flying them throughout the Solar System. They were in perfect working order, but hopelessly outdated. Any modern warship would scythe them down in seconds.

"There's nothing we can do," Amanda said. "We don't even know what is going on."

Roman blinked. His implant hadn't been able to access any information, but he'd assumed that was because he was just a cadet. But the proctors were clearly just as much in the dark.

"I suggest that you use your implants and study for your tests," Amanda continued. "I assure you that if you die you won't have to sit them."

Roman snorted at the bad joke and then caught Raistlin's eye, trying to let the man know Roman agreed with him. All hell was breaking loose out there, and yet here they were, stuck in the Safe Lock and unable to do anything, even run if necessary. Above them on the Luna surface, something was going on.

Cadets weren't trained to sit on their hands. So why was it that they hadn't been ordered to battle stations rather than the Safe Lock? Something wasn't right here.

He looked away, hoping to conceal his expression from Proctor Amanda. Feeling helpless wasn't pleasant, but what else could he do? In hopes of distracting himself, he called up the data for the tactical exam and started to run through it. It didn't work. His thoughts kept returning to the battle above, where the future of the Federation was being decided.

After all, why else would anyone attack Earth?